A Time To Pray

Obadiah Ariel Yehoshuah

WestBow
PRESS
A DIVISION OF THOMAS NELSON

WestBow Press books may be ordered through booksellers or by contacting:

WestBow Press
A Division of Thomas Nelson
1663 Liberty Drive
Bloomington, IN 47403
www.westbowpress.com
1-(866) 928-1240

ISBN: 978-1-4497-2835-9 (sc)
ISBN: 978-1-4497-2836-6 (hc)
ISBN: 978-1-4497-2834-2 (e)

Library of Congress Control Number: 2011917651

Printed in the United States of America

WestBow Press rev. date: 10/13/2011

Chapter 1

THIS SUMMER WAS HOTTER THAN any Newark had ever experienced in a long time. The flowers were wilting and the people were miserable. Al Gore was sure there was a global warming problem and he must be right because the temperatures were reaching over a hundred degrees and this was just unheard of in these parts. There wasn't much rain, water levels were low across the country and the California wild fires were out of control. Announcements went out that the odd number houses could water on one day and the even numbered houses on the other day. If you had a swimming pool then too bad because it just wasn't enough water to fill them all. But who listened to that warning. Oh how the people fussed and moaned about that. The middle class just had to have their swimming pool filled and their flowers watered. They didn't care about having water for the basic nessecities like bathing and drinking.

New Jersey occupants are used to it though so the children played in the water hydrants to keep cool. If you used your imagination and the man on the hydrant knew what he was doing you could make that water shoot high in the air and the children would run one by one under it like it was really a waterfall. The local swimming pools were filled to capacity with the people from the neighborhood. Even when it closed people would sneak back in with their lawn chairs until the wee hours of the morning. Oh how wonderful it is being a kid you never worry about anything. The farmers had it even worse. The drought didn't help them much. Their crops were failing and that was not a good sign. It was so hot they had to water the cattle. In some places cows were dying from the heat and lack of water. It was a disaster area. The Governor had to do something quickly before the effects were deadly. Some of the larger cities in New Jersey set up cooling centers for the elderly who could not afford air conditioning. Some of the local stores put their money together and bought air conditioners for those who could not afford them. The area that Sam and his wife lived in was full of elderly people but there was no cooling center in his neighborhood. It seemed like in the ghetto no one cared about the people there. The house they lived in Sam had lived in all of his life. His mother and father bought that house many years ago and would leave it to Sam when they moved south. It used to be a great neighborhood but of recent many new families moved in and they just didn't care about the neighborhood like in the old days. When the blacks moved in the whites moved out and when the Hispanics moved in the gangs moved in with them. The gangs wanted to have their own territory to control the flow of drugs and women in the area. Things had changed rapidly it wasn't safe to walk the streets anymore. Mothers and daughters were afraid of being out by themselves. The children couldn't play in their yards for fear of drive by shootings. Men had abandoned their responsibility as fathers and husbands to one wife.

When Eddie and Mabel purchased the house things were different and much less expensive. Even people were different back then. It was like one big family. The men gathered together during the summer months to go fishing together. The women looked out for one another exchanging recipes and taking care of one another's children. The children all played together never caring about color or religion. The world would be a different place for Sam's children.

The house was getting old and like all old houses there was no central heating or air conditioning. The house was getting old and there were many things starting to break down. Sam had to do lots of repairs. He just couldn't let go of the house it just had too many memories. The pipes were bursting all the time and the hot water heater needed to be replaced. It was home nevertheless. Some of his childhood friends still lived in the neighborhood or had family that still lived there. Sam remembered his first Christmas in the house with his parents. Being an only child had its advantages. Eddie worked as a maintenance man in a hospital. It was steady work and by the time that Eddie retired he had been working there for over 40 years. Although Eddie didn't make much money they always had a real Christmas tree. In those days the men would go out and cut down their own trees with their sons. It was a family tradition. Sam looked forward to Christmas. The neighborhood was bustling with kids riding their new bicycles, so many treats to eat at all the houses. The competition was on just after Thanksgiving which street would have the best Christmas light extravaganza. It was what life was all about for the children. Every year on television the family would sit down together and watch their favorite movies. Sam liked "The March of the Wooden Soldiers" the best. As a little boy the soldiers were tall and so real to him. But as he got older perspective seemed to change and they didn't look so scary after all.

Life for Sam was good in Newark. He heard all the terrible stories about the riots that happened in the 60's and you could still see the affects in some neighborhoods. Newark would never be the same but many of the businesses stayed and that was a good thing. A lot of the churches had since closed their doors and more and more were closing all the time. It was a sign that times were changing when churches turned into discos and restaurants. His father would say "son things are changing in the world. People don't care much about God anymore. They just live like they want and that won't be good in the long run."

Eddie's father started their church. As a youth it was his responsibility to play the piano for the services. His father even allowed him to preach every now and then. He looked so funny as a youth mimicking his father in the pulpit. But that was the duty of a father to teach his son how to take over the church after he was gone. The people in the neighborhood loved going to church back then. They loved their families but life was centered around God. The services were alive and the presence of God was felt in each service. The men got dressed up on Sunday morning and the women wore their fineries to church as well. They were called "holy rollers" because when the power of God hit the place they fell out under the power of God and rolled on the floors. Sam remembered as a young boy not truly understanding what was happening but he enjoyed going to church to play the piano and see his friends. Sam's father took over the church after his grand-father got too old to do all of the services, visit the sick at the hospital, dedicate the babies and all the other responsibilities a pastor had to do.

His father loved preaching. He would say "son preaching is the best thing ever. When the power of God hits you its like you feel like your floating on air." Sam would just smile at his father not truly understanding what he was saying. But he did know that he felt something great when he was singing and playing the piano. The tradition of playing the piano passed down from his father. It was like the angels were singing with him and Jesus had his arms wrapped around him. He felt like he was on top of the world.

Eddie and Mabel didn't grow up with a silver spoon in their mouth so they really wanted to start a mission that would help those less fortunate. Eddie went to every business in the area and asked for donations to start a mission. The mission would start off small at first just giving out sandwiches, juice and cookies so that they would have something to eat every day. Sam met his good friend Oliver the first day out for the mission. Oliver had fallen on bad times and was living on the street. There were so many men and women homeless that Sam just couldn't believe it. What had happened to these people? Why didn't they have jobs and a place to live? Eddie explained to Sam that times were getting hard and according to the Bible it would get worse the closer it was to Jesus return. His father said that in the last days that there would be wars all over the world, famines, pestilences and earthquakes in diverse places. He said that there would be economic collapse in the government and people would lose their jobs and homes. Sam wasn't much on reading his Bible but his father made him memorize a scripture verse every week. Sam hated it but whatever dad said he would do. He was a good son and he wanted to please his father and mother. But he couldn't understand how what the Bible was saying had anything to do with people being out of work. His dad also said, "son many of these people have fallen away from God. They are all searching for something that is lacking in their lives. Every man and woman has a desire to know who they are and what is the meaning of their existence. The only way for them to get this answer is to ask God, for God is creator of all things including man. But instead they turn to sex, drugs, alcohol, power and money. And then when they exhaust all of this they hit rock bottom. These are the lost one's that Jesus said He came to save son." This made a lot of sense to Sam.

One day when the mission went out to feed the homeless Sam met a man named Oliver. Oliver was no different at first glance from any of the other men that lived on the street. His clothing was old and looked like he had gotten them out of someone's garbage. He had not shaved in forever and certainly had not taken a bath in God only knows when. All that he owned was in a duffle bag that read U.S. Army on it. But Sam noticed that he wore an army jacket. He had seen them on television. So he wondered whether Oliver had been in the military before and decided to ask him about who he was. His father taught him to have compassion for the people who were less fortunate. "So Oliver you have on an army jacket were you in the military?" He just came out with it. That's the good thing about being young you don't have to think about what you say. "Well yes son I was in the military. I fought in Vietnam. Do you know anything about war son?"

"Well no I really don't. I think I saw some pictures in a magazine though about Vietnam. They were really gruesome. People were blown apart by bombs and it was terrible."

"Yes Sam it was terrible. You see this medal. They gave me the purple heart because I saved some of my buddies from getting killed. It was the best thing that I've ever done with my life. But Sam I just can't get the smell out of my nose and the noise out of my head. We did drugs to keep the day going. Many of us did things that we wouldn't want our family to know about to survive in the jungle. I can't kick the habit. Anyway my life is over Sam. Make good with your life. You only get one chance at it. "

"Come on Oliver. You're still alive. Your life is not over. Why are you giving up?"

"Sam I was a young man when I went to Nam. I went over there to fight for my country you know. I came home half a man with no legs. My fiancée just couldn't handle it and she left me. Oh Sam I wanted more for my life. But I don't have any skill but to kill people. I'm almost 50 years old now. I can't walk. What can I do now? Can you see me going back to school for some trade or something? Nobody wants a bum like me. I don't have any friends or family. Sometimes I wish I would just not wake up in the morning. That will take care of everything."

"Hey maybe my dad can help you out. He has a big heart and he knows a lot of people. Maybe you can get into a program or something. If you really try Oliver I know that you can make it out of this. Living on the streets is no place for a war hero like you. Think about all the lives that you saved? I bet they care about you but don't know where you are."

"Yeah. I sure would like to see some of those guys again. No, no Sam its over. Thank you anyway for the food you're a great kid."

Sam just couldn't help but think about how lonely Oliver was and so many other soldiers that came home from war to nothing. There was something wrong with what had happened to them. Sam and Eddie talked about war and the affects of war on the nation and on individual people like Oliver. It was then that Sam dropped the bomb on his father that he had been thinking about going into the military after school. "When did you make this decision son?"

"Well dad I was just thinking about it. I know I want to go to college but I'm not sure what I want to do. My teacher says I have an aptitude for numbers and should think about accounting but it sounds so boring. I'm not an old man. Maybe I'll think about that when I have to support a family or something. But I want a little adventure you know what I mean."

While growing up Sam had always had a desire for the military. His school had a recruiting day and he got a chance to talk with some young men and women from all of the various branches. He knew the girls would swoon when they saw a man in uniform. Sam felt like any other young man that people would look up to him if he was wearing that uniform. He told his father that when he grew up that he would become an officer in the military and when he graduated from high school off he went into the wild blue yonder in the Air Force. His father and mother were so proud of their son. Sam did pretty well in school and had good scores on the military exam. He did unfortunately have to serve in Desert Storm and his mother worried every day whether her son would come home as did many of the other women in the neighborhood. Sam's mother and father were avid prayer warriors and so they prayed over their son and every other soldier that they would come home safely. Sam's father gave him his special bible that he carried around with him all the time. By the time he passed it on to Sam it was worn out from all the time Eddie spent reading that bible but Sam didn't mind. He loved his father and that was a way that he had him with him all the time. For a young man Sam loved the word of God and he loved reading the word. So while he was away he read that word and stood on the word like his father and mother had taught him.

Sam enjoyed the military very much and made lots of friends. After two years he met Ruth while home on leave and it was love at first sight. He was out doing his Christmas shopping and he bumped into an angel. Sam had never dated much when he was a young man. He was always feeling awkward around girls. But when he met Ruth he didn't feel awkward at all. To him she was the most beautiful girl he had ever seen. After all he was a big military man she would just have to fall in love with him. He was tall and lanky and his uniform fit him very well. When she first saw him she took a double take he was so handsome and walked so cool. She felt like a school girl again. He had to figure out a way to get her attention but didn't know the right words to say. "Hi". He said to Ruth. "My name is Sam."

"Hi my name is Ruth. Are you home for Christmas or do you serve in the area?"

"I'm home for Christmas with my family. Just doing a bit of shopping. Wow I don't usually do this but it sure would be nice if you would join us at my church we are having a Christmas celebration. The kids usually put on a nice program and I play the piano for them. We also have a day in which the mission we started does a big Christmas dinner for those less fortunate in the neighborhood. Maybe you might like to come and volunteer your time."

"Oh that sounds great. I've never volunteered for a mission before. Sure. Give me the information and I will be there."

"Okay. Let me write it down on some paper. Don't forget I would really like to see you again Ruth."

"I'm looking forward to it myself Sam."

"The program is Saturday evening and the mission lunch is that afternoon. Here is all the information you will need and my phone number just in case something comes up. It was nice to meet you." Sam just kept looking at Ruth until she had walked out of sight. If she looked back at him that would tell him that she wanted to see him again too. She looked back. Sam smiled and walked off feeling like a new man.

Sam couldn't wait until Saturday came and bugged his mother to death about Ruth. He was concerned that she would not be able to make it but would pray that she would come. His mother was getting sick of him but she understood young love. She had been young once but that was a long time ago. "Sam don't worry. I'm sure that if she can't make it she will call and let you know. For now just relax and hope for the best."

Saturday didn't come quick enough. Sam looked through his closet a million times to see what he would wear on Saturday. He didn't have much clothing and he couldn't wear his uniform. That would be too conspicuous. He did look really handsome in his uniform though. He had a nice suit but he had worn it so many times before. But then again Ruth never saw him in that suit so maybe she would still be impressed. That morning he got up early because there was so much to do for the Christmas lunch that afternoon. He didn't have to worry about the play that night. He had been playing those same Christmas carols for years now. He knew his part well and they had been doing the same play for the last five years.

It was just like every year. Sam had a lot of running around to do. The businesses in the area had done so much for the mission since it first started. Imagine they went from giving out sandwiches to having a place for Christmas lunch and plenty of gifts for the children and the families that attended. It truly gave Christmas time a new meaning. When Sam was just a little boy he cared only about his family but now he was a grown man and he realized that life was about more than his family and his toys. Now he could serve the community by giving the joy of Christmas to others who could not afford to do it for themselves. It gave him so much joy. He hoped that Ruth would feel the same way.

The first stop would be to go over to the church and make sure that it was clean. The ladies spent a lot of time the evening before decorating the tree and putting all of the presents around it the best way they could. The businesses gave so much that they couldn't possibly put them all around the tree. They brought in all of the cookies, cakes and pies from the bakery. The churches in the area donated the turkeys, hams and fried chicken. What was Christmas without a turkey? There was certainly enough food to feed an army. Sometimes they would miss some things and it was Sam's responsibility to come in and clean the floors just one more time before all the people arrived. Sam looked the place over like he had so many times before and thought about the many people that would be served there that day. He thought about his friend Oliver that had finally accepted a place in a newly renovated building for the homeless. Now instead of living on the street, Oliver had a real apartment complete with furnishings and a social worker who came to see him and make sure he was being taken care of. He had even started attending church so Sam could see him whenever he came home to visit.

The next stop would be to the church. Sam would go to the church just to pray with some of the other young brothers for the coming new year. They had started a small prayer group just before Sam had left. The power of prayer was emphasized so much by his father. There were so many in the neighborhood that had all kinds of problems. It gave them strength to know that there was someone who was constantly praying for them. It was kind of a fellowship as well. He got to know some of the other young men like himself during this time of fellowship and prayer time. Although Sam was away from home he wanted to be in touch with what was going on at home. He loved his church and all of its members. One day that church would be passed on to him maybe. He didn't want to think much about it. He just didn't feel like that was his calling but he would see.

After the prayer group had ended Sam went home to get ready for the lunch that afternoon. The prayer meeting took his mind off of Ruth for a moment anyways. He was still very nervous about meeting up with her again but the lunch would break the ice because they would be busy from the time they entered the door until the last person left for the afternoon. Then off to the church for the play. Sam loved this day. It was the greatest day of the year for him and his family.

Sam had not noticed that Ruth had walked into the room because they were so busy feeding the people that came for Christmas lunch. Sam had not counted but it seemed like it was well over two hundred people that came that day. The fellowship hall was all decorated with Christmas lights, a huge tree and all the gifts that were donated. The kids couldn't wait. Traditionally they would eat first and then they would all gather into the fellowship hall where Pastor Eddie would tell the story about the baby Jesus and give out the presents to all of the families. No one would leave that day without having received something.

"Hey Sam there is a young lady out here looking for you."

Sam quickly ran towards Mabel without even noticing that he had not taken his apron off. "Mom is it Ruth?"

"Yes. She is beautiful. I see why you are so tongue tied about her coming. Just be yourself son. You'll do just fine."

"Thanks mom." Sam gave his mom a big bear hug and a sloppy kiss.

Sam tried not to act nervous as he walked out to greet Ruth. "Hi Ruth. Wow I am so glad that you came. Welcome to Christmas at the mission."

"Thank you Sam." Ruth had a gleam in her eyes. She had never volunteered at a church mission before. She felt bad because it seemed like they were having a lot of fun. She could not believe the number of families that didn't have money for Christmas dinner or presents for their children. She had been born again that day and wished that every year she could spend Christmas with Sam and his family. "I had not realized how many families would not have Christmas without people like you. I feel terrible that I had not thought about this until now. This is what the church is all about huh?"

"Don't feel bad Ruth. If it were not for my father starting the mission I would not have realized a lot of things myself. By the way let me introduce you to my mother and father. You can meet the rest of the team later." Sam and Ruth walked into a kitchen full of working hands. The team consisted of most of the sisters from the church and many others from churches all around that area who came to help. They all turned around and waved really quickly because if the mob didn't get fed things would get ugly pretty quickly.

Sam took Ruth's hand and led her over to his father who was filling up a pan with some more turkey and dressing to put out on the table. Eddie looked up with those endearing eyes and beautiful white teeth and saw his son with the most beautiful angel he had ever seen. She reminded him of his Mabel when she was just a young girl before they got married. He quickly wiped his hands on his apron and reached out to shake her hand. "Are you the young lady my son has been talking about? He is really stricken with you girl."

"Nice to meet you sir. I hope he hasn't gone on too much."

"Well, he does get a little excited but I can see why. I'm Pastor Eddie. You are welcome here anytime. We can use all the help that we can get. Sam will get you an apron? I hope you know your way around the kitchen. If not these ladies will get you started."

"Sure. I can do something. Sam get me an apron. You heard your father. There is work to be done. The people are hungry." Sam just smiled and handed Ruth an apron as they walked over to his mom for instructions.

"Sister Mabel I would like to introduce you to Miss Ruth Green. This is the young lady that I spoke to you about. Dad says to give her an apron and put her to work."

"Oh that man don't you worry about him none Miss Ruth. We are all family around here. But you can start with something easy. Put those biscuits on the table and mingle a little bit. You'll get the hang of it."

Ruth was a natural. She walked around talking to the people and making sure everyone was taken care of. She filled the glasses with tea and cleaned off the areas where people had finished eating and had gone into the fellowship hall. It took several hours even after she had arrived to feed the continuous flow of people coming in and out of the dining room area. But Ruth had the time of her life. She couldn't imagine that she had been missing all of this fun. She noticed as she worked how diligently Sam, his mother, father and all of the other brothers and sisters worked to make the lunch a success. It was certainly a privilege to be a part of this family.

Sam had been noticing how Ruth seemed to love working with the mission. He would tell her the whole story about how the mission came to be. His father had a love for people and his love for people and God is what started the mission. Jesus said that if you do it for the least of these my brothers you've done it for me. After everyone had eaten it was now time for Pastor Eddie to tell the story about baby Jesus to the families and give out the gifts. The look on the children's faces when he talked was nothing less than miraculous. Pastor Eddie had a way of making that age old story come to life in such a way that the children thought it was a new story all the same. Sam and Ruth stood to the rear of the fellowship and watched Pastor Eddie in rear form. After the story he gave a prayer for all that God had given to them that day. He prayed that all would be good for the new year and then Sister Mabel and the team had everyone to line up so that the presents could be given out. It was another successful Christmas to end with the play at the church that evening.

Sam had tears in his eyes but he didn't want Ruth to see him crying. The mission was hard work but Sam loved to see the look on the families faces after the dinner was over. There was love in their eyes, and the peace and joy of Christmas was felt by all. No one was left out in this neighborhood Pastor Eddie made sure of it. After everything was cleaned up Sam invited Ruth to drive with him to the church to get ready for the play. Ruth knew in her heart that Sam was a very special young man and was glad that she didn't chicken out from coming to the mission that afternoon.

Both Ruth and Sam didn't say much for the first couple of minutes into the ride to the church. They were both deep into their thoughts about what the mission was all about and how important it was to the community. "My father started that mission because he saw the plight of the homeless person in America today. He realized that if the church didn't do something that so many people would die on a daily basis. We didn't have much when he started the mission but the people in the community have all taken a front seat in taking care of the people. All in all its been a great success and we know that Jesus is definitely in it."

"I see. You know what I was thinking Sam. I was just thinking what a terrible person I have been. You know at my church we don't have a mission. What is church really about? Isn't it about being like Christ and not just reading about Christ?" Ruth felt in her heart that she needed to make some changes in her life. She was feeling good but she thought about all of the years she had not even ministered the love of Christ to another person.

"I know how you feel Ruth. But today is your day and now you have a mission and a new family. We do lots of things at my church. We have prayer meeting and you are welcome to come and be with us anytime. We have groups that do prison ministry, they go to the hospitals and they also go to the nursing homes. It might be a bit different from what you are used to we are not the traditional church but we love the Lord Jesus Christ and that is all that matters."

"I would really like that." Just at that moment Sam pulled into the church parking lot and parked the car in his father's parking space marked pastor. Ruth felt giddy inside she had met the pastor's son. Her father would just eat that up. He was trying hard to get his little girl married and to a pastor's son that would be rich.

It wasn't as large a church as Ruth went to but it was a good size nevertheless. Ruth was taken back with all the beautiful decorations for the play. Her church went all out for Christmas. There play had been running for so many years they had to give out tickets to make sure that everyone had a seat when they arrived. But she didn't know that she was in for a treat that evening. Sam had been playing the piano for many years and all of the churches came to their play no matter what they had at their own church. .

The play was a story about a young lady who was having problems growing up and had gone to prison. While she was in prison an angel came to her to tell her that if she did not straighten up her life that she would end up in jail forever and that was not what God wanted for her. Many of the congregation had come as a result of the prison ministry. Pastor Eddie put this together to minister to them and their families. There was so much that needed to be mended from when they had been in jail and after coming out. The families were in disarray and this was a way to mend it and get them back on track. They could see that there was a light at the end of the tunnel. The angel took the young lady back to the beginning when the baby Jesus was born. But he didn't stop there he went through Jesus life to show all of the miraculous things that he did for so many people during his ministry. There was the woman with the issue of blood that was healed by Jesus. He showed her the men who were blind and received their sight back from Jesus. He showed her the many people who had received a blessing from Jesus that changed their lives. Then the angel showed Jesus death, burial and resurrection. The story of Christmas was not just about a baby being born but it was about the King of Kings and Lord of Lord that was born that day. The play was complete with all kinds of animals and at the end Jesus came riding through the church on a big white horse. It was a show stopper every year.

Ruth couldn't believe it when she saw that huge horse walk into the sanctuary. They had a good play but nothing like this. The people were cheering and crying and she couldn't help but get up and start screaming herself. A birage of emotions came over here all at once and she started to cry too. All of a sudden Ruth could see a host of angels off to the side cheering and shouting as Jesus rode into the sanctuary. She blinked and then blinked again. She couldn't possibly be seeing what she thought she was seeing. She had an epiphany that day and Jesus became bigger than life for her. Ruth didn't want to leave the church when it was all over. She just sat there soaking up this great feeling that she was having. She never told anyone about seeing the angels. She didn't think that anyone would believe her anyway.

Ruth and Sam had a special relationship after that day. It was only a few days later that Sam would have to return to his home station in Virginia. It was really hard for him leaving this time. He never had a hard time before but he knew that he wanted to see Ruth again and that being long distance was never going to be enough.

Chapter 2

SAM WISHED THAT HE HAD more time to spend at home but it was time for him to return to his duty station. He promised Ruth that he would write and she said that she could email sometimes too if he had one. Sam was quick to give her the address and email to his office. He wasn't inside much but he would make sure that he checked it everyday. He knew he had made an impression on her but he wasn't sure whether there might be someone else in the picture. He would have to move fast if he wasn't going to lose what they had already started. Leaving was never so hard but he had an obligation and if Ruth was to be his in the future then time would tell.

Sam didn't know why but Ruth was the girl for him. She was bright, funny and his mother and father seemed to have taken to her right away. He had butterflies whenever he looked at her. Sam had brought home girls before and maybe his mother wasn't ready but she seemed to chase away every girl he brought home. He dated Ramona for two years before he left for the military. She and his mother never got along. She would always say, "son that girl is not the one for you." His father just tried to stay out of the line of fire. Ramona wasn't from their side of the tracks. She grew up with a silver spoon in her mouth. That's probably why his mother didn't like her. They didn't have anything in common. Ramona didn't know how to cook, she didn't know how to wash dishes or do anything around the house. She had a nanny and a maid growing up. Ramona's father and mother were both doctor's and had practices in several locations. Ramona had a bit of an attitude not so much because she was rich but she grew up different from the other children at church. Bartholomew her father came from the neighborhood. He was blessed enough to have wisdom from above from the time he was a little boy. He always loved playing doctor when he was a kid so his parents scraped and saved to send him to college. Low and behold he had the brains to make it through. He met Cindy in med school and then came Ramona. But like many who made it out of the ghetto they still came back to the old church to make sure that Ramona had a good foundation growing up.

Ramona had lots of things but she was chubby, knock kneed and she wore the craziest coke bottled glasses which didn't make her very attractive. And on top of that she wore braces on her teeth. Sam kind of felt sorry for her and so he befriended her so that she would not be alone. Being a friend to Ramona had its advantages for a kid like Sam. Her father and mother were busy most of the time taking care of patients so they were not home most of the time. Ramona had a nanny and a maid to answer to her every whim. And the two kids took advantage of the situation the best kids knew how.

Bartholomew gave his little princess everything a girl could want and then some. She had her very own bank account to buy whatever she wanted and go wherever she wanted. On the weekends they would pick special places and the nanny would take them wherever they wanted to go. During the winter they would go into New York and have lunch and go ice skating at Rockefeller Center. Sam loved to ice skate, Ramona wasn't very good but she would do anything Sam wanted to do. She just couldn't get the hang of it. But she was a better bowler than Sam was. She enjoyed beating him at every game. They just had lots of fun together growing up. Every Christmas both families went to Radio City Music Hall to see the Christmas show and the Rocketts. Ramona loved the lights and all the excitement. It was the one time she had with her parents together. She would have been very lonely without her friend Sam.

When Sam finally got the nerve to tell Ramona he was leaving for the military she was very sad but she knew how much Sam wanted it and she wasn't really ready to commit to a relationship yet. She decided that she would go off to Europe and continue her schooling there. Sam was happy for her and that was the end of the romance. They were still best friends and Mabel was happy that nothing else had come of it.

Sam returned to Virginia and before he could put his things away he had to call Ruth and tell her he had returned home okay. What should he say? He was tongued tied when it came to her. He mustered up the courage to make the phone call. Maybe he could just say I'm calling to just say hello. That wouldn't be so bad. She would expect that. After all they really had a good time together. He was sure of that. It seemed like forever till someone picked up the phone. "Hello this is Sam Robertson is Ruth at home?"

"Oh yeah. I think she told us about you Sam. This is her father. You have made quite an impression on my daughter. She wants to teach the Bible to the whole world now son. She made the rest of us feel guilty and now she wants the church to start a mission. She's a monster but she means well."

"Oh gosh. Sir, I didn't mean to start any trouble."

"I didn't mean it that way son. I'm glad that my daughter has a true heart for people. She has never sounded so compassionate about anything in a long time. She's a good girl. I'm glad she has good friends like you."

Sam was happy to hear her father say that. This was a step in the right direction. Maybe he will give her permission to see him again. "Is she there that I can speak with her?"

"Yeah, hold on a minute. Ruth it's that guy from the military you was talking about. Come on girl don't keep the man waiting."

"Sam, Sam is that you?"

"Yeah Ruth how are you doing?"

"I'm doing great. I didn't know when I was going to speak to you again. How was your flight?"

"Oh it was good. It didn't take but a few hours to get here. I just had to call you. I hope you don't mind. I really wanted to tell you how great a time I had when we were together. Everything went well that day. I hope you had a good time too." Sam was like an inexperienced young boy on a first date. He didn't have a clue how to talk to girls but he was doing a good job.

"Wow it was the best day of my life. I don't do very much but go to school and church. I have a few girlfriends but we just do regular stuff if you know what I mean. I never thought much about ministry type stuff. I don't know a lot of people who do stuff like that. I'm really glad that I met you and your family. When do you think you'll be coming back home?"

Sam was excited that she wanted to see him again. "I'm not sure. I was really thinking hard and long on the flight home about my military career. My mom has been getting on me about getting married and having a family. But military life is difficult. My crew works long hours. I'm a crew chief and we are gone all the time. If I have a wife and children I won't see them very much. I think that if we are going to be serious about one another Ruth that I might have to leave the military and come back home, get a good job and then we can see how things develop from there. What do you think?

"Well Sam my father is trying hard to get me married too. He brings them home to me its embarrassing. He means well though. But I understand what you mean, I never thought about it but I would like a husband who could be home every night with me and the children. I would like to have children too."

The conversation was getting serious kind of quick but the two knew what they wanted and it was good that they could be honest with each other about it. Sam was feeling uneasy because he loved the military life but he never thought he would find a young lady like Ruth to tug at his heart the way she was. He would have to talk with his mom and dad. They always helped Sam make big decisions when he didn't know which way to turn. He loved his parents.

The days after Sam returned were all very difficult. He had a big decision but he wasn't sure which way to go. He thought it was time for him to call his dad and have a long heart to heart with his mentor. Eddie was the glue that held the family together. He always knew the right thing to do even when Sam didn't. Eddie was always delighted to hear his son's voice although he knew from the sound of Sam's voice that something was troubling him. "What's going on son?" he would say and then Sam would let it all loose.

"Well dad I've been thinking about leaving the military. I've been talking to Ruth, you know the girl that came to have Christmas with us. I really like her dad but there is something tugging at my heart about leaving the crew. I'm not sure what to do. Its time for me to sign my reenlistment papers and I've been putting it off. If I leave I leave a big part of me behind and if I stay I risk losing what could be the best friend of my life. What would you do dad?"

"Well son, there are many people who have to make this very decision every day. It all balls down to what is important in life. Is a career more important than family? If you have a big career and no one to share it with then what is it all about? You know lots of people who have big jobs and lots of money but without people it's nothing Sam. Don't make that decision. You can have your cake and eat it too.'

"How do you figure dad?"

"What I mean is that you can have a great career here and have a family too. The transition won't be easy son because you are in a totally different world from us civilians but I'm sure we can keep you busy and when you see Ruth and maybe walk her down that aisle you will forget all about the guys."

"Oh dad. I think that you are right about that. You always make me feel better. She really liked the mission and wants to do more work with us. I really miss that about being home and you and mom too but I miss working with the people and seeing the changes in their lives. That's what life is all about. Right now I guess the work side of me likes what I do. The crew are great too. But like you said we have great friends and I can come back to playing the piano at church. I don't get to church much because we are always working. Okay dad well you still got my room ready. Don't tell mom just yet. I want it to be a surprise. I'll tell her just before I come home. It will be a few weeks. I have to talk with my commander."

"Oh son. I'm so glad you are coming back home. The whole congregation will be so excited to see you back for good. And you know your mom misses you terribly. I love you son."

No matter how big Sam got his father always told him that he loved him. "I love you too dad."

Sam's talk with his dad had really made him feel a whole lot better. Now it was time to talk with First Sergeant Gordon. Sam knew that his first sergeant would understand. He was having problems keeping things together with his family as well. He would just march right into his office and tell him that he was ending his career. It was a bitter sweet moment when Sam knocked on the door and asked permission to enter. "Hey Sam come on in what's on your mind?"

"Well good morning sir. I hope you had a Merry Christmas."

"Yeah it was great. This was the first Christmas that the family has had together in quite while. You know how it is we are always gone and my wife Katie hates that. But when she signed up to be a military wife she knew the ins and outs. And with all the war now it's getting even tighter." Sergeant Gordon pulled out a big cigar lit it and sat down at his desk.

"Well sir that's what I've come to talk to you about. It's time for my reenlistment and I've decided not to reenlist. I talked at length with my dad about it. I met a girl sir. I think that I would like to get married and have children. I don't want to be away from my family. She's not as understanding as your wife is. She wants a husband that will be home every night. I think that she is right and that I can find something else to do that will make me feel as complete as the military and have my family too."

"Well son it sounds like you have made up your mind. You know you will always have a job here if things change. I'm not going to give you a hard time. Your not like the rest of these guys. Many of them Sam need to be where they are. The military gave them a career that they would not have had otherwise. You are a very intelligent young man, go home and get into college. Use that money the government has given to you and get a good job on Wall Street or something. You will do great no matter what you are doing. Maybe one day you will be playing at the Metropolitan Opera House or Carnegie Hall or something. There is so much that you can do with your life." Sam had never had a conversation like this with the sergeant. He had no idea that he felt that way about him. It made him feel proud.

The conversation was over so Sam got up from his chair and went over to his sergeant and shook his hand. "It was a pleasure working with you sir. And thank you for understanding. If my wife to be changes her mind I'll definitely give you a call and return to duty." He put his hat on and left his office.

Well it was all settled and Sam would be on his way home in just a few short weeks. His mother would be excited. He couldn't wait to tell Ruth the good news. What would he go to college for? He had some time to think things through. Ruth was in college maybe they would see each other walking through the halls of Rutgers University. It had a good name and he could use his benefits there. Rutgers was a good school.

Now that Sam had made his decision he felt better and better about it as the days went on. They had a long mission so he didn't get a chance to speak with Ruth very much. He spoke with her and then every night he would send her emails from the plane. She really had a good sense of humour and she said she was counting every day until he would be coming home. She and his mom were doing work together at the mission. Sam couldn't believe that his mother was really into Ruth. That was definitely a good sign. Mabel didn't like anybody. Ruth sent Sam a picture of them that was taken at the church that evening of the play. He didn't even remember when it was taken. Sam and Ruth were standing near the manger with his mom and dad. He would treasure that picture always.

Chapter 3

SAM HAD CALLED HIS MOM the day before he was leaving to come home. He told her that she didn't have to come and pick him up because Ruth wanted to come and pick him up from the airport. He wanted her to stay home and fix his favorite meal. Mabel didn't mind she hated Newark International with all the cabs and cars it made her nervous. She loved Newark, she had lived their all of her life but she was ready to move South and settle down to some peace and quiet. She and Eddie were getting on in years and they had raised their son, pastored the church and started the mission. There was so much to be grateful for but at the same time she was tired.

The trip to the airport was uneventful to say the least. Ruth got there just moments before Sam's plane was to land. She found a parking space and rushed in so that she could be there when he got off the plane. Newark International was busy as usual that day. The terminal was actually somewhat quiet in the evening. Most of the business travelers flew during the morning hours. Ruth had no problem making it through the terminal to where Sam's plane would come in. It was quiet so she just took a seat and waited patiently. There was only about twenty minutes before the plane touched down.

All of the shops had already closed and there was a scarce amount of personnel at work that evening. There was a woman and two children also waiting for someone to come in along with Ruth. The children were running around and Ruth looked at them and wondered what life would be like in a few years when she and Sam had children. It was kind of exciting thinking about how quick they grow up. She didn't know what it was like growing up with a brother. She and Sam had that in common that they were both the only child in their family. Sam said that he didn't really worry so much about not having a brother or sister because he did a lot with his dad and they had so many children in the congregation that he had lots of friends to play with. Ruth felt a bit different about being an only child. She longed to have had a sister that she could do things with. She had been in the same church but she didn't make friends that easily so it was a while before she had good friends that she spent time with.

Ruth thought that it would be better that she and Sam have at least two children. Would they look like her side of the family or his side of the family? She just wanted that they be healthy. She really didn't care much whether it was a boy or a girl. The minutes went by quickly and after an announcement Ruth could see the plane outside of the window. Her heart started beating quickly. She had not seen Sam since he had left after Christmas. It was such a wonderful time she couldn't wait until he came back home so they could spend time together and see what else they had in common.

Where should she stand? Should she be right outside the door or stand back where he could see her afar off? She decided to stand in the aisle where she could see everyone coming off of the plane. When she saw Sam she had the brightest smile that she could muster up. Sam had on his uniform and he looked so handsome in it. She would never forget seeing him come off the plane. Now he would be home for good. She was glad that he had on his uniform maybe that would impress her father. She gave them the phone number and address so that they would be there when they arrived. Her father was sending mixed signals just before she left the house. No one would ever be good enough for her little girl but someone that he had picked out.

"Sam, Sam."

"Ruth. Wow you look great. I hope you didn't have to wait very long." Sam didn't know whether it was right to hug her yet so he just shook her hand.

"No I just got here a few minutes ago. But it wouldn't matter I came here to get you. I would have waited all night." Ruth was overwhelmed how smitten she was with Sam. She hoped the evening would go well with her parents. Eddie and Mabel were easy but her parents were much different from them. She was really nervous but she didn't want Sam to know. "Let's get your luggage and get on to the house. My parents should be there waiting for us for dinner."

"Oh yeah. I hope that the evening goes well. I'm sure it will let's not worry. Most parents don't get along right away. We'll just have to convince them that I'm a great guy." Ruth smiled when Sam said that. How could anyone think anything otherwise. He has served his country. He had a great future although he wasn't sure what that would be. He had a very likable personality. And Ruth liked him that was all that mattered.

The couple walked over to the next terminal where they picked up Sam's bags and made their way outside to the car garage. Ruth drove her mother's car to the airport. Her father said that after she finished college he would purchase a vehicle for her graduation present. Being so taken with her beauty all Sam could do was stare at Ruth most of the ride going home.

Ruth and Sam came through the door all smiles. It was time for the whole family to be together. Susan and Johnny were sitting in the living room with Eddie and Mabel when the couple came into the house. "Well, well you two it's about time you got in here the dinner is getting cold." Mabel broke the ice and Sam was happy about that. Ruth took Sam's hand and took him into the living room to meet her parents. "Mom, dad this is Sam. Look how nice my military hero looks in his uniform."

"Yes, that's my son. He is a hero in this house."

"Well Sam I finally got a chance to meet the man that stole my daughters heart. You had better be good to my baby."

"Oh Johnny. It's nice to meet you Sam I'm Susan. I'm sure you are a wonderful young man. Your mother and father have been so very courteous to us. I'm looking forward to eating some of that good smelling stuff in the kitchen. I'm not a good cook but I know good cooking when I smell it."

"Come on Susan. Let's get everything ready." Susan and Ruth went into the kitchen with Mabel while the men sat down to talk men talk."

Eddie felt the tension in the room so he asked Sam to play something on the piano. That way he would have time to relax and hopefully it would tame the beast in Johnny. He understood that he was just acting like a father but he wanted to bridge the gap and slow the tiger down a bit so Sam could get his composure and show Johnny what a wonderful young man he really was. "Son why don't you play something for us on the piano. Show Johnny what you got. Johnny loved music but he didn't want to like Sam. He had a nice young man he planned on marrying his daughter to and it wasn't Sam.

Sam motioned over to the piano and started playing some music from the old days. His father allowed him to play all types of music not just gospel. When the women heard the music they made their way from the kitchen into the living room. Before everyone knew it the couples had made it to the floor and they were dancing and having a good time. Ruth sat on the bench by Sam. She just looked in her man's eyes with amazement. Her father was having a good time and that was a good thing. Thank God for Eddie. After a few songs the whole family sat down to eat and Mabel's cooking topped off the evening. She had made a special cake but they would have coffee and cake after a time.

Everyone sat down to the dinner table and Eddie did the honors of blessing the meal. Sam and Ruth started to relax now that Johnny had already gotten up and shook it around a little. Ruth had not seen her mother and father dance ever and could not believe that her father even knew how. They talked about the mission and asked Susan and Johnny to come and visit with them whenever they had the chance. They could always use a few more hands to cook or build something or whatever was needed at the moment. Like Ruth her parents were pew potatoes and had not thought about doing any kind of volunteer work. She was surprised to hear her mother say that before she got married when she was a teenager in college that her sorority sisters used to volunteer all the time. Her favorite thing was volunteering with the inner city children. The evening was a great success and Mabel wanted to do it again really soon.

Sam and Ruth snuck away from the grownups for a nice walk outside. Sam took his new girl to his spot in the backyard where he still had the swing he and his father made when he was just a young boy. He thought it would be romantic to give her a swing and just look at the moon. He was right she was eating it up like fresh chocolate donuts. Women liked the small romantic things guys did. Sam didn't have a lot of money so he had to put on the charm real strong. "I was thinking about enrolling in school for the next semester."

"That will be great. I'm going to Rutgers how about coming there? We can have lunch together sometimes and maybe we might have a course together. That would be fun."

"Yeah I was thinking the same thing. Do you think your fathers warming up to me? He looked pretty good out there."

"I was amazed to see him dancing myself. I don't get a chance to see much of that in my house. We are kind of stuffy. Maybe your family will put some life into my family. I think we are doing okay. But with my father one can never tell. Let's just ignore him and see what happens."

"Okay Ruth. I sure think you look really pretty tonight." Ruth just smiled.

"We had better get back inside before your father calls the cops on me or something. Mom might have that cake ready. I sure am ready for some. You know my mom is the greatest cook ever. Oh I'm sorry. Don't worry she taught me everything she knows. When we get married I don't mind doing the cooking. Or we can do it together."

"I like the way that sounds. I love a man that can cook. My father sure can't but he's a good dad. He loves me and that is all that matters."

Sam and Ruth joined their parents in the house and they were talking about old times and how they met and how things have changed from when they were young. Mabel and Eddie met while youngster in school. Eddie said he used to walk Mabel home every day and he just knew she was the only girl for him. Johnny and Susan didn't meet until college. He said he had to beat out a whole lot of guys just to get a date with her. Then her father didn't like him. Nowadays young people shack up and then get married. Most of those marriages don't last past the wedding day. "Let that be a lesson to you young people. None of this shackin up business. We won't allow it. You date like decent folk and then you get married and then have children. None of this not having children business. That's what God put us here for. We gotta have children to keep things going." Johnny had said his two cents and everybody just shook their heads in agreement. The flow of the evening was dwindling down now so it was time for cake and coffee. The ladies went into the kitchen again and left the men alone.

Sam thought it was his turn to ask Johnny what he did for a living. He was trying to make an impression by acting as if he was interested in what his future father in law did for a living. But he seemed to be more interested in talking with Eddie than with him. Sam couldn't get a word in edgewise. He couldn't wait until this evening was over. Not that he wasn't having a good time. But he noticed that Johnny was ignoring him. The ladies came back in with the cake and coffee. Mabel asked Sam if he would play the piano again which he quickly obliged. He felt like he had no reason to be in the room at that point.

Sam played a few songs and watched them dance again. After a time his father took over so that Sam could dance with Ruth. His father had a way of knowing what his son was thinking at all times. Sam was glad he had taken over so he could stop feeling like he had two left feet at their first meeting. After all was said and done Sam and Ruth had a good time that evening but there was a lot of work to be done to win her father's affection.

Chapter 4

SAM WISHED HE WOULD NEVER have to have an evening like the night before. He so enjoyed being with Ruth and her mother was great but her father didn't want anything to do with him and he knew it. He was feeling so bad that he had to speak with his mom about the situation. How did his father win her father over that was the question? He spoke with his mother that morning at breakfast about how he was feeling about the situation. She told him to do what his father did go over and speak with him man to man. She said that Johnny just wanted a good man for his daughter. If Sam went over and spoke with him about his future and how he planned on taking care of Ruth that might just calm him down. He seemed to have had a pretty good time that evening and Susan was a good woman.

He felt that his mother was right and so he called Ruth up and told her that it was time for him to have a man to man talk with her father. Ruth didn't quite know what to say. She wasn't used to her boyfriend coming over and speaking one on one with her father. She didn't know whether she should be there or whether she should let Sam do this all by himself. Maybe this would make her father respect him more. Her father's problem was that he wanted her to marry someone rich and Sam didn't have any money, he didn't even have a job at the moment. She asked her mother what she should do. Susan told her that when she started dating Johnny that her father didn't like him either. Her father liked playing golf and Johnny would come over every week to play golf with her father. That was one way he won her father's heart. He spent more time with her father than he spent with her for a while. She wondered whether he cared about her or not. But it was his way of getting into the family. Susan said that she would have a heart to heart talk with Johnny and see whether she could help things out.

With great apprehension Sam came over to the house to speak with Johnny. He was shaking all over but he was gonna get this off of his chest. Johnny came to the door to let Sam in. "Come on in son. How you doing today? My baby said you needed to talk with me about something."

"Well yes sir. Well sir you being a college professor and all I thought you might give me some tips on the best career fields to go into. I hope that soon me and Ruth might get married and I want to be able to give her everything that she could possibly want. I will be starting college in just a few months and there are so many fields that I can go into. Bartholomew thinks I should become a doctor like him and his wife. I don't know whether I want to put that much time into school. What do you think?"

Johnny was really surprised that Sam came over to talk with him about a career field. He kind of liked that. Well he had been in the military and that was a good thing. He had a lot of respect for the young men and women who gave their lives to serve their country. At least he wasn't lazy. "Well son I'm a college professor but I see lots of students every day. You don't necessarily have to know what you want to be long term. There are some classes that every student must take. But within a period of time you must figure it out. What do you like to do? What do you have an aptitude for?"

"Well I do love music but I don't want to get a degree in music. I've been playing the piano since I was a little boy. My teachers say I have an aptitude for mathematics. But what great career field can I get into with mathematics?"

"Oh my boy have you ever heard about the actuarial sciences? These guys make lots of money. You have to study really hard. I can have you talk with some of the students that are in the program. It's difficult stuff but you seem like a diligent young man."

"Actuarial sciences huh. I had better look that up when I get back to the house. Do you think that Ruth would want to marry say an actuarial science major?"

"Well I don't know but maybe I might put in a good word if you do good on your exams my boy. But I can't say what my daughter would like you know. There is this guy that is trying to get her affections at the church. His father has a very large business and he stands to inherit the whole shebang you know. A father in law can move into the big house when he gets old and tired you know. But I can maybe put in a good word. We'll see about that."

Sam could not believe what he was hearing. Johnny was more worried about his daughter taking care of him when he got old and gray than what would make her happy. He was pitiful but Sam thought he would play the game anyway. Sam was just glad that at least there was a conversation going. He wasn't being ignored because there was no one else in the house but the two of them. "Well sir I had better go but can we get together sometime and just hang out the two of us. What else do you like to do? Fishing, bowling, golf?"

"Well do you play golf?"

"I don't usually have much time for golf. We were in the air most of the time but I would love to play if you have some time. As a matter of fact I have some friends that are still in at McGuire AFB and we can go up there have lunch, go up in one of the plane's and play golf on the base what do you say?"

"Wow on the base. That sounds like fun. I'll let you know when I'm available."

"Okay sir that sounds great. Tell Ruth that I will call her this evening.

Johnny started getting nervous he would have to get his young man in quick otherwise all would be lost. He got on the phone and called young Barney to get a spark going otherwise he and Susan would end up in a nursing home.

Johnny had a slew of boys lined up to meet Ruth but she would have nothing to do with any of them. She wanted to pick her own husband. The next day after Sam came to visit Ruth came home from school and her father had a young man sitting in the living room waiting for her to come home. She would often come home for lunch and return to school after having a sandwich or something. She could not believe that he was so bold as to have him there for lunch knowing that she would be coming home. Ruth was never so embarrassed in her life. He looked like pee wee Herman this guy. His suit was too tight. He was short and his hair looked rather strange. But then he was on the usher board and his family gave regular tithes and offerings to the church. His father had offered at one time to build a new church since the one they were attending was old and had been in use for over 100 years. They had just celebrated the church's birthday and pee wee made eyes at Ruth the whole time. She just hated him. Anyway dad invited him over for lunch to try and set things up. That was a lame way of getting a girl to ask her father.

When Ruth came through the door they both jumped up like they were just having a men's conversation or something. "Ruth honey, you know Barney, Ted's son."

"Well yes I do. Hi Barney it's nice to meet you." The whole time Ruth's skin was crawling and she just wanted to get out of the room as soon as she possibly could. But dad had other plans. "I thought that maybe we could all have lunch together. Unless you have other plans." Ruth didn't have the nerve to say no. Although she wanted to. She didn't want her father to be angry nor Barney to feel bad. It wasn't his fault that he looked the way that he did. He was probably a really nice guy.

"Well lets all go into the dining area for lunch." Ruth couldn't believe it her dad had a four course meal waiting. She could not believe he was going all out for this geek. His father must have a lot of money for her dad to do all of that. Her mom had somehow made other plans, she knew that Ruth would be upset about the whole arrangement. Anyway they all sat down and then the phone rang. Her dad jumped up of course after he told them to continue with the lunch. He had this whole thing planned and now he was going to leave her alone with the guy. What a family she had?

"So tell me Barney about yourself. I see you at church but I've never gotten a chance to talk with you." And she never planned on talking to him. He was just too weird.

"Well Ruth there isn't very much to tell. I work along with my father in the family business. I'm on the usher board as you know. I'm looking for a wife but it's hard to find a girlfriend. Most of the girls don't like me. I hope you don't mind my coming over for lunch today. Your dad said that you were not dating anyone and that maybe you might want to go to a movie sometime."

"Oh Barney thanks for thinking about me but I'm not interested in dating right now. I'm going to college and I want to stay focused on my studies. You should think about going to college or in the military or something. Plenty of women and I know they would love to see you in a uniform." She was lying through her teeth. She didn't feel very good about this but there was no way that she was going out with Barney. Nothing would help this guy but Ruth really believed there was someone for everybody out there. It just took time to find them. She had eyes for Sam and didn't want to mess that up. She really hoped that her father would like him despite the fact that he didn't have lots of money like Barney.

Lunch was a strain but Ruth made it through. She made idle conversation with Barney and then quickly excused herself because she had to go back to school. "Barney I hope you don't mind but I have a class in just fifteen minutes. I really will have to go. I'm sure my father will have lots for you guys to talk about once he gets off of the phone."

"That's okay Ruth. I really enjoyed your company today." She left Barney sitting in the dining room. She went over to her father who was still on the phone talking to probably her mother and told him she had to go. He quickly ended the conversation and went in to talk with Barney.

Ruth couldn't wait to see Sam again. Sam had called her the night before to tell her that he had a talk with her father and things seemed to have gone well. He had somehow talked him into playing a game of golf with him. He thought that might break the ice. He wasn't looking forward to it but if he wanted to marry Ruth he would have to win her father first. Sam invited Ruth to come to church on Sunday. He was looking forward to seeing her again.

Ruth really liked Sam but what kind of guy invited a girl to church all the time? Ruth grew up Baptist and so she wasn't quite sure when she and Sam walked into the little church what she was to expect. The first time she came it was for the Christmas play. The people were all so pleasant like all other churches. Sam walked straight down front and asked Ruth to sit in the front row. Oh gosh she had not planned on sitting in the front row but Sam insisted. Sam played the piano for the church so this way he could play and look at Ruth all at the same time. He wanted to make sure that the other guys knew she was spoken for. Ruth wasn't much on singing, dancing and certainly could not play an instrument. She really liked this about Sam though. She could imagine that at times he would play the piano and sing songs only for her. She was sure that everybody was looking at her as she walked in the church with Sam. He was such a handsome young man and the girls were certainly jealous that he had brought her to church once again. She felt really out of place, but she was there and they would just have to deal with it.

Eddie and Mabel had not arrived as yet but they knew that Sam was bringing Ruth to church again that day. They both walked right up to the front and sat down next to Ruth. "Hey darling you doing okay today? How are your parents? Tell them to come by again anytime."

"They are doing well. I think that you guys should come to our house next time. My dad has a wonderful art collection that he loves to show off." Ruth was a pretty little girl and had good manners so it wasn't hard for Eddie and Mabel to take to her right away. They sure hoped that this would be the one. Sam was taking a long time finding a wife. When he set out for the military they were sure that he would come home with a wife right away but Sam was too busy working. When he decided to leave the military and return home both his parents were so excited.

The service started as would be expected with the pastor praying and reading the scripture for the morning. After prayer the pastor asked if there was anyone that was new to the congregation so that they could be officially greeted and welcomed into the family. Well of course Ruth was right up front so she couldn't hide. She stood up and turned around and gave a nice wave to the congregation. All of a sudden the members came up one by one and hugged her and kissed her and she felt like one of the family right away. What a warm and loving church Sam belonged too. Ruth started to feel more comfortable. The pastor made several announcements and then the church choir stood up to sing. Ruth recognized many of the songs and felt like this must be a Baptist church, there is nothing different between this church and the church she grew up in. The ushers came and lined up in front of the church so Ruth thought it was time to take up the offering but instead the pastor asked if there were any in the congregation that needed prayer for sickness or anything else they wanted the congregation to pray for. She had never experienced anything like this before. While Sam played the music many of the members came up for pray. But they did an interesting thing the pastor had a bottle of oil and he would put it on his hands and he would lay his hands on the persons head and then he would pray and then sometimes the person would fall on the floor. If it was a woman they would lay a cloth over her legs and if it was a man someone just stood by to watch over him. Ruth didn't know what this was all about she just watched and thought she would ask later. She wanted to be polite. She must have had a strange look on her face because Mabel reached over and took her hand. "Don't be frightened child. This is the work of the Holy Spirit."

"The Holy Spirit."

"Yes the Spirit of Jesus Christ. In the bible it says that if there is anyone sick amongst you to call for the elders of the church, anoint them with oil and pray. The bible says that they will be healed."

"Really."

"Yes."

"We don't do that in the Baptist church."

"Well you should honey."

Ruth had seen something different in the holly roller church that day. But she didn't see anything wrong with it if it was in the Bible. She sure wished that they did that at her church though because for such a small church they had over fifty people in the church with some form of cancer. Maybe if they prayed they wouldn't have so many sick people in the church. She would have to ask Sam more about this oil. Ruth was really enjoying herself at the church. It was different but different could be good sometime.

After the service was over Sam invited Ruth to come back to his parent's house for supper. They always had a few people from the church over. It was like a tradition in their house to have people over after church. Ruth was delighted and drove with Sam to his home. It was a small house, nothing fancy but cozy. Like all mothers Mabel put an apron on Ruth and gave her several chores to do. Sam was used to his mother so he went about taking care of his chores. He knew how to set the table and get the cups and drinks ready for the guest's arrival. This gave Mabel a chance to talk with Ruth and see what kind of a girl her Sam was getting involved with. "So Ruth I heard that you and Sam might go to the same school."

"Yes maam." Mabel liked that she was really a polite young lady. "What are you planning on being when you grow up?" They both smiled when she said this.

"Well Miss Mabel I just really want to find a nice young man, settle down and have children. I love writing and so I'm taking some English and writing classes right now. I thought that maybe one day I would write Christian books for children. Maybe I might even be a school teacher or something. I'm really not too sure right now."

"Well that sounds marvelous." Mabel wanted several grand children. She had so many complications when she had Sam that the doctor told her that she should not try to have another one or she and the baby might not make it. So Mabel was grateful that she had at least one child. "You know that sounds just like me when I was your age. I just always loved babies and wanted to have a baby as soon as I got married. Eddie and I had a hard time but God gave us Sam. He is my life."

"He seems like a very nice young man. I was taken back when he asked me to church. I thought it strange. Usually boys ask you to the movies or out to eat. But instead he brought me to church and to meet his family. That truly means a lot to me. I hope my father will calm down and give him a chance. He's trying to get me married but I don't like his pickings if you know what I mean."

"Oh child. What we will do is invite them to church and have Sam give the message. That will win them over. Oh and he is a marvelous cook too."

"Really. I think he might have mentioned something about that."

"Trust me Ruth, Sam will make a fine husband. If he were a bum even as his mother I would tell you the truth. I'm not like some mothers no matter what there children do they will lie for them. I don't have to lie about Sam he's a fine young man if I may say so myself."

"I'm sure that he is Miss Mabel. He sure knows his way around the kitchen. A girl could get use to that." Mabel just smiled. She was sure proud of how she and Eddie raised their son. He was a good boy.

The guests started to arrive slowly but surely. It seemed as if they saw the fried chicken come out of the pan. Mabel loved macaroni and cheese, corn bread and fried chicken. The church said she made the best fried chicken in the church. They poured through the door anytime she was cooking. She was just a natural. She could bake all kinds of pies and cakes. Sam liked her cheesecake the best. She had truly missed her calling. She had talked about a shop at one point in time but she just stayed small baking for the church and anybody who wanted catering for weddings and other occasions. She made a good living at it. She and Eddie were saving their money for the day that they could move to Florida and retire never having to work again.

Deacon Flake and his wife were the first ones to arrive at the Robertson home. The others trickled in slowly. Ronald and

Samantha were nice enough but they always managed to come over every Sunday. Ronald could live off of Mabel's cooking if he got the chance because as he said it "Samantha could burn a boiled egg." Mabel felt sorry for him so she let them come over every Sunday so Ronald could get at least one good meal for the week. Samantha could have taken the time out to get some cooking lessons but she was too busy shopping and spending Ronald's money. He was at least 15 years older than her so everybody knew she didn't marry him for his good looks. Ronald didn't mind though he worshiped the ground that Samantha walked on. It was shaky ground but he managed. Ronald was a very gifted young man and although his family came from meager beginnings he won a scholarship to Seton Hall and graduated magna cume laude. He was making six figures but really loved his little church and remained faithful to his pastor. He and Eddie grew up together in the neighborhood. Eddie was happy because he always took care of the church financially. It was good to have at least one member he could count on. Ronald was a geek but he tried so hard to be cool. "Hey Eddie how you doing? That was a good sermon today man. I wish I could preach like that. I would probably put everybody to sleep."

"Now, now Ronald. You have been a deacon with us for a long time. I think that maybe you should think about giving a sermon. Don't worry I will help you prepare and you will see how easy it is."

"Are you kidding me. I don't think that I could do it. But let me think about it." Ronald knew full well he was just itching for the chance to get in the pulpit. He loved Eddie but all the men wanted a chance to preach. It was a position of power and he could probably get more cooking from Mabel too. All the people in the congregation gave you gifts and complements even when the sermon was the worst they had ever heard. He wanted it so bad he could taste it.

The dinner went off well as usual. Ruth and Sam went out side for a walk. He was feeling so shy. Up until now he didn't have to say very much. But he was watching Ruth work beside his mom and that was a good thing. He was sure that his mom was taken with Ruth's charm just as he was. It was now his turn to woo this young lady.

He didn't know that she was already smitten with him. "I bought you some flowers Ruth. I hope you like them."

"Thank you Sam they are absolutely beautiful. How did you know I like roses."

"Well I figured all beautiful women liked beautiful things." Ruth was smiling like a chessure cat. "Well what did you think about church and my parents they are great, mom sure knows how to cook." He put his head down took her hand like a young school boy. She didn't object. She liked how he was so shy.

"I thought the church service was nice. It was quite different from what I am used to in the Baptist church. We are not as loud as your church. It was different but I could go back. Your mom reminds me of my mom and she can cook. That food was so good. You think I can come back again for some of that corn bread?"

"You sure can anytime. And just for the record I have the recipe for that cornbread. I can make it just like mom." Ruth looked up at him as if to say this guy certainly cannot be real. What kind of man cooks? But she sure liked the idea. Her father didn't know how to boil water let alone make corn bread.

"So what are your plans for the future Ruth? You seem like the kind of young lady a man could marry and settle down and have children with. I'm not old but my parents keep reminding me that I'm not getting any younger. I left the military so that I could go to school and get a good job. It takes lots of money to raise a family these days. Mom and dad had it good because they only had one child. I think I would like to have a house full. How about you?"

"Well I don't know about a house full but I do want to have children. My Sam this is happening all so fast. I want to get married and my father is trying hard to marry me off to one of the boys at church. But until now I have not found anyone that makes me heart beat fast you know. I feel something for you and I hope that one day we will be married and have children together. Let's just take it one step at a time. If it was meant to be it will be. I'm not going anywhere."

"Oh don't worry. You'll see it will all work out. My parents are planning on moving to Florida soon and they are going to leave me the house. The house is all paid for so we won't have to worry about that. I will be finished school and already have a job lined up working with one of those large firms on Wall Street or something. Your dad said that I can make top salary as an actuarial somebody. I have not looked it up yet. But he seems to think that it will be a good career for me. You can stay home and we can have babies right away. Am I moving too fast. I'm sorry Ruth but I just don't want you to get away from me. I feel something wonderful about you." Ruth just smiled in that girlish way that only she could. She was pure and Sam could see it. "That sounds great Sam. Now enough of this talk you didn't tell me that you were so good on the piano. You must have started very young?"

"Oh yeah. My father didn't let me go out and play until I had learned my lessons. At first I hated it and then after a while I kind of liked it. Well the girls liked it at church and that made me want to play even better. Maybe one day you can come over for lunch and I'll play just for you Ruth."

"That sounds great. I hate to break up our time but I'm sure my father is wondering why I'm out so late. I don't usually go out much. Maybe you had better take me home."

"Okay Ruth. Your right. I don't want to get him mad before the wedding is set." He just smiled at Ruth and he knew she was the one.

Chapter 5

By the winter the couple had gotten engaged and the mother of the bride and groom could not wait to start making wedding arrangements. Ruth was so excited about her upcoming wedding. Mabel, Susan and Ruth planned every little detail. They didn't want to spend too much money because they didn't want a lot of debt after the wedding was over. Ruth wore her mothers wedding gown from when she got married and this made her mother very happy. The gown was just stunning. It had a long train down the back. It was decorated with what looked like rose petals around the bodice and down the back of the dress. It was accentuated with very tiny pearls around the rose petals. Ruth knew that one day she would wear that dress too and the time had arrived. The affair was catered by Mabel of course and the food was exquisite. At the wedding reception would be served stuffed cornish game hens, glazed ham and turkey. The first course was tossed salad, and then the second course would be a choice of three different vegetables, with either rice or a baked potato. The wedding cake was made by one of the sisters in the church. She had a bakery and made the cake to look like a church. It had about 10 layers on it. Mabel was afraid that it was going to fall but it stood up pretty well despite how big it was.

The wedding took place at Ruth's church only because it was larger than Sam's church to accommodate both his and her family and friends. But Eddie had the honors of doing the sermon for the young couple. Oh it was a day to remember. Sam looked so handsome in his tuxedo and the bride was just stunning. Mabel couldn't contain herself when she saw Ruth and she just broke down crying. Oh how she longed for this day. "Ruth how beautiful you look. I never imagined this day would be so wonderful."

"Oh Miss Mabel you look rather stunning yourself. I am blessed to have found such a wonderful man as your son."

"I know I told you he was a good catch." Mabel stayed with Ruth for a while. Her mother was busy making sure that everyone was in place and that the wedding was ready to start. After all the guests were seated and Eddie and Sam were in place she rushed to make sure her baby was ready to walk down the aisle.

"Ruth now remember all the things we talked about. You are about to make the most important step of your life. Well that is until we start getting the grand-children."

"Oh mother, we haven't even gotten married yet and here you are talking about children. Sam and I want to have children right away. Let's get through the wedding first." Susan had tears in her eyes. She was only fussing like a mother hen would. She was so overjoyed that finally her little girl was growing up and leaving home. She didn't know what she would do without her. But now was the time to let her go and be with the one she loved. Johnny walked through the door to escort his daughter down the aisle to be married. He had a lot of feelings but he truly wished that it was Barney she was marrying. He liked the Robertson family and Sam really loved Ruth but he didn't have much of a future like Barney did. His father had lots of money and Ruth could have had anything she wanted. But then he figured young people didn't have much sense anymore. He managed a big smile so that Ruth would be happy.

"So is the bride to be all ready to get hitched oh I'm sorry ready to be married?"

"Oh daddy. You know that I am. I know that you wanted me to marry that bozo. But I refuse to marry someone I don't love for money. You know me better than that. Your gonna just have to accept Sam. I'll never love another man. Except for you that is." That put a smile on his face. He loved that little girl more than life. He could remember the day they brought Ruth home from the doctors he was giving out cigars even though he didn't smoke. He was the proudest daddy on the block. Now his little girl was leaving to take up with some bozo he didn't really like.

Ruth could hear the music as she and her father approached the church door. All of the guests stood up as the flower girl and boy walked down the aisle. Marie and Pedro were just five years old but they took it all in stride. Marie threw out rose petals as she walked down the aisle and Pedro fussed with his tie all the way down the aisle but they made it. Ruth was so nervous her butterflies had butterflies but she was determined to make it down the aisle without passing out. Her father was doing pretty well and didn't fall down like he did during the rehearsal. She was sure that he might have been drinking before the wedding. But he was smiling and all was well.

She wanted to just walk quickly but counted a few seconds before taking each step. Ruth and her father were all smiles. She could see the faces of all the young men who had tried to date her but Ruth wasn't interested. They had lost one of their finest women to someone that wasn't even in the congregation. But they couldn't resist seeing the bride in all of her glory just one last time. At the front of the church was aunt Kristy. She watched all of her sisters, brothers, nieces and nephews get married but she never married. She was definitely going to be a spinster. A rich one at that though. She was more interested in working and travelling all over the world. She was a good Christian woman though. Ruth was glad she had taken time out of her busy schedule to attend the wedding. She couldn't wait to see what she had bought her for a present.

Sam stood down front with his father and Doug who was his best man. Doug and Sam grew up together in the same neighborhood. He was a few years older than Sam and was a little jealous that Sam had found a girl before him but he was happy for the young couple nevertheless. Eddie was smiling from ear to ear and was so proud of his son that day. The bride finally made her way down the aisle and took her place next to her husband to be.

As everyone took their seats Eddie started out with "dearly beloved we are gathered here together on this occasion." You could hear a pin drop in the sanctuary. All of a sudden Mabel started to crying "my baby". Then followed Susan right after her. You would have thought it was a funeral or something. The way mothers act you would think that they would never see their children again. It was a wonder they made it through the ceremony. Eddie tried his best to keep a straight face but every now and then he would look up at Mabel and give her the evil eye. She was acting like a big baby.

Eddie gave a heart wrenching story about a young couple who spent many years of their lives loving one another as man and wife. They had several children together and they had all married and had children of their own. The couple felt blessed in their older years to be able to travel and see the world together. But one day the woman was diagnosed with Alzheimer's and after a while she didn't even know who her husband was anymore. For quite a while he kept his wife at home taking care of her every need. He woke her up each day and gave her a bath and fed her breakfast. Each day he would take her for a walk in the park because she loved watching the children play and just being out in the fresh air. He took her to visit her children and grand children so she would not forget who they were. After having dinner he would sit her down and read her favorite scriptures to her and they would sing hymns together. Amazingly so she had not forgotten her favorite songs. Then he would brush her hair and they would retire to bed after watching one of her favorite movies on television. This went on for years until her health issues were such that he could not do it all by himself. Now it was time to visit her at the nursing home. His heart ached not having her at home with him every day. She was like his heart beat he couldn't live without her. He was like one of the staff their every day taking care of the needs of his wife. He was there when she woke up in the morning until at night when she went to bed. The nursing home set up a special room where he would come and stay at the nursing home with his wife. This way he could be with her just like at home but he would have the staff there to assist him when he needed it. They loved the couple so much and Henry really appreciated the care they gave to him and his wife. One day Myrtle went home to be with the Lord and Henry moved back home to his house.

"Ruth, Sam a husband and wife are not just two people who love each other when the times are good. They are two people who walk through this journey through good times and bad times. There will be great sacrifices that will have to be made in life. These sacrifices will be made together. Never stop loving one another because one has an infirmity that the other does not have. The two of you together will have the strength to make it through if you work together."

With that the couple said their vows and the church exploded with applaudes, tears and cheers. Sam and Ruth were one. "You may kiss the bride."

After the wedding was over the church went to the family life center for the festivities. The tables had all been decorated with a centerpiece of silk flowers complements of the Green family. The musicians played soft music while the guests mingled and the bridal party took pictures to last a life time. Mabel and Susan had since stopped crying long enough to get the people seated and the meals served.

Chapter 6

WELL IT WAS OFFICIAL SAM and Ruth were expecting their first child. Ruth was sick every day but her excitement overroad any thing that she was feeling. Sam walked around like a peacock. The grand parents couldn't stop smiling since this would be their first grand child. The women just used it as an excuse to go out and spend money. Mabel and Eddie decided that after the baby was born they would stay a few months to help Ruth get used to motherhood but then they would move out of the house and leave for their new home they bought in Orlando Florida. They had been wanting to move south for many years but just could not see themselves leaving the people and the church that they had grown to love. Who could they possibly get to run the church like Pastor Eddie? He was a natural and he had literally put his whole life into the church and the whole neighborhood. These were all his family as he put it. He was just a good guy and there was not one person who would say anything otherwise.

Sam and Ruth made some changes everyday to the baby's room. Sam went to the store and purchased the paint, the baby bed and dresser. He wanted it to be a surprise so he had it delivered after Ruth's mom snuck her away for lunch one day. Ruth loved going to Priory Restaurant. It was one of the truly eloquent restaurants in all of Newark. It had been a Catholic church at one time and an entrepreneur turned it into a restaurant. It was kind of weird but it was done very tastefully. When you walked in there was nothing different about it the stained glass was still in tact but there were no pews. It was divided into three separate dining rooms. The tables were decorated like a three star restaurant. You could eat off the floors the place was so clean. Ruth loved the fried chicken. They really had the best fried chicken outside of Mabel. So Sam didn't have much time to prepare but his dad was waiting to help him get the room ready.

First they wanted to get the furniture ready and then they would cover it over so that they could paint and not get any paint on the furniture. They reminisced about the day that Sam came home from the hospital. They didn't have a lot of money even though it wasn't many years ago. What an occasion it was. Mabel and Eddie knew most of the people in the neighborhood. Eddie had no idea that the women at the church had planned a shower for Mabel the day she came home from the hospital. She and Sam stayed in the hospital for three days. That was the time when having a baby was a big thing. Nowadays the women come home right the day after because the insurance companies don't want to pay. Hopefully she won't have any complications. So Eddie came driving down the street but it was blocked off. He couldn't imagine what could be going on so he went up the street and around the corner so that they could get in. He was sure going to give somebody a piece of his mind once they got into the house. What could be wrong he just couldn't figure it all out. All of a sudden as they turned the corner there was this mob of people complete with enough food to feed an army, banners, music and all types of gifts for mother and baby. Mabel was overwhelmed as was Eddie.

It was one of the best memories of Eddie's life. He told his son about the ins and outs of fatherhood and that life no longer is about him but about his wife and son. All Sam could do was laugh. He had heard all of these stories before but his father was so funny about some of the stuff he used to do that he had to laugh again and again. Baby Sam ran the whole household until Mabel thought he was big enough for her to get a switch off of the tree outside. That stopped his shenanigans quick. But he was just the average little boy and his mom and dad loved him just the same.

It took quite a few hours to get the furniture put together because Eddie refused to read the instructions. He just knew how to do everything so he put pieces where they were not supposed to go. They didn't realize it until it was just about put together. So they would start over and over again until Sam finally convinced him to read the instructions but they got the room together before Ruth and her mom returned home.

Sam didn't tell her about the room. He just welcomed her home as if nothing had happened. She never went into that room. Mabel had gone out to the store to pick up the frilly stuff. Eddie and Sam had done their part. Mabel was to come home and sneak into the room and put all the frilly stuff up and then they would take her in after dinner. Sam had a hard time not telling her about it. He was not one to keep a secret when it came to surprises.

It was Ruth's turn to cook dinner that night but she wasn't feeling very well so while Mabel worked on the room Sam made dinner for the family that evening. He didn't know whether she had eaten too much or whether she was just feeling sick as she normally did. He just made a light soup with bread so she wouldn't have anything too heavy before going to bed.

When it was time for dinner Sam went up to wake Ruth to see if she wanted something to eat. She had this really strange look on her face like she had seen a ghost. "Sam I had a really strange dream."

"What happened?"

"I had a dream that we were leaving the hospital with the baby. Oh Sam we are going to have a son. We have not even talked about names yet. I guess I just assumed that we would name him after you. Is that what you want?"

"Oh darling I'm not worried about names, a son, really?"

"Yes. I'm not one on having dreams but maybe that was God's way of talking to me Sam. But why now? He has never talked to me before. It's kind of taken me back a bit. That God would take the time to speak to me about our son."

"Well you will have to talk to my father about that. He has dreams from God all the time."

"Really I didn't know that. Yeah he has told dad a lot of things they have a really close relationship. He told me just the other day that he was praying to the Lord about him and mom moving and he was asking God who would take over the church. I guess he always thought that it would be me that would take it over."

"Well aren't you going to take over the church?"

"I had not really thought about it. I would if dad said that the Lord wanted me to but it seems like God has chosen someone really special to take over the church. I will remain in the position that I already hold. I'm okay with that. God knows best you know. Hey we have dinner ready and then the family has a big surprise for you."

"A surprise. Are there people coming over? I look terrible."

"No honey. Just me and my parents. Your mom and dad know about the surprise but they won't be over until tomorrow. It's just the family. Don't worry just wash your face and come on down."

Ruth got up and went into the bathroom to wash her face. She couldn't get the dream out of her mind. She had never had an experience like that before. What did it mean? She would have to speak to Eddie about it. Maybe he could shed some light on what God was trying to say. Sam had done a good job with the soup and the family always sat down to eat together. Ruth was truly blessed to have a husband and extended family like she had. She couldn't imagine her life any other way. She wished that Eddie and Mabel would reconsider about leaving New Jersey. She loved having them around the house and she would need someone to help her with the baby. She didn't know anything about raising a baby.

Eddie and Mabel were like two little children in a toy store without any grown ups present. They couldn't help but keep on looking at Ruth to see whether she had any idea that they had started preparing the baby room for her. She didn't have a clue. But as soon as dinner was over they couldn't wait to put the blindfold on her and lead her to her room. "Come on baby." Mabel kept saying. "Just a little more, just a little more ways to go."

"What are you guys doing? I can't wait to see my surprise."

The closer they got to the room the more they would snicker and giggle and laugh. It was pitiful. Sam had run ahead to turn on the light so by the time they got to the room he was smiling like a cheshire cat. Mabel held Ruth's hand while they scooted her through the door and then they took the blind fold off. "surprise" everyone shouted. Ruth opened her eyes and she couldn't believe how beautiful the room looked. Ruth liked butterflies so Mabel got them small and big to put all over the room on the walls. She looked around and a flood of emotions came from the pit of her stomach all at once. Ruth just began to wail and cry out loud. Sam started to panic but Mabel caught her first since she was closest to her. "What's the matter child? Are you not feeling well?"

"No mother. I'm just so overwhelmed about the room. How did you all do this without my knowing about it? I didn't have a clue. It is beautiful. Look at the baby bed and the butterflies. Now me and my son will have something in common. He will love butterflies just like I do. I can see us now singing songs to him as he goes to sleep in his butterfly wonderland." They all started to smile and think about what it will be like having a little one in the house again.

The nine months seemed to have gone by quickly yet slowly. But once it was all over Sam was taking that walk that many had taken before him. It was time for Ruth to go into the hospital to have the baby. It seemed like between his and her family and the church they took up the whole hospital.

Ruth and Sam were on top of the world. It was now time to bring their little baby into the world. Bartholomew and Cindy both came to the hospital when the beeper went off. This was their family too and Cindy didn't want to miss the birth of their new son. When they arrived at the hospital Eddie said "hey man we been waiting for a long time for you to get here."

"Don't worry Eddie. Cindy and I have been delivering babies for a long time now. Piece of cake."

"I'll give you a piece of cake. That's not just anybody in there. That's my daughter and grand baby. I want them to have the best treatment there is. Go on in there and check on her." Bartholomew didn't argue with his pastor and friend he just did what he was told.

All the parents acted like that with the first one. But so far Ruth didn't have any complications and he believed that it would be an easy birth.

Bartholomew opened the door and Ruth was laying down in the bed and Sam was at her side. "Hey you two. How is the little mother feeling?"

"Hi Doc Bartholomew and Doc Cindy. I feel like I'm gonna have this baby any minute. I wanted it to be natural but the pain is getting to be too much. I think I would like to have some help if you don't mind?"

"No problem. I think that I can help you with that. Let's see how you are doing. The doctor took the time to check Ruth before he left the room to tell the nurse that Ruth wanted something for the pain. The baby would be born possibly within the hour. Sam looked like he was about to pass out so Doc Bartholomew told him to take a walk and get some water. After the drugs took over Ruth would be sound asleep. Sam took the opportunity to take a walk down the hall to get some water and he would come right back.

The walk down the hall was a difficult one. The hospital was a terrible place to be even if your sick. The first door to the right there was a woman sitting next to a man in the hospital bed. Sam assumed that was her husband. Poor thing he looked so old. He didn't look like he was going to make it. Sam resisted but he wanted to go in and ask her if she needed prayer or anything. He had worked in the mission for so many years it was just a sixth sense to know what was on people's minds. Just before he got to the water fountain he saw a woman walking with her daughter. The little girl was no more than about ten years old. She was walking with an oxygen machine very slowly. What could possibly be wrong with her Sam thought. He just couldn't resist asking this time. She was right in front of him. "Excuse me maam what is wrong with your daughter?"

"She has cancer. The doctors don't give her much time to live. She has been in the hospital for about six months now. They are sending her home to die. I feel so helpless."

"I'm so sorry. I'm here for the birth of my first child. I cannot imagine what it would be like to lose my child after only a few years. I don't mean to be insensitive.'

"No your not being insensitive. Not talking about it will not make it go away. I'm Roxanne and this is Leslie."

"Hi Miss Leslie. I heard that you are not feeling so well today. I hope that you will be feeling better soon. Keep the faith it will take you a long way when times are hard." Leslie tugged at Roxanne's blouse.

"Mommy, mommy this is the man that I saw in my dream last night. My dream mommy, my dream. Leslie was getting excited and started shouting. People were looking and coming out of their rooms to see what the commotion was all about.

"Honey what are you talking about? What dream? You didn't tell me you had a dream."

"I didn't think that you would believe me mommy. Jesus came to me in my dream last night. He told me that I would meet a man and that he would pray for me and that I would get healed after he prayed. Mommy he is the man, he is the man."

"Honey. Well if he is the man then you had better ask him if he will pray for you." Sam was taken back at what the little girl was saying. He couldn't wait to tell his family what had happened. That he was in this place not only for the birth of his son but for a divine assignment from God.

Roxanne invited Sam to come into Leslie's room so that they could pray. Leslie had made such a fuss people were watching them. So Sam went inside the room with Leslie pulling at his arm. Leslie sat on the bed and her mom sat on the chair that was near bye. Sam sat in the other chair. He pulled out a small bottle of oil. Since they started the mission he didn't go anywhere without that oil. He believed what the Bible said because he had seen so many people get healed. His father taught him to believe in the word of God. So after a brief prayer he left little Leslie and her mom knowing that the word would heal that little girl.

Sam had just about forgotten what he had come to the hospital for. He rushed to get some water and return back to his wife's side.

When he arrived back into the room Ruth was already starting to push. "Ruth, Ruth I'm sorry. I got hung up outside."

"That's okay. Cindy is here and Bartholomew. Everything is going to be okay. I didn't know it was such hard work having a baby. My mother said it would be a piece of cake. I don't know what kind of cake she had but this one is hard work." Sam only smiled but he was worried about her and the baby. He said a brief prayer under his tongue while he wiped the sweat off of her brow. Doc Bartholomew told Ruth that when he said that she could push and that they would soon see the baby's head. Ruth started to push and low and behold a little head emerged from its mother. "Wow, I can't believe it." Sam and Ruth both started to cry. Ruth was getting tired but she was hanging in there.

"Doc is the baby okay. I'm getting tired."

"Your doing great Ruth. Just a few more pushes and you will have your little crumb snatcher. And remember when it starts acting up you can't bring it back to my office. We don't give refunds." The couple just smiled.

After a few more pushes Sam Jr. was born and Doc Bartholomew put the baby on Ruth's chest. They both looked at the little squiggly thing in amazement. It was crying and their was blood and gook on it. Cindy came over after the umbilical cord was cut to take the baby have him weighed and cleaned up to meet the whole family. Bartholomew ran out into the waiting room to tell Eddie, Mabel and the rest of the crew that little Sam Jr. was in the world and doing great. Everyone was crying and shaking hands and dancing. It was a time to remember.

While the nurse and Cindy was cleaning up Sam Jr. all of a sudden he stopped breathing. The nurse ran out of the room to bring Bartholomew back into the delivery room. He had barely gotten a chance to tell the family that they would be able to see the baby in a few moments. They moved the baby out of the room for Ruth's sake so they could do CPR on him in hopes to revive him. Cindy, Bartholomew and the nurse could not understand what was happening but after some time had passed by the baby would not be revived. "Call it!"

It was one of the saddest days that Bartholomew had ever had. Not like they had not lost a patient before but this one was too close. Most of the church was standing in the waiting room waiting for that little baby to come into the world. How would he tell Ruth and Sam that there little boy had not survived. He couldn't breath and Cindy fell into his arms in a ball of tears. When they had gotten themselves together Bartholomew decided to tell Eddie first so that he would be there to help his son and daughter in law. "Eddie I need to see you for a moment."

"Hey Doc what's the good word?" He could see the pain on Bartholomew's face. Eddie collapsed in a ball of tears on the floor and Bartholomew had to get him together before he could call the other grand parents in the room. When Mabel walked through the door she thought that she was about to see her grand baby but Eddie met her at the door with a flood of tears like she had never seen before. She also collapsed and Eddie had to get a hold of her before they could tell the rest of the family what had happened. "I'm sorry everyone but the babies heart must have been weakened somehow and he just couldn't breath on his own. We didn't get to him in time. It happened so fast. I wanted you to know first before I told Sam and Ruth. This is going to be very hard on them."

There was silence in the room for quite a while before anyone had dared to say a word. Eddie spoke first. "I had better tell them. You guys just stay here and I'll be back. I'm sure they will have many questions for the Doc. We will give them some time alone and then we will come in to speak with them when they are ready. Eddie left the room after splashing some water on his face. He didn't want his son to see him like this. He needed to be strong for them. There was nothing worse than the lost of a first child. The walk down the hall was the longest walk that Eddie had ever taken.

Eddie stood outside of the door for approximately two minutes before gently pushing the door open. Ruth was laying in the bed and Sam was at her side holding her hand. "Hi son."

"Dad. They just took the baby out to get him cleaned up. Dad he is the most beautiful boy I have ever seen. I'm sure that I was not so beautiful when I was born. Now as for my wife I'm sure her dad would say that she was the most beautiful baby. Have you gotten a chance to see him?"

"No son. I have not seen him. Ruth how are you feeling?"

"I'm feeling a bit tired dad but I'm doing okay. That was hard work. I think it will be a while before I have another one. You know dad I never told you but I had a dream about the baby one night. God showed me our son and I could not understand why he would do that. What do you think?'

"Well I don't know but God works in mysterious ways I guess. Ruth, Sam I have something to tell you. Let's say a prayer first and then we need to talk." Eddie didn't make it long but short and bittersweet. "Son, Ruth we just had a talk with the doctors and I'm sorry to tell you but little Sam's heart is weak and he couldn't breath and he didn't make it son. I'm sorry." Eddie broke down crying. Ruth just looked at him as did Sam. They were in shock and could not believe what he had just said.

"Dad did you just say that our little boy is dead. What happened dad? I don't understand. It took a minute for it to sink in but when Ruth realized that her little baby didn't make it she burst out in tears and tried to run for the door. She collapsed at the door before Sam could catch her. Just then Susan walked through the door to comfort her baby girl.

"Mama, mama it can't be. Tell me this is not true. Where is my baby? Please let me see him. Please mama. We can pray and it will be alright." Susan could not keep herself together and so she layed on the floor with her baby in her arms. Eddie ran out to get the doctor so that they could give Ruth something to calm her down. Sam was just in shock and everything was happening so fast. Mabel came into the room next to console her son and daughter in law. Johnny was overwhelmed with grief and went outside to take a walk. It was all too much for the family to absorb. After quite a few hours Ruth had fallen asleep from the sedative the doctor gave her. Susan would not leave her side. Eddie and Mabel had taken Sam out of the room despite his disagreement to leave Ruth. But there was nothing that he could do. Susan was what she really needed at that moment. She was asleep anyway.

Obadiah Ariel Yehoshuah

It would be a long road ahead. There was the arrangements for
the funeral and Sam couldn't even think so Eddie and Mabel would
take care of the arrangements. Ruth had taken it pretty hard. Mabel
thought immediately that maybe they had gone too far making up
the baby room and all before the baby came home. What would they
do now? She and Eddie would definitely put off their plans to move
until Ruth was herself again.

Chapter 7

THE TRIP HOME WAS THE longest trip that Ruth had ever had. She didn't feel like living anymore. She knew that she loved her husband but yet she could not be comforted by him. Her son was the most important thing in the world and she had not gotten a chance to even know him for a few minutes. Why did God show her and Sam with a son and not let them have him? She was angry with God and she felt that she could never enter a church ever again. What kind of God would do such a thing? She had carried that baby for nine months just awaiting his entrance into the world and she had been robbed of it.

Sam loved his wife dearly but the person who walked out of the hospital was not his wife at all. She looked exactly like her but something had died inside and she was no longer the Ruth that he knew. He had no idea how to comfort her. She would not let him get near her. She didn't want to talk, eat or release the pain that was inside of her. Sam knew that if she did not that she would be angry forever and they would no longer have a marriage. Things were going so well. Eddie and Mabel were all ready to move on and leave the house to the young couple and now this. As much as Sam was hurting at the lost of his son he didn't want to lose his wife too. It was time for some motherly and fatherly help in this matter. His father and mother always knew the right things to say and do in every situation. He sure hoped that they knew what to do now.

One day after Sam had returned home from work his mother told him that she had a talk with Ruth. He couldn't believe that she could talk with his mother but not him. "Mom how could she talk to you and not talk to me? She won't even sleep in the bed with me as though I did something wrong to her."

"Son I know. I'm sorry but you must understand that she has gone through a traumatic situation."

"She has gone through it. What about me mom? I lost my son too."

"I know son but you didn't carry the baby. It is a different level of commitment. I know that you love your son and your wife but she died with that child. We must get her through the funeral and then we must help her to rebuild her life. She feels like she has lost a part of her that cannot be replaced. Please just understand. Be there for her. Don't be angry with her because she has displaced anger that she doesn't know how to cope with."

"I'll try. Have you finished with the arrangements. Yes we will be having the funeral in just a few days."

The day of the funeral was very difficult for everyone. Ruth didn't want to go but Susan talked with her and told her that she had to do this. It would be wrong for her not to say goodbye to her own son. Ruth thought about it and she didn't want little Sam to be alone. She was his mother and she would be there to say goodbye and send him to the Lord. She still struggled with why the Lord needed him. She needed him not the Lord. He had plenty of people in heaven why this one little baby. Why could he not let her have him?

There wasn't a dry eye in the congregation during the funeral. Eddie decided to sit this one out and let a good friend of his do the funeral. He would not be able to keep it together this time. He had lost his grand son and it hurt like nothing he could imagine. After the funeral was over everyone came up to Ruth and Sam. The funeral had somehow helped her because Ruth was actually hugging and kissing all of the guests. They had not planned on having people over after the funeral because they didn't think that Ruth would be able to handle it. She had at least taken Sam's hand while they were sitting in the church. It really touched his heart that she was starting to work through her feelings.

Sam and Ruth stayed back after they had put their son in the ground. She had stopped crying long enough to ask Sam a question. "I wonder whether Jesus is looking down on us now. He had to come and take our son home." Sam was startled he had not heard Ruth's voice in quite a few days.

"Yes Ruth he came to take our son home. I'm sure that when we get to heaven God will explain to us why we couldn't keep our son and why he had to take him. There are just some things we will never understand. I want to know the answer to that one too Ruth." The two just sat in silence for a while before Ruth said that she was ready to go home.

How could life be so cruel? Ruth knew that things would never be the same again. She kept pondering on how to go on. Sam had his work but she had chosen to be a mother and now she had no child to mother. One day she decided that she would just end it all. No one had to know that she had planned on killing herself. She went by the house to say good-bye to her mother and father. There was no one at home so she drove the car to a park that she went to many times before when she needed to pray. It was nothing much just some trees and flowers and some benches to sit down on. The sorrow was just too much for Ruth and she just didn't want to hurt anymore. She thought about leaving Sam and all of the people that she loved but she wanted to be with her son. If she died then she could go to heaven and be with him and he would not be without his mother. It seemed so simple but for some reason she felt that they would be angry with her and very sad if she left them too. They were all hurting and she wasn't paying any attention to how much they were all hurting at the lost of their little boy. What should she do should she stay or go? "Jesus if you are real please tell me what I should do?" Ruth cried out to the Lord for answers but she didn't hear anything from him at first. She fell down on her knees and cursed the day that she was born that she would have something like this happened to her. She loved life, she loved her husband but something was missing and she needed a plug to fill the emptiness in her heart. All of a sudden the wind started to blow a little. Ruth was startled by a figure that seemed to walk right out of the trees just behind her. It was Jesus and he was as beautiful as Ruth could ever have imagined that he would be. He was very tall, and he had on a white garment that was whiter than any white she had ever seen. He had brown hair and his white teeth glistened with the sun. She didn't know quite what to say. She had so much she wanted to tell him but at that moment she couldn't say a word. "Ruth why are you crying?"

"Lord why did you take my son? I loved him Lord and I wanted to keep him. You showed me a picture of him and then you took him. I don't understand."

"I understand Ruth. Ruth your sons heart was not developed and so he died. I know you cannot understand that right now. But Ruth until my sons and daughters receives the new body they will always be sick and will sometimes die. It's unfortunate but he is with me and I will take good care of him until you come to be with us in heaven. As for now you have a husband that loves you and he needs you too. Please let me take this hurt from your heart and you must not take your life but return to your family. But I have one other thing to tell you. In the future you will get pregnant again and you will have a son that I have anointed to be a prophet to the nations." Jesus leaned over and took Ruth in his arms and stroked her hair like a father would do to his daughter that was hurting. Ruth felt the virtue go from Jesus body into hers. From that moment on she felt the love of God like she had never felt it before. She no longer felt like dying but living and she wanted to hold her husband and tell him that she was going to be okay. That they would be okay and that they would have a son that would speak to the nations on behalf of God.

"It's time for me to go now Ruth. Don't forget what I have told you. Remember I am only a prayer away don't be a stranger." With that he got up from the bench where they were sitting and he walked away out of sight. Ruth could not believe what had just happened.

One minute she was ready to kill herself and end it all but after she spoke with Jesus she was feeling more like herself again. She would never forget her little baby but she was secure that he was with Jesus and that she would see him again. It was time to return home to her husband. Ruth realized all at once how much pain Sam was in and the rest of the family. Her silence had made them worry even more about her. It was time for them all to heal. She would call her mom and dad to the house and tell them that the family would be okay.

When Ruth reached the house she could see the pain on Sam's face. "Ruth where have you been we were all so worried about you." He wanted for the first time to scream at her but he kept his cool.

"Sam I'm so sorry that I didn't leave a message where I was going. I was feeling really low and just needed to get some air." She went over to him and hugged him and kissed him for the first time in many weeks. He didn't know quite what to say. "I have something that I need to tell the whole family. Let me call my mom and dad over. Ask mom if she can fix dinner for a few guests okay?"

"Okay Ruth." Sam had no idea what was happening but Ruth looked better than she did in a long time. He was anxious to know what she wanted to say to them. Ruth didn't have to say much to her mother. She was just glad to hear her voice. Johnny was in a terrible funk and she was grateful for the invitation just to get him out of the house. When the couple arrived Mabel, Eddie and Ruth were all sitting in the living room waiting for them. When the door bell range Mabel jumped up to get it. "Hey you two. Long time no see."

"Hey Mabel." Susan gave Mabel the look like what is going on. But Mabel didn't know so she couldn't tell her. "I'm so glad to see you."

"Hi Mabel." Johnny said in a low voice. He was still struggling with the lost of his grand son. Johnny didn't say much so you never knew what he was thinking most of the time. But this situation was more than he could deal with. The couple came into the living room where Ruth, Sam and Eddie were sitting. No one seemed to want to breath. It was quite difficult. "Hi everyone. Ruth darling are you starting to feel better."

"Much better mom. Hi dad. Come on in and sit down for a while. I have something I want to say to you all." The couple took off their coats and sat down. "Before we have dinner and want to first say that I'm sorry for the way that I've been acting. When the baby died it was as if something in me died and I didn't know how to handle it or put it into words." Susan took out a kleenex and started to dab at her eyes. "It's okay darling."

"No mother it's not okay. Mabel and I have been doing a lot of work at the mission and I see women, men and children who are in crisis all the time. And it's easy for me to comfort them but when it came time for my crisis I didn't want to be comforted as if that was going to be the cure of my pain. Actually it only made the pain feel worse. I wanted to reach out to my husband and I treated him as if he had done something wrong. The man that I promised to love for better and for worse. Eddie was right when he spoke about the man who was there to comfort his wife when she was ill. Sam I'm sorry that I shut you out. I'm sorry that I shut you all out. The baby is gone but we are going to make it through this. I have something else to say but I hope you don't think that maybe I'm talking through the medicine that I'm taking. I'm not going to need it anymore. But today I went to the park with the mind to end my life." The whole room burst forth with a resounding sound of awe and dismay.

"Ruth how could you think of something like this?" That was the first time that Johnny had said anything much in quite a few weeks himself. "You know how much we love you girl. Please don't talk like that anymore. You cannot fix anything by running away.

"Dad your right. I'm sorry for even thinking about it. But something wonderful happened daddy. I saw Jesus today. Yes he came to me and told me not to take my life. He said that I may not have liked his decision but that our baby was with him in heaven and that he would take good care of him. He said that one day I will be there with him too. He also said something really awesome everyone. He said that Sam and I would have another son and that he was anointed to be a prophet to the nations." The whole room was silent. They looked at Ruth as though she was a martian. "I know that it is hard to believe me but it is true. Jesus is real and I saw him and he spoke to me.

"Ruth are you sure it was Jesus?" Eddie broke the ice. He was a prophet of God so it wasn't difficult for him to believe Ruth.

"Yes Pastor Eddie. It was Jesus alright. When he hugged me Eddie I knew what the bible meant when it said that virtue went out from him. The power was so strong that it just moved the pain out of my soul. I never felt so good in my life. All I wanted was to go with him and be in heaven with him and my baby. But Jesus told me to go home. It's not my time to die. I have a son to raise although he is not here yet. I believe the words that he gave me. Sam and I will have another son one day." Now the whole room was shouting and laughing. Even Johnny had tears of joy in his eyes. He had his little girl back. And more than that Sam had his wife back.

Now that the couple was back on their feet Eddie and Mabel thought that it was a good time that they leave the nest and let the young couple go it alone. So after a few weeks they packed up all the belongings that they wanted to take with them to Florida. Pastor Eddie had a good friend that was ready for his first church. After much prayer he sought the Lord who would be the one to take over the church and the mission. Sam didn't feel that he was ready to step into his father's shoes so Eddie asked Daniel a good friend of his to take over the church. Daniel was a young minister who had come several times to give the message for Eddie. He was assisting at one of the other local churches. He and his wife came all the time to work at the mission so Eddie knew that he had a heart for the people. Many of the brothers were upset over the decision but how could he pick one deacon over the other. He thought it best to bring someone from the outside. These decisions are never easy to make.

On the last day that Eddie and Mabel had their big send off a new pastor came to town. The congregation didn't quite know how to take it. Eddie and Mabel meant so much to so many people. They had started the mission and many lives had been changed and restored. Sam and Ruth were back on track now. They would only be a phone call away and Ruth's parents were still in the area just in case.

Chapter 8

THIS PARTICULAR EVENING AS SAM dosed off to sleep he had a dream of being in a house and there was lots of smoke and he could see himself walking through the house looking from room to room but finding no one in the house. The fire was blazing and the smoke was thick. As he walked through the house he could see flames shooting from some of the doors and he was frightened but he continued to walk through the house why he did not know. All of a sudden he could hear cries of children coming from a bedroom and he raced into the bedroom to get the children out. There in a small closet in the far corner was a small boy and girl holding each other and crying. He picked them up one in each arm. When he tried to get out he couldn't see to get out of the house but then he saw what looked like a fireman motioning him to follow him. He followed the fireman who led him and the children out of the house. He woke out of the dream feeling quite uneasy about it but he said nothing at this point to Ruth about the dream. Maybe someone was in trouble or going to be in trouble and God was telling him about it before hand. His father had the gift of word of knowledge. The Holy Spirit would tell him before hand many things that were going to happen that his father could pray over these matters. There was a young man in the community who was very troubled. Many called him crazy but he was troubled nevertheless and had spent some time in jail. When he was released he lured one of the young boys from their church up to a building, raped him, burned his body and threw it off of a roof. The mother was used to sending her son to the neighborhood store and didn't think anything of it. At the time no one knew what had happened. He was just missing for a few hours. But when he didn't show up for supper his mother immediately knew something was wrong. He would never miss supper or run away. Lacie called Eddie right away when she suspected that something was wrong.

Eddie got together with his wife and they started to pray and seek the Lord. Eddie had a very special gift and he could see in the spirit. The Lord showed him that Byron was lying in an alley in between two buildings not far from where he lived. He immediately went out to look for him after calling the police. The authorities were able to find him after only a few hours that he was missing. The boy was still alive when they found him but unfortunately he still died a few hours later. This troubled the community and the boy's mother for sometime. His mother was devastated. The worse funeral is a young person who never had the chance to live life. The young man was quickly arrested and sent to prison.

Sam knew how important dreams were especially if they were coming from the Lord. Sam didn't dismiss the dream but didn't pay a lot of attention to it either. But then the dream kept coming back night after night. He thought it was time to discuss it with Ruth for her to tell the prayer group that they attended. They were a great bunch of people who had learned the power of prayer. If the Lord was trying to talk to him he wanted much prayer to back him up. What if there is a family that would lose their home and maybe their lives if they did not pray? The Bible is very specific about how the people of God should humble themselves and pray before God and he would hear and he would heal.

"Ruth, Ruth."

"What is it Sam?"

"Please wake up Ruth. I have something important to tell you."

By this time Sam had had the dream three times and he could no longer sleep.

"What's wrong Sam?"

"Ruth I have had the same dream three times already. Jesus is trying to tell me something."

"What happened in the dream?"

"Well I am in this house and there is a fire. I managed to find the children but then it got so smoky that I couldn't find my way out of the house. I saw a fireman and he led us out of the house and that was it."

"Well it sounds like that there is maybe a fire to take place and Jesus wants you to pray about it so that all will go well and the family will escape unharmed. Let's pray about it now and then maybe you can go back to sleep. Okay?"

"Okay. Yeah. It's starting to get to me. I can feel the heat in the house and the smell of the smoke is unbearable. The children are crying and if the fireman had not shown up we would not have made it I'm sure of it."

"Okay let's take it to the Lord in prayer. Father, we come to you this night. You are an awesome God in that you allow us to see what you see in this world that we cannot see. Thank you Father for this revelation of that which is to come, speak to us Father that we might know what we should do about it. Thank you for the fireman or the angel of mercy that you have sent to get them out of the house. Father you are gracious to us with this word. Now give Sam rest in his spirit that he might sleep tonight. In Jesus name we pray."

"Thanks Ruth. I didn't want to bother you with this but please take it to the prayer meeting tonight and have them pray again and again. I need some rest. I can't stand it any more. You know I know now how difficult it was for my father receiving words of knowledge all the time from God. He was always praying about one thing or another. He was always burdened with the things that were on God's heart. Lots of people want to have the gifts of the Spirit but they don't know that there is a great responsibility that comes with it. I'm sorry honey. Go back to sleep I believe that the Lord will let me rest now."

"Okay honey. Are you going to the men's fellowship tomorrow you can bring it up and they can pray for you as well."

"I almost forgot all about that. I guess I had better go. Aaron is looking forward to it."

Sam was Aaron's buddy. Aaron had lost his dad a few years ago in a car accident and he really needed a buddy, someone not to take the place of his father but to be a role model for him. Sam went back to sleep and prayed that he would get a bit of rest before getting up to go to the men's fellowship at their church. They met once a month for some kind of event. Last month they all took their sons to a big car show they were having in New York City. What man doesn't like to see all of the newest cars that were coming out for the next year. They might not be able to afford one but they sure could dream.

The prayer with Ruth worked and Sam was able to go back to sleep. They were going to have a big day today with the brothers. The men decided to take them to the Pennsylvania Dutch Country. Sam had gone there when he was just a young boy on a school trip. They thought it would make for a good day out with their young sons. Sam had fond memories of the stores where he could buy plenty of candy. They had the best shops ever. The Amish were major craftsman and had really established themselves in the world although they had decided not to be a part of the mainstream society. He knew young Aaron would enjoy the day out seeing how the Amish people lived. It taught him how some of God's people have decided to live without some of the excesses that modern day people use. Sometimes he thought that they really had something. As he read the bible as a young man Sam believed that there would be a day that these modern day accessories would be more trouble than a little bit and that learning how to live without them would be a plus for the Amish people. He had a friend that lived in New York City when they had the blackout. He remembers him saying that they lost all of their food from the freezer, they had to do everything by candlelight and they could not of course watch television. He said that his family thought that it was Armageddon. They were Jehovah's Witnesses and they do not believe in the rapture. What if something happened and that took place all over America? The ramifications would be endless. The Amish people were not bound to the modern day things such as cars, electricity and such. They were able to subsist without these things. It was a great lesson to learn just in case.

Ruth didn't have any plans for the day. Despite Doc Bartholomew's advice Ruth and Sam got pregnant again right away. Ruth was sure of what she heard the Lord say and she wasn't going to wait one minute. She wanted to be a mother. When she got the good news that she was pregnant again she couldn't wait to tell all of the family and Sam was so excited but he was scared that they would lose the baby again despite what Ruth said. He knew that he would just have to have faith since Ruth was so sure of what she had heard. Mabel and Eddie were having the time of their lives in Florida and the kids promised that they would come to visit real soon.

Since Ruth's recovery she had started a group for women who had lost babies like herself. She realized that there was a group of women who were in need of comfort and that maybe it would be a help for her as well. She wanted to celebrate the life of her son and not be in anguish because of his death. The more she talked with the women at the mission about it there were more and more women who had similar experiences. She also put up flyers at the hospital so that the other women would know where the mission was and what time they met at the church. All in all there were about twelve women in the group. Every week was a celebration for the women and they really enjoyed themselves. Maria was the first to sign up for the group. Maria had already had a child and she and her husband decided that they would like an addition to the family. So after trying for over three years to get pregnant they finally got the good news that they were going to have a baby. They had prepared and the room was ready. After a long bout with cancer their little bundle of joy died at home with all of her friends and family around her. Maria and her husband Rafael knew that they had enjoyed the eighteen months that their daughter Sophie was alive. They missed her but they knew she was in a better place and that helped to soothe the pain some.

This particular day a new member joined the group. Carmen and her husband Josh were like Ruth they never had a baby before. Carmen had cancer and the doctors told her that there was a good chance that the baby would live and also a chance that it might not live but they decided that they would not terminate the pregnancy. She had just lost the baby a few days before coming to the meeting so she was a basket case. Ruth and the others welcomed her with open arms. "Hi are you looking for the Angels of Heaven Ministry.

"Yes. I got this flyer from the hospital. I'm Carmen."

"Well welcome Carmen. Come on in. Would you like something to drink or eat?"

"We like to eat around here so forgive us. This is Maria and the rest of the group will be here any minute. While you are waiting let me show you our Angel Tree. This tree represents all the babies that have gone on to heaven. If you didn't get a chance to make a picture then we can just put the babies name up here on one of the angels. Every week the tree gets bigger and bigger. Heaven is just too crowded with angels."

Carmen seemed to have been overwhelmed by what Ruth said and she began to cry. "Ruth why did God have to take my little angel? If heaven is too crowded then he could have let me keep her for just a while longer." Ruth put her arms around Carmen and wished that she could impart the love that Jesus had given to her but she could not.

"Carmen I can only tell you that your baby is resting in the arms of Jesus right now and that when you reach heaven she will be there waiting for you." Ruth hoped that this would make sense to Carmen. Those words once turned her around when she didn't want to live. Ruth was amazed at how many broken people there were in the world who has lost loved ones. She now had a reason beyond her family to live.

The meeting was always difficult but it got easier as time went on. People now had a place to go to celebrate the life of their babies. This particular month Maria thought it would be great to release balloons into the air for each baby that was represented. They all went up to Ruth's favorite park where she saw Jesus. They had a big picnic. It was a beautiful day for the angels and a prayer was given that all of the angels would be watching over their families.

When Ruth got home she was pondering over what Sam had mentioned the night before about the dream that he had. She thought that maybe she would call Pastor Eddie and ask him what he thought about it. After all he was the prophet in the family. Surely the Lord would give him some insight. After ringing the phone several times with no answer Ruth decided to just leave a message and wait for them to call back. She was deep in prayer when all of a sudden she felt the presence of someone in the room. She was almost afraid to open her eyes. Just then Ruth could see in the Spirit her Lord. She was wide awake but it was as if he were standing right there in the room with her. This is known as an open vision. It was as though he stepped through the portals of heaven through a door and stepped into her living room. Ruth was scared at first, she didn't know quite what to say. Most people who have a vision of God fall on their faces before God because His power is so great that they cannot contain it. Ruth was just frozen in place she couldn't move or say anything.

He stood there at first as though she wasn't in the room. He put his hands up to his face and began to weep so uncontrollably that Ruth stood up and went over to him slowly and started to embrace him to console him. She could hear his cries from the bowels of his being. It was like he was unleashing years and years of anguish at that moment. He looked up at her with big brown eyes that were greatly troubled. She was afraid to say anything. She said "My Lord why are you so troubled?"

He said, "Ruth the tears that I shed are as the former rain and the latter rain that shall fall just before my coming. Read for me the Book of Joel."

Ruth went back to the table and got her Bible. She read from the Book of Joel. Be glad then, ye children of Zion, and rejoice in the Lord your God; for he hath given you the former rain moderately, and he will cause to come down for you the rain, the former rain, and the latter rain in the first month.

The Lord then proceeded to speak to Ruth again.

"Ruth these are the last days before I shall return to this earth to set up my Kingdom. Ruth my children have become sluggish and the world does not even know who I am any more. What has happened to the power gifts that I have given to my church? This nation was founded on my word and the generations of today do not even know my word. This has caused me great anguish. I want that you should go to your church and your prayer group. Tell them to pray for there is great calamity that will befall this nation because they have forsaken my word. My word is not for bondage to the people as some may think. But my word is to be a lamp for this nation. Because my word is no longer here this nation has ceased to be the lamp that she was created to be to the world. For this reason will many nations rise up against her because she is no longer light but she is darkness."

With that the vision ended and Ruth sat in her living room in amazement that Jesus would take the time to come to her. She sat there with the Book of Joel still opened up and she read the following: "And it shall come to pass afterward, that I will pour out my spirit upon all flesh; and your sons and your daughters shall prophesy, your old men shall dream dreams, your young men shall see visions: And also upon the servants and upon the handmaids in those days will I pour out my spirit."

Ruth was now sure that God was speaking to her that she should warn the people about what is about to come to the earth. What if anything this had to do with Sam's dream she did not know but she could not wait to get to the prayer meeting she would have to call the pastor right now.

"Pastor Daniel how are you doing today?"

"I am doing fine Ruth how can I help you."

She immediately began to cry. She was so overwhelmed by the situation and being seven months pregnant didn't help the matter any.

"What's the matter Ruth? Are you ready to have the baby? Is Sam there? What's wrong?"

"No I'm not ready to have the baby. I'm doing fine. Sam has gone to the men's fellowship and I just had a vision from God."

"A vision from God. What has he told you?"

"Oh Pastor Daniel. I have never thought in my wildest dreams that Jesus would take so much time to talk with me, me Pastor Daniel. But he has and I don't know where to start."

"Well start from the beginning."

"Well I was just sitting here doing my Bible reading and writing my notes for Bible study tomorrow. Sam had a dream that was really bothering him and I thought that if I sought the Lord he would give me the interpretation of what he was saying to Sam."

"What dream did Sam have? He has not told me anything about this."

"He was going to bring it up at the men's fellowship to have them pray with him. I knew you wouldn't be there because you are still recuperating from your operation. But anyway he had a dream that he was in a house and there was a fire in the house and he saved some children from it. He said that there was a fireman that helped them get out. He believed that if the fireman wasn't there that they would have died."

"Oh my goodness. Go on."

"Well in any case I was just seeking the Lord. After reading and studying my word I had an open vision of the Christ. Pastor Daniel he was sobbing and weeping and he said that his tears were flowing as the former and latter rain that would be poured out in these last days."

"Glory to God. Go on I'm sorry."

"Yes and he said that the Body of Christ has become sluggish and the world does not know him any longer. He says that great calamity will come upon this nation because they have ceased to be the light that he has called her to be to the nations. He said for this reason may nations shall come against us. Pastor Daniel what does all of this mean?"

"Oh Ruth. God has come to you in a mighty and special way to speak to the people of our church. We have much prayer and fasting to do that he might reveal how we can be used to accomplish his will in these end times. I will call the prayer group together and we must travail in prayer and fasting for the people of this nation and the church as we have never done before."

"Okay Pastor Daniel. I am available. Do you think that you can make it to the prayer meeting tonight? I know you are still recuperating.

" I sure can. I will start calling around right now to make sure everyone can be there. Start praying right away okay?"

"Okay."

With that Pastor Daniel started at the top of the prayer list to get everyone together for prayer. Lucille and Bob Danville were his strongest supporters he would call them first. Bob would probably be at the fellowship but maybe he could catch Lucille at home.

While he was trying to dial her number his private phone started to ring so he took his cell phone out of his pocket to answer it.

"Hi this is Pastor Daniel. Hey Lucille I was just trying to call you. How are you doing today?"

Just then Lucille started crying hysterically. Pastor Daniel was alarmed because Lucille was a very strong woman. Whatever was bothering her had to be of alarming proportions.

"Lucille what seems to be the matter?"

"Pastor Daniel I had a vision of Jesus. I can barely talk to you right now. But I knew that I had to talk to you right away. We have to meet for prayer tonight we cannot cancel for any reasons. Something terrible is about to happen. I'm not sure what the vision meant but he is trying to warn this nation that something big is about to occur.

"Okay sit down, take a deep breath and start from the beginning."

"Okay. In the vision he was as tall as one of these skyscraper buildings you know. And he was just standing there looking out over New York City. I could see many of the buildings and the Empire State Building and the Statue of Liberty as well. So then I could see these very large birds start flying over the buildings, just circling and circling around like vulchers. Just then they plunged into the buildings and they started to crumble. It was horrible. I could see the anguish on the people's faces down below as they watched in disbelief. Then I could see what looked like people in churches, schools and in their homes just crying out to God and praying for our nation. It was incredible the amount of people that were praying and travailing to God. But then there was an empty space like they had cleared everything away after the disaster and the people started to rebuild. I think that after time Pastor they had forgotten about what happened. I don't think that God was happy about this. It was as if they had forgotten what had happened and just went back to business as usual."

Pastor Daniel was beside himself at this point. He knew that God was talking to Ruth and Lucille about an impending situation. He had allowed this church to receive this information that they could pray for this nation. They had been meeting for quite a few years now and God had been hearing their prayers. This was time to go to battle for the people of this nation. He would continue calling the list of prayer warriors and he would also have a special day of prayer the next day instead of the regular service. This was serious. Oh how many times pastors and leaders have missed God and not sounded the warning. Many were too afraid to say that God had said anything. They didn't want to alarm the people as though not telling them would do no harm.

"Lucille you take half the list and I'll take half. Let's call everyone and meet tonight as usual. I have something to tell you as well. But what I believe that God is saying is that something terrible is about to happen to this nation. He was warning us so that we could pray. After this event a great revival of prayer will break out all over the nation. The people will turn to God for help and comfort. But what will happen is that after a time they will forget what has happened and they will start to rebuild their lives. This is what happens to us. When something terrible happens we turn to God for comfort and help. That is how selfish children are. They do not love God and speak with God when things are good only when things are bad. They then forget him and go back to the way things were. But this cannot keep happening before God will not take it any more.

"Lucille, Ruth just received a vision from God as well. The bible says out of the mouths of two or three witnesses let everything be established. She had a vision of God right in her home as well. She said that he was crying and sobbing about the church and the world.

Lucille God is burdened about the state of the church and the state of unrepentance in the world. "

"Pastor Daniel we have got to fast and pray before God. If we don't the situation that is about to unfold can be disastrous. I will see you tonight. I'm waiting for my husband to come home. He will probably be very tired but I will try to get him to come anyway."

"Do the very best you can Lucille. This is an emergency of the highest proportions."

Pastor Daniel continued to call around to the rest of the congregation members on the list. His heart was pumping so fast he thought he was going to be sick. He had just had minor surgery and had been recuperating for quite a few weeks. It was time for him to get up going again. God needed them now more than ever. The group had been praying together for several years now but this was the first time anything of this magnitude happened. He wanted God to know that they were there for Him and they wouldn't let him down now.

Chapter 9

RUTH COULD NOT WAIT UNTIL Sam got home to tell him all about what had happened and to ask him to join the group tonight. She didn't know whether there was any connection to his dream but if it was she wanted to know. They would have to spend as much time in the presence of the Lord as possible. She didn't want anything to happen to him, not now the baby was coming and everything was going well. It was like a bad dream was about to unfold. Jesus warned the Body of Christ about the last days but most people that she knew believed that the rapture would come soon and no one would have to go through the tough times that Jesus spoke about. But it seemed that maybe this was a false sense of security. Israel was going through hard times and perhaps America might go through some hard times as well.

When Sam got home Ruth tried to keep her composure. He was already burdened by the dream that he had been having. This was going to bring him to his knees. His father had the burden of a prophet and Sam lived with it all of his life. He knew how hard it was for Eddie. He literally lived and breathed God's heart all the days of his life. He was a true man of God. Sam told her about how his father would go out in the country and fast and pray for days on end. He could fast 21 days straight just on water seeking the voice of God for his family and the church. Sam never talked about having this type of anointing in his life. He was somewhat relieved because of the burden that his father carried. He didn't know whether he had the strength to walk with God that way. But when a person is called of God there is no turning back. You don't say no to God. You do what he asks of you. Sam had the gift of help. He would help anyone at any time. It didn't seem strange to her when he said that in his dream that he was in that house trying to get those people out. This was the gift that God gave to him. She wondered what that dream meant in the natural and how this would all come together.

"Sam tonight we are having a special prayer meeting. I have already talked with Pastor Daniel about it. I think that you ought to come."

"Oh Ruth I am so tired. We had a 3 hour bus ride there and back. Aaron and the boys had a good day. Tomorrow we have church and then back to work. I know that sounds selfish especially since I'm asking you to pray for me."

"Yes Sam it does. I'll tell you why. Today when I was preparing my lesson and praying for a sign from God about your dream I had a vision of Jesus."

"A vision?"

"Yes. Jesus came to me and spoke to me about the church, the world and Sam he is heartbroken about what is going on in the world and even more so he is saddened by the state of the church today. He says that we don't even know him any more. We have lost our way and followed with the world. We are no longer light but darkness."

Sam sat down now. He put his face in his hands as if to say that he felt terrible that he could even say that he didn't have time to pray. Prayer is just one of the most important tools that the church has to fight against everything. When there is sickness we are taught to pray. When we have any needs we are taught to pray. Prayer is our communicating to God what needs we have. Without God there are no answers to life dilemmas. Without prayer there is no wisdom coming from heaven. Unfortunately, man believes that they can govern themselves but history shows that this is not so. Without God nothing can be accomplished in this world. Only God can make water which is the basic necessity of life. If it so much as stopped raining all life would cease to exist. So all Bible believing Christians understand the power of prayer. Even people who do not believe in the Bible or God will actually allow someone to pray for them because somewhere deep inside they understand that they need help in times when a situation is beyond their ability to change things.

Sam took Ruth's hands in his and said, "honey I'm sorry. I had not realized the gravity of the situation. I repent before you and God for my sluggishness. God has blessed me with a beautiful wife who loves the Lord. He has given us life and now we are expecting a new addition to our family. I will just take a quick shower and we can go together to the prayer meeting. Did Jesus say what he wanted us to do?"

"Yes, he said to "pray".

Lucille was totally beside herself by the time that Bob came through the door. As he walked in he could sense that something was wrong with her. She just sat there saying nothing as though something really terrible had happened. He calmly walked into the room so that he would not startle her. He knew that the prayer meeting was that evening and usually Lucille was really good about preparing herself for the time spent in the Lord. He tried not to make any noise but there was a sense that she was praying about something serious and he didn't want to disturb her. He understood the sensitivity of praying in the Spirit. If you so much as make a wrong noise the Spirit will depart and breakthrough could be coming at that very moment. He remembered that he and Lucille had gone to a prayer meeting because he had broken his leg during softball practice and it didn't quite heal properly. He had been having problems and so they heard that there was going to be a large prayer and healing meeting in Atlanta, Georgia. Oral Roberts, Kenneth and Gloria Copeland would be at Creflo Dollars church and they just knew that the same healing anointing that he had when he was young was still with him. So they decided to go. He and Lucille had already prayed all the scriptures that they knew before hand and was believing in God for a miracle that night. The choir had started off the service as usual and the Spirit of the Lord was in the house strong. You could feel his power in the air. Bob always heard about the glory cloud and although he couldn't see it he just knew that it was in the air. So the Pastor of the church came out to introduce Oral Roberts but he said that they should prepare their hearts for God to do miraculous things in the house that evening. Well the expectation was high, people were speaking in tongues and the fire fell in the place even before Bro. Roberts came out to speak. Bob could feel the power of God surging through that leg that had been broken and he knew that his healing was happening and Bro. Roberts had not even come out to speak yet, let alone pray for healing. When all of a sudden a young lady decided that she needed to go to the bathroom just at the moment when the anointing heat of God starting moving up that leg. She startled Bob so that he nearly jumped out in the middle of the aisle. He looked at her harshly like this is not the time for movement, the Holy Spirit is moving. This is the thing about the anointing power of God you cannot be moving around, talking and doing foolishness otherwise he might get offended. You must stay in the Spirit or interrupt the flow of the Spirit. Well although the flow of the Spirit was interrupted God still healed the leg.

Bob opened the door quietly just enough that she would know that he entered the room but not enough to disturb her concentration. She turned around and he could see the terror in her eyes. He almost didn't want to ask her what was going on but he knew that he had to. There was so much going on in the world maybe something terrible had happened and he needed to join her in prayer. The Lord had blessed them with this ministry of prayer. They were so glad when their fellowship started the prayer meetings every week. Thus far many in the church had received healings from God, many were being delivered from all types of bondages and God was just blessing the fellowship. This is what God wants to do in his church. He said that he was coming for a bride without spot of wrinkle. The renewing of the mind is only accomplished by the Holy Spirit dwelling in and amongst his people.

Lucille looked up at Bob and reached out her hand to him. He reached out back and knelt down on the floor so that he could hear all of what she had to tell him.

"Bob, Ruth and I have both received visions from the Lord today. We are all going to meet tonight to talk about what God is saying and to pray."

"Bless the Lord. What has he been saying to you?"

"He came to me in a vision Bob. He was standing tall, very tall like a skyscraper. He showed me New York City. I could see the buildings as clear as your standing in front of me. It was so awesome Bob. But then I could see these very large birds just circling, and circling the skyway. All of a sudden they plunged into the buildings and the buildings began to crumble right before my very eyes. I could see the people running, screaming and crying below. Then it changed and I could see people in churches praying, in schools praying and in their homes crying out to God. I thought this terrible catastrophe has brought a great revival to New York City. But then I could see that the rubble had been cleared away and there was just an empty place with a memorial for those that had died but then the people started to rebuild and I no longer saw anyone praying anymore. Bob do you think that this is a sign that something terrible is going to happen in New York City?"

"It most certainly seems like it is? Let's start praying now and get ourselves ready for tonight. Have you alerted Pastor Daniel about this?"

"Yes. He was the one who told me that Ruth had a vision as well."

"Father God, thank you for allowing us to see what you see. Thank you for giving us this warning that we might come together in prayer and agreement with you. We know Father God that you do not desire that anyone should perish but that all should have everlasting life. Pour out your Spirit upon all flesh that they might see their sins and repent and turn unto the one true God. Warn your people Father God that many shall not perish in this catastrophe. We plead the Blood of Jesus Christ over New York City and its surrounding cities Father God. Call unto your church to fast and pray Father God. We thank you and we ask these things in Jesus precious and holy name. Amen."

Lucille and Bob prepared themselves to be at the church promptly at 6 pm to get the doors opened and the lights on for the rest of the beloved to come and pray before God. They always started with praise first to give thanks before hand to the Father for what he would be doing that evening. It was all about the Holy Spirit. Most prayer meetings aren't prayer meetings at all. It's all about what the believers have come to ask of God instead of what God might ask of them. They come in with their prayer lists and they go one by one and then when they have finished they go home. This prayer group when it was started immediately saw what God was doing in each and every vessel present. God first taught them how to repent of their sins before him. He wanted that each vessel be a vessel of light cleansed from all iniquity. Then he started to reveal to them his purposes for the church and the community in which it sat. Many of the families were broken and needed much repair. The purpose of the church was to spread the Gospel of Jesus Christ to those families and bring them into fellowship with their Creator. He could then fix whatever problems they had and give them the abundant life that he wished for them to have.

The world is caught up into all types of programs to fix the worlds problems. These programs are all good but no one can change the nature of man. The Lord God said in his word that the inclination of man's heart is evil all the time. In order for the world to be healed God has to change the inclination of man's heart from evil to good. The only way for this to be accomplished is for man to come back to God.

The prayer group attendees started coming in one by one. Lucille and Bob opened up the church as usual and Pastor Daniel came in shortly there after.

"Hey Pastor Daniel. Your looking better and better every day."

"Thanks Bob. I'm feeling like the Holy Spirit is really going to do something in here tonight. He has already manifested himself to us twice today. I'm not sure about it but I think that something is going to happen and he wants us to join him in prayer."

"You are sure right about that. You know I was so busy listening to Lucille about her vision I had not asked her about Ruth. What did God tell her?"

"She said that he appeared to her while she was doing her bible study. He was crying and distraught about the state of the world and the church Bob. I think that the church thinks she's okay with God but she's not. We have got to get this through to the church that we must also repent before God and get right with him."

"You know what the word says he said that many will say I have healed in your name, I have caste out demons in your name and he said that he will say depart from me you workers of iniquity. This is the church he is talking about. Wow man I feel sick."

"Let's get everything set up. They should all be getting here soon."

"Okay."

"Lucille just get your seat. We'll take care of the rest. I think we are going to be in for a few hours tonight."

"Okay Bob."

The rest of the group started to filter in. Pastor Daniel was at the door. He wanted that no one came in without a heart of reverence to God. Sometimes when they came for prayer they were talking about all kinds of things and then they got started. He already sensed the presence of God in the place waiting for them and he didn't want to keep God waiting. He admonished everyone to take a place in quiet and just get on their knees, their faces or whatever posture they chose and start calling on God. He felt that whatever God wanted them to do he wanted him to tell them. He didn't want to take anything for granted tonight.

Ruth sat on a chair since it would be hard for her to lay down or kneel down. Sam knelt down a few seats from her. Pastor Daniel's wife Suzie usually played the piano so she stayed close by just in case God told her to play. Bob and Lucille were already overwhelmed and were lying face down on the carpet. The heaviness of the Lord had already made it's way into the sanctuary. It was as if a heavy weight had been placed in there. There was a campus chaplain who heard about the prayer group and he brought some students from

Seton Hall to join the group. These young people were on fire for God. Pastor Daniel loved having them. Mark, Joni, Kyle, Samantha, Bonnie and Jacob truly put all of themselves into their prayers. The church was amazed at these young people.

As the group entered the building they too could sense that something strange was happening that had not happened before. They all came in quietly for the group was already in prayer. They usually came in around the time that Suzie started playing the praise songs. They had not heard yet what had happened to Lucille and Ruth. All of a sudden you could hear people crying the power of God was so strong. They had started travailing by means of the Holy Spirit. Suzie started screaming like a woman who was about to give birth. It was quite scarey. This had not ever happened in the prayer meeting before. Pastor Daniel was rocking back and forth as though he was in great pain. The young people had started to pray in tongues. The language of the Spirit was coming forth in great force. God was praying. No one was doing anything in the flesh but the Spirit had taken over the meeting that night. This is when things are really done. When we do it in the flesh we can accomplish some things. But when the Spirit is praying he prays to the Father things that we know not. When in the Spirit times passes without your knowledge of how much time has passed. This praying in the Spirit went on for one hour before it finally lifted and God allowed Suzie to get up off the floor and play something on the piano.

Everyone stood up at this point and began to worship God openly in praise telling him how much they loved him and wanted to do his will in their lives. Samantha one of the students gave a word from the Lord.

Word of Knowledge: "Why have you forsaken me? Why have you not gone out to the people and preached my gospel? What has happened to the power in the church? How will the people know me if you do not tell them about me? I have sent many messengers and you have forgotten about them. I sent my son William Branham and you have forgotten about him. I sent my son A.A. Allen and you have forgotten about him. This is the word that I sent him long ago and much has still not taken place. You must go back and research the prophetic words that I have spoken over this nation.

Pastor Daniel said "I have a prophecy that A.A. Allen gave many years ago if the Lord will permit I will bring it and read it tomorrow. We will see what the Lord had to say." With that the heaviness lifted and they just rejoiced in the Lord. A total of two hours had past without them even realizing it.

Chapter 10

THE GROUP COULD HARDLY SPEAK let alone walk after the visitation from the Lord. Many of them just layed out on the floor until they could get up. They spent a total of four hours in the sanctuary that night. They wondered whether that same power would be there still the next morning for the church service and bible study. They didn't think that things would be normal if it were. That was okay. They had heard from the Lord and that's what the church needs. It's time that the church stop talking so much and listen for a change. God is alive and he is well and he has much to say to the church, the world and to his people Israel. But the church has so many programs just like the world that she doesn't have time to listen to her master any more. In the early church the Book of Acts shows that the Holy Spirit was moving and breathing all over his church and many signs and wonders followed thus causing massive amounts of people to turn to the Lord. What has happened today? God is still the same God, yesterday, today and forever more. So the problem seems to lie in the church. The signs and wonders are not flowing in the church because she has become a works church. She has decided that God doesn't do miracles any more so they have to do it all themselves and they are doing a lousy job at that. The church belongs to God and the church needs to recognize that.

Pastor Daniel found in his study a copy of the prophecy given to Prophet/Evangelist A.A. Allen in 1954. He decided that he was going to read it to the church. Many had heard of him but have since forgotten the word that the Lord gave to him. He believed that the glory in the sanctuary from last night still lingered on and that the church needed to hear a message of the cross. It was time that the church returned back to her original beginnings and preached the cross at Calvary and the blood of Jesus so that people could get saved for real. He had heard a message that one of the evangelist had preached on a tape that he brought. He noted that the church had stopped preaching the cross, hell and heaven. No one seemed to care about that anymore. The Gospel that was being preached from the pulpit didn't have anything to do with the cross but had everything to do with prosperity. If you read the words of Jesus he says take no care about what we are to eat or to drink. But the church has gone on a quest to tell people how to be successful, how to be beautiful and all of the things that we can get from the world system. Not that these things are not important but the Father says to seek ye the Kingdom of God and His righteousness and all other things will be added. So we are doing things backwards. The church is the only entity on the earth whose prime responsibility is to preach the Gospel of Jesus Christ. Pastor Daniel prayed that the Holy Spirit would move upon the hearts of the congregation through the Gospel message and that many would repent and be saved.

Pastor Daniel held Bible study that morning same as usual and his lovely wife Suzie lead in worship. They were all still amazed at what happened the night before in that very sanctuary. The people came as usual but Pastor Daniel hoped that today they would leave different from when they came in. He could still feel the power of God in the room. He was glad that the Holy Spirit had come and was staying in that place. It was indeed an honor to have his presence in such power there.

There was a brief intermission between the bible study and the main service. The choir was moving into place as usual and nothing seemed different for the most part. Pastor Daniel was still looking to see some changes in the congregation. He and the others still sensed the power of God but he didn't see any outward show of change in the rest of the congregation. He just prepared to start the service.

"Good morning beloved. Last night my wife and I met with the prayer group because God has chosen to reveal himself in such a magnificent way to a few of our prayer group members. It is apparent that he is answering our prayers and has chosen to reveal some very important things to us. I have here in my possession a very important prophecy of which I am going to read to you today. I believe that it will have some bearings on what the dreams and visions that he has given to Sister Ruth and Sister Lucille. Let us pray that he will continue to reveal himself to us and what we need to do for him. But at the very least we need to continue to pray church for our nation and for our president that God will reveal to him his wisdom on how to move this nation forward despite the adversities she is receiving from outside sources.

After reading the prophecy Pastor Daniel felt like he had swallowed a watermelon. He was absolutely sure that God was telling them that great destruction was coming to American and that if the church didn't pray that it would be disastrous consequences.

"Church I feel now more than ever that God is telling us that if we don't pray that terrible things are going to happen in America. The good news is that we who are in Christ Jesus have been given power in the name of Jesus Christ. If we would pray then he who is our advocate before the very throne of God will intercede and many of these things can be stopped. Think about that church. We have the power to stop many of these things. Let us not be slothful in our works for Christ Jesus. For we know that it is not by works that we get saved but by faith but we also have a job to do for our Lord. When Jesus came to the earth over two thousand years ago he went about the region preaching repentance and preaching the Kingdom of God is at hand. Well that message is still the same today beloved. Many of you have been in the faith for many years now and have forsaken the Gospel. Yes, many of you have forsaken the Gospel. It seems like when the church is going through persecution she is much stronger. Maybe God is saying that we need something to bring us to our knees so that we can remember that we need him.

The Gospel of Jesus Christ is a Gospel of hope to the nations. Why this hope? This hope is because this kingdom ruled by Satanic forces is quickly coming to an end. But the hope that we have says that if we side with Jesus Christ that we do not have to perish but have life eternal. I know that most of you here grew up poor just like I did and it sure made the family pray more. We had to pray that God would put food on the table and keep daddy in a job. Times were hard and they are not getting any better. But we do have a lot of things that we didn't have back then. Now we don't have to go out to the well to get water and most of the population don't live on farms anymore where you have to plant or else there won't be anything to eat. The people of yesterday lived hard lives and they depended on God for everything. Now we go to the grocery store and we complain when the line is too long. Our society should look at how fortunate we are that we have computers, cars, telephones and good jobs that we can depend on today. I think that we need to reach deep inside our hearts and see where we personally have failed God. Perhaps we are not praying enough. Maybe there is someone here that has unforgiveness in their heart. You know that Jesus was very big on us forgiving one another. He said that if you have ought against your brother that you should leave the offering and go make things right.

Let's look at Matthew 24 and see what this Gospel is that Jesus preached to the world: "Take heed that no man deceive you. For many shall come in my name, saying, I am Christ; and shall deceive many. And ye shall hear of wars and rumours of wars: see that ye be not troubled: for all these things must come to pass, but the end is not yet. For nation shall rise against nation, and kingdom against kingdom: and there shall be famines, and pestilences, and earthquakes, in diverse places. All these are the beginning of sorrows. Then shall they deliver you up to be afflicted, and shall kill you; and ye shall be hated of all nations for my name's sake. And then shall many be offended, and shall betray one another, and shall hate one another. And many false prophets shall rise, and shall deceive many. And because iniquity shall abound, the love of many shall wax cold.

But he that shall endure unto the end, the same shall be saved. And this gospel of the kingdom shall be preached in all the world for a witness unto all nations; and then shall the end come.

Well this seems to be a different kind of Gospel than we are hearing about today. This is a Gospel of the sacrificial lamb. This is the Gospel that Jesus Christ came here to the earth to die for the sins of the world. This is a Gospel that says the Father of glory came from heaven and gave of himself to be a servant for us whom he loves.

How many of you can say that you truly have this type of Gospel in your heart? Or are you one of those who have forsaken the true Gospel of the risen Lord for the prosperity gospel. The Gospel that is about self and not about the Lord Jesus Christ or about others. When was the last time that you witnessed to someone at work or along the way about what Jesus has done for your life? This is not just about coming to church every Sunday because this is what your parents taught you to do. This is about a life change that says we are about doing the business of the Father as Jesus was about doing the business of the Father. When Jesus was just only twelve years of age he was in the temple ministering to the rabbis the wisdom that the Father had imparted to him. They were astounded at the teachings of such a young boy. We must study the word of God that we might minister it to others. Matthew says that this Gospel should be preached in all the world. We need some people who are willing to forsake all for the sake of the preaching of the Gospel. Let us seek God today and ask him what we can do to get the Gospel of Jesus Christ out. Maybe you are not called to pastor a church but what about going into the prisons, the hospitals, the nursing homes and places like this. There are people who are old and on their way out and they have never heard the Gospel or made a confession of faith that they are with God. Do you know that these people will go to hell because we as the church failed to minister salvation to them? This is blood on our heads and I for one do not want that innocent blood on my head.

Jesus spoke about false prophets and people who will profane the gospel and many innocent people will follow them. So it's up to us who have the real Gospel to get to them first or else they will perish.

We know beloved that we are living in the last days. The disciples thought that Jesus was coming back in their time but there was still too much prophecy that had to be fulfilled for that to be true. But we know as we look at what was prophesied by many of the Old Testament prophets that we are undoubtedly the last church age. There will not be another church age. This is it. We have a big job to do and we are literally holding Jesus back from returning. I for one want my Jesus to come and rule and reign over us. Oh what a glorious time that will be saints of God. "

Just then a member starting speaking in tongues. The interpretation was given directly after.

"This is the Gospel that I have given to you. This glorious Gospel that my Beloved Son in whom I am well pleased came that you might have life and have it more abundantly. He came that you might have a way back to my heart. I have not forsaken you but you have forsaken me. Continue to pray for this nation is going to suffer great peril by forces of darkness but if you pray there will be help from heaven for you. I have dispatched my angels due to your prayers, my heavenly forces to combat the darkness that is headed your way. You my beloved will suffer many things for my sake but he who endures for the end will receive the greatest prize. You will sit with me in high places. You who endure till the end will have everlasting life in the Kingdom of God."

Pastor Daniel stood in silence. The rest of the congregation was in silence as well. They could all now feel the presence of their holy God in the place that morning. They all knew now that something had taken place that had not taken place in that church ever before. Their faith in God was revived and many just starting praying and praising God.

"I think that we have heard from heaven again today. Let's just all take some time to praise God today. We need to come here more often and expect to hear from God. "

There was silence in the place and many came to the altar to get right with God.

Chapter 11

WHEN SOMETHING TRAUMATIC HAPPENS IN the world most people can remember for years on end where they were when it happened. Those who were alive when J.F. Kennedy was assassinated still remember exactly where they were when they heard the news. When Martin Luther King was assassinated most people who were living remember exactly what they were doing when they heard the news. That is just how life is. When the news hit that morning that several planes had crashed into the World Trade Center, the Pentegon and missed Washington it was like a bomb had gone off. Many people just could not believe it until they saw the actual footage on television. Even then it was like a bad dream, or a bad movie. How could this happen in America? How could we have missed this? What was our intelligence people doing that they didn't get wind of this before it happened? Well these questions would be answered eventually but still many thousands of people's lives were taken because they were not answered before hand. If there was a warning we didn't get the warning or didn't heed the warning. Was this possibly what God was telling the church and maybe countless others that could have done something about it? Many would like to still have the answers to these questions.

Sam had already left the house for work while Ruth slept. She was getting more and more tired as her due date got closer. Sam

worked in an office at the Trade Center and had no idea what was
going to happen that morning. He had taken the Erie Lackawanna
train as usual and got on the path train to the World Trade Center. It
was around 6 a.m. he had some work he wanted to get finished that
day so that he could get off early. They had a doctor's appointment
and he didn't want to miss seeing the baby on the ultrasound.
They really got a kick out of seeing the baby move and stuff. It
was amazing to see what God was doing with their little one. No
one can make a baby no matter how much science tries to mimic
what God has created they just can't do it. Sam and Ruth were so
excited about their son that was coming into the world. They had
already planned names and that they were definitely going to have
him circumcised by a Jewish Rabbi from the Messianic synagogue
in that area. They truly believed that Jesus would have wanted that
for their very special son.

There was nothing out of the ordinary for Sam that morning. He
had no idea that the dream that God had given him was a warning
of that which was to come that very morning, September 11, 2001.
The train was not too packed that time of the morning. It was always
nice getting ahead of the crowd. It would take approximately one
hour from home to work. Sam was able to get a seat and he usually
brought his Bible along that he might get a bit of reading in before
getting to work. When he got home he always liked spending some
time with Ruth before doing other things so this train ride was the
best time to have a bit of private time with the Lord.

This particular morning there was a young man that sat down
next to Sam. He looked up and bowed his head good morning as is
usually the custom on the train. His train partner looked like he had
just graduated high school and probably working his first job ever.
Sam always liked to see the young people taking responsibility in life
and working towards a future for themselves and later on a family.
These day's young people seemed to be spoiled and selfish because
of parents who wouldn't allow them to grow up and be responsible
adults. This is part of the decline in our society today. When Sam
left high school he went immediately into the military for a few
years. He was a decorated soldier when he was discharged. He was

so proud of his military career but wanted to settle down and have a family. He knew that it would not be easy to raise children and be on the go all the time so he got an honorable discharge and came home and got himself a good job working in Manhattan. The train ride was difficult every day but he got used to it after a while. It was kind of exciting for him a young man who thought that he would never amount to much of anything. The job was steady and he was able to take care of his family.

His train partner had pulled out one of those video games the young people were playing these days. Sam was amazed at the things young people had today that he didn't have growing up. He didn't know whether they had it better or worse. This generation had so many gadgets. They were all involved with their cell phones, video games and chat rooms on the internet. He thought that it was best that he didn't grow up with all of these things. It is truly getting the young people in trouble. They bring them to school, to work, the supermarket and they walk down the street with that cell phone plastered to their heads. It's a wonder they can get anything done. It certainly was a different society than he knew growing up. Sam returned to reading his Bible when the young man interrupted him.

"I'm sorry to disturb you but do you really believe what you read in the Bible?"

Sam was startled that he had asked him a question. He was taken off guard.

"Yes sure. I believe every word of it. Why do you ask?"

"Well I've been brought up in the church but for some reason I don't get it sometimes. Maybe I'm just not paying attention like I should. I don't really get excited about it like my parents do."

"I understand. By the way my name is Sam. What's yours?"

"I'm Benjamin, Sam it's nice to meet you."

"It's a pleasure to meet you as well Benjamin. When I was a young boy Benjamin I didn't get the Bible either. It just seemed like who are these people and what does this have to do with me, you know?"

"Yeah, that's what I'm talking about. Like they lived thousands of years ago. Jesus came and died on the cross and here we are thousands of years later still waiting for him to come back. What's the point?"

"Benjamin the bible has so many points you really have to take the time to study it to understand what it's all about. Number one it's a blueprint for every Bible believing person to live by. It teaches us how God wants us to live in the world. For example he tells us to love the Lord thy God and to love your neighbor. That's not hard to understand right?"

"No. That's pretty straight forward."

"You see Benjamin if you will just read the word you will see that most of it is not hard to understand. You went to school right?"

"Well yeah."

"So much of what you learned in school was about the history of this nation right, math, science and such."

"Yeah a whole bunch of irrelevant stuff. They lived a long time ago too and we have a totally different society and way of doing things than they did."

"Well we have to look at that statement a bit closer. The people who came here before us do have a great relevance on how we live our lives today. For example, when this nation was first formed there were no laws. They had to make them up as the need arose. There was a time when an employer could do just about anything they wanted to.

The employees had no rights. But the people came together to fight the employers and now we have laws today that say a person has rights. You see what I mean. The federal government has legislated that there is a certain salary that must be paid and that people have a right to sick days, vacation days and in some cases even medical benefits and it's getting better every day for workers in America. You see the link between those people that lived before and you now. If they had not fought for these things you would not have the rights you have now. Well it's the same with the people in the Bible. When God created the first man and woman what they did and didn't do definitely has an effect on your life now. When Adam and Eve the first man and woman disobeyed the law of God, God punished them and took away their privilege to live in that Garden. This is how sin entered into the world."

"So are you saying that I am paying for what they did back then?"

"You sure are."

"Well that's not right. I didn't do anything wrong. I think that I need to have a talk with God about this."

"I'm sure everyone feels the same way. But you know Benjamin unfortunately we do the same thing that Adam and Eve did. When we don't read God's word to tell us the difference between right and wrong we are being disobedient to him the say way. We must read the word of God that we might know what is right and wrong. We cannot use our own judgment. We just are not capable of that. For people in this world right and wrong seem to be questionable."

"Yeah like in some countries if you murder someone it's still punishable by death of hanging or getting your head chopped off. We don't do that here in America. Even though that electric chair thing is pretty gruesome."

"That's right. Now your thinking Benjamin. So do you see the connection now of how sin entered into the world?"

"Yeah. Through one man sin entered into the world."

"So what's God gonna do about it?"

"Okay that's the next point. Well the Bible says that through one man sin entered into the world but then again through one man we have been saved."

"Oh man thank God we have some way of getting this thing turned around. So what's the plan, and whose the man?"

"Jesus is the plan and the man. Now this is going to be difficult to understand but you have to understand God to understand his plan."

"Yeah that's a mouthful. I don't understand God. I don't know that I ever will understand him."

"That's okay Benjamin. At least you acknowledge him. That's the first step. First you must acknowledge that God exists and then we can work from there."

"Okay."

"Let's say for example someone breaks into your home and steals your video game. You call for the police to seek retribution for what was stolen right?"

"Well yeah. I want my video game back or payment for another one?"

"Exactly so that person now has a debt to pay to you for that which was taken?"

"Yeah."

"Well this is the same system that God used for the sins of man. He used his sons death on the cross to pay the debt that we all have to God."

"So your saying that when Jesus went to the cross he paid the debt that I owe to God."

"Yes."

"Why would he pay my debt? It's my debt not his. He didn't do anything. It's my sin that I inherited."

"Wow, that's a mouthful. So then Jesus is paying a debt that he didn't even incur for you. What a wonderful and kind God that he would do that?"

"Yeah. I guess it's like a long time ago me and a few of my buddies were playing softball outside which we were not supposed to do. We broke a window and my mom and dad had to pay for the window. I guess it's kind of like that huh?"

"It's exactly like that. But Jesus death paid for the sins of all mankind. Isn't that amazing?"

"Yeah it sure is. You know I never heard it quite like that before. I think that I just might start reading that Bible to see what else I can learn from it. "

"Benjamin you know I don't usually have conversations like this every day. I must ask you have you accepted Jesus Christ as your Lord and Saviour? The next day is not promised to anyone. Why don't you pray with me and let Jesus be your Lord. If he were to come today you want to make a confession to him so that you can spend eternity with him in his Kingdom."

"No I have not made that step yet. I've been feeling something tugging at me though. Maybe that's why I asked these questions today so that I can be sure that I understood what it was really all about. I feel better than I have felt in a long time. I can't wait to tell my mom and dad that I understand Jesus finally and that he gave his life because he loves me."

"I like you Sam it would be a pleasure to pray with you. What do I do?"

"Just bow your head and repeat after me. Father, In the Name of Jesus Christ of Nazareth. I believe that Jesus Christ died and rose from the dead to pay the debt for my sins. I come to confess my sins before the throne of Almighty God today. Forgive me of my sins. Cleanse me with the Blood of Jesus Christ of all iniquity. Fill me with your Holy Spirit. Satan I renounce your kingdom today. I will no longer serve you. Father I am now born again of the Spirit of God and Jesus is my Lord." Benjamin prayed with Sam by faith after each line.

"Benjamin I am so proud of you. You make sure that you tell your parents you are now ready for water baptism. Remember the bible says that you must be born of water and Spirit."

"Okay. My mom will be glad that I met you today Sam. Do you take this train the same time every day?"

"No I'm trying to get in early today. My wife and I have a doctor's appointment this afternoon. We lost our first baby and I want to see how he's progressing."

"Oh that's cool. You guys pick out names and stuff yet?"

"Yeah we are thinking about naming him Samuel like the prophet in the Bible. You should look him up you will find his story very interesting. Hey looks like we are here. I hope that I will see you again Benjamin. It was really a pleasure talking with you."

"It was a pleasure talking with you too Sam. Have a good day."

Sam went to get his coffee and bagel, same as every day. The building was crowded as usual. No matter what time you go through that place there are always people coming and going. Sam made his way up the elevator to his office and sat down to read the paper for a minute and have breakfast. The place was so still. You can hear the walls talking when there were no other sounds in the building. It was a beautiful morning and Sam wanted to get out of there as quickly as possible. There had been so much going on at work these days. They were talking about actually moving out of the building. When they had that bombing a few years back many were afraid and wanted to move just in case they decided to try again. But as usual it was only talk. They were glad though because it would take so much time to box everything up and move to another location. Sam knew about moving from the military. It's never easy.

Sam worked for an investment company. He would really need to start investing a little more with the baby coming and the repairs for the house he didn't know how they were going to support a family. He truly believed in his wife staying home to take care of the children. Society had changed so much and women weren't staying home like when he was a boy. He enjoyed coming home and his mom being there to greet him when he came home from school. He didn't like the latch key kid concept. That's the reason why the children are getting into more and more trouble. There are no grown ups at home to supervisor the children when they return home from school. Most parents are just paying the bills and the children are raising themselves. They won't take them to church on Sunday because they have the bus or van come and take them to church. It's a wonder that they don't listen to their parents. They don't spend any time with them. Sam thought it amazing that young Benjamin wanted to talk with him about the Bible. If parents took the time out their children would go to church and talk with them about the Bible if they would just take the time. That young man gave his life to the Lord. Who knows how long his lifespan will be. The next day is not promised to any one. Many have given their lives to the Lord just in time to meet their maker. He hoped that Benjamin would have a good life. At least he had parents who took him to church and encouraged him in the Lord.

Sam gathered up his papers to go and make some copies, send out some faxes and do the dreaded filing thing. He had been in the copy room for about 45 minutes when all of a sudden he heard a great sound that sounded like an explosion. He was never so scared in all of his military career. He dropped to the ground just in case the ceiling was collapsing. Nothing happened right away but he could then hear another series of explosions. It was now time for him to get out of the building. He just dropped everything and made his way down the hall to the stairwell. He was on the 21st floor so it would be quite a ways down. He was in good shape so he scaled those stairs like a young man still. He heard the screams of other people who had obviously heard the explosions as well. He didn't know what was happening but he knew that he had to get out of the building. The people were running down the staircase and asking questions at the same time but no one had any answers.

When Sam finally got to the bottom of the stairwell and out to the street he saw all the faces of the people looking up and then he saw what looked like a plane sticking out the side of the building and then he saw another plane come toward the other tower and plunge into the tower. He thought this couldn't possibly be happening but it was. He then remembered Lucille's vision, could God have been telling them about this before it happened? God did it in the Old Testament times why would he not warn New York City of an impending attack upon the World Trade Center.

All Sam could think about was the people who were in the building as he could see it just burning. He didn't think about himself but he found himself running with the emergency medical people and the fire fighters to help the people. There was smoke and fire and people just screaming and yelling. They were frightened and he could see the desperation on their faces. His heart was breaking but he couldn't just stand there. He needed to do something to help with this utter chaos that was unfolding before his very eyes. He thought about that dream he had. God had warned him that something was going to happen. He just didn't know what or when but he believed that this was most certainly it.

What kind of person would do such a thing to another human being? There is just no excuse for this type of attack. These people didn't do anything wrong to anyone. What could have motivated this? He found himself fighting back the tears while helping the people. The place was a disaster area. He tried to keep his composure and use his military training to help the fire fighters get people out of the building. He had gone back and forth several times and the smoke was getting into his lungs and he was coughing.

He could hear sirens coming from all directions and what sounded like explosion after explosion. Glass was breaking, stuff was falling everywhere. He never thought he would ever be in such an horrific situation at home. Sam had been in the Gulf War and that was awful but he was in a war and he expected what he saw there. They went into combat situation after another but there was some order because they were literally fighting the enemy. This was chaotic because the enemy did a sneak attack that no one was ready for. They had the advantage. No city could have been ready for such an attack so quickly. There weren't enough emergency vehicles in all of New York City to take care of all the casualties that happened that day.

Sam had run back into the building again one more fateful time. He could hear some screams but with the smoke he didn't know what direction they were coming from. He tried to see but he couldn't see. All of a sudden he saw a fireman motioning him to follow him out. Just then the smoke overcame Sam and he fell to the floor. Unfort-unately Sam had suffered some burns and had not even realized it because he was so busy helping the other injured people. The fireman quickly went over to get Sam when some building fragments fell upon Sam and he had to go and get help to get Sam free. By the time they had returned Sam was barely alive.

When Sam went down he couldn't see anything but he was going in and out of consciousness. He found himself saying, "I plead the blood of Jesus" over and over again. His father had taught him that when he was in trouble that he should plead the blood of Jesus for his protection and this is what he was doing at this most crucial time in his life. At one point he didn't know whether he was alive or dead. All that Sam knew was that he could see a very bright light. It was like it was a tunnel and then he could hear the voice of God speak to him just as clear as if he were standing right in front of him.

"Sam I am here. You are safe now. Come and join your brothers and sisters, they have been waiting for you. You don't need to fear you are home."

But Sam was saying in his spirit "home". I'm in this building what home, what are you talking about."

Just then he could see Jesus standing there with his hand out. He said "Hi Sam".

Sam said to him "Master, have I come to heaven?"

"Yes Sam you are in heaven now. Come your many friends await you."

Sam was overjoyed but at the same time saddened because he now knew that he had died and that he would not see Ruth or the baby until they reached heaven some time in the future. But it was so beautiful and he so missed his mom and dad as well. He walked over to Jesus and then he could see angels all around and many other people who had died that he knew. They all came to embrace him. There was a young boy looking up at Sam and he knew in his heart that was his son that had passed only when he was a baby.

He walked on streets of gold just like the bible said. Many think that this is not so but the streets of gold are really there. He saw the most beautiful grass and trees that he had ever seen in his life. The grass seemed too beautiful to be real. It was as if they had diamonds in them. But they were not like diamonds like we know in the material world but they were diamonds nevertheless. The trees were as if they were alive so to speak. They had fruits on them of so many different varieties and all one had to do was go over and just put their hand underneath it and the fruit just dropped off. The people were so happy there and the children played like they had no worries in the world.

The whole heavenly city was full of peace, love and joy that no man could ever know. This Jesus said was the way that the earth was supposed to operate before the devil came in and polluted it. He said that when he returned that he would return the earth to its original glory.

At that moment Sam knew that he was safe and in the arms of his Lord forever. He would see his family again in the new Kingdom when he returned with Jesus, the angels and the rest of the saints.

The firemen managed to find Sam again and pull the fallen objects off of him and carry him out to safety. At this point no one knew who Sam was to get in touch with his family and let them know that he had in fact been injured and that he was on his way to the hospital.

Sam had no vital signs by the time they got him into the ambulance. They pronounced him dead in the ambulance. They checked his pockets and found a cell phone and all of his identification. They would have someone call from the hospital to tell his family that he had passed away.

The firemen had noticed that Sam had been helping people to get out of the building. They wanted to make sure that the City of New York knew that this young man had given his life to save many other people. When they received word that this young man had died they looked at him as if he were one of their own.

Chapter 12

RUTH HAD GOTTEN UP THE morning of September 11, 2001 not realizing that her life would be altered forever. She fixed a cup of tea as was usual for her. It seemed to settle her stomach. The baby was getting bigger and bigger it seemed every day and so was Ruth. She decided that she would turn the television on and check the weather and see the news report. It was about 8 a.m. she had a doctors appointment for 1 pm and Sam promised that he would be finished at the office and back home to take her for her appointment. They were looking forward to seeing the ultrasound, hearing the baby's heart beat and seeing its little form on the monitor. Sam was so proud and Ruth just wanted him to be healthy and full of the spirit of God.

It was 8:45 in the morning when the news reporter came on for a special bulletin. It was then that Ruth heard the news of what was unfolding at the World Trade Center. She nearly fell off of the chair. She tried not to panic but she didn't know whether Sam had gotten out of the building or not. She thought to call his cell phone but she was too afraid that he would not answer and it would cause more panic for her. She picked up the phone to call the pastor. She could not go down there, it was all shut off.

"Pastor Daniel. Have you heard the news about the World Trade Center?"

"Yes Ruth. This is terrible. Did Sam leave for work yet?"

"Yes. He went in early this morning to do some work. He wanted to get back in time for my doctors appointment."

By this time Ruth couldn't contain herself. She was worried of course and expecting the worse.

"Ruth keep yourself calm. Until we have heard something conclusive Sam might just be okay. Many people were able to get out. I and Suzie are on our way. You sit tight."

"Okay Pastor Daniel."

Ruth immediately started to intercede for Sam that God would bring him out of this situation okay. She remembered his dream and felt that all along between Sam, herself and Lucille God had unfolded this whole thing to them so that they would pray. She didn't know what the outcome would be but she knew that her God was able.

Ruth was a nervous wreck by the time that Pastor Daniel and Suzie walked through the door. She opened the door and just collapsed into Pastor Daniel's arms, balling and screaming at the top of her lungs for Sam.

"Suzie I can't lose Sam too. I can't loose Sam too. The baby is coming. Why is this happening?"

Pastor Daniel and Suzie got Ruth to the couch and tried to calm her as best they could. They wanted to call someone but calling 911 probably wouldn't help. With all the commotion unfolding they would not have any conclusive answers for them at this time. Pastor Daniel and Suzie thought it best to start interceding for Sam and the rest of the people. It was the best thing to do until they could get some answers. In the meantime he would call Sam's mother and father to intercede as well.

After some time the praying seemed to calm Ruth down. They thought it best that she not think about going to the doctor but to lay down and keep herself calm. The baby was due in a few months. They didn't want her to go into labor before it was time. She had already lost one child and if something bad had gone wrong with Sam she would need something to look forward to the future. The baby would give her a reason to live.

Pastor Daniel and Suzie had started calling some of the hospitals in the World Trade Center area to see if maybe he was in the hospital. He had not called and this was not a good sign. He must be hurt and unable to call. They knew that he would have called as soon as he could. It was quite early so they didn't want to panic but for some reason they didn't feel good about it.

Ruth had layed down but was of course unable to go to sleep. She was so worried and she just layed there praying to God that Sam would be alright. She somehow with the help of the Lord had dosed off and went to sleep. It was a good thing though so she could stay calm for her sake and the babies. Little Samuel was due in a few months and she had gone so far in the pregnancy. Jesus had told her he would be born and she was going to do everything possible to make sure that he was okay. Just then she saw herself sitting in her favorite garden where she had seen the vision of Jesus. But this time it was a beautiful day and she and Sam were sitting together talking. He held her hands in his and he was looking up at her with such peace in his eyes but he was a bit troubled.

"Ruth. I have come to tell you that I am in heaven with Jesus now. Don't be troubled. Remember that you have a great responsibility to raise our son as Jesus has instructed you. I'm okay. I just wanted to make sure that you are okay and that you promise me that you will not worry for me. When Jesus went to the cross he took the stain of death away from us. Remember you will see me again when the church is raptured out of this earth. Please don't worry for me. You will be okay. Pastor Daniel, Suzie and the church will be there for you."

"Sam. I'll always love you. I will bring up our son. You pray for us okay. I don't want you to go but our Father Jesus knows best about all things. I will see you soon if Jesus does not tarry. I will tell Samuel how great a man his father is. Say hello to our son. Now I will not worry for him because you are there with him. Tell him that I love him. I'll always love you."

When Ruth woke up she had tears streaming down her face. She wanted to scream and holler but she had a sense of peace that she knew Jesus had placed in her heart like when the baby died. Sam was right when Jesus went to the cross he took the hold of death and it should no longer have the same affect for Bible believing followers of Jesus as for those who didn't have the hope which is in Christ Jesus. Christians know that when they die they will go to heaven for Jesus said that he would go to prepare a place and there they would be also with Him.

Just then the phone rang. It was the hospital calling to tell them about Sam. They found his personal items and cell phone. They were able to locate the family that way. It was a terrible thing to have to tell someone but it was their duty and the family would want to know so that they could put it to rest. Pastor Daniel and Suzie hated having to tell Ruth the news but they were glad that she would have someone with her at a time like this. Pastor Daniel would go to the hospital the next day when things calmed down to verify the remains and help Ruth make the funeral arrangements. He wanted to let go but he had to be strong for Ruth and Suzie and the rest of the congregation.

Ruth came out of the bedroom with kind of a glow on her. They had not ever seen her with such peace. Pastor Daniel and Suzie could not imagine what was going on. She must have had another visitation.

'Pastor Daniel, Suzie I just talked with Sam."

"You did. What happened? Tell us all about it."

"Well he came to me to tell me that he was okay. He said that he was with Jesus. He wants us to be strong and go on with out him. He knows that it will be hard but we must for the baby's sake. God has given me a job to bring him up and I must do that although he will not be able to be with us."

She started to cry but she was not hysterical like she was before she layed down. It was a good thing that God had allowed them to speak with each other one more time. It sure helped her alot to cope with his departure. Pastor Daniel and Suzie just looked at each other. They were amazed but they both started to cry because it was now final for all of them. They would not have to struggle with giving her the news that the hospital had already called.

"Ruth the hospital called a few moments ago to tell us that Sam had been taken to the hospital. Apparently Sam had gone back into the building to help other people out. He is indeed a hero. He saved many lives and gave his life for them."

"Remember Pastor Daniel the dream that Sam had. This is what God was trying to tell him. He did show us that Sam got out. And he did show us that Sam would be the great hero that he is. He did give his life for those people. But you know that's just what Jesus did for the world. He gave his life so that we might live. I know that he is proud of Sam for what he did. He said that there is no greater love than a man should give his life for another. It hurts but it makes me appreciate Jesus all the more."

"Do you feel like you want to be alone? We can come and check on you tomorrow and help make all of the arrangements or Suzie and I can come and be with you for as long as it will take. We don't want you to feel like you are alone."

"I would like for you to stay with me at least until my mom and dad can get here. I had better contact her. They are out of the country on vacation. She may not have heard yet what is happening. I told them all about what was happening with the prayer group and all. They will be heart broken. They loved Sam like he was their very own son. And I don't know how I will tell his mother and father but they are strong people. We will all make it through this somehow."

Mabel and Eddie came back home as soon as they heard the news. Ruth's mom and dad cut their vacation short to be with Ruth during this terrible time. Mabel was uncontrollable. She tried to hide her feelings for Ruth's sake but Ruth knew that she was devastated. She had lost her only son and a piece of her died that day.

Ruth picked out Sam's military uniform to lay him to rest in. Because his body had been so bruised they decided to have a closed casket funeral. Ruth wanted it that way she wanted everyone to remember him the way they last saw him. He was always smiling. They did put up a huge picture of him and Ruth in better times.

Pastor Daniel did the funeral at their local church. Sam was sent home with full military honors and the mayor of New York sent his condolences when he found out that Sam had gone back in the building several times to help other people. Ruth's group at the mission put an angel on the tree for Sam. It was a sad day but Ruth believed that this was only the beginning of what Jesus talked about in Matthew 24. She believed that there would be more terrorist attacks to take place before it was all over.

Chapter 13

RUTH HAD GONE THROUGH SO much turmoil in the past few months. She had just lost her husband and now she was faced with raising her baby all alone. Little Samuel finally came into the world around 3:30 a.m. one Friday morning, but he was premature and very sickly. After resting Ruth went to see her little bundle of joy. He looked so much like his father. His face was all wrinkled. They had him all dressed up in a baby outfit and she was so proud. How she wished that Sam had lived to see his son come into the world. They had planned this baby, he was not a mistake but a blessing from the Lord. But she would have to bring little Samuel up all by herself in this big world. But Ruth held onto the vision that she had of Jesus. He came to tell her that her little Samuel would one day grow up to be a mighty man of God. It reminded her of the story about Hannah. According to the bible Hannah could not have children. In those days it was almost a curse to not be able to have children. So Hannah cried out to God to bless her womb. She went to the High Priest Eli and when he first looked upon her he thought that she had been drinking. But she told him her problem and he prayed for her. She promised God that if he gave her a son that she would bring him to the temple for the service of the Lord. After her Samuel was born she would do just that and bring him to the temple to serve under Eli. Ruth thought that God gave her the name Samuel because God said that he would have the anointing of Samuel. She didn't know what that meant but she knew that Samuel was a mighty man of God. It would give her great pleasure to name her son after the Prophet Samuel.

In the days of the Bible people didn't just name their sons any old thing like people of today. Their names meant something. The name of Samuel has various meanings. One of which is "heard of God" or "God has heard". Another translation can be "Son of El" or "Son of God". Samuel was the last of the judges and the first prophet. Samuel was the one whom God sent to anoint King Saul and King David.

It was important for Ruth to understand who Samuel was because her son's life would be patterned after Samuel. She read in the Bible that when Samuel was perhaps about 12 years of age that God spoke to him for the first time. Samuel used to sleep by the ark of the covenant when he heard the voice of the Lord. He called to Samuel several times but because Samuel had not yet known the Lord he thought that it was Eli calling out to him. Each time he would run in and ask Eli what he wanted. After a few times Eli discerned that it was the Lord calling to Samuel and so he said "when he calls you just say "speak Lord for your servant has heard." This is what Samuel did and the relationship was formed between God and his prophet from that day forward. Samuel would be the one called of God to speak to his people on his behalf.

Does God still actually do this in this way today as he did back in the Bible days? Ruth could not fathom this. She had her beginnings in the Baptist church and she never remembered ever hearing about a prophet in her day. It was not until Ruth had married Sam that she learned more about the bible and that God was doing miraculous things even in her day. Mabel and Eddie were a lot different from her parents. She was so glad to have them in her life. They believed that the Holy Spirit was and is still working in the lives of every believer today. They held the Book of Acts as a guide for the church today. The church was to have the Holy Spirit in full measure just like the early church did. They spoke with other tongues, they believed in divine healing and the other gifts of the Spirit as it was given to the church. She believed that one of the reasons why the church had ceased to operate the way it should was because it had ceased to believe in the very power and authority that Jesus had given to it from its birth. Perhaps this was the reason that God was raising up her son. She thought about little Mary when the Angel Gabriel came to her to tell her that she would have a son and that as recorded in the scriptures "And, behold, thou shalt conceive in thy womb, and bring forth a son, and shalt call his name Jesus." Mary could not have possibly understood that her son would be the Messiah, the one that all of the Jewish people looked for to establish the Kingdom of God. The prophets were very important men and women called by God to call the people of their time to repentance. Ruth marveled over these things that she was thinking about concerning her son. But all that she knew was that God had entrusted Samuel to her and that it was her responsibility to lead him in the commandments of the Lord. If he was to call the people to repentance then he must know the commandments of the Lord through and through and so Ruth set it in her heart that she would teach her Samuel the very best that she knew how.

When Hannah weaned her son she took him to the temple to be taught of Eli the High Priest. There was no such thing today so Ruth would seek the Lord and see what he would tell her to do. Ruth was a praying woman. She always had been a praying woman since many years ago when she entered a prayer group. They started with just a few church members but the hand of the Lord was on that group. Soon after just a few months the group grew to about 12 members. They would set days for fasting and praying over all manner of situations. They prayed over the President, the Vice President and the government officials that God would give them wisdom. The United States of America was a large nation and they were sure that when God birthed this nation that he had great purpose for it and they wanted to make sure that it stayed on track. Many great nations rise and fall very easily when they get off track of their purpose and especially when they take God out of the picture. They wanted to make sure that this didn't happened and it was the church that would make petition to God for this purpose. They also prayed for all of the members and their loved ones to receive salvation from the

Lord. This is at the very heart of what God is doing in this world today. Because the world has fallen into such sin God has from the beginning of creation sought to redeem mankind. This has been no easy task since the devil is trying to destroy what God has made. But when God sent his son Jesus redemption for the sins of mankind had been fulfilled. Now it is the task of every Bible believing person to shout the Gospel of Jesus Christ to the mountaintops because there isn't much time left. Jesus is coming back and very soon.

Ruth watched her little baby breathing so shallowly in that incubator. The proud grandparents were in awe of the new addition to the family. Having them around would be good so that they could help Ruth to adjust to having a new born baby at home. It would probably be several weeks before she could actually take Samuel home so she could get a bit of rest and fix the place up for his arrival. With Sam's untimely death and the whole 9-11 destruction Ruth couldn't get that out of her mind but she had to go on for Samuel's sake. The nurses at the hospital were extra hospitable because they knew that Sam was a decorated soldier killed in the World Trade Center. Sam was a good man. He did so much for so many people it seemed so unfair that this should happen to him. Ruth was angry and hurt but she didn't want to sin against God. But she did feel that one day she would get the strength to have a good conversation with Jesus about the whole mess. How could this have happened? The prayer group prayed so for this nation and this happened? What was Jesus trying to say if anything? She was sure that he knew about this before it happened? Why did the government not know what was ahead so that they could warn them ahead of time so that all of those people would not have lost their lives? Some people are taught when they are young that its not our place to question God but Ruth wanted to have a little talk with him she knew that he could handle it.

Within just a few days the hospital allowed Ruth to go home but little Samuel would have to stay in the hospital until he had gained some weight and they were sure that he was strong enough to make it on his own. It was so hard for her to leave him there. She wanted to stay but her mother Susan beckoned her to go home and get some rest. The little guy would need a lot of attention when he came home. But Ruth, Susan and Mabel would come every day to pray and sing to him. They knew that would make him strong right away. The prayer group was praying and they knew that all would be well. Jesus had already come so they didn't have to worry.

The house felt so different now without Sam. Mabel and Eddie promised that they would stay with her as long as she needed them. It was helpful for them as well. Mabel had lost her only son but had gained a grand son. She too felt that she had a reason for living although she loved her husband very much. The house was nevertheless quiet without him. Sam had such a sense of humour and he would have things going all the time. But Ruth knew that once Samuel reached their little home that the place would feel alive again. He looked like he had a good set of lungs on him. She didn't mind he could keep her up all the time it would give her something to focus on other than Sam.

"How are you feeling Ruth?"

"Mother I don't know sometimes. I feel good that Samuel is here and then I feel bad that Sam is not here to see him. I know that he's in heaven with Jesus but I want him here at the same time."

"I know. When the first baby died I was very angry for quite some time and your father was very sad also. But I know that there was nothing I could do to bring him back so I had to let go of him. Oh how I wanted to die too but I guess it was all in God's hand. I'm glad that I am here right now to be with you and see my grand-son. You have to take it moment by moment. If you take in too much you feel like you will explode. That won't be good for you or Samuel in the long run. I'll be here for you I promise."

"Thank you mother. I know you will. Hey I didn't get a chance to show you some of the beautiful letters I got after the funeral from so many concerned people from all kinds of organizations. One day I will have to organize them so that we can send them thank you cards. I don't care what people say but this is a great nation and the people do care a lot about each other during the difficult times."

"Wow you mean that people are writing you letters and sending cards?"

"Yes. I got many letters from many veteran organizations and their families. Some have even sent donations that their children collected at school. I have started to log each and every one of those. The children's cards are the most precious. "

"There are certainly still good people in the world."

"Yes mother there certainly still is. But you know being good is not what gets us to heaven. We need Jesus in order to get to heaven. This is what I believe the Lord was trying to tell me is that the church must get their focus back on the cross of Jesus Christ. Without him there is no remission of sin and no way into the Kingdom of God. He and my husband will not have died in vain mother. My son has no father. I want their death to have meant what it should mean. There is a war going on and if we don't wake up and start fighting we are going to lose many more brave soldiers like my husband."

"What do you mean Ruth?"

"Mother the devil is using everything he can to keep mankind at war with each other. He knows that as long as we are fighting each other we are not fighting him. It's the oldest trick in the book."

"I have never thought about it like that."

"Yeah. He can't whip Jesus because Jesus is God and he has all power. But he can keep us fighting one another. This is one way that he gets to us by taking out as many people as possible. He knows that he only has a short period of time and so he's taking as many people to hell as he can. I'm not going and neither is my son. My job now is to make sure that my son learns the commandments of the Most High God. He is called to be a prophet to the world. Jesus said that he is going to put a sword in his mouth. That sword is the word of God. This word is a word that will wake up the nations if they have ears to hear."

Within a few weeks Samuel had gained enough weight to come home. Oh the prayer group held a vigil for their little soldier. They already heard the word of the Lord but they knew that he needed a lot of prayer to bring him through these crucial hours. When Ruth brought Samuel home the whole neighborhood was waiting. Samuel was the light of his mother's world.

Chapter 14

IT DIDN'T TAKE LONG BEFORE Samuel was ruling the whole house. Whenever he so much as blinked his eye his mother and grandmother were both running to see what was going on. He was having a good time with them too. If mom or grand-ma didn't come after the first cry it just got louder and louder. They loved every moment of it to. Samuel was well on his way to winning the heart of the whole congregation. In no time he had taken over his mom's life and she was so grateful to have him. Ruth had received so much financial assistance that she was able to stay home and raise her son. She didn't like the idea of having a baby and then putting him most of the day in day care while she worked. It was a blessing to be able to stay at home and raise your children. Mabel and Eddie had gone home. She immediately started getting information for home schooling. She believed that a lot of the problems for Christian parents today lies in the fact that they have to send their children to a school that does not believe in God, that will not teach the children to pray and do not have the moral foundation of the Holy scriptures as she did. If her son was to become a prophet of God then this was no place for him to be taught. There were many good Christian schools but she would put it off as long as possible. If she could set a good foundation in him before he started school she thought she could lay a firm foundation for when he entered the world without her.

Samuel was just like his father always following Ruth around trying to help although he was too small to push the vacuum cleaner he tried his best to help her with the chores around the house. She would find little things for him to do. She sure hoped he would stay that way when he was big enough to really do chores around the house. She would have it made. Most men don't like doing chores when they get big but when they are small they are nice to have around the house. He was just like any little boy always wanting to play and get into mischief. Ruth didn't like him playing outside in the neighborhood because times were changing and parents had to be careful of leaving their young one's alone outside. She tried her best to be watchful of him when he was outside playing in front of the house. His best friend David would come over and they could play for hours. She thought a lot about selling the house and moving to a nicer neighborhood but she didn't have the heart to sell the house. Sam grew up in that house and there were so many memories of him there. She wanted Samuel to know as much about his father growing up as possible. She would leave the house to him and let him make the decision of whether to keep it or not. She had a feeling that God was going to take him places that he could only dream of.

When Samuel was just a young guy Ruth started to teach him the scriptures. He was at the head of his class in church. He could read the scriptures and pretty soon he was able to stand in front of the class and explain what his mom had taught him about many of the people in the bible. Ruth kept it in her heart what Jesus said and she took it seriously. Children these days can learn all kinds of things if parents would just take the time to teach them. Instead of barney she wanted him to know Jesus and the patriarchs of the faith. Samuel loved reading and learning. She tried to make it fun for a child. But it was like he just loved reading the word and whatever she taught him he took it right in.

Ruth just enjoyed watching her son grow and enjoy life. She told him as much about his father as she could. She wanted to make sure that he kept his father in his heart and didn't forget him. One day Samuel came down with a horrible fever and Ruth took him to the doctor after a few days because he was just getting weaker and weaker. He was a sickly baby when he came into the world but he had been doing pretty good up until now. She didn't want to worry but mothers have a way of doing that. She went to the emergency room but after taking some tests and giving him some medicine to stabilize him they said that she should definitely take him to his regular doctor for testing.

The doctor couldn't see at the time anything that could be wrong with him, he suspected that it was just a bug that was passing through. He would probably get over it in a few days. If he didn't she should bring him back and they would order some more tests. But after a few weeks it seemed as though Samuel wasn't getting better. He said that his body just ached and he felt sick all the time. He was unable to go out and play with the children and Ruth had to stay home with him and he was bedridden and unable to do anything. She took it to the prayer team of course and they began to pray.

When Pastor Daniel realized that Samuel was not getting any better he had a group to come over to the house to lay hands on Samuel, anoint him with oil and pray the prayer of faith that he should get better. The Bible says that if there are any sick amongst us to call for the elders of the church, and let them pray over him anointing them with oil in the name of the Lord. And the prayer of faith shall save the sick, and the Lord shall raise him up; and if he have committed sins, they shall be forgiven him. They really believed it and it worked. The word of God works but the people don't believe. So they all came over and anointed and prayed over little Samuel. God had a work for him to do and they were not going to mess it up for God.

However, at first Samuel did not get any better. The doctors finally told Sister Ruth that Samuel had cancer. She could not believe that her son had cancer. She was standing on the word that God had given to her.

Sister Ruth started praying and interceding for her boy like never before.

"Devil you take your hands off my boy. I plead the blood of Jesus Christ over his body, over his mind, over his heart, over his blood and you cannot have him. He is God's son and God has spoken a word over his life and it is going to come to pass. Thus saith the Lord that I shall put a sword in his mouth and he will speak of me to the nations. This has not been fulfilled and you cannot stop it."

After months of praying and fasting Samuel seemed to get weaker and weaker all the time until Ruth had to put him in the hospital. The treatments were just taking its toll on his little body. Samuel would look up at her after his treatment and say:

"Mama don't worry I have seen Jesus and he told me that I'm going to be okay just have faith. He told me that this affliction will be healed and that I will have a great healing ministry. From this I will have compassion over those who are sick in the world."

Ruth would just break down and cry. She didn't want her son to see her this way but she couldn't stand to see him sick like that. What did the devil get out of doing this to her son?

She thought about Job. How the devil told God that Job was only serving him because of all the blessings that God bestowed upon him. He told God that he had a hedge around Job and that was the reason why Job was so faithful to him. So God allowed for Job to be tested to show the devil that Job loved him and served him because he loved his God and that he would serve him despite God taking away his blessings. The Bible says that after Job had lost all of his children, his livestock and his houses that he didn't sin against God but he still worshiped him.

It was not easy for Job for he had lost everything that he held dear. Job was a great man of faith and he worshiped God every day making offerings to him like he was taught to do. There are various lessons to learn about the beloved man of God but this one thing all people must remember is that the Lord blesses with all blessings and gives us power to have wealth and good life. But these things must not be put ahead of God. We must not sin against God when we have bad times in life. Job suffered physical afflictions and he stood the test that was before him. Ruth realized that it was during these tests that every Christian would know whether they loved God because times were good and hated him when times were bad. The Lord thy God should be loved and reverenced no matter what the circumstances are because he is the one that will bring a person out of the hard times. It is during the hard times that a person can see what they are really made of. If they don't have what it is going to take then they must examine why. Have they enough word in themselves to persevere. It is the word of God that must be used to fight the enemy. When Jesus was being tempted of the devil he used the word of God to face Satan. Battles in the spirit are not fought with guns and knives but with the sword that is the word of God. It is through fasting and praying that every Bible believing Christian can stand against the wiles of the devil. One should study and show themselves approved and then when the test comes they will be able to win. The Bible says "but they that wait upon the Lord shall renew their strength; they shall mount up with wings as eagles; they shall run and not be weary; and they shall walk, and not faint."

Ruth decided that little Samuel had more faith than she did. After all she had received a word from God and Samuel also received a word from the Lord so that should settle the matter. She should walk by faith and not sight. Yet Samuel seemed to be none the better.

On the days that Samuel would have his treatments he would get a chance to see some of his friends that he had made while coming for his treatments. There was little Bobby who had leukemia also. He and his mom had to travel several miles to get to the treatment center because they didn't want to move from the country to the city so that they could be closer. Oh how the boys enjoyed seeing one another. It was like they had a kindred spirit or something. Ruth would sit with Mona and they would laugh and cry and laugh and cry some more. Bobby didn't seem to be getting any better. But Ruth promised Mona that she would put his name on the prayer list that she had started of all the little children that were coming for treatments. Ruth had not realized the gravity of the situation that there were many parents that had been coming to that center for many years now with their children before she had even started bringing Samuel. She felt terrible that there was so much sickness and pain in the world and she was totally oblivious to this very big problem. People don't pay attention to the vast problems in the world until it touches their very own family.

Mona felt the same way. She didn't know anyone who had cancer until Bobby was diagnosed with it. She was so hard on herself. She blamed herself for the fact that Bobby had cancer. She was sure that she had done something wrong or that God was punishing her for her sins. Ruth tried to tell her that sickness and disease didn't work that way. She was sure that the devil picked on every family on the face of the planet and that she was nothing special. This was the test that she would have to bear and Ruth was glad that she was there to help her. She seemed to have more strength for other people than for her own situation. Ruth had been through many trials and tribulations and had it not been for the Lord on her side she didn't know whether she would have made it to that point. Mona was a sweet young lady. She and Bobby were all alone in the world. Her husband had run away when Bobby was just a baby. It was ashamed that she had to bare this all alone. Ruth was certainly salt and light in the dark place that Mona and Bobby were living in at the time.

She and the children would get together when they could. Samuel didn't feel like much getting out of bed sometime. But when he felt like it she would drive to the country and see Mona to make sure they were alright and let the boys spend some time together. They really didn't expect either one of the boys would make it but they just kept on surviving. Ruth wanted to make sure Bobby had a friend he could depend on just in case he didn't make it. Samuel told her that he had asked Jesus to heal little Bobby so they could go into ministry together. He told Bobby Jesus told him he was going to be a preacher and so he would sit in the chair and read the Bible to little Bobby and try to explain it to him the best way he knew how. Ruth was so proud of him and Bobby loved hearing the story's from the Bible. It gave him hope. Bobby learned how to pray to the Lord and believe in him for the miraculous things that Samuel told him Jesus could do for him. He made a believer out of a little boy who had nothing but despair in his life.

Samuel and Bobby were both real troopers but Samuel got really sick one day and had to be hospitalized. Ruth called the pastor and the prayer group to hold a vigil for him, he was very weak. She was holding on for dear life to what Jesus had told her and so she knew that he would come out of this too but the prayers would make it that much easier. She had fallen asleep by his bed that night after praying for quite a few hours and just reading the healing scriptures over him. Samuel told her that Jesus had come to him and said that it was time that he received his healing. He said that Jesus came and there was a bright light in the room. She was sleeping so peacefully that Jesus said "we musn't wake her she is very tired."

He said that he sat on the bed and began to tell him many great things about his future. He told him he would have a healing ministry and that if he would lay hands on little Bobby that he would heal him too. He told him not to get involved with the things of the world like smoking, drinking and having sex with women. He wanted him to stay pure before the Lord because he was his high priest and the high priest must be pure before God. He said then Jesus got up and held out his hand and Samuel was able to get up out of the bed and walk to Jesus. He put his hand upon his head and pronounced him healed. Samuel said that he felt like lightning rushing through his body and he felt cleansed and there was no pain or sickness in the stomach like after he had his treatments. He knew that he was healed and Jesus had done it for him. He was so happy.

When Ruth woke up that morning Samuel was asleep in his bed so she just thought that it was good that he was able to sleep through the night for a change. Most nights he couldn't sleep very well. She would have to give him a nice warm bath and rub his aching body down for him to sleep even a few hours. But he was fast asleep and there was a peace on his face that she had not seen before.

When he woke up he sat up and said "mama Jesus came and healed me last night."

She said "what?"

"Jesus came and healed me last night. He told me of the great things that I would do for him. He told me to stay away from smoking, drinking and women and that I should stay pure for him. Mama we must go over to see Bobby soon, really soon, like tomorrow. Jesus said that if I layed hands on Bobby that he would heal him too."

Ruth just looked at him to see if maybe he had a fever and was delirious or something. But she could see that something had happened. Samuel got up and said look mama I feel fine. Jesus really healed me. Let's ask that doctor if we can go home. Ruth was not sure but she just started to rejoice. If Samuel said that Jesus came perhaps he did. She would see what would happen from there.

"Well let's tell the doctor that you are feeling better and let's go and see Bobby."

She called Pastor Daniel to thank him for the prayers and to tell him that Samuel had seen Jesus. He was dumbfounded at first but thought why not. He had heard about that many times how Jesus would come to people in the hospital and heal them. What a tremendous testimony. He couldn't wait to see Samuel so he could tell the whole congregation about it.

Samuel and Ruth went to see Bobby and Mona. Mona could see right away a difference in Samuel's face. He was walking like he had strength not like he was barely making it. She told her about the visitation and she just started to cry.

"Why can't my boy get a visitation from Jesus? Does he love your Samuel more than my boy?"

"No Mona. The reason why we came so quickly was that Jesus told Samuel that if he would lay hands on Bobby and pray for him that he would heal Bobby too."

"Oh my God. Oh my God. Bobby, Bobby."

Mona went screaming and crying into Bobby's room. She half scared the boy to death.

"Bobby today is your day for a miracle."

They all gathered together and layed hands on Bobby and prayed the prayer of faith and anointed him with oil and just praised God for the miracle that was happening before their very eyes.

Chapter 15

SAMUEL GOT BETTER WITH EACH passing day and never looked back to the time he had cancer. He set out to do what Jesus had called him to do. Pastor Daniel and the whole church stood behind him in all that he did for the church. He enjoyed ministering with the young and even the toddlers loved Evangelist Samuel. Samuel had never been so nervous in all of his life. Pastor Daniel worked diligently with him and the time came that Samuel would give his first sermon at the youth conference. He had more confidence in Samuel than Samuel had in himself. The church had a great youth department that empowered the young people to learn how to preach the gospel to school mates, to have leadership roles in the congregation and to prepare them for what God anointed them to do. He knew about the vision Ruth had from Jesus so he watched Samuel more closely than all the others.

Samuel had such a way with the people. He just seemed to have a compassionate spirit. The people felt comfortable with him and they with them. His mother certainly taught him the word of God just as Jesus told her too. He went on all the mission's trips during the summer, he helped out after school with things to do at the church and he really enjoyed working with the younger children on Sunday. He had truly become a real servant of God. He loved God's people and he loved God.

God had given him a burden for the prophets. He studied them from the biblical standpoint and read countless numbers of books on each one. Whatever he could get his hands on he studied. His first love was Isaiah and so he decided to speak that day about Isaiah.

Isaiah was a prophet whose name meant Yahweh is salvation. It is his book that is known for the prophetic word of the coming of the Messiah. He is believed to have been about twenty years of age when he started his public ministry and is believed to have come from high culture. The Talmud held that he was the nephew of a king. He was a citizen of Jerusalem, was married and had two sons.

Samuel saw in the Book of Isaiah the story of a nation called of God for a special purpose in the world. But through the course of time this nation had fallen into idolatry thus displeasing God. Because of their disobedience time after time God allowed them to fall into the hands of the enemy that they might see the error of their ways. He always counseled them about allowing the ways of the enemy to come in and pollute the people. Light and darkness do not mix. The Nation of Israel had specific instructions from God of how they were supposed to live their lives. If God had allowed them to continue this way the whole plan of God's salvation would be in jeopardy. The people of God had become polluted and the leadership had become polluted. These were the one's that were supposed to teach the people God's ways and they had become polluted and had forsaken God and the commandments of God. When Moses was on the earth and sent to lead the people God warned him that if the people turned away from the commandments that judgment would come to them. This is what God came to tell Isaiah. But he also spoke to Isaiah about the Messiah that was to come to redeem the Nation of Israel. Isaiah had the awesome privilege of seeing the Lord of Glory high and lifted up in the heavenly place. There would be a time when there God would put an end to all the war and that the people would be blessed and be at peace.

Samuel believed that there was a great correlation of this story to the church today. The world has become so full of hatred and war is everywhere. It seemed to Samuel even as a young man that when his father died that this nation called the United States of America is a great nation that was called by God to spread the Gospel of Jesus Christ to the nations of the world. But unfortunately she has forsaken the call by which God ordained her and she has fallen into idol worship and the things of the world. Because of this great judgment has come to her not only because of her disobedience but because God wants to draw her unto himself. This is done by allowing her to see the error of her way when she turns her back on righteousness and replaces it with unrighteousness. Like the Nation of Israel she gives God false praise and worship while on the other hand she bows to idols made with man's hands. The United States of America besides Israel is the greatest nation that God has ever birthed. But she has a purpose and like Israel is in jeopardy because of failing to complete the task that she is called to accomplish for God.

For a young man Samuel was very wise. You could see the anointing power of God on him when he ministered to the young people at the youth conferences and in church. The Lord said that he would put a sword in his mouth and you could hear it when he preached the word of God. He was going somewhere and God was going to take him all the way.

Samuel decided that he would look over his sermon one last time. For some reason this sermon had some great significance to him. He didn't know why but it just made something well up inside of him. It was as if the Holy Spirit was giving witness to him that this needed to be said and that the young people he was ministering to needed to hear this message. Many of them would be going on to college, missions, pastorates and maybe even government. They needed to have more of an understanding of what this nation meant to God. They would be the leaders of the world someday and they were ill prepared to deal with the many challenges they would face. They needed to know that God was in control and that they were not alone in this world. They needed to know that if they put God first and kept his commandments that he would continue to do great things in this nation because there was much more that was to transpire before the Messiah would come to save the world from destroying itself.

While Samuel was sitting in his hotel room he looked over his sermon and he fell asleep at some point he didn't know how long he had been sleeping. He had a dream like the vision of Isaiah where he saw the Lord high and lifted up sitting on his throne. There were angels all around him crying, holy, holy, holy, the earth is full of his glory. Samuel just looked on in awe. This was the first dream that he had of this magnitude. He had been having dreams for a long time where God would show him things that he would do in the future. Sometimes they would be just a picture of a person who God wanted him to pray about sickness or salvation. He had never seen the Lord like this before. It was such a humbling experience. He heard the voice of the Lord say:

"Samuel you have been called for such a time as this. The people have forsaken me but I will send you to the nations to tell them that I have heard the cries of the people who are in bondage in satan's kingdom. Many are crying who are homeless, hungry, and being afflicted in ways that break my heart but the world is too busy to hear their cries. But I have heard their cries and it shall not go on much longer. I will come to save them just like I came to save my people Israel when they were in slavery in Egypt. I cannot stand the bloodshed of war anymore, I cannot stand to see innocent babies killed every day in America, I cannot stand to see innocent children kidnapped, raped and killed every day in America. Samuel this bloodshed must stop and I am the only way that this will be accomplished."

Samuel woke up in a cold sweat. He didn't get a chance to speak to the Lord but he had heard loud and clear what was on God's heart. He didn't know whether he could preach now. His mind was in another zone. He had seen the Lord. Was he to tell the people about what God had told him? Should he tell Pastor Daniel? He would tell Pastor Daniel but he would wait until the youth conference was over so that he could tell him what he was supposed to do now.

Pastor Daniel came to knock on the door to pick Samuel up for the conference. Samuel was all dressed and ready to go.

"Hey Pastor Daniel you all ready to go?"

"Yeah. How you feeling son?"

"I'm feeling okay. I guess I do have some butterflies in my stomach."

"Well that's okay. Just keep your mind focused on the text. You can look at me that might make you feel more comfortable. I remember when I gave my first sermon I kept my head down the whole time. But as time went on I became more confident and didn't have to look down any more. You'll get the hang of it. It will really get interesting when the Holy Spirit takes over the sermon."

"What do you mean takes over the sermon?"

"Well it's like you are not preaching but God is preaching through you. You receive power. Remember in the Book of Acts when the Holy Spirit came upon them they spoke with other tongues and they received power. Well that power is to give men the boldness that they will need to give that message power. You won't be afraid any more but the power of God will be working in you."

"Oh. Well I need some of that power tonight. Can we pray before we leave that God will give me that power that he gave the apostles?"

"We sure can son. Father in the name of your precious son Jesus we come. We thank you Father for each of your sons and daughters that have come for a special time in your presence today. We thank you for your servant Samuel. Father give Samuel power in the Spirit that he might bring forth the word from heaven with power. Send your Spirit to abide with us in this meeting. Touch each and every one today that we might see some saved, healed, filled with the Spirit and renewed by the power of God. In Jesus name we pray. Amen."

"Okay I think that I'm ready to go now. I hope this goes well."

"Oh you'll be fine."

The youth conference was held for their denomination once a year. Youth from all over the country attended, it was truly magnificent. There were about 25,000 youth in attendance this year more than in previous years. God was truly doing something in his young people to prepare them for the latter day outpouring of the Spirit. Pastor Daniel was so excited. He could feel the power of God in the air when he walked into the auditorium. He would make sure that he continued to pray for Samuel as he gave his sermon to the youth that evening. The praise team was already getting prepared to start. He would open in prayer and exhortation for the group and then the praise service, Samuel would speak and of course whatever the Holy Spirit had in mind. The prayer group had been praying for this conference. They wanted the Holy Spirit to transform each and every youth there that weekend. Pastor Daniel remembered when he was a young boy going to tent meetings and seeing the power of God working in his people. People got saved and many were healed of all manner of diseases. This was a true testimony that Jesus is alive and that he is the same today as he was in the Bible. It's unfortunate that many of our young people don't have those kinds of preachers to sit under anymore. There seems to be a different gospel being preached in the last days before Christ return. Pastor Daniel talks to God all the time about what has happened to the power in the church?

At 7 pm Pastor Daniel came out to exhort the young audience of Holy Spirit charged warriors ready for great things to happen. They had come to worship their King and he wasn't going to wait another moment. He was excited as well. After prayer, the praise team got up and the young people joined in song to the Lord Most High. The excitement was building with each song. There was nothing so beautiful to see than a group of teenagers worshiping God. Pastor Daniel believed that the youth of today were in trouble because there was no one showing them that they can be free in Jesus Christ. They didn't have to take drugs, have pre-marital sex and put a ring in their belly to be free. What they needed was to know that God loved them and that was freedom. By the time the praise team sang his favorite song "How Great Is Our God" the natives were wrestles and he didn't know whether he should interrupt or not. Sometimes we get in the way of what God is doing.

One by one people were coming to the altar and Daniel just looked on and let it happen. He remembered when he was just a young boy how when the praise started people would just start coming out of their seats and crying down to the altar. These were usually the services where the pastor never preached a sermon but just let the Holy Spirit do what he wanted to do. So that's what they did. The word would come forth when God allowed it to come forth.

Samuel was enjoying the flow of the Spirit and he quickly learned not to worry when he had to preach maybe the Lord would let him preach and maybe not. He would keep his sermon tucked away for the next night if necessary. The people of God were being blessed just with the presence of God in the room. Maybe the church was making the Gospel of Jesus Christ too difficult for people to understand. It seemed like God could speak to his people even without words being said. Maybe there needed to be a lot less talking in the church and a lot more of God.

The youth started to do an amazing thing. They got together in groups and just started praying for one another. Pastor Daniel was astonished to see them doing this. Had they been taught this at their local churches or were these young Bible college students? It was just amazing to see them praying for one another. He and Samuel just went down into the crowd and started praying with group after group and laying on of hands that they might receive the Holy Spirit. This went on for five or six hours with the praise team hanging in all the way.

When the night was over there were young people layed out in the presence of the Lord. He had surely come in a powerful and mighty way for his people. The word of the Lord tells us "if my people which are called by my name shall humble themselves and pray, and seek my face and turn from their wicked ways, then will I hear from heaven, and will forgive their sins and heal their land."

Chapter 16

SOMETHING SUPERNATURAL WAS HAPPENING TO Samuel and he knew that he needed to be alone with God for a time to see what he needed to do next. He wanted to make sure that he was doing exactly what God wanted him to be doing. He enjoyed speaking at the youth conferences but it just wasn't enough. He knew that God wanted him to be in full time ministry. Was he to pastor a church like Bro. Daniel or would he truly be an evangelist going throughout the world ministering to the lost people of the world? Things were going great though miracles were happening the young people were giving their lives to Christ what could be better. He had done what God told him to do he didn't get himself involved with the world and kept himself holy unto God.

He decided that he was going to try a 21day fast like the prophet Daniel in the Bible. He was another one of Samuel's favorite prophets. He loved the story about how Daniel, Azariah, Mishael and Hananiah were taken captive during the exile to work in the king's palace. Because they were Hebrew they had strict dietary laws and although they were in exile they wanted to adhere to the commandments that God had given to them. They refused to eat of the meat and drink of the wine that may have been offered to the Babylonian gods. They would have defiled themselves if they had done so. So they asked that they be given a different diet from the rest which was granted. The Bible says that God blessed them and gave them knowledge and skill in all learning and wisdom and Daniel was given a special gift of God in the understanding of visions and dreams. When King Nebuchadnezzar had a dream that was keeping him from sleeping, he called for all the astrologers and sorcerers and the Chaldeans to give him the interpretation. He promised that if they did not give him the interpretation that it would be death for them and their houses. But if they could give him the interpretation he would reward them greatly. Because they could not give him the answer all the wise men of Babylon were to be put to death. So Daniel went to King Nebuchadnezzar and asked for more time. He Hananiah, Azariah and Mishael fasted and prayed before God to give them the answer for it would have meant sure death for them all. The God of Abraham, Isaac and Jacob honored them with the answer to the dream. Daniel had a night vision and God told him all that the king saw in his dream. He was able to tell him down to the very minutest of details. Only God knows everything that will happen in the future.

On an occasion Daniel went on a 21 day fast because he wanted to hear from God. Samuel had only been fasting for a few years but knew that if it worked for Daniel that it would work for him. When Samuel first decided to go on a fast he had been reading the New Testament where when the disciples had a problem casting out the demon he said that this one came out by fasting and praying. He knew that if Jesus said it that it was for every believer. Most people think that they don't have to fast because they are not casting out any devils. But the fact of the matter is that every believer should have a fasting lifestyle because it moves heaven and earth. So Samuel fasted on all pleasant bread, meat and fast food for 21 days of consecration before God. It wasn't as difficult as he thought but it wasn't as easy either. It's amazing how difficult it is to give up some things that you are so used to eating. Samuel liked chocolate donuts and giving them up was like giving up his right arm. But he knew that he had to do this for God. He needed a breakthrough in his life.

When Queen Esther found out that Haman was plotting against the nation of Israel to kill them she called all of her people to a three day fast without any food. This was a cry to God to help the nation or else they would be eliminated. God heard their cry and he turned what Haman was going to do on him and his house. Her uncle Mordecai was rewarded for his diligence in fasting in prayer and sackcloth before God as well.

During the time that Samuel fasted before God he had a regimen of getting up every day and praying and seeking God for two hours that day. Fasting and praying should be looked at as a holy time before the Lord. The Lord Jesus Christ said that when you pray don't let man know what you are doing. But wash your face and go before the people with gladness that they not know that you are fasting. Some people while fasting don't really spend time with God but they spend most of their time telling everybody that they are fasting. Jesus would say surely they have their reward. So fasting should be a secret between you and God.

Within three days of starting his fast Samuel had a dream that night. It was as though he were hovering over the room. He could see down into the room but he knew that his mom could not see him. She was kneeling down at her bedside praying to God. He could not hear her conversation but he could see her praying. He could see every detail of the room. The bed sheets were the ones that she had on her bed. He could see the picture of his father and his mother shortly after they were married that sat on the table stand next to her bed. It was so weird. Why was God showing this to him? What did it all mean? The dream then shifted to a hospital. He and his grand-mother were in the waiting room and his grand-mother was crying. Pastor Daniel was there and he was sitting down with his head down and his hands over his head. Samuel knew that something was wrong but what he couldn't understand. He then had a dream where he was hovering over a funeral home. He could not see the person in the casket but it all somehow fit together. What did this mean? Was his mom in trouble? She wasn't sick so he could not see what this all meant. He woke up in a cold sweat. He felt anxious so he got up and got dressed and went for a walk to talk with God.

Within a week after his dream Ruth had a massive stroke and died. Samuel was heartbroken. He couldn't understand why he had to lose both his mother and father so young. He didn't even get a chance to know his father and his mother was his life beside Jesus. He felt so all alone and confused. What would he do now? Besides his grand parents she was all that he had. He wanted them to grow old together. He didn't want to be offended but he was offended at God for taking his mother. Now he knew for sure what the dream meant.

"Why God? Why did you take my mother and my father too? I have no one now except my grand parents. I love them but I feel all alone God."

Samuel just cried and cried. He had not cried so much in his life. He didn't know that he had so much anger and hurt inside of him. Since he had been sick when he was just a young boy he didn't even cry then when he felt so weak and sick that he couldn't even walk or eat on his own. His mother was there for him the whole time and he had a special bond with her. He didn't feel like he could go on. He felt for the first time in his life that he truly wanted to die and didn't care whether he saw the next day or not.

Samuel thought of so many ways that he could kill himself. He wasn't a fan of pain so he thought about driving the car off of a cliff or something surely this would be fast and painless. He could take some pills to make him really sleepy and that would calm him so that he would not lose his nerve. Maybe he would buy a gun and kill himself that way. That was supposed to be quick. But there was a little voice inside of himself that kept saying "you can make it through this just trust in me."

"No I can't make it through this. My mother was always there for me in times of trouble. Now I'm in trouble and she's not there."

The voice said "I'm here now and I have always been there for you Samuel. Remember when you were sick in the hospital and the doctors said that you would not make it. I came to you and healed you and set you forth to do my work. I was there then and I will be here now."

"But why Jesus, why did she and dad have to go? I didn't get a chance to even know my father."

"There are some things Samuel that it's not for you to know. But if you need an answer then try this one. This kingdom is not my kingdom. As long as you live in it there will be sickness and death. I never meant for the world to be the way that it is but when Satan stole the rights to this world from Adam he corrupted everything that I made. Everyone has an appointed day to die and this was your mother's. You too will die someday. Most people don't look at it but unfortunately it's true.

Your mother never told you this but a long time ago she had a baby that died before you. The baby was sickly and it died Samuel. She felt like she couldn't make it without the baby despite how much she loved your father and all of her church family. But I came to her at a point when she wanted to take her life and told her that I loved her and that I could help her with the depression if she would just let me. Make the choice that she did because if she didn't you would not be alive today."

"I don't feel much like being alive today."

"I know Samuel. But remember little Bobby. He was a very sickly boy. If you had not believed in my miraculous power to heal he wouldn't be alive today. Do you know that someday he is going to have a family and three healthy children. This is the power that you will take around the world."

"Wow I have not thought about him in quite a few years. We lost contact when he and his mother moved away. I'm glad that he is doing well. And no I didn't know that my mother had thought about suicide like I am right now. Oh but Jesus it hurts so much."

"Yes my son. I know that it does. But in time if you will allow time to heal you you can be healed of this. Your mom and dad are together again. He was waiting for her arrival. They are both praying for you and know how difficult a time this is but trust in me Samuel you are still going to do great things for the kingdom of God."

"I will try. Please Jesus don't ever leave me. I won't be able to do this without you."

"Oh Samuel I will never leave you nor forsake you. Just trust in me, lean not unto thy own understanding in all your ways acknowledge me and I will direct your paths."

Samuel felt a warmth in his heart like Jesus had just touched him in some supernatural way and he felt like he could make it. He had not eaten much in quite a few weeks. The 21day fast had actually been in God's timing because Samuel had no idea that he was going to go through what just happened. The fast actually put him closer to God at a time when he was truly going to need a great level of strength from Jesus.

Chapter 17

AFTER SAMUEL'S MOTHER PAST AWAY he was confused, lonely and desperate for God. He decided after talking with Pastor Daniel that a time alone with God was needed to get him back on track. Samuel packed some equipment and went away for a month to fast and pray before the Lord. He needed revelation of what God wanted him to do with his life and he followed after Jesus example after he was baptized of John how he went into the wilderness to fast and pray before God.

Samuel's grand-parents Mabel and Eddie lived in Florida and he remembered as a young boy going to visit with them and how much he enjoyed the tranquility of God's country. It was certainly a beautiful place with all of the trees, flowers, creeks and the beautiful ocean. He even got a chance to go and see the amazing spaceships at the NASA space center. How he enjoyed going fishing with his buddies. There was so much to do in Florida. The people were always so courteous and the churches were awesome. How he enjoyed that down home country preaching and singing. He really needed to be in a place like that where he could hear from God and get healed of some of the terrible pain he was feeling inside. Why had God taken his father when he was so young and now his mother who was his best friend? It was difficult leaving his grand ma and grand pa in Newark. They had just lost their baby girl and now he decided that he needed some time away. But they understood that he was hurting and that Mabel and Eddie would do their very best to help him.

Samuel arrived at his grand-parents with a warm welcome from them, the church and some neighbors who came to see the little boy they once knew. Samuel used to run around that neighborhood with some of the other young boys when he was young. Many of them had already gone off to school or had jobs. Samuel wasn't quite sure what he was supposed to do after school had finished. His mom always reminded him that he had a call of God on his life and that what the world was doing was not for him. This caused great anguish for Samuel because he was waiting for God to tell him exactly what he wanted him to do. To date he had not heard exactly what he was to do for God so of course he was confused. His good friend Pastor Daniel had exposed him to preaching and he enjoyed preaching and teaching the word but he wanted a word from the Lord where he should go next now that he was out of school. He could be a missionary but he didn't even know how to get started. He could go to Bible college but he had just finished school and didn't want to sit in classes right now. He wanted to get right into what God wanted him to do. He knew that he would be happiest if he was in the perfect will of God for his life but what was that? He figured this is a question that many are asking God. Perhaps he will find someone who had figured it all out and they could tell him what to do.

Determined to find the answer Samuel took some camping equipment and told his grand-mother that he was going out to his favorite camp sight to commune with God. He hoped that at the end of his fasting time that he would hear from God. Fasting is one of the most best kept secrets of the Bible or maybe one of the most forgotten secrets of the Bible. When Samuel first started fasting it was so hard for him, but then of course he started off with water and no food at all. He asked Pastor Daniel whether he fasted and how should he do it. It seemed like he just couldn't get through the day without feeling light headed. He had to sleep most of it without praying because he didn't have the strength. But Pastor Daniel gave him a great set of tapes and some books that taught all about fasting from the Biblical perspective and then he was able to put it in a better perspective. After studying he realized that he could start off with just one meal a day until he got stronger and that it had to be done by means of the Holy Spirit. This is why it was so hard for him because he was doing it on his own strength and not God's strength. There was no way that Moses could fast for forty days and nights if not for God's help. Jesus also fasted for 40 days and nights after his baptism of the spirit and water. Fasting opened up Samuel's sensitivity to what the Spirit was saying to him. He needed to hear from God and he needed to hear from him now.

Samuel had some friends that lived in the country and thought that he would go up there and see whether they were still around. He loved going up there because it was nothing but farms and trees and the river. He remembered when they would get in the boat and sit on the water for hours and hours. The birds would be flying back and forth and you just knew that God was watching over the place it was so tranquil. He could really hear from God there. Luke's father had a farm and as young boys they would chase the chickens and the goats around the farm. It was so much fun. He liked being out of the city. He wished that he lived on a farm like Luke. He knew so much stuff that most people in the city didn't know. Samuel felt as a young boy that some day God would call him out of the city and he would move south. He started to feel already that this was a part of the answer he was looking for. Already he felt a sense of peace that he didn't have in the city.

"Lord is this what you want me to do? Should I sell the house and move south to live from Mabel and Eddie? I would be happy and so would she? But mom and dad worked so hard on that house she might be angry if I sold it? What do you think Lord?"

A still small voice inside of him said "My son your mom and dad are here in heaven praying for you. They want you to be happy. If selling the house and moving to the south will make you happy then so be it."

Samuel felt like wow I haven't even started fasting yet and already I feel like I have a part of the answer that I was looking for. He knocked on Luke's door. He didn't see the truck but there was a car out front so someone was at home.

"Hi. I'm Samuel I used to play with Luke when I was a young boy. I haven't seen or heard from him in quite some time. I came down to visit my grand parents. Is he still living here?"

"Yeah. He sure is. He's out back doing some farming. Hey I think I do remember you from long time ago. How you doing?"

"I'm doing okay I guess. My mom just past away not a few months ago so I'm thinking about moving down here."

"Oh that's a fine idea. Come on let's find Luke. Luke an old friend of yours is here to see you."

Luke was a lot bigger now but he had that same boyish face that Samuel remembered. He remembered Samuel as soon as he saw him also. He ran to the house to greet him.

"Hey man. How you doing? Long time no see. How is everything?"

"It's going okay. Lost my mom. I'm thinking about moving down here. How are you doing?"

"I'm doing great now that school is finished. I've always wanted to work on the farm but dad wouldn't let me quit school. But now I'm done and I can do what I've always wanted to do."

"Hey that's great. I'm trying to figure out what I'm going to do. Hey would you mind if I camp out here on the farm a few days. I just need to clear my head and seek a word from the good Lord if you know what I mean."

"Well now me and God haven't been talking much but that's my fault I guess. Hey your more than welcome to camp out as long as you like. That old barn is good for laying down in. I go in there myself sometimes when I want to get a way from dad. He can sure get me going sometime. If you'd like you can help me out around here. I can use all the help I can get. The old man is working me to the bone. But I love it. This is where I will be forever I guess. The country is all I know and all I ever want to know."

"Hey I sure would like to help. I told my grand-mother that I was coming up here. I'll give her a call and tell her that I'm okay. And the barn sounds great. Did you know that Jesus was born in a barn?"

"Yeah I think that I recall hearing something to that affect. Well if it will make you feel closer to Jesus then have at it."

"Okay. I want to go over to the river later you game?"

"Sure. We can get the old boat out. Remember the good old days when we just sat on the water fishing all day?"

"Yeah. I sure do. Luke I came up here to do some soul searching. My mom told me that before I was born Jesus came to her to tell her that he had something for me to do and I need to find out what that something is you know?"

"No. But I'm with you and I'll help you anyways I can my friend. Remember I'm backslidden all the way back to the beginning. You will have to help me out. Maybe there is a reason you came back here. I need God but I don't know quite how to get back to him you know. You think that he'll forgive me for having stopped going to church and all?"

"Oh Luke, Jesus is not like that. He came for them that are lost. If you are lost then Jesus came for you. The Bible also says that all have sinned and fallen short of the glory of God. He will forgive you and not remember your sins anymore. Oh Luke I'm so glad to see you and I'll help you find your way back to Jesus if you are sincere."

"I'm sincere but I got a lot of sin. Will you take your time?"

"Sure will. I got all the time in the world. What do you want me to do first?"

"Well why don't you just go and put your stuff in the barn. Now you can stay in the house but you might feel closer to God in the barn. I'll teach you how to ride the horse so you can take it out whenever you like. I can take some time off in a few hours and we'll just go fishing. Sound like a deal?"

"Sounds great. I'll see you in a few. I'm going into the barn and relax a while."

Samuel went into Luke's barn and there were horses in the barn. He remembered the days when he was so little that he was afraid of the horses but now he just felt at home. He went up to one of the horses and he petted him and he wasn't afraid of the horse anymore. He started to feel more and more confident that this was the divine will of God that he move from the big city of Newark to Florida to be with his grand parents. He didn't know where he would go from there but this was a start. He pulled out his cell phone to call his grand-mother to tell her that he was okay. The reception was terrible so he stepped outside to call her.

"Grand-mother this is Samuel. I've found Luke and he has invited me to stay as long as I wish and help out at the farm. Will you be okay?"

"Oh Samuel I'm just fine. I'll miss you. Make sure you call me every day okay?"

"Okay grand-mother. I sure will. I love you."

"I love you too."

Samuel went back into the barn. He was feeling happier than he could ever have imagined due to the circumstances. He put his gear down and made a make shift bed in the hay. He would try to get something a bit more comfortable in the days ahead. It could not have been easy for Mary and Joseph when Jesus was born so he didn't expect that it should be for him either. He must have been tired because no soon as he layed his head down he was fast asleep. Must be that clean Florida air that did it.

Samuel feel into a deep sleep when he was awakened by someone tapping on his foot. He woke up thinking that it was Luke coming to fetch him to go fishing but when he looked up there stood Jesus.

"Get up Samuel and walk with me."

Samuel got up quickly to walk with the Lord. Jesus climbed up on one of the horses and beconed Samuel to join him by putting out his hand. It was easy as pie. He just took Jesus hand and he pulled him up on the horse. It was amazing.

"Where are we going Lord?"

"Don't worry just hold on and listen."

"Samuel I have been waiting for you to get to this point in your life. I knew that you would come to ask me what I wanted you to do with your life. Samuel before you were formed in your mothers womb I called you to be my servant. You are called to be a prophet to the nations. The prophet is my special messenger. Samuel being a prophet is not an easy job but as long as you give the message as I give it to you then you will not have the blood of the people on your head. But if you fail to give the message their blood will be required of your hand."

"Father I don't know how to be a prophet. What do I do?"

"Do not worry. I have trained many prophets before you. Before you I trained Elijah the Tishbit, I trained Moses and Aaron, I trained Ezekiel, Isaiah and Jeremiah. All of these were my prophets, my sons. You too will be like these and more than these for I will put a mighty sword in your mouth and you will speak of me to the people and speak of that which is to come. And you will receive a special anointing and people will be healed of all manner of diseases and you shall caste out demons and raise the dead in my name."

After Jesus had finished speaking Samuel found himself right back in the barn laying down. It was as if Jesus had somehow transported him back into the barn. The horse that he was riding on was no where to be found in the barn where he lay. Just then Luke came into the barn to see if Samuel was ready to go fishing.

"Hey Samuel are you ready to go fishing now? I can get us some sandwiches and stuff to take for lunch."

"Luke that sounds great. Let's go."

Samuel dared not tell Luke what had just happened to him. He would have thought that he was crazy. He almost felt crazy for a moment. What did God want him to do? He could not even fathom what a prophet was supposed to do in this day and time. He had been burdened to know about the prophets and now he knew why. God was working in him in ways that he could not understand. But he knew better than to say no to God. He would do whatever it was that God wanted him to do. He had faith that God would show him the way just like he showed his other prophets the way. But he knew that it would not be an easy journey. His favorite was Elijah. He remembered how Elijah was chosen of God to speak to his people Israel and to show them the evil that had crept into the people's worship and their heart. He was chosen to turn them around and it wasn't easy. But the hand of God was on Elijah's life and he gave him power that when he spoke the people would know that God was behind him. Elijah called down fire from heaven and when it was time for him to leave this earth God sent the chariot of fire to take him to heaven.

Chapter 18

SMALL WAS STARTING TO FEEL better already. He called his grand-mother and told her that he was here to stay. She was of course overjoyed that her grand-son would be there. Samuel made the arrangements to put the house in New Jersey up for sale and hoped that he would make a good sale. He wasn't sure what God had in store for him and he didn't have a paying job anyway. He was helping Luke and his dad on the farm but he wasn't asking for any money from them. He was just glad to have his old friend back again and some peace of mind. The Lord had been revealing himself in some mighty ways and he wanted to stay free to go wherever the Lord asked him to go. He was just hoping that God didn't want him to leave Florida anytime soon he was having such a tremendous time with Luke and his father. His father needed salvation as well so it was a goal of his to see them saved.

He was looking forward to going to church on Sunday and hoped that he would be able to get at least Luke to go with him. That would be a good start to getting him back on track with God. They were young but so was his father when he died. The next day is not promised to anyone and yet most people live as though they don't have a care in the world.

Samuel didn't want Luke to feel out of place so he just put on a pair of pants and a shirt. He would usually put on a suit and tie

Obadiah Ariel Yehoshuah

but he thought for this first time he would be less formal. They were having a traveling minister name of John to preach the service that day. He was on fire for God. Samuel wanted the fire John had. There was just something different about him. He preached a sermon that day on heaven and hell. He didn't mess around he just came right to the point and people were flocking to the altar. What power he had? John was at least 75 years old and had been in the ministry since he was 40 years old when God called him to go into all the world.

John talked about things that Samuel had never heard about in his church. Pastor Daniel was good but this guy just had something that he had never experienced and he was determined to find out what it was. Oh there was singing and praising God in that little ole country church that moved heaven and earth. Samuel loved the church and he loved God. He was still feeling confused and a bit sad over the past few months experience but he knew that Jesus was right and he needed to get himself together for all the people who were waiting for him to get into the ministry that God had called him for. Maybe John could shed some light on what Samuel should do next. He would ask him after the service was over.

John was a character. He was born and raised in Tennessee but you would never know that he had already ministered in over 120 nations across the world. He was a prophet of God sent into the world to minister an end time message that many of the Body of Christ did not want to hear. The first night of the revival he spoke about a dream that God had given to him many, many years before. It was a dream he said that changed his life. When he was just a young man he fell away from God and didn't want anything to do with the church. He as a young man of course wanted to see the world because the church was all he knew from his youth. He wanted to travel, have a big job, make lots of money and have many girlfriends. All of this he did but through all of these years God was showing him things in dreams and visions that he didn't understand. Of course, there was no one that he could talk to about what God was showing him that would understand what God was trying to say. He went to his pastor to tell him some of these things and he told him that he had a devil and not to give place to the

144

devil by talking about what the devil was saying. This confused John all the more so, so he did just that he prayed that the devil would stop bothering him but since it was God that didn't work. He had dreams about major earthquakes that would take place in America. He had visions of war in America and he had visions of great pestilence, suffering and famine in America. His family was by no means rich but they got by with what they made on the farm and his dad would take odd jobs whenever they needed something extra. Overall they made ends meet. The Lord gave John the ability to build things so he learned how to build houses and do electrical wiring and he made a very good living doing that for a long time. He got married eventually and had a family and was doing well in life. All the while the dreams kept coming and coming. He never talked much about them because he knew that they would tell him that he had a devil and he didn't want to hear that any more. One day he heard about a man of God by the name of William Parham and he had the testimony about how when he was young he used to have these dreams and he was told that he had a devil. He went out to pray to God to take the dreams away because he did not understand that they were from God. Well this peaked John's interest and he went to see this brother that he might help him to understand what God was trying to say. Well Bro. Parham told him that this was of God and that he went through the same problem growing up. He told John that they should pray together and he should turn his life over to Christ and God had the call of a prophet on his life and he was to go and tell the world about what God was saying to him. Well John didn't know whether he was excited or not. God had been talking to him all his life and he didn't even know it. But now he had to make a decision. He didn't really want a call of God on his life. But how could he tell God that. Anyway he and Bro. Parham talked for quite a while. He poured out his heart to William about the things that he had saw. Bro. Parham told him that he had had similar dreams and that it is a hard anointing to tell people what is about to befall this great nation. After pouring out his heart he was amazed that he felt better, clean if you will than he had ever felt in his life. He understood that God had chosen him to take a very hard message to America and he had to prepare himself to do just that. He knelt down with Bro. Parham and prayed the sinners prayer and received Christ that day.

This of course was just the beginning of what he had to do next. So he went home to tell his wife what had happened. She wasn't against Christ but she was like him she wasn't for him either. She loved her husband and had to date supported him in all that he did and so she had to support him now. John was a good husband and if he wanted to now serve God she would go along. She had no idea the pain and suffering they would go through in order to do so. John wanted to sell the business and go on the road to preach the gospel. She wasn't ready for all of that but what could she do. John was sure that God was talking to him and he had to go and warn the people of America that some terrible things were about to happen to her and she needed to prepare.

They had never in the 20 years of their marriage even stepped foot into a church. But that Sunday they found themselves in the church of one of the biggest preachers of their time Bro. B.B. Springer. John was amazed at the energy this young man had when he preached. It was like he was floating on air or something. He would come out on the platform and command the audience with his preaching etiquette. John prayed that God would give him that same charisma to preach like this brother did. He had totally forgotten everything about that word of God so he knew first he had to start reading the word again. He was a good businessman and had studied volumes of books about electrical wiring and building houses and stuff. This would be no different just a different book. He had to get to know this God that had been talking to him all this time and how to talk back to him so they would be on the same page. He of course had given him the power to do what he had been doing all these years so he should continue to trust him now.

John had already prayed the sinners prayer but Bro. Springer talked about receiving the Holy Ghost. He had remembered them talking about the Holy Ghost when he was a kid but he didn't put much stock into it. All he knew was that he didn't want it. He didn't want no Ghost living inside him. What did he need a Ghost for? But

Bro. Springer said that the Holy Ghost was the Spirit of Christ Jesus that lived inside every believer that he might be born again. He said that you cannot enter into the Kingdom of God unless ye be born again. Well he knew that he wanted to be in the Kingdom so he went up to receive the baptism of the Holy Ghost. All he remembered was that he fell to the floor and when he woke up he felt different but he couldn't explain it. He didn't know how long that he was on the floor but someone was trying to help him up but his legs just weren't working and he just kept laughing and laughing and trying to walk but he felt like he was floating on a cloud. If this was the Holy Ghost they needed to put it in a bottle and sell it over the counter. People would pay out the nose for this stuff. John had been quite a drinker so he knew the good stuff when he had it.

His wife was looking at him with huge hazel eyes. She couldn't believe how crazy her husband was acting but she thought he was having a good time so why fuss. She still wasn't convinced that she needed God. Bro. Springer had the gift of healing and so after each service he had a prayer line for the sick. She remembered on one particular day that there was a man who she remembered had a large tumour on his left cheek. That thing was the size of a cantaloupe. It was huge. She always thought how in the world can he stand that thing on his face. You couldn't help but stare at it it was so big. Anyway she felt sorry for him. But this particular Sunday Bro. Springer called him out and told him that God had given him word of knowledge that he would be healed that day. Well that man came out of his chair and went to the front of the church. Bro. Springer took some oil from a bottle and placed his hand on that tumor and prayed. All of a sudden that thing just evaporated before the congregations eyes. That skin was like baby skin as though there was no tumor there at all. Robin could not believe her eyes. She had seen it herself. Many of the healings he had just prayed and she never saw for herself the after affects of the prayer. This was a true miracle. She could not believe what she had seen. This had to be God.

Betty began weeping uncontrollably because she had suffered with cancer for many years and had gone through all the treatments. She was in remission for five years and then the cancer came back.

She was struggling with this but she had no one to help her. Maybe there was hope after all. She would talk to John about it and see if Bro. Springer would pray for her one Sunday. She was afraid and felt bad because she had been so skeptical about this whole thing. She had not given her life to Christ or received the Holy Ghost or anything. She felt that she was not worthy of the love that Christ was showing all these other people who truly believed in him. But John told her that Christ loved her too and that all she had to do is believe in him and he would heal her too. She just cried in his arms and could not wait until Sunday came. As soon as Bro. Springer gave the altar call she dashed down to the front dragging John with her to receive Christ. Bro. Springer just said the Lord told me that you would be coming soon. All the congregation just praised God because they had been praying for weeks that she would come to the altar. Bro. Springer also said and he said that you need healing. Lift up your hands and receive it in Jesus name. She could feel the power of God going throughout her body. She understood what the woman with the issue of blood felt when she touched the hem of Jesus garment. The power of God went through her and she knew that she was healed. Betty went to her doctors the next day to have some tests done and the doctor was amazed that there was no cancer. She had been healed by the power of God.

From that day forward John didn't have a problem with Betty. She was sold out on Jesus and wanted to tell everybody they knew and met about how Jesus healed her and saved her and forgave her sins. The couple was ready to serve the Lord but didn't know how to get started. Neither one could preach, sing or anything. They just had a testimony. Bro. Springer introduced them to another brother who had a great tent meeting who was needing just some extra hands. They knew they could help so they sold just about everything and went out on the road with this evangelist. They did everything from putting up the tent, to cleaning the portable potties. It was hard work but they were glad to work for Jesus. The evangelist would let them give their testimonies, pray and sing with the group. They never felt so good in all of their lives. God was using them and they were learning about ministry from a great man of God.

This was the beginning of John's ministry. To date he has not looked back yet. He eventually brought his own tent and Bro. Thomas would call ahead that the congregations in his network would receive John. The Lord blessed the ministry and later took him overseas to many different continents to preach the word of God.

Chapter 19

Samuel couldn't wait to talk with John after the service. He felt that he would definitely have the answer to some if not all of his questions. He knew that God had called him but he didn't know what to do next. When the service was over Bro. John and his wife were in the fellowship hall and when Samuel got a chance he walked up to Bro. John and asked for his guidance.

"Bro. John that sermon was awesome tonight. I'm looking forward to your next sermon."

"Son I got plenty more where that came from. God has put a burden on me son and I'm wide open this week."

"What has God burdened you with Bro. John?"

"Well son you will be the first one to hear about this. I had a terrible dream a long time ago. I had all but forgotten it but God has brought it back to my attention. I believe that it must be coming to past really soon for him to be telling me again. When I was just starting to search for God I had a dream that I had a met an older gentleman and he was talking to me about my life and how I had forsaken God and the call of God on my life. I was listening to him and I thought it was a strange dream but you know how dreams are you have to go with the flow. Anyway there were all of these people that we were meeting along the way that were kind of ministering to me as well about the Lord and how the time was short and all and I was just like okay. So anyways eventually I gave my heart to the Lord in the dream but in reality I was not saved yet. Then son the dream changed and God showed me all these horrible things that were to take place in America. He showed me that there was going to be a major earthquake in California, Tennessee, Oklahoma and other places and many people would die. He also showed me that our government had turned from the Judeo-Christian values that our founding fathers had come here to establish in this country and that because of it America would cease to be the free nation that God had held up for her for so long. He showed me that many organizations like Al-Qaeda, Hamas and Hezbollah would come up against us. He also showed me that a time was coming when Russia would turn against America and wage war against her. Son you look like you swallowed a watermelon. There are some heavy things that I must tell the Body of Christ and it is not easy. But there are lives at stake. He also told me that there will be several volcanic eruptions and that the earth would be darkened for 90 days. This will cause major food shortage in the world such as man has not seen in a long time."

"Hold on Bro. John. I can't breath. Did God tell you all of this?"

"Yes he has."

"Well what are we supposed to do?"

"Well my friend I have told you too much already. But now is the time to pray."

Samuel couldn't help but think that this man must be out of his mind. He wasn't feeling too good about him any more. How can he make up such foolishness? This nation would never allow the Russians to wage a war against it. And all this stuff about volcanic eruptions, no sun for 90 days and famine. Where is he getting this stuff from anyway? He must be reading some of those magazines they have at the checkout at Walmart or something. He had never heard anything like this from the prophecy experts. Surely if this were going to happen a bunch of them would have been talking about it. He watched Christian television and no one he listened to was talking about it at all. Well maybe he would just ask the Holy Spirit for some kind of confirmation and if he said that any of this were true he would pack his bags and follow this man anywhere that he went.

Samuel was so dumbfounded by what Bro. John had told him that he didn't even get a chance to talk about his problem. He would wait until he could speak with him again. The revival was to go on as long as Bro. John was hearing from God. Tonight would be the second night. He couldn't imagine that he would tell the people this stuff but he was going to wait and see. Well surely the night came and Bro. John began to pour out his heart about what God had supposedly shown him and the people were on pins and needles listening to him. There were some that were crying, some walked out of the church and yet others fell down on their faces before God crying, repenting and praying for forgiveness. Samuel didn't believe one word and just slipped out the side door and hoped no one noticed. Luke had a hard day on the farm and decided that he would stay home that night.

Samuel was somewhat distraught about what he had heard and decided to call Pastor Daniel to see what he thought. He didn't want to mention it to his grand-mother. He knew that she would tell him not to go back to that church. He wanted to talk with someone more objective than her.

"Pastor Daniel this is Samuel. How are you doing? I'm sorry it's been so long since I've contacted you. So much has happened."

"Yes Samuel. I am doing great. I'm so glad that you called. I was wondering how you and your family were getting along."

"Well actually I'm staying with some friends in the country. I feel closer to God here. Hey I got a question to ask you?"

"Go right ahead."

"How much do you know about dreams and visions?"

"Now that's an interesting question. Well all I can say is that before your father died he gave him a dream of what was coming. Your grand-father also from what I heard had an awesome anointing in that area as well. He worked very closely with God through dreams and visions. Many people were greatly blessed through his ministry. Sister Lucille also received a dream on the same topic and your mom actually talked with Jesus about some coming events. If you are asking me whether I believe in dreams and vision then I will tell you emphatically that I do."

"Have you had a dream?"

"Well I have had many dreams but I have never told anyone about them. I have also seen Jesus quite a few times of which I have kept that to myself as well. I thought that people would think that I was crazy. But this is not about me Pastor Daniel there is a brother here that is having a revival at one of the local churches. He told me some things that will shock you Pastor Daniel."

"No Samuel after 9-11 I'm not shocked by anything anymore. There are some terrible things that are going to happen to this nation and we had better get ready for them. God is warning us and we are turning our heads away from the truth because it is so horrific that we cannot fathom it."

"You sound like you are convinced of this."

"Yes Samuel I am convinced of this. Might I ask what the brother had to say."

"Well I had gone to him just to ask about what I should do now to break into a new level of ministry. He began to tell me some things that would make you sick and shake all over. He told me Pastor Daniel that Russia was going to wage a war against us in the future and that many would die. He also said something really strange about some volcanic eruptions in the United States and that it would bring a great famine to the U.S. and that the sun and moon would be darkened for 90 days causing terrible problems with the weather. He also said that the dollar would be replaced by a new monetary system. I didn't believe a word of this but now I'm starting to think that maybe I had better not throw the baby out with the bathwater you know what I mean?"

"Wow. I think I had better sit down. This man may well be a prophet of God. If he is you had better be careful with the word that he is giving. You see Samuel all through the Bible God gave his word to his prophet. The prophet is the most important person in the Bible. To date many of the prophecies given to Daniel and John the apostle still have not come to pass. This is how it works. God gives the word to the prophet and he or she is to give the word to the people. Many times the timeframe is a long timeframe and it is such a hard word for the people that they don't receive it. Many of the prophets actually die before the word even comes to pass. But this does not mean that the word is not going to come to pass its just that God gives it and we have to wait until it does come to pass. It would not surprise me if we went to war with Russia at some later date in time or Iran for that matter. We can see just from the news reports what is going on in the world. The Bible says that there would be earthquakes and tornadoes and such things like this we see all the time. So no it does not surprise me that God would tell the prophet that there would be volcanic eruptions as well."

"That's not what I was hoping you would say. So you don't think that he's a phony?"

"No Samuel. I'm afraid not. I wish you could send me some of his tapes if he has a tape table. I would like to document what he is saying. I will bring it all to the prayer group and then we will just have to watch and see if they come to pass. If they do we are in for a long ride here in the U.S. If this 90 day thing is for real the church had better start putting some food aside. Do you remember Joseph?"

"Yes I remember Joseph. God gave the king a dream. Joseph told him that there would be 7 years of famine and 7 years of plenty. During the time of plenty they saved up enough grain to last through the 7 years of famine. This is during the time when his brothers came to Egypt because of the famine to buy grain."

"Exactly. I'm proud that you are reading your bible. Well if it worked for them then it will work for us. You see the reason for the prophetic word is for the people to fast, pray and prepare. Many people hear the word and then they just hear it. The word is for them to prepare."

"Yes you are right. Okay Pastor Daniel thank you for your input. I'm going to go to church tonight and hear what the man of God is saying. If he has any information I will send it to you. In the mean time tell the church to pray over these matters. When God hears he will answer."

"I love you Samuel. And be careful."

Samuel went again to the revival that night to hear Bro. John. He gave another hard message about the great commission that God had given to the saints before he went back to heaven. He admonished everyone that the time was short and that these things that God was speaking to him about were only signs that we were in the last days. He told them that God was delaying things as long as possible that many more people should repent and be saved. Samuel's heart was so moved by the compassion in the man's voice. He didn't come across smug or anything but that he had the love of God for the lost in his heart and he wanted so for others to receive Christ as he and his wife did. This man had given up a great business and position in the world to take this gospel out and Samuel felt nothing but love for him. He didn't have an earthly father and he would love it that Bro. John would be his spiritual father and show him how to move to the next level in ministry.

Samuel knew that Bro. John only had a few more days before he was to go on to the next city. He had to make his move or else he would be gone until the next time. He went up to him and asked him point blank if he could use a pair of willing hands to go on the road with him. Bro. John saw the look in Samuel's eyes and immediately said no problem we could always use a strong young man to help put up the tent and other things.

"You know how to preach boy?"

"A little sir. Well not like you do but I can learn?"

"You got parents boy?"

"Yes I have two set of grand parents. My mother and father have both gone to heaven."

"I'm sorry to hear about that. You make sure they're okay with you going. We'll be moving on to Georgia in just a few days. Pack and get ready to go. When the revival is over you meet us the next day right here by the church at 6 a.m. sharp. Okay?"

"Okay."

Samuel had never been so happy in all of his life. He would have to tell his grand parents that he was going out to evangelize for God. They would just have to understand. He hoped that they would understand. He had only been there a short time and they so wanted him to be around but that was not what God wanted for him. He would pray that God would speak to them first and that would make things a lot easier on him.

That night Samuel said a special prayer for Bro. John and his wife. He knew that this was the thing to do. God had called him into the ministry and now he was on his way with a great man and woman of God. They would show him what he needed to know about ministry. Bro. John had a great anointing on his life and he hoped that it would rub off on him like Moses and Joshua, like Elijah and Elisha.

Samuel went to his grandparents to speak to them about his leaving and he had hoped that the Lord had spoken with them too so that they would not be upset.

"Eddie God has called me into the ministry. You remember what he told mama before I was born. It's time for me to go out now and do what he has called me to do."

"I knew the day would come that you would go out Samuel. I will miss you but you must do what God has called you to do. You don't want to be like Jonah being disobedient. God does not like disobedient servants. You go with God and keep in touch so we'll know that you are okay. Do you have plans?"

"Yes. There is a brother and sister who are having a revival at a small country church not far from here. I believe that he is a prophet of God and I would like to go with him. We are on our way to Georgia and who knows where from there."

"Oh that sounds marvelous. Make sure that you behave yourself and write me and call me whenever you get a chance. If you need anything let me know and I'll help you get it."

"I love you. And don't worry. Bro. John has been doing this for a long time. He is no youngster I'm sure he'll keep me in line. I had better go and get prayed up. I'm so excited."

When Samuel came home he told Luke and his father that God had answered his prayer and that he would be going on the road with Bro. John. He thanked them for their hospitality and he took the time to very gently tell them both that the time of God was about to end and that they really needed to look deep inside and reconcile with God. That it was now or never. What Bro. John had told the congregation was no joke and all who listen to the words of God given to the prophet will be ready for the trials to come and those who did not listen there would be weeping and gnashing of teeth.

Monday morning and 6 a.m. could not have come quick enough. Samuel was already at the church and rearing to go at 5:45. He believed in being prompt always. He had received his grandparents blessing and he knew that God was in this with him. He could feel it. Bro. John and the rest of the group were already waiting at the church.

"Well son. You ready to go?"

"Yes sir."

"Well take your last look at Florida. It will be the last time you see her for a while. We got a tough itinerary from here. It won't take long to get to Georgia and then on to Texas I have a lot of ground to cover. Your young you'll be okay. I hope you have some money with you. We don't get large offerings most times so I ask people to help themselves and we'll help you when we can if necessary."

"Oh I'm fine with money. I sold some property my parents left me so I'm okay with finances. Samuel didn't believe that God would answer his prayer that quickly but he did. It was like a dream come true. He had a whole new family and he was about to fulfill the purpose that God had for his life.

Bro. John didn't give them much time for rest. As soon as they touched down in Macon, Georgia they had to pitch the tent and get everything ready. Bro. John was starting the revival that very night. He didn't use the tent all the time. Many places they would go he would be speaking in the church so there was no need for the tent. But many places the tent was necessary so they could fit more people in the tent. This took quite a few hours and to get the sound equipment set up and the chairs. By the time it was all done it was around 4 so they had a few hours to get something to eat and maybe a quick nap. It was going to be a long night he supposed. Samuel had never been to a tent revival before. He was excited. He couldn't believe how big that thing was. It reminded him maybe how the tent of meeting God instructed Moses to build may have looked somewhat sitting in the wilderness. It was more glamorous than this one but it was a thought. He prayed that the Holy Spirit would show up in a mighty way that night and that many souls would be saved. He dosed off to sleep very quickly for a few hours and got up just in time to run and get something to eat. He didn't want to be sitting in the back eating or sleeping while the man of God was preaching.

Around 6:30 the praise team came out to start getting ready. There were already quite a few hundred people already filing into the tent. Bro. John was praying and had not given him any specific instructions but Samuel already knew how to jump in there and do something. Bro. John had quite a group with him. Samuel had already introduced himself to a nice young man his age by the name of Benny short for Benjamin. He had started with Bro. John the same way. He too wanted to do ministry but wasn't satisfied with what he was doing. When Bro. John came to his church he just knew that he had to follow this man of God. He felt that many in the church were false and that they were not feeding the sheep with the true word of God. He wanted more and he prayed and God told him to go and serve the prophet and that he would receive the anointing of the prophet to preach. He had been with him now for 3 years and he was loving every minute of it. His job was to help with the tent, to keep the man of God in prayer, to take up the offerings and whatever the man of God needed that was his job. He said that so far the man of God was pleased with his work and promised him that soon he would let him give testimony before he started preaching. He was excited and said that he was already preparing to give that testimony. He had never preached before that many people before. It scared him but he had to get over that fear. Samuel had already begun preaching to large crowds and he was looking forward to preaching again.

The praise team leader had opened the service with prayer and you could feel the power of God hit the place as soon as they started singing the first song. There was just something about being in the night air that summoned up a power surge that Samuel had never ever felt before. He was hooked forever on the tent ministry. People were dancing and praising God and the night was still young yet.

There was such a freedom in that tent that Samuel never felt in the church for some reason. He would have to ask the others if they felt the same way. Some churches were just stuffy. Maybe that's why so many people have stopped going to church. Jesus came to set the captives free not to put them in chains. Now that's not to say that anything goes because there are some like that too. But there was a fresh Holy Spirit in this place. No walls to keep him from operating in his own magnificent way. The women and men were shouting. The babies were crying but nobody noticed. Even the young people were having a time in the Lord. The Holy One was happy Samuel could feel it.

After a time in praise the praise team leader gave the service over to Bro. John's wife. She got up there and gave her testimony about how God had healed her of cancer. Samuel didn't know anything about that. If he had the chance he would testify about how Jesus healed him of cancer too. It's funny he had not even once mentioned that in all the time he was preaching. He would minister from the word but he didn't give his testimony. How precious are the testimonies of the saints. And then he remembered that the Book of Revelation said "and they overcame him by the blood of the Lamb, and by the word of their testimony; and they loved not their lives unto the death." It was through the blood of the Lamb and the testimonies of the saints that Satan is overcome. He would have to repent before God. All this time he had been keeping from the saints the very thing that God wanted him to tell the people. He noticed the looks on the people's faces. He knew that these testimonies built the faith of those people who had come there to get a special touch from God. There wasn't a dry eye in the place.

Samuel had not heard many women preachers in his short life span. He truly liked it. He wished that his mother was here to see Sis. Betty preach and testify. After her testimony she turned the service over to the praise team again and then the praise started all over again. Bro. John didn't come on for some time after that and by the time he started to pray there were literally thousand of people under that tent. Samuel was dumbfounded at the people who turned out for this man of God.

Bro. John had such a special way of addressing the Holy Spirit. He spoke to him as though he knew him personally. He reverenced him with each and every word that came from his mouth. The Holy Spirit was his God, his Lord, his friend, his King, his confidante and his Saviour.

"Holy Father, King of the Universe, Bright and Morning Star, Lamb of God, Prince of Peace. We humbly come before you this evening to give you the praise, honor and glory that is due you. Thank you Holy Spirit for blessing us with all blessings. Thank you for blessing us with your presence. Thank you for your abundant loving kindness and tender mercy. These are your people Father God and we are here to serve you and to hear from heaven. Mighty God, Mighty God, there is none like you in all of the earth.

Thank you for your Son, Jesus. He is the author and the finisher of our faith. He is the only-begotten of the Father sent to this earth to die on the cross for our sins. He is the one of whom you spoke through the Prophet Isaiah "he was wounded for our transgressions, he was bruised for our iniquities; the chastisement of our peace was upon him; and with his stripes we are healed." Father God heal your people today, forgive us our transgressions today Father God.

Thank you for the precious Holy Spirit. For he comes not to speak of himself but of the Christ. He comes to comfort us Father God. He comes to speak all truth to us Father God. He comes to abide in every believer Father God that we might live like the Christ lived when he was here upon the earth. As we go into this revival this week Father God minister to us in a powerful way. Minister to us about the 7 Wonders of the Blood. Like Moses sprinkled the blood of the lamb upon your people. Cleanse us of all unrighteousness. For we are made righteous not of our own works but of the blood of the Lamb.

May your Son not tarry but let him come quickly. And we cry "even so come Lord Jesus." May your Spirit fall fresh upon us today as we hear your word. But let us not be just hearers of the word but doers of this word also that we might be found ready when the bridegroom comes for his bride.

It's in the precious name of Jesus that we pray. Let all the people say amen and amen. The Lord has set it upon my heart to minister over the next seven days about the "Seven Wonders of the Blood."

Chapter 20

THE NIGHT WAS WARM AND the people poured into the tent just like the night before. All of the attendants took their places as the praise team got in position to start the service. Samuel was thinking about what he was going to say tomorrow but he knew to just let the Spirit move and he would tell him what to say. After a few songs Benny came up to the podium to give his testimony.

"Praise the Lord everybody. I said Praise the Lord everybody. I would like to start out with a word of scripture if you would all rise for the reading of the word of God: "I will bless the Lord at all times: his praise shall continually be in my mouth. My soul shall make her boast in the Lord: the humble shall hear thereof, and be glad. O magnify the Lord with me, and let us exalt his name together."

You may be seated. I don't have a great testimony of physical healing like Sis. Betty but I have a testimony nevertheless of how Jesus saved me. I was lost and on the streets doing drugs, prostituting my body for a fix and some money to eat and sometimes have a place to stay. I was like the demoniac sometimes sleeping in the tombs to keep warm when it was cold. I saw a lot of terrible things in that place. Nevertheless, when I was at my lowest I starting robbing for a living and ended up in jail. My parents were beside themselves because I did not grow up in a bad home. My parents were both Christian but

I had decided when I turned 13 that I wanted to do what I wanted to do. I got in with the wrong crowd doing drugs, drinking and cutting school. We just wanted to have fun so we thought. But as I got older the drugs had a hold on me and I couldn't get out. I dropped out of school and became a junkie full time not doing anything with my life. I really didn't care about working, going to school or anything good it was just about hanging out and having fun. When I finally hit jail I knew that I had to do something. I didn't want that for my life. I never thought that I would end up in jail. We were just a bunch of kids having fun. We didn't want any trouble. Or should I say we didn't want to take responsibility for our actions. So my parents told me about a program called Teen Challenge. I figured I had better do something or else I would be in jail or worse dead. I went to the program where I met a bunch of really nice people but I was not ready to commit to the program. I stayed all of three weeks and ran away. That was how I ended up on the streets. I stayed on the streets for about 3 years before I hit rock bottom again and ended up overdosing and in the hospital. This time I almost died. As I was laying in that hospital Jesus came to me and asked me why was I trying to kill myself. He told me that he loved me and that whatever was wrong that he could fix it if only I would allow him to. I couldn't believe that he would actually take the time out to talk to me. First of all I didn't really believe in him. But when I saw him for myself I said wow this is what happened to that guy Paul. He believed in God but he didn't believe in Jesus until he experienced him firsthand. I think that's what the world needs. They need to see more of Jesus. What they are seeing is a bunch of self-righteous Christians who have never really experienced Jesus either. If they would experience Jesus and give the world the Jesus of the Bible then Jesus could come a whole lot sooner. He's not here because the world nor the church is ready for him.

Well to end my testimony I called my parents and told them that I needed to try that program one more time and that I really wanted to get sober. This time I finished the program and became a counselor for a while. I came to Bro. John's tent revival one night and I've been with him ever since. I know that I want my entire life to be about serving God and telling people about the Jesus of the Bible who loved a loser like me enough to save me and give me another chance."

The crowd was cheering and crying all at the same time. This is the message of the cross that whomsoever believes might have everlasting life in the kingdom of God. God will take you as you are and he will change your life forever.

Bro. John came out and hugged his prodigal son. He loved Benny and wanted nothing but to see him make it. Benny was doing great with him and he knew that he was truly born again of the Spirit of Christ Jesus that lived within him.

"Before I get started tonight I want to release to you tonight a vision that God has given me for this nation. It is so horrible that I tremble as I bring this word to you tonight. People you don't understand how difficult it is to walk with God as I walk with him. I wish that many of you could walk with God in this way and then you will appreciate this life, this salvation this blood that was shed for us. We are not like the world, we know what is to come in this world because Jesus our Saviour is talking through his prophets to bring this word to the Body of Christ. I have been holding onto this word for sometime but God has told me that it is going to happen soon. There will be lots of volcanic activity very soon. The Lord has said that the sun will be darkened for 90 days around March or April is what he said. This will be at a very bad time of the year. The crops will fail and there will be wide spread food shortage of mass proportions. The weather will be terrible all over the world. People you must get ready and put food away just prior to this or else you will not have enough food to feed your families. If you can put some away for someone else as well. I heard Yellowstone and Mt. St. Helen. There will also be 10 major hurricanes coming. People we have got to listen to what the Spirit of the Lord is saying or else suffer with the rest of the people. Let he who has an ear to hear let him hear. This is not easy to tell you but if I don't God will require my life.

Let us pray to receive a word from heaven today. Gracious and glorious Holy Father, King of the universe. We thank you for this day Lord and we thank you for your people that are here today. There are many who are in great need today Lord. We know that there is nothing too hard for God. But we just want to praise you for what you have already done God. We want to praise you because you are God. We want to glorify the Father, the Son and the Holy Spirit because you are our righteousness. This day Father please, pour out your Spirit upon us to cleanse us of our iniquity, our sin and our transgressions. We want to be just like your Son, Jesus. We want the world to see Jesus in us. May our lives be a living epistle to the world. May our praise be a sweet fragrance before you Almighty God. There is none like you. We worship you oh Prince of Peace. This is our life's desire. It is for you and you alone that we gather here today. In your Son's precious name we pray. Amen.

Let us read the text today: "And these things write we unto you, that your joy may be full. This then is the message which we have heard of him, and declare unto you, that God is light, and in him is no darkness at all. If we say that we have fellowship with him, and walk in darkness, we lie, and do not the truth: But if we walk in the light, as he is in the light, we have fellowship one with another, and the blood of Jesus Christ his Son cleanseth us from all sin. If we say that we have no sin, we deceive ourselves, and the truth is not in us. If we confess our sins, he is faithful and just to forgive us our sins, and to cleanse us from all unrighteousness. If we say that we have not sinned, we make him a liar, and his word is not in us."

From the time we are youngsters most parents teach their children the necessity of washing the body. When we are born again we must be also taught about the washing or cleansing of the soul and the spirit man within. There are many here today who have at some time or other through life have gone through some things that you would rather not speak about today. I have had the blessed privilege of doing quite a lot of counseling as my wife and I have been in ministry for many, many years now. I have seen many young people like Benny who have literally lived on the streets while they were on drugs. For many of them it is a horrible experience. There are people out there in the world who would use that situation to make these young people do terrible things to support their habits. But when we get a hold to them some of them literally need a good bath, some new clothing and lots of love to cleanse them and heal them of the terrible lives they lived without God. This is what the blood of Jesus does for us when we come to Christ Jesus. It literally washes away the stain of the sinful life that we lived outside of the will of God.

First and most importantly in this process is the confessing of our sins before God. It is such a cleansing experience to lay our burdens at the foot of the cross of Christ Jesus. Just to be transparent before God and tell him all of our sorrows and our pains. Many people are carrying around burdens that happened to them when they were just 5 or 6 years of age. Carrying around such burdens have affected them way into their adult life. So for many when they come to Christ and they are able to take all of those cares and give them to the Lord healing can take place in their lives.

Secondly, we are cleansed from our sins by the word of God. When we as believers in Jesus Christ consistently read the word of God it changes our outlook on life as a whole. These young people and many others have been told a lie about who they are for so long they actually believe that they are nothing and will never amount to anything. Well these things were told to them to keep them enslaved to their masters in the street. As long as someone tells you something negative and you don't know anything different you will believe them because they are the only role models that you have. But when you read the word of God, God will tell you that you have been made righteous not because of anything that you have done but because the shed blood of Jesus Christ has made you righteous. We are his righteousness because of what he has done for us.

The word says that he has given us a name that is above every name. We can caste out demons in that name, we can heal the sick in that name, we can call on that name and be saved. So the reading of the word tells us who we are in Christ Jesus. This changes the way that we look at ourselves. Now we know that we can do all things through Christ who strengthens us.

This word is a word that renews the mind. The word says that whatsoever a man thinketh so is he. The word of God renews that sin stained mind and gives us the mind of Christ. The Body of

Christ must be careful after becoming born again what we take into our minds. Many of you are watching things on television that you should not watch. It's a wonder you cannot sleep at night. The devil is pounding you and not letting you rest because you have just spent 2 or more hours in bed with him. Many of you are reading books and magazines that you should not be reading and then you are wondering why you have thoughts that are not of God. You need to repent and throw that material away and then you can keep your mind on Christ Jesus. We must also be careful of the movies and the music that we listen to. There is just so much that is going on in the world that is certainly of the devil and we must not tarnish the pure temple of God with garbage. In order to stay cleansed we must stay in our word so that the Holy Father will tell us what we are to do to build ourselves up. The world is not interested in building up the people of God but the devil is seeking every day to keep you from reading the word of God and keeping your mind on the things of the world.

Thirdly, we must not forget the Holy Spirit. The Holy Spirit washes us spirit, soul and body. Remember that when Moses came from the mountain that his face shown in such a way that the people had to cover his face. The presence of God affects the physical person as well. There is nothing more beautiful and more powerful than a saint who has the power of the Holy Ghost rescinating through them just like Moses. You can usually tell a person who has drank liquor for many years. But God can change that and heal their body through and through. Many of God's people you can tell who they are because the Holy Spirit will keep you young and full of life.

The Holy Spirit will cleanse you not just of your iniquity but it will cleanse you and heal you of the affects of sin. You will not even remember that sin anymore. When Jesus healed the leopards of leprosy we have no idea what that meant to them. Leopards were the outcaste of society. They could not live with their families and were caste outside of the city. When they were healed they were not only healed physically but societally as well. Now they could go and be pronounced clean at the temple and they were able to go back home again. Imagine being caste away from your family. This is what the blood of Jesus did for us all. It cleansed us outwardly but inwardly as well. They no longer had to hold their heads down, be laughed at and feel like they were nobodies in society. We too can hold our heads up. We don't have to worry about what people are saying about us because of who we once were.

The Holy Spirit living within us cleanses our spirit and we now have the Holy Spirit living within us. We have a new spirit. We have the spirit of love, joy, peace, longsuffering, gentleness, goodness, faith, meekness and temperance. We no longer have hatred in our hearts when someone does something bad to us but as Jesus taught us that we should pray for them that despitefully use us. We would not have had this attitude before but Jesus teaches us a new way. He teaches us to love our neighbors and love our enemies. He gives us peace in the midst of the storm because we know that he is our strong tower and the righteous run into it and they are saved. And not only that but we are peace makers not kicking up strife but bringing peace to the storm.

Oh my beloved there is so much that we can say about what the blood of Jesus does for us. There is someone here today that needs the cleansing blood of Jesus to save you, some need to be washed by that blood and some of you need the Holy Spirit to give you new life. You got saved but you are not living the life that Christ has promised to you because you refuse to let go of some things that happened over 20 years ago and you are still carrying them with you today. Perhaps some of you still have unconfessed sin in your life that you need to confess to God. He cannot forgive you until you confess. And because of it you are still feeling the condemnation that Jesus said you should not have. Come to the altar all of you before we pray for the sick and confess your sins unto God."

The altar was full that night. People were on their faces before God confessing their sins. Bro. John just left them there all night to get clean before God. He would pray for the sick the next night. The work of the Lord was being done that night. He didn't want to interrupt what God was doing. Samuel and Benny and a few others stayed for over 4 hours waiting for them to finish repenting but this is necessary for true salvation to take place in the lives of the believer.

Jesus died so that his people might have an open heaven before God but they do not because they do not do what the word of God tells them to do repent before God.

Chapter 21

SAMUEL WAS FINALLY ABLE TO get some sleep around 3 a.m. that morning. He was thinking what was he going to say for his testimony that night at the revival the crowds were bigger than he had ever seen. He was nervous but he didn't want anyone to know. He prayed God would take the fear away from him that he might say something that would change the life of someone at the meeting that night. As he dozed off to sleep Jesus appeared to him in a dream.

"Samuel, Samuel wake up. I have something I wish for you to do for me tonight at the meeting. You must tell the people the day of the Lord is come. Tell them I shall not wait any longer but I will be coming for my bride and that they must get ready. I have been pleading and pleading with my bride and the world so they will not lose their lives. But I shall not strive with man much longer. But as the days of Noah were, so shall also the coming of the Son of man be. For as in the days that were before the flood they were eating and drinking, marrying and giving in marriage, until the day that Noah entered into the ark. And knew not until the flood came, and took them all away; so shall also the coming of the Son of man be."

Samuel woke up saying "Lord I will tell them." Well Samuel didn't have to worry any longer what he was to tell the people. He would tell Bro. John that he received a word from the Lord for his people so he wouldn't be amazed.

At the same moment the Lord visited Samuel he visited Bro. John. The dream was in three parts. Bro. John saw himself high atop the Empire State Building in New York City. He knew it well he had been there several times. The Lord showed him many cities in the United States. There was a sign in the sky that said E.M.P. he said Lord what does this mean? The Lord said "Electro Magnetic Pulse". What is that my Lord? He told him that many cities in the United States would be hit with this E.M.P. and that it was a form of warfare the terrorists would use against the cities to completely wipe out the electricity in the city. It would put many cities back into the dark ages when there was no use of electricity. It would be devastating. This attack was to last two weeks. How will the people make it Lord? Please Lord, Bro. John cried out to the Lord that he would not allow this to happen. The problems would be endless. People who lived off of oxygen machines would not be able to use them. Hospitals, nursing homes and many places would not be able to keep patients alive without the electricity. Cash machines, stores with large food supplies and gas pumps would not be functional. There would be no way that television stations or radio stations could communicate in these cities. Bro. John began to cry before the Lord.

The dream changed and Bro. John began to see these camps. He thought that they might be camps for detainees but then he saw people that he knew in these camps. What are these camps for Lord? The Lord said "these camps are for Christians, Jews and anybody who comes against the beast when the persecution of the saints comes to America." America Bro. John said. "This cannot possibly be true. The Lord said "Yes my son there will be persecution in America of the saints. Tell them they must be ready. If they are not ready they will deny the faith out of fear." Bro. John cried all the more so.

The last part of the dream the Lord told Bro. John, see this man, this man is a prophet of God sent by me to take the mantle that I have placed in your life. Your days are numbered and you will soon come home to heaven to be with me. I want you to train him and you will pass the mantle on to him. The Lord had showed him Samuel in the dream. He has a word for the people. He will tell you in the morning. The dream ended. Bro. John struggled to go back to sleep.

He needed some rest otherwise he would be no good to finish the revival. He wanted to go and wake Samuel up but knew that God was wrestling with him as well. He should get some rest he had to speak to the people that evening.

The next morning Bro. John got up to get the day started with prayer. He heard a knock on the door first thing. He knew that it would be Samuel for the Lord had already spoken. "Come in he said."

Samuel opened the door. "Good morning Bro. John."

"Good morning Samuel. How are you doing this morning?"

"Well I didn't sleep very well last night. The Lord spoke to me in a dream that which I should speak to his people tonight. I was struggling with what I should say in my testimony."

"Yes. I understand. The Lord also came to me last night. I have much to say tonight as well. I cannot speak about it right now. But he said that you would have something to tell me."

"Oh yes. He said that he will not strive after man much longer. I am to tell them that the day of the Lord is come. I don't know what this all means Bro. John but he was pretty firm when he said it. What do you think it all means?"

"I believe that it means son that the rapture could take place any time now. But I also believe from what God has said that there are going to be some terrible things that will happen before the rapture will take place."

"I think that I can speak for the rest of the body we want to just go up you know."

"Well my boy we must go with the masters words to us in Matthew 24. He gives a great list of things that are to transpire before his return. And he said that these are just the beginnings of sorrows. The birth pangs are just beginning. Unfortunately, son there is a lot more to come. The Lord has told me that my mantle will pass to you and that I must train you to take over the ministry. Have you ever preached a sermon before?"

"Yes sir. I used to preach at the youth rallies for my church. I truly enjoy preaching."

"Well good. How about you go back to your room and talk with God. See what he would have you to minister tonight. I want you to give the word from heaven tonight. Go on and get to work."

"Okay Bro. John. Are you sure? If God has given you a word you should give it."

"Yes, but he has given you a word also. I can wait until tomorrow. I want to ponder over this word. It is not an easy word to give. It will give me some time to think it over."

" Okay. I'll go and get to work."

Samuel took off like a bat out of a cave. He had not given the word in quite a few months and was very excited. He ran into Benny and told him the good news. Benny was excited for him and told him that he would pray God would give him the right word for the people that evening. Pastor had been preaching about the blood of Jesus Christ and so he prayed that God would give him a word about the blood to keep it flowing. He looked through his Bible and he came up with Exodus 25:10-22. God showed him that when God brought the children of Israel out of Egypt into the wilderness that he told them to erect what is called the Tabernacle of Moses. This tabernacle had many meanings but they all pointed to Christ Jesus as the Lamb of God which takes the weight of the sins of man on his shoulders. He wanted Samuel to minister to the people about the mercy seat that was covered with the blood of the goat. The animal was slaughtered and the blood was poured upon the mercy seat. Mercy seat in Hebrew literally means bloody covering. What was this blood to cover? On the day of atonement the blood was put upon the mercy seat to cover the sins of the people for one more year. For us now it is the blood of Jesus that was shed that covers the sins of every believer for all time.

That blood stayed on the mercy seat always pleading before God in the Holy of Holies for the sins of the people. Christ sits at the right hand of the Father in heaven always pleading and making intercession for every believer in heaven. Samuel felt something big was going to happen tonight. God wanted the people to know that he was pleading before the Father to forgive them of their sins and that they should accept his pleadings before the times of the Gentiles ended and no more Gentiles would be saved.

Samuel didn't want to get nervous so he layed down for a while to take a nap before preaching that night. All of a sudden he saw what looked like a host of angels behind what looked like a tape measure. He had never seen anything like it before. He was certainly afraid. Samuel saw what had to be thousand upon thousands of angels. It seemed that they were an army ready to go out and do battle. He could see several names underneath them. He tried to read them but he was too busy looking at the angels. They are the amazing workmanship of God's hands. There were some in the back that seemed to have stood over 30 feet tall. The wing span was enormous. The one's that stood in the front looked like regular men but they were huge like the guys that you see in those competitions with huge chests and arms. They were ready for warfare. You could see that they were not preparing but that they were ready to go out and do what God had called them to do. Then another angel that must have been perhaps the Captain of the Host came out and cut the string and all of the angels took off. He was then able to see the names of the cities that they were sent to. Some went to Washington D.C. and then others went to Miami, Florida and then some were going to New York City and others to various other parts of the world. The Captain walked over to Samuel and said "these are the messengers of the Lord thy God. Some have been sent to take messages to various leaders in your government. Some have been sent to hold back the persecution of the saints. Many have been sent to stop some of the people who are working in the terrorists factions that bombed the World Trade Center where your father lost his life. Many have been sent to hold back the winds, the storms and the earthquakes that Lucifer has sent to kill God's people. Go back and pray. Tell the people tonight that God is with them. Samuel woke up in a cold sweat. He didn't know how to tell the people what he had just seen. But the final word is that "God is with us."

There seemed to be a heaviness in the camp that evening. Samuel had so much to tell the group he didn't know whether he could get it all out. The Spirit of the Lord was heavy on him and he could feel it in the air. He couldn't mess this up. The Lord had given him a word and he meant to give it to the people. He was nervous Bro. John and his wife was sitting right down front. He got a chance to rest and hear from the Lord. He was always fasting, praying and preparing for God's people.

The praise team came out first as usual with much praise and expectation for what God was going to do that night. The people came out in record numbers. Bro. John and his wife were well liked in these parts. After the worship portion Bro. John got up to introduce Samuel. Samuel felt so honored that this great man of God would open his pulpit for a young man who clearly had not the experience with the Lord such as Bro. John did.

"Praise the Lord everybody. We have all gathered here together to hear from heaven. I have been struggling with many things that the Lord has put upon my heart but this one I struggle not with. This young man that will be coming up here to give the word tonight has also heard many things from the Lord that he must and he will tell you tonight. I want you to receive him just like you would receive me as a true man of God called by God and anointed by God for this work in these ends times. Come on up here Samuel. The other night while receiving the baptism of the Holy Ghost this man received a word in tongues that we are getting the interpretation of right now. I hope that we will get it by the time the revival is over so that you can hear what God spoke through him. I had not experienced that in such a long time that I knew there was a special anointing on this young man's life. I am honored to be working with him and to be called by God to mentor him. God has told me that this young man will be blessed to take the mantle from this ministry and that he will take it to the world. Love on him and pay head to what he has to say tonight."

With that Bro. John hugged Samuel's neck and sat down.

"Bless the Lord. Forgive me if I am a bit nervous. The Lord has given so much to me that I am full and don't know where to start first. Many, many years ago the Lord came to my mother and told her that she would have a son and that she should name him Samuel. This son was to receive the anointing of Samuel, the prophet that had the pleasure of anointing David to be King. This son was born after her husband died while trying to save many people during the tragedy of 9-11. So it gives me great pleasure to have Bro. John as a spiritual father being that my earthly father has gone on to be with the Lord many years ago. It was after this tragedy that I fell ill with cancer at a very young age. My mother and I thought that I would die many, many times but we held onto the word from the Lord that I would go to the nations of people with this Gospel of Hope which is Christ Jesus. After a long battle with cancer the Lord came to me in my room at the hospital and he told me that he would heal me and to go minister this healing Gospel to the sick. He healed me, I came out of that hospital and I had a friend that was sick also in the hospital and the Lord told me to go and lay hands on him and that he would recover. We serve a mighty good God. I said we serve a mighty good God."

The crowd shouted "we serve a mighty good God."

"I have been struggling for some time now with who I am and what God wanted me to do and then I was blessed to hear the testimony of this great man of God and I believe that I will follow him all the days of my life until Jesus tells me to do something else."

Samuel could see the angel of the Lord walking through the crowd. He had something in his hands and he would go through the crowd and pour oil upon the heads of certain people as he walked through the crowd.

"There is an angel walking in our midst today. I could act as though he were not here but he is doing something and I feel blessed to be in the midst of this crowd tonight. I believe that some people are being healed right now. I believe that some are being set free from bondages tonight. I believe that some are being anointed to go out and do the work of the Lord tonight. Just receive it and do what the Lord is going to ask you to do.

I wanted to minister along the same lines as the minister of God but I feel the Lord tugging me in a different direction for this evening. This is a very special evening and we want to get all that God has for us today. Amen."

The crowd responds with a resounding "Amen."

"Let us read from the great man of God, the Apostle Paul in the Book of Romans. How many of you know that the Book of Romans has mysteries that we have not even begun to unravel? Praise the Lord. And the text says: For we know that the whole creation groaneth and travaileth in pain together until now. As I read this passage it made me ask the question why did Paul interject this statement in the middle of this sermon. When we look at Romans 8 this is the chapter that all Christians use to minister the Gospel of Jesus Christ to the sinners. He starts out with "there is therefore now no condemnation to them which are in Christ Jesus, who walk not after the flesh, but after the Spirit." We use this passage that when we as believers fall into sin that we know we who walk in the Spirit know that the devil nor anyone else can continue to convict us of the sins that we commit for we have the blood of Jesus Christ that washes us of our sins and whatever sins we committed before we became born again we no longer have to walk around with the weight of that sin because Jesus took that sin with him on the cross. I'm glad about that. I know that you are too.

He also tells us though that this is not a license to sin because we must mortify our flesh my brothers and sisters. We must die to the fleshly desires that so easily entangle us still in this life. We have the Spirit of him that raised Jesus from the dead that liveth within us and quickens our flesh that we might no longer sin against God. I believe that the Body of Christ has forgotten what the blood of Jesus was shed to do. It was not just shed for the remissions of our sins but to wash us totally clean of sin. One might say well I don't think that we can totally be clean from sin. I am here to tell you today that we can and should be clean of sin when Jesus comes to take his bride away to the heavenly city that he has prepared for us. There was a man of God who had a car accident in Nigeria. This man would die of his injuries and he lay in the hospital awaiting his family to make the arrangements for his burial. The morgue received the body and his family was making the arrangements for his burial. But Jesus had another plan for this man. The story goes on to say that when this man died the angels came to him and showed him first the very gates of hell. You see God did not want that this man should die because he although a pastor did not take care of his sin properly before he died. He thought that he was okay with God and that he would surely go to heaven. The angel told him that before he had died he had some sin that had not been forgiven of God, one of those sins was that he had ought against his wife. They had a fight prior to his death and he did not forgive her of this. God was not pleased with how he had treated his wife prior to this terrible accident that took his life. The angel told him that if not for the forgiveness of God that this would be his fate. He saw not only the gates of hell but he saw some of the people who had been sent there. He went on to say that he even saw some other pastors who were there and cried out to him not to come there. You see hell is a real place. We preach about so many things from the pulpit now but nobody wants to talk about the blood of Jesus, hell and the consequences of sin in our lives. We must return back to the cross of Jesus Christ. We must tell the people that there is a place called hell and that they do not want to go there. That this place hell is a place of torment and great sorrow.

The angel then took him to heaven. He showed him the streets of gold and how beautiful the heavenly city is. He saw the saints and how happy they were. He saw the marvelous light of God and he wanted so to stay but he could not. He heard the most beautiful music that he had ever heard. The angel told him that this was the flowers and trees singing. They are awaiting the arrival of the saints. Oh the pastor could not contain all that he had saw. He knew that he had sinned before God and that if it were not for the abundant mercy of the Holy Father he would have gone to hell and missed out on all that Jesus had for him. It was three days before this man of God was sent back to earth to tell of what he had seen.

My brothers and sisters God does not want that anyone should perish but that all should have everlasting life. This account made me think about what Paul was saying here in Romans 8:22 how the whole creation groaneth and travaileth in pain together until now. When this pastor went to heaven he said that it seemed like all that God had created was singing and praising God. The trees was praising God, the flowers was praising God, even the many mansions he saw was praising God. Paul says that the creation down here is groaning. That's not what the man of God said was going on in heaven. This means that there is something wrong with what is happening here on the earth. In Tennessee the world heard a story about a mother and her two children who were mauled by a bear. The mother in desperate attempts to get the one child free from the bear was mauled and the other child as well. She lost one child and lay in the hospital barely alive as well as the other child. The Bible says that the earth was given to man and that Adam was to be the master over it. There was no such thing in the Garden of Eden of God's creation reaping havoc such as this. This is the result of sin. Even the earth knows that it is not in alignment with the perfect will of God.

Jesus says in Matt. 24 that there shall be famines, pestilences, and earthquakes. We can just look at the news and see that what Jesus said over 2,000 years ago is certainly coming to pass. Look at the weather all over the world. Not just here in the United States of America but all over the world. We cannot keep up with what is happening. The prophets have heard the word from the Lord that there will be a major earthquake in America and that there will be several volcanic eruptions. The earth certainly is groaning. I believe that Paul knew a lot more about our times than we even know. We must fall on our faces before God and begin to do what he says next. He says that we also must groan but this is a groaning unto the Holy Father to forgive us, to save us, to bring us unto Himself.

We are blessed my brothers and sisters that the Lord Jesus Christ has not forsaken us but Paul says that we don't even know how to pray but that the Spirit helps us in that He groaneth and makes intercession for us before the very throne of God. I believe that we need to go back to the olden days when people just came together to pray. We need to fall on our faces with sackcloth and ashes like Mordecai did when Haman set out to kill his people. We talk about Esther but Mordecai was the one who was on his face first before God. He was the one who was making intercession for his people before Esther was even aware of what was happening. How many of us take the time out to make intercession for the saints? We need to be making intercession for the whole world because we are living in perilous times. The church has become too relaxed in this time. We are truly the Laodicean church. Christ said to her, "I know thy works, that thou art neither cold nor hot: I would thou wert cold or hot. So then because thou art lukewarm, and neither cold not hot, I will spue thee out of my mouth. Because thou sayest, I am rich, and increased with goods, and have need of nothing; and knowest not that thou art wretched, and miserable, and poor, and blind, and naked."

Unfortunately, history shows that when the church gets too popular and when it gets too rich that it looses its way. The church has lost her direction in many ways. We want the people of God to be prosperous. But not at the expense of the Gospel of Jesus Christ going into all the world as Christ commissioned us to do. Most Christians are spending more time worrying about money than worrying about God. He never told us to do this. He said in fact do not worry about these things but in every book store there are more books about prosperity than about the blood of Jesus. There are more books about losing weight than about the consequence of sin. People don't want to know about anything else but healing and money. The Holy Father says to "seek ye the kingdom of God and His righteousness and all these other things will be added." What ever happened to this scripture? We are failing our Holy Father and we had better get it right or else the gates of hell will be widened not because of the Holy Father, for He is merciful but because we have tainted the Gospel and sold Him out for the prosperity Gospel that He did not preach.

My brothers and sisters I am sorry if you are not excited about this message but this is the message that I have for tonight. If you don't have a ministry whereby you are preaching the true Gospel of Jesus Christ and you are just here because you need healing then shame on you. Do you know that the anointing will keep you young and healthy? Do you know that the anointing will break every yoke? Do you know that in the anointing is everything that you will need for this life? Christ the anointed one that lives within you has everything that you need. But you seek after Him for the things that He says don't worry about. If we would seek after His righteousness and His kingdom and do for Him what He tells us in His word He will make sure that you get everything you want and you need.

The Bible says "eyes have not seen, and ears have not heard neither has it entered into the hearts of the man the goods things that God has for them who love Him and are called according to His purpose." We are the called out ones. We are the ones who are called to the purposes of God, not the people of the world. We are called to bring in the Kingdom of God to this earth by going out and making disciples of people of all nations baptizing them in the name of the Father, the Son and the Holy Spirit."

I had a dream last night and the Holy Father gave me a word for the saints tonight. This is a hard word for the saints because there are many things that are coming for the testing of the saints to prepare the bride for His glorious coming. But the Lord has said that He shall not strive with man much longer. He is ready for His kingdom to come and we had better prepare ourselves for His return. He is pleading with His saints and pleading with the world to receive Him but we have turned our backs on Him. We don't have much longer saints. Please tell your family members, co-workers that the day of the Lord is come."

Samuel became overwhelmed and the Spirit of the Lord began to travail within him. He fell onto his knees and began to groan as though his body, his soul and his spirit were in agony. It was the Spirit of Christ that was in agony for the people of this world.

The people in the crowd one by one overcome by the Spirit began to cry and to pray in tongues unto the Lord. A spirit of repentance had hit the place and the musicians joined in praise before God. It was a night where the glory of God hit the hearts of every person in attendance. The people went home changed that night.

Chapter 22

SAMUEL COULD NOT SLEEP A wink after the service. He asked Bro. John if he wanted to just take a drive. It always cleared his head to just get in the car and drive for a spell. He could have a little bit of quality time with his mentor as well. He wanted to see how well he had done. It was now or never to hear his comments. This was a bit unusual for Bro. John. He never left the camp site during the revival but it wouldn't hurt. He knew that he would not be able to sleep either. The Spirit of the Lord had moved in such a mighty way that evening. He didn't quite know what to say to Samuel. The people stayed on their faces until 3 in the morning just moaning and groaning before God. This was a true revival. Many would have come to the altar that night but Bro. John didn't want to interrupt the Holy Spirit. These were His people and He knew exactly what He was doing. He didn't need preachers, He could do all the work Himself but He gave them the privilege of working along with Him. It was so much better when the Holy Spirit took over or should we say that we allowed the Holy Spirit to do only what He could do. God changes hearts not people. He knew exactly what to do and say that would get the people in order. What most pastors, ministers and evangelists do is try to go in and work things up in the flesh. No one gets saved from that. It's only by means of the Spirit that people repent and turn to God.

"Bro. John do you know that pastor was dead for three days before the Lord allowed him to come back to his family? It was the most amazing story that I had ever heard. I could not imagine praying over a person for hours and seeing the life come back into him after he had layed in the morgue for three days."

"That was an awesome story my boy. I had not heard that one. It is truly a miracle. I had to look inside of myself and wonder what sins I had in heaven that I had not repented of. I must take some time to weep before the Lord about this matter. That was amazing what you said about the quickening blood. When we look at the blood of Jesus so much has been given to us. It's the power of the blood of Jesus that quickened that man's body and brought it back to life. The blood of Jesus has given us power. If it were not for the blood of Jesus he could not have told the disciples in Matt. 10 heal the sick, cleanse the lepers, raise the dead, and cast out devils. This power is given to the believers.

I believe that tonight we should have a prayer meeting tonight. You were right my son that we spend too much time working things up ourselves instead of letting the Holy Spirit do what He knows how to do best. He can get to the heart of the people much more effectively than we can but we feel if we are not taking up every minute that the people won't be happy and God will be grieved. I think it is the other way around, we should not worry for how the people feel and we should let God have every minute and we have less.

Samuel didn't know what to think. He thought Bro. John was going to criticize his message and tell him what he did wrong. Instead he was repenting openly and agreeing with what the Spirit of the Lord did that evening. Samuel felt relieved and he felt confident he had been obedient to what the Spirit wanted him to do and it was indeed a successful revival. Most of what people call revival is not revival at all. The church brings in a minister for quite a few nights and they call that a revival. It's no different from a regular Sunday or Wednesday night bible study. Maybe they get excited, run around the building a couple of times and they had a revival. True revival is when the Holy Spirit comes down and meets with

His people and change takes place in the heart of the believers. And even more so revival is when the Spirit is poured out and many unbelievers get saved and receive the blessed salvation of the Lord. Many of these spill out like in the Book of Acts and go into all the world. If we look at the history of the church true Holy Ghost revival is orchestrated by the Holy Spirit Himself. The Azusa Street Revival was orchestrated by God. The Lord is great and many were spilled out into the world from the Azusa Street revival."

Bro. John and Samuel saw a Catholic church opened and thought they would get out of the car and stretch and bit. It was a good time to pray and just sit in the presence of the Lord they would sleep later. They parked the car and went into the sanctuary to pray. There were a few not many that had the same idea they had that morning. Jesus prayed all the time in the wee hours of the morning. There must be something to it if the Holy one did it. God is calling many of his saints to get up in the wee hours of the morning to pray with Him. There is so much that is happening in the world and God wants His people to pray. Because of the many demands of work and family this is the best time for many to pray. The children are in bed and the house is quiet. Many have found that this is the time when God comes to them most often to give them dreams and visions.

Bro. John and Samuel both found a place to kneel down before the Lord. All was quiet because in the Catholic church you must be very quiet. Bro. John could see a young man to his far right and he was just sitting there on the pew just staring into space. He could see the trouble on the young man's face. As he knelt down they made eye contact and he could see him raise up and head in his direction. Perhaps they had come here for God to do a work in this young man's life so he sat down on the pew instead. The young man came over and sat down next to him.

"Excuse me sir. I don't mean to trouble you but I need to talk with somebody. You wouldn't happen to be a priest or anything?"

"Well as a matter of fact I am of sort. I and my friend over there are here doing a revival in your city. You ought to come over and visit with us tonight. We are planning on having a night of prayer for the city. We just feel that God will like us to do that. My name is Bro. John by the way."

"Hi I'm Bro. Raymond. Bro. John I need to confess my sins. Doesn't it say somewhere in the Bible to confess your sins one to another?"

"Yes Bro. Raymond it does at that."

Bro. Raymond began to sob terribly and he just fell into Bro. John's arms like a small boy who had need of help from the Lord. Bro. John was taken back but just allowed Bro. Raymond to cry. He knew that he needed to get cleansed from whatever was ailing him.

"Bro. John please don't think that I'm crazy but I just feel so overwhelmed. I don't know where to begin."

"Well would you like me to start and maybe once you hear what I have to say things will seem a bit brighter."

"Okay. That sounds good. I cannot find the words right now."

"Okay Bro. Raymond. Let me tell you a bit about myself. When I was a young man I learned about the Lord but I turned my back on Him and went out into the world. I did some things that I have told no one but God. I still don't want to talk about much of it although I know better. I just feel so bad about it. Does that sound familiar?"

"Yes. Bro. John. Yes it sounds familiar."

"Okay. I and my wife turned our lives over to the Lord many years ago and I have not turned back to my sinful life again. I have no taste for sin anymore. Our young preacher over there gave a great sermon last night. You should have heard it. It would have made you feel better right away. In the Book of Romans 8 Paul say that there is now no more condemnation in Christ Jesus. My Bro. whatever sin you committed you can go to the throne of God, confess your sins and be forgiven. You can tell me what it was but you can take it to God and he will be quick to forgive you. How do you feel about that?"

"But Bro. John you don't know what I have done. The Catholic church is very strict about a lot of things and they will ex-communicate me if they find out about this. It's all that I have. My family and the church are my whole life. If I lose them I'd rather die."

"Bro. Raymond, who is your Lord?"

"C h r i s t   J e s u s ."

"So then why are you afraid of man? The Bible says if God be for us He's more than the world against us. If the Catholic church and your family cannot forgive you then don't worry about it. They are not the one's that went to the cross for you. You have this thing all mixed up. You see when Jesus died on the cross He and He alone died for your sins. You are redeemed because of His blood that was shed for you. Confession doesn't mean that man can absolve you of your sins one way or the other. It is a way of cleansing our souls of the stain of the sin and also we are being accountable to the Body of Christ. It is a good thing to do. You feel better once you have gotten it out of your system. Also the beloved are here to help one another through the process of being born again. You don't have to feel that you are going at it all alone. We are here to help one another not judge one another like some have the custom of doing."

"But you don't know how people can be."

"Oh my brother I've been around long enough to know that yes people will turn their backs on you when you are at your lowest point. But let me tell you another thing that I have most recently learned. It is the blood of Jesus, the word of God and the indwelling of the Holy Spirit that has quickened us in Christ Jesus."

"What is quickening?"

"This means that we are made alive in Christ Jesus. We are dead to sin. Just because you sinned one time does not mean that you have to persist in sin. You are to die to sin. Maybe that is what is bothering you too. How could you have done what you did?"

"That too. I have been a good Christian all of my life. I never thought that I was capable of falling like I have. I don't know how I even got here."

"Well Bro. Raymond how we get into sin is quite complex. This world is full of sin and if we don't watch it we will be entangled in it as well. Just look at what they have on television today. There was a time when a person could not even smoke on television and now they have people having sexual intercourse on television. Oh, oh I think I struck a bell."

"Yes Bro. John. I don't know what they call it but I got involved with pornography on the internet. One day I was just doing my work and this website popped up. I didn't look at it at first but then I found myself thinking about looking at it every time it popped up. So one day I did. I couldn't believe that it was so easy. I found myself doing it more and more. It seemed as if it had a hold on me. I never ever cheated on my wife but I found myself thinking about call girl service. It wasn't enough to just see the women on the website I started having fantasies about them. I feel so horrible. Then I started seeing women outside of my home. How can I ever get free from this thing?"

"Bro. Raymond God can take care of that. Let me continue with what I was saying to you. The Psalmist says that God quickened him by His spirit. You see when the Spirit of God enters us and dwells in us he quickens us in the matter of sin. This does not mean that we will never commit sin but he will convict us of it. He allowed you to go into that sin because you have free will but he is convicting you of it and you feel bad about what you have done. This is a good thing. It could be the other way around. If you didn't feel convicted by the Holy Spirit you could be in sin for much longer than you would like. The fact that we are having this conversation means that you want to be free from this sin that has you in bondage.

"Yes, Bro. John I want to be free. I don't want my wife to leave me and I don't want Jesus to be angry with me."

"Bro. John Jesus is not angry with you. The reason why He came is so that you can be free. He doesn't like to see His precious children in sin because He knows the affects of sin. The Bible says that the wages of sin is death. He wants you to confess your sin and repent of your sin and get back on track. You first must get more in touch with what the word has to say about who you are and even more so who Jesus is in your life. The word also quickens us because it tells us who we are in Christ Jesus. We are more than conquerors in Christ Jesus. You too are a conqueror but you have unleashed something in your life that must be removed. The devil is just waiting for the opportunity to entrap us in sin. You are not the first person that this has worked on but you don't want to stay in it.

Also Bro. Raymond I believe that if you confess this sin to God and ask him to give your wife a forgiving heart towards this situation she will forgive you and you and she can get marriage counseling and move forward in this thing stronger than ever before. Has she ever told you anything about sin that she has asked God to forgive her for?"

"Yes. As a matter of fact before we got married we confessed to each other all the time. I had forgotten about that because we just don't do that anymore. I don't know why not. But we took them to God and we asked Him to forgive us our sins and when we got married we felt the love so strong in our marriage. I didn't mean to do this it was enticing."

"Yes that is how sin is. It is very enticing but when we get into it we know right away that we got in something that we should not have gotten into. It's like when I started smoking cigarettes I thought it was cool. I didn't know that you could get cancer from it because I was young and not informed. But now we know so much more about it. Thank God I never got cancer but my wife did. She kicks herself to this day because of cigarettes and she is a big advocate of telling young people never to start this terrible habit. You see Bro. Raymond a Christian who says that they have never sinned is a liar. The Bible has a list of sins that were committed at one time or other by faithful Christians who were quickened by the word, the blood and the Holy Spirit. They were not always dead to sin but they enjoyed the sin that they were in.

Right now Bro. Raymond you can confess your sins to God right now and he will forgive you for them. Then you must repent by turning around from what you are doing. If you feel you cannot by yourself you might want to seek treatment or someone you can further talk to about the matter."

"I'd like to do that. Will you pray for me?"

"I sure will. Bow your head with me. Father God we come to you this evening in prayer. Thank you Father God that Jesus died on the cross so that we no longer have to walk in sin but that we can walk in the spirit. Father I thank you that you have so moved upon my brother's heart that he has come into the house to lay his sins at the cross. I cannot forgive his sins but the word says that you will be quick to forgive if he repents before you. I know that his heart is broken over this matter. The devil has set out to rob, steal and destroy the harvest that you have made in this man and his family. I cancel the plan of the enemy today in Jesus name. I plead the blood of Jesus over his family to wash, cleanse and rebuild their lives. Please Father God hear us today. In Jesus name. Amen. Now you confess your sins to God."

"Okay. Father God I thank you for this man of God that you sent in my path to listen to me tonight. I hear the word that you have spoken through him. I thank you for your loving kindness and your tender mercies. I come tonight to confess my sins before him and before all of heaven. Father I have sinned before you and have done what is heinous in thy sight. Father please forgive me of my sins. I will seek help in this matter. I pray that my wife and my family can find it in their hearts to forgive me for this sin that I have committed. Give me the strength that I need to put this thing down and never, ever return to it again. In Jesus name. Amen."

Bro. Raymond started to sob again uncontrollably. This was a good thing. He was being cleansed of the Holy Spirit of this sin. Bro. John hoped that all would be well with him. Samuel saw that Bro. John was praying with this young man so he decided not to interfere. He was now feeling refreshed and ready to sleep. When they had finished praying he came over and collected Bro. John so they could get some rest before the evening service again.

"The work of the Lord is never ending. That young man needed to talk with someone and I was glad to have been there for him."

"Yes you are right. I have done a lot of ministry that way as well. Just going to and fro from one place to another I have met people and God has spoken to me to impart something to them."

Bro. John and Samuel went back to the hotel to get some rest. They were excited about what God might do that evening in the service. They had decided that this evening would be a time of nothing but prayer. It was to be the Lord's night and Him only.

Chapter 23

It was a bright new morning and Bro. John called the whole group together for breakfast. He wanted to tell them that things would be different that evening. He felt the need to allow the Holy Spirit to just take over the whole service from beginning to end. There would definitely be some praise and worship for it is due to the Lord but he wanted to pray and call out to God like had never been done before in his meetings. He felt that the time had come for a change in the meetings. The night before he felt that he too needed to spend some more time on his face before the Lord. Many ministers get so caught up in doing ministry that they forget that they can fall into sin just like anybody else if they didn't stay close to the Holy Spirit. The times of the Gentiles is about full. When that time comes and the church is taken out of this world it will be too late to repent before God. The Day of the Lord is come. He is working diligently to bring His Kingdom into this world and it is now or never to get it right.

Through the blood of Jesus God has called out a royal priesthood unto Himself. This royal priesthood is sent into the world to speak of the Christ. The Lord has given the church over 2,000 years to preach the Gospel but His day is about to come when he will not strive after man any longer. The Kingdom of God shall come to this world.

Bro. John realized that when he was a babe in Christ that he spent so much time with God. Each day he woke up the Lord was on his mind first and foremost. He made sure that he took the time out of his schedule to pray, read his word in fasting every day. There was not a day that he did not spend time with God. Now that he had been in ministry for a time he found himself working for God instead of taking time to show his love to his Father. Most of the Body of Christ does the same thing. They believe that if they are working for God it's the same as walking with him. This is not true. A person can work for an employer that they never get a chance to see. This should not be with the children of God. It is a love relationship between children and Father, between husband and wife. No relationship between husband and wife or children and parents get stronger by not spending time with one another. It is important to show love to the Father in word and deed. Bro. John would find himself just singing to the Lord at times. He would go into the woods and sit under a tree and talk to the Father about how wonderful he was and how much his life was blessed just being in his presence. He just admired what he saw the Father doing in His creation and in his Bride. The Father has feelings just like anyone else. Everyone must remember that. He does not like it when His children just come in prayer for what they need. These are selfish children. But He loves those who just come to say "thank you" or just to say "hello" and even more so those who come to say "what can I do for you Father today?" This makes the Father's heart glad.

One thing that the Body of Christ talks about is the high priest's role. The Body of Christ are made up of high priests. This needs to be looked at much closer. The role of Aaron and his sons was not just to the people but to God. There responsibility was to minister to God. They took care of God's house, God's people and God. Most miss the and God part. Who ministers to God when things go wrong in the world? The Bible says precious in the sight of God is the death of His saints. Missionaries are being killed in record number and it grieves the very heart of God. The world is full of hatred, violence and death. This grieves the heart of God. Most people don't think about the feelings of the Lord and should take the time out to minister to God when difficult times happen instead of always looking to God to minister to them.

The group realized that what the man of God was saying was absolutely true. They realized that they had been selfish and had only been thinking about themselves and their part in the meetings and not what God wanted to be happening in those meetings. The gifts of the Spirit were not flowing as they probably could if they would just get out of the way and let God be God. There needed to be a change in the meetings and tonight would be the first night for the rest of their time on the earth. They wanted meetings like A.A. Allen, F.F. Bosworth and Maria Woodworth Etters. The Lord would send her into trances and many others. They would see the Lord, see hell, see heaven and many other ways that God would minister to them. Many talked for a long time about the glory of God. The prophets have talked about it and many experienced it and they wanted to see the glory of God working in these meetings so that people would get saved for real. Not just healed in their bodies but still walking in sin. The day of the Lord is come and the church must wake up or else she will be ill prepared for that which is to come.

That afternoon Bro. John went in seclusion to spend some time with God. He had not gone on an extended fast for quite a while but he needed to hear from God. He needed to repent for walking ahead of God and not being as a little child before God. He took some time to get away from the group to seek the Lord. He found a nice little bed and breakfast on the outskirts of town and got a room there. The people were so nice he wanted to make sure that he prayed for them and left his peace in that place. It was people like them that made life worth living. He went to his room and instead of taking out his bible he just layed down a few comforters on the floor and layed on his face before the Lord. He did not know how long he had been praying before he fell asleep and had a dream. He saw himself walking in a market full with people. They had all types of items that they were selling in the market. There were shoes, clothing, food items and much more. He didn't know where this place was or what he was doing there. He walked around for a while and then he stopped to have small talk with some of the people there. He then found himself coming out of the market and getting into a car and driving for a while. He could see a long bridge with people walking across that bridge. The strange thing was that there were the dead carcasses of many cows on the left hand side of the road. The people walked past them without even so much as looking down at the carcasses there. Then on the other side of the road people were walking with cows that were alive. They were quite sickly but alive nevertheless. After they passed along the road he proceeded down the road to cross the bridge. The dream changed and he found himself walking into a church, he noticed though that the pastor was standing at the pulpit, there was no one else in the church but him. Bro. John just walked into the church and when he saw the pastor standing there with his head between both hands he immediately felt that something terrible had happened or was going to happen and he fell to the floor prostrate on the ground and started to intercede before God. Another brother entered in from another part of the church and he saw them both and he fell down as well praying before God. Bro. John did not know whether there was any connection to what he had seen before. The next portion of his dream was what troubled him more than anything he remembered that he was in a room with some believers, a church perhaps. There seemed to be a loud noise outside which caused them all to run outside to see what was happening. As he got outside of the door he could see smoke, but he was more alarmed when he heard this very loud explosion. Everyone started to panic and started running. He started running too and found himself trying to climb over a fence, but on the other side of the fence he could see buildings on fire and he thought there is no need in going over there. It was at this point that he woke up in a cold sweat. He was quite surprised at how quickly the time went by. He had not had much time to spend with the Lord. He would have to cancel some upcoming events. He was too busy to even talk with God. This was not the way he had wanted things. His life was out of control and he did not even know it. He would have to call his wife and tell her he needed some time in the Lord and to have the meeting without him. It was Gods meeting and he would understand.

Bro. John walked that room and walked that room trying to figure out what God was saying. He cried out "Lord what does this mean? I have preached and preached this message to your people for many years now. I feel like I have let you down and I'm not sure what to do next. Please Lord tell me what you want me to do? I think something terrible is about to happen and I don't know what or where. Why are you telling me? What can I do? I'm only a preacher of the word."

All of a sudden the Lord Jesus Christ appeared to Bro. John in the room. He said "John you have been called to another assignment. Many people around the world have not heard this gospel and I want you to take it to the world. There is a place that you should go and take this gospel to these people. Do you know that there are many people who hunger after righteousness yet they do not even so much as have a bible to read? They are hungry for the word, they are hungry for me and I am sending you to them."

"Lord I will go if you send me. I know there are people who are hungering after righteousness. Lord I feel that I have not done as much as I could be doing. Maybe this is the answer that I am looking for. Thank you Lord. Where are we supposed to go?"

"I have a people, a group of people who have been forgotten in Sudan. There is much turmoil in the government and the people are crying out for help. I want you to go there and take the gospel to these people. Many of them are Christians but many are still looking for the Messiah. You must go and tell them that I have already come and that I will soon come again."

With that the Lord left Bro. John. Bro. John had not ever seen the Lord before. He was excited, awe struck and terrified at the same time. He had seen the Lord. He could not wait to tell the group what had happened and what the Lord has told him that they should do next. The first thing he thought about was that they did not have the money to take the tent overseas. But he knew that if God had told him to go that he would prepare the way for him in every way.

Bro. John's wife carried out his wishes and had prayer meeting instead of the regular meeting. She explained to everyone that Bro. John had to go away unexpectedly for an emergency and that they should pray for him that he returns safely. The whole crowd was wondering what the emergency could be. She didn't want to tell them that he felt that he needed a touch from God and that he was not going to stop praying until he had received it. Being in the ministry is not as easy as some people think that it is. Many go into the ministry without realizing that one must put all of oneself into the service of the Lord. When Jesus came to the earth he was totally devoted to the service of the Lord. Everything that He did was about saving the lost. Each day He woke up was about preaching the gospel of salvation. This is how every believer should look at his or her life. That life is not about eating or drinking and having a good career. Perhaps raising a family and then you die. But life is about ministering the gospel of salvation to the lost world.

After the praise team got up and lead into worship Sis. Betty came up to address the beloved:

"My beloved brothers and sisters. This evening Bro. John wanted to see another mighty move from God such as we experienced the other evening. Many of you who came the other night when Bro. Samuel spoke a true word from heaven realized that something awesome happened that night. Well my husband and I have been on our faces before God ever since that evening. He and I have not spoken much to each other since then. We are not only praying but confessing our sins before God that we know our relationship is right with Him. We must all do this tonight. Let's not make this meeting about ourselves, but let it be about Him. Often times we are always going to God for what we need, but we don't think enough to ask Him what he is needing. We need to take more responsibility for what is not happening in this world. The world as we know it is going straight to hell because we as the beloved of God are more worried about our healing and our prosperity and our families and not about the lost that are going to hell every day. Right now as I speak there is someone that is dying and we don't even know about it because we don't spend enough time with God. He would tell us who to intercede for if we would take the time to ask Him. I know people right now who spend countless hours every day just interceding and walking and praying over all kinds of matters in cities across the world. Let's join with them tonight. Perhaps God will come and visit with each and every one of us and take us to a new realm of prayer."

Just then a woman spoke in tongues. The crowd fell silent as the Lord spoke through the woman. Sis. Betty gave the interpretation.

"Oh for joy my heart is full tonight. My people are awaiting a word from me tonight. Oh how I long to walk with you and talk with you but my people are too busy with the cares of life. Did I not tell you to take no account for what you are to eat, what you are to wear for each day has its own needs. But I told you to caste your cares upon me and I will give you rest. I have told you that I will bless you so that you can be a blessing but you ask me for small things. Ask me for the better things. Ask me for my glory. Ask me for robes of righteousness. Ask me to breath upon you that you may be filled with my Spirit. Ask me that the church would be revived with tongues of fire as in days of old. Why is it that the dead are not being raised, the lame are not walking, deaf ears opened and blind eyes being opened? My people who are called by my name are not humbling themselves, they are not praying, they are not seeking my face. This is the problem with my beloved she does not seek me. Ask and it shall be given, seek and ye shall find, knock and it shall be opened. It shall be done if you would just ask."

"My beloved we have heard from the Lord. This is what we are wanting to happen from now on in these meetings. We want the Lord to take control of his church. We have for far too long taken the helm from the Holy Spirit and this is to the detriment of the Bride of Christ. She is now left weak and having no effect on the world as she should. Let us all take our places before the Lord and pray for a true revival to take place all over the world, not just here in America. God loves the people of the whole world. When Jesus died he died for the sins of humankind across the globe. Amen. So let's cry out to God and let the Holy Spirit continue to have control over this prayer meeting."

The voices of the crowd grew louder and louder as the people fell on their faces before God to pray. They started to realize that the day of the Lord's return was upon them and that the wrath of God was being poured out in various ways around the world. The scriptures specifically warned about all of these things but the people are not heeding the warnings as they should. For this reason terrible disaster will befall many and many will lose their lives. The prayer meeting went on for several hours and many left the meeting totally drained for crying and weeping before the Lord.

Chapter 24

By the time Bro. John returned to the camp that next day his wife was quite worried about him. She was so happy when he appeared that afternoon. She noticed quite a difference in him but she didn't know what it was. She had a feeling that he must have heard from the Lord. She let him take his time telling her all that God had revealed to him while he was in prayer.

"Hi darling. I'm so sorry that I did not return for the meeting last night. I just needed to spend some time with the Lord. I think we need to take a couple of weeks off and spend some time with the Lord. We can all go to Dallas for the revival and then after that we need to take some time and spend with Him. You know how it gets we get so busy working for God we don't have time for God. We should never fall into this type of sin. I'm somewhat taken back by God's words to me the other day."

"Why honey what did the Lord say to you?"

"Well he has definitely said that we are going to leave the United States and go to Africa to help the people of the Sudan. I don't know why he has chosen us but that we must do exactly what He is asking us to do. It does tell me that the time is getting closer for the Lord's return. You know that there will be a time when the times of the Gentiles is full and God is going to turn his face towards Israel again. He has already launched a great effort to bring all of the Jewish people around the world back to Israel. But there are several places where there are still many Jews who have not returned for one reason or another. But there are also so many people that have not heard the gospel. We have to launch out into the deep and bring the fish in."

"To Africa. We don't have that kind of money to go to Africa. How will we get the tent and the workers there? This will cost more money than we can have faith for John. Did you tell the Lord that?"

"Oh honey you know that the Lord doesn't want to hear that. No I didn't tell Him that. If the Lord wants us to go to Africa He will provide the money for us to go oh ye of little faith. Do you know how many times Jesus said that in the Bible and we still don't get it. God has been providing for missionaries for centuries now. He knows what He is doing."

"Your right. We had such an enormous prayer meeting last night. We received a word from the Lord. I believe this is part of what He was talking about. You know that Kris Brogen in Africa has so much of the gifts operating in his ministry. We don't see as much of this in our meetings as we would like. I think that when God sends ministers to places like Africa where many of the people don't know the Lord you see more miracles. He said last night that we don't have as much faith as we should that He would do the very things that He said that the apostles would do. He said why are blind eyes not being opened and people being raised from the dead. You know I don't know why. But I know that I don't have the faith that I should have. Before I got healed of cancer I really didn't believe in the healing power of Jesus Christ. Well for one I didn't know that I could believe. It's not like I knew about it. Many of the body of Christ don't even know what they should believe in. The Church is not operating in the gifts of the Spirit like they should. It's a wonder we don't have any faith. Faith comes by hearing and hearing by the word of God. When you hear the word of God on a matter it tells you what you can expect from God."

"Now you are talking my dear. Perhaps its time for us to go to another level in our faith walk with God. Let's take some time from now on to read more of the New Testament and see what it is that

Obadiah Ariel Yehoshuah

God was doing in the world while He was here. He said that we would do greater things and we are not even doing what He did. Let alone the greater things. I want to be able to be a blessing to the people of God. Many of these people are suffering from malnutrition, terrible poverty and sickness. We cannot just go in there with the gospel of Jesus but we need to take some of their needs as well. Even Jesus fed the 5,000 with some fishes and loaves. So must we. I don't know where the money is to come from but God does. He told us to go and we are going to obey."

"Oh honey. I could never have imagined when we got called into the ministry that God would call us to do missionary work. I'm so glad that you took the time to pray about further direction from God. And He has answered and we will be obedient to His calling to Africa. Let's wait a while before we tell the group. But we can tell them that after Dallas we are all going to take some time to seek the Lord's direction for the future. Agreed."

"Agreed. I think that tonight we will finish the lesson on the blood of Jesus and then have a time of prayer and seeking the Lord again. Maybe He will give me further direction for this last meeting. Let's take everyone to breakfast this morning."

"Okay. I'll go and round everybody up. Tomorrow we'll be heading out to Dallas."

"Why don't we give them a day to rest. It's been a tough time for everyone. We have time. I'll meet you at the car."

"Okay."

The group went out for breakfast that morning and Bro. John told them some of the things that the Lord told him but not all. They were all excited about his latest visitation and informed him of the great things the Holy Spirit was doing in the meeting. After breakfast they all had time to prepare for the evening. The praise team was putting together their music, Bro. John was putting together his notes and Sis decided that she should take some time to pray over the things that she and her husband had spoken about that morning. She wondered why God was sending them to Africa at this time. She had some doubts as to their ability to minister to the people of God. She didn't know a lot about Africa and thought that when

200

they had some down time she should look up some things and start preparing for this new ministry. She also wanted God to tell her how the money would come for the meeting. These days because of small crowds they barely had enough to go to the next city sometimes. Tent ministry was a dying art with the large churches that were being built now. Most of the people didn't come out anymore. She was quite worried.

Sister Betty had not slept much the night before. She was worried about John and it kept her up most of the night. Also she was thinking over and over again what the Spirit had said in the meeting and how it related to her at that time. She decided that she would do what John had done and take some time away from the group.

"Honey I think I would like to take some time away from the group to pray. I feel a need to connect with the Lord myself."

"Oh honey you will feel so much better tomorrow. Don't worry you took over for me last night. We will take care of things. There is a little place not a few miles from here. Go and talk with God. See if He will give you any further information about this new journey that He is sending us on."

"Yes darling. Thank you so much. Have I told you lately that I love?"

"Well."

They both laughed. Ministry sometimes can be a strain on a marriage but John and Betty always had a strong marriage and this just made it even better. They understood that the marriage between man and woman here on the earth was just as the marriage between God and the Nation of Israel. The covenant is never broken no matter what. When Betty got sick with cancer John was with her all the way. She had times when she couldn't use the rest room on her own and he would pick her up and take her to the rest room like a parent taking care of a child. It was hard for her to take but she needed that much help. The chemotherapy left her weak all the time. He took her to her doctor's appointments and waited on her hand and foot every day. He cooked the meals, washed the clothing and did all the chores around the house while she was ill. It was not that he didn't help before but she couldn't do anything so he had to do it all. He enjoyed doting over her and taking care of whatever she needed.

There were so many books of the bible that speaks about that covenant relationship that God had with the Nation of Israel. The most profound was the marriage of Hosea and Gomer. Gomer was supposedly a prostitute. Hosea would run after her time and time again. She even had babies out of wedlock. But the word of the Lord told Hosea to continue to be married to her and to help her. At one point Hosea left his wife because of her infidelity. This is a type of the marriage of Elohim and his bride Israel. Israel had left their God and had taken up with other gods. She is called an adulterous wife. But throughout all of this God continued to love her and take care of her. But at one point God had gotten so mad at Israel that He divorced her only to take her back time and time again. The Lord loves His bride but even God can take only so much. He is a jealous God and does not want to share His wife with any other gods.

The time is coming very soon when the Lord will not continue to fool with the adulterous church or a world of people who will not love Him and obey Him. The Kingdom of God is coming in whether man wants it or not. Those who choose the wrong side will pay with their lives. Those who choose Jesus Christ will receive the reward of a lifetime.

Betty made her way to the little hotel that John had gone to just the day before. But she saw a little community park and just wanted to sit down and smell the roses for a few hours before checking in. She remembered when she was just a little girl how she so enjoyed going to the park with her mom. She would take her and her brother and they would just play and play. These were fond memories that she had of her family. Her mom and dad got a divorce when she and her brother were young teenagers. Her father drank a lot and couldn't hold down a job for more than a few months at a time. This caused great stress in the marriage and they were always arguing. It seemed as though she was doomed to marry the same kind of man that her father was. Her first husband would drink and was very abusive to her. She stayed in the marriage for many years because she had promised God that she would never get a divorce. But after so many years she just couldn't take it any more. She felt as though she was going to have a nervous breakdown and she finally left. She would later meet John and they had a good marriage. She took the covenant of marriage very seriously and so does God. The covenant that He has made with His creation is forever. God is not slack concerning His promises. He says that there is no end to His Kingdom. He says that He is coming back and He is coming back.

Betty sat down on a bench near an enormous tree. The tree was so beautiful and the nice flowers they had all set around it. The air was fresh and there were a few people with their children in the park. Betty didn't have a book or a walkman with music she just wanted to sit quietly so that God could speak to her. She realized that she had not done this in a long time. Most often times she was so busy helping John prepare for the meetings or some task of that sort. She had not taken the time in years to just spend time with the Lord. When she and John first met they used to go out to eat and to the movies every week. They chose a night to go out and do something special together. She realized that the covenant marriage she had with God should be executed the same way. She needed to at least once a week break away from the group and take care of her marriage to the Lord. Perhaps it was a walk in the park, or maybe a time out on the water in a boat. Maybe she would just get a sandwich and sit by the pond and sing Him some praise songs. And most certainly she needed to spend more time in prayer over the world. Just some place where it was just the two of them to have quiet time alone. She knew that the Lord would love that. She would definitely have to do this. Many people think that just because Jesus is a Spirit that He doesn't have the same feelings and emotions as when He was in the flesh, quite the contrary. He enjoyed His time with the disciples. She thought about how they spent so much time together. They went to the feasts of the Lord together at times. There was so much that you had to read between the lines but Jesus had a full life with the disciples, His friends and His family. He had many brothers and sisters that He grew up with. They must have had some great times together. He is still that same Jesus. If His children would take the time to spend with Him they would see how great a guy He can be in fellowship. He is Lord, He is Comforter, but He is friend.

Betty was wondering in her heart what it was going to be like to work for the Lord overseas. To date she had not done much traveling out of the country but always wanted to see more of the world. She had never been to Africa. She didn't remember John saying what part of Africa they were supposed to go to. She would not worry about it for the Lord knew where He wanted them to go and He would tell them more about it as the time drew nearer. They certainly did not have the money to go so they would take it one step at a time.

From the corner of her eye she could see a young lady enter the park. She wore tattered clothing and looked like she had not eaten in quite a few days. She was headed in Betty's direction and Betty thought that if she sat down she would minister to her and perhaps buy some food for her if she wanted. When Betty and John first started in ministry they used to go to the soup kitchen and help give out meals for the homeless. Betty knew what a homeless person looked like. They looked like they did not belong anywhere. It was a kind of look that most of the people that they served had. Oh how she wanted to just take them all in and wash them up and make everything brand new. It was not so easy but this is what the gospel of Jesus Christ is all about. It is about taking broken lives and making them new and preparing them for marriage to the King. The great thing about marriage to the King is that He will take anyone. It doesn't matter what socio-economic status you have, where you were born or how many sins you have committed. It's all about the King. He will forgive anyone of their sins. All you need to do is ask.

The young lady sat down a bench away from Betty. Betty knew that she wanted to say something but was ashamed to say anything. She looked in her direction and smiled so that she could feel comfortable.

"Hi would you mind if I sat with you?"

She had come there to minister to the Lord but Jesus said "if you do it to the least of these ones you have done it for me." It was her responsibility to minister to the lost people of the world. They need Jesus and she knew that Jesus was looking on and He wanted that young lady to hear the gospel.

"No I wouldn't mind. I kind of need a friend today."

"My name is Betty. It's nice to meet you."

"I'm Awan. It's nice to meet you too. You live around here?"

"No actually my husband and I are having a tent revival not too far away from here."

"Oh wow. That's great. I have not been to one of those in quite a long time. I went to one while I was staying in Warner Robins, Georgia. It was great. I really felt the power of God in that revival. For the first time I believe that I felt the Holy Spirit in a way that I had not felt Him before."

Betty could not believe what she was hearing. This was an open door, a wide open door. She could not leave this young lady until she found out what was going on with her. She was almost sure when she saw her that she was a homeless woman but now she was not too sure.

"Wow that's awesome Awan. So do you live around here?"

"Actually I stay over at the shelter in town. I have not gotten a job yet. It's kind of hard after you get out of jail to get a job right away. But I'm looking though. The shelter won't let you stay there long if you are not looking for a job."

"Oh. I understand. What type of job are you looking for?"

"I'll take anything I can get. Have you tried looking in the newspaper? They seem to have a lot of hotels around here. One thing I've learned about the hotel business is that they will give you a chance. Might I ask what your charges were?"

"Prostitution. I mean I wasn't on the streets or anything. I was going to college and some of the girls told me about this place that I could make some extra money while going to school you know. It was a dating service if you know what I mean. I was doing really well. The dates were really high level businessmen. I didn't have to do anything that I didn't feel comfortable doing. Then I started going to these parties and doing drugs. This was my fatal mistake. Eventually I started sleeping with the men and the rest is all down hill. I got really strung out. There was a police raid at one of the parties and more down hill. I was in jail and they bailed me out. Of course eventually I got kicked out of school because my grades started dropping because of the drugs and the late night parties."

"It sounds like you got in over your head. But Awan you can pick yourself up from here and get your life back on track."

"Oh Betty, how can I? I have done some things that I cannot even tell God about. I am so ashamed."

"No Awan that's not true. You have forgotten that God is with you all the time. He already knows about the things that you have done and will do in the future."

"Yes I guess you are right. I just cannot bring myself to talk to Him about it. How can He love somebody like me who has wasted so much time on drinking, drugs, stealing and terrible things?"

"You know I've said that very same thing at one time in my life. When I first started going to church with my husband, I thought that everyone in the church knew about my sin. I thought that they all were better than I was and that I had no right to sit in that church amongst all of those holy people you know."

"Yeah, that's how I feel too. I feel as though they are all judging me. I just can't take it."

"Well Awan you know what turned me around. It might not sound so good but this is what really happened. I used to watch a certain minister on television all the time. I really like him. Our pastor actually purchased our church from that ministry after they built their new church. In any case he was one of the most influential men in our community and he fell into sin. Oh my it was in the newspaper and everything. I felt so bad for him and his family that they were going through this. But my point is if he could fall into sin then anybody could. You see the devil is always looking for some way to push our buttons. The bible says that all have sinned and fallen short of the glory of God. This means that when Jesus went to the cross to bare our sins he went for everybody no matter how big or small the sin that was committed. Everybody in that church has sin no matter whether you think they do or not."

"But they look at you as though they are better than you are."

"Well don't let that look make any difference to you. You just walk into the church and sit down and receive from heaven like the rest of the people. Hold it in your heart that Jesus died for your sins and their sins and you have just as much a right to be in the presence of God as they do."

"Wow. Thank you Betty. That certainly makes me feel a whole lot better. Where did you say that tent revival is at?"

"It's not too far from here only about a mile down this road. Do you have a way to get there?"

"Yes I do. I think I have a few friends that might want to hear your husband preach as well. They need Jesus too."

"Don't we all, I'm so glad that I met you today Awan. I hope you'll come to the revival. We have only one more night. I came here today to spend some quality time with God. I have some issues that I'm dealing with as well. Don't think that you are the only one who needs to talk with God."

"Well I hope that all goes well for you. I think I'm going to go and make a long awaited phone call home. Maybe I can reconcile with my mom and start going back to church again. I feel like I can talk with God now and make some needed changes in my life."

"That sounds great Awan. I will pray that you and your mom will reconcile. Jesus can help you both do that. Maybe you might want to go back home and start all over again. A mother never stops loving her child no matter what. She is just waiting for you to want her in your life again."

"Your right Betty. I'm sure you are a great mom. My mom is kind of difficult to talk with but then I did some really terrible things that I need to apologize to her for. I hope to see you again soon."

"Me too Awan. I'll be praying for you."

"Thanks Betty. I'll pray for you too."

The two ladies hug and then Awan leaves and continues to walk through the park. While Betty was contemplating on what to do next she decided that she would do better talking with the Lord in the hotel room. There were too many distractions sitting in the park although she was glad that she was there to give a word of encouragement to Awan and hoped that she would make it to the revival. This was the last night. She didn't know whether she would be there but she knew that God would be there and He would take care of Awan and her friends needs. Right now she needed a talk with Jesus all by herself. It was not easy being a minister's wife. Sometimes she felt that her husband didn't have much time for her but she understood why. John wanted to put most of his time and effort into praying for what God wanted him to be doing in connection with the ministry. She couldn't argue with that. She had a good husband and he loved the Lord. She walked across the street to the hotel and checked in. It was a nice place, very quiet and she knew that John had reached the Lord here only the night before. She hoped He would come and visit her as well.

Betty didn't bring many things with her because she didn't know whether she would stay the night or just a few hours. She decided that she would just sit in the nice chair next to the window and talk with the Lord.

"Lord I thank you for this time that we can share together without any distractions or any demands. Today there is always so much to do yet we seem to not get much accomplished. I guess that's why we get seven days to sort it all through. But John and I have realized that we have not been spending as much time in prayer as we ought. He took some time out last night and you gave him a word that we would be changing course in our ministry for you. I am excited about it but I am not sure whether we are the one's that should be doing this type of work for you. We are used to tent ministry, praying, laying on of hands and ministry like that. Is this what you want us to do in Africa? What would be the best way to minister to the people? I'm just concerned that we don't have what you need?"

Just then it was as if Betty was transported out of her room and she was walking down a dirt road with her bible in her hand and there was a man walking with her. She had never seen him before and asked him "where are we?"

The man turned to her and said "I am the Angel Gabriel. The Lord has sent me to show you the ministry that you will be doing when you arrive here. These are the people of the Sudan. Many of them have lost their homes and are looking for a way to return back to them. Some have already accepted the Messiah but many of them still adhere to the old religions of their people. Your assignment is to teach them the word of God. You do know how to do that don't you?"

"Yes we do. But what about the tent?"

"You can take the tent or leave the tent behind for now. Remember the days that you spoke to Awan about? You used to go into the prisons, nursing homes, hospitals and on the street. The Lord had not even started the tent ministry. Now you can't think of anything but that. Remember your beginnings and use those skills here. The people are not looking for much. They need many things but they really need the Lord. He has said in His word that He will provide all things and for you not to worry about these things. You just obey God and do what He tells you and He will grow this ministry in ways that you cannot see right now."

"Okay. I guess I am afraid."

"That's okay. God will be with you. Here come with me to this house. I want you to go inside and minister to the people inside."

Betty walked up to the door while the angel stood outside. It was a small little place and there was no door or windows so the people could see her walking up.

"Hi how are you today?"

"We are doing fine. How are you doing?"

"I am doing well. My name is Betty I am a missionary would you mind that I come in and sit a while?"

"No we don't mind. We are Christians too. From where did you come from?"

"I am from the United States. The Lord has sent me here to minister to you. Is there anything that I can help you with today?"

"Well my mother is very ill. We have been praying that God will heal her. We need a miracle or she will die."

"Well you know that Jesus is still the same healer that He was when he walked the face of the earth."

Just then Betty could see Jesus standing in the room with the same angel that brought her to the house. Jesus motioned to her to go and lay hands on the woman. While she was laying hands on her Jesus came over and he layed hands on her as well. Just then she opened her eyes and starting praising the Lord. She shouted "I'm healed, I'm healed. I saw Jesus laying hands on me at the very same time that you were laying hands on me. This is truly a miracle."

Betty was so amazed at what was happening.

"Well I told you that God is still a miracle working God."

With that she was transported back to her hotel room. She could not believe what had just taken place. The angel of the Lord took her to Africa so she could see the type of work that she and John would be doing there. It was right out of the bible. She didn't think that God still did that type of thing. God used the angels all through the New Testament to speak to the disciples to help them. They even saw them in prison and came to rescue them many times. Betty always prayed that the angels would be encamped round about her so that if she ever got into trouble they could help her.

Before she could get her composure she heard a knock on the door. She went to see who it could be, no one knew that she was there except John. She opened the door and there stood Jesus at the door. She just smiled as he entered the room.

"Ruth why are you amazed at what just took place? It amazes me that my children read about me but they don't think that what the disciples experienced in the New Testament is the same that it should be for them today? I am going to show you things that you never thought possible."

"Lord I believe. I guess I'm like most Christians I just have not experienced the bible quite like that up close and personal if you will."

"I know and I'm going to change that. When you and John leave here you will experience me in ways that will increase your faith to a new level. I have been preparing you and John for many years for this assignment. This will be your last assignment and then you will both be coming to be with me in heaven. Don't be startled this is another thing that most Christians are not ready for. Until my Kingdom comes death is still a part of life. But for my children you should not be afraid. If you run the course of this race with diligence and obedience you will win the prize of everlasting life in the Kingdom of God. The saints in heaven are praying for those of you who are still working diligently like you and John. I am so proud of you both and what you have accomplished but this assignment is very important to me Ruth. These are my people. I made a covenant with Abraham and it is an everlasting covenant. I want to see these people receive the gift of salvation."

"Yes Lord. I understand. John and I will do everything you tell us to."

With that Jesus had just disappeared. How many people get the opportunity to get an assignment directly from God? Betty felt like Moses must have felt when he was out tending to his sheep and he saw a great sight and went to investigate what it was that he was seeing. When he got to that mountain he saw a bush that was burning but the fire did not consume the bush. He then heard a voice from heaven that said to take off his shoes for he was standing on holy ground. God gave him an assignment that no one else since that time received. He was the one chosen by God to lead the people of God out of the bondage of slavery in Egypt. Moses led 3 million people out of slavery into the wilderness to be consecrated and sanctified for God. This assignment given to Betty and John was a continuation of the same covenant that God had made with Abraham concerning his people. He never forgets a promise that He has made. Betty felt better than she had when they first received the word from the Lord. She felt inadequate just like Awan felt going into the church after she had fallen away from God. She felt that certainly there was someone else that could to the job better. Moses felt the same way when God told Him that he was the chosen vessel to be used of God. But God reminded Him that it was not about Moses but about the power of God working through Moses. Betty needed to be reminded that God was the one that was going to do the miraculous things but she and John just had to be faithful and walk with God. He would show them the way to minister to the people.

As soon as Betty started to feel better about the whole thing she started to doubt. They were paying salaries and she couldn't see how they would be able to sustain the group if God did not reveal a way. But then she thought well she would talk to John about liquidating all of their assets to fund the mission. God had blessed them over the years and the missionaries of the past did that very same thing. Why should it be any easier for them? They had some property and other assets and they could use that to get started. These were poor people and they would definitely not have any money to help them while they were there. Even Paul had to work to take care of himself. If God could feed Elijah during the drout then He could take care of them when the money ran out. She would not give place for the devil to bring doubt into her heart. She knew that Jesus gave them this assignment and He would take care of them.

Chapter 25

SINCE BETTY HAD NOT EATEN for the day she decided that she would have some dinner at the hotel and retire early. They would be packing up the next morning to leave for Dallas. There was so much that she and John needed to talk about before the revival in Dallas started. They would also need to talk with their staff about what God wanted them to do next. Perhaps some of them would not want to go. God did not say that the whole staff had to go but that Betty and John had to leave for this assignment. Maybe she had better ask the Lord about this as well. There was so much to do and they wanted to get going when God said to leave.

After dinner she took and shower and she knew that she could hear the Lord say "earthquake, earthquake". She said "when Lord, where Lord?"

The Lord said "Dallas, you must warn the people, Dallas, you must warn the people."

Ruth became frightened. She didn't know whether the earthquake was going to be today, tomorrow, next week or what. She got out of the shower quickly so that she could pray. Over the years the Lord had told her many things and she knew that before she started asking Him more questions that she should just pray. Before she could get dressed the phone rang. Who could be calling her at this hour of the night? She hoped John was okay. It was probably him checking on her to see if she was okay.

"Hello."

"Hello darling. I just called to tell you that I miss you. Are you okay?"

"As a matter of fact I've never been better. Hey I'm glad that you called. Please look out for a young lady and perhaps some of her friends. I met a young lady today and she said that she might come to the revival. She needs prayer. I have so much to tell you."

"Well start from the beginning."

"No honey. I can't talk right now. I got a word from the Lord and I was just getting ready to pray. Please say a special prayer for Dallas tonight. It's not good John."

"Oh!?"

"I cannot tell you right now. God needs me to pray. I'll see you in the morning bright and early okay?"

"Okay darling. Don't worry. God has us praying because He wants all to go well with whatever the situation is. We've been through this many times before. Don't worry, pray. Love you."

"I love you too."

Betty got on her knees as soon as she hung up the phone with John. This was something important and she was not going to miss God. God was talking with His children in these last days like never before. There was a lot that was going to happen and He needed someone to pray. The Body of Christ still does not realize the importance of prayer. Like one minister said that many have gotten really excited about praise and worship but most do not know how to pray. When you ask people in the church to come just for prayer you may get one or two out of hundreds of members. This means that they don't pray at home. Prayer is the lifeline of the church. Prayer is the power of the church.

"Father God, I thank you that you have spent this time with me today. I thank you for all that you have done for my family and the ministry team. I pray Heavenly Father that you are pleased with our service. Father I have heard your sweet voice tonight that there is something terrible going to happen in Dallas and that you want us to warn the people. I thank you that you and the Holy Angels are watching over us and all that is happening in the world. I thank you that you have entrusted this word to me today and many others around the world to pray over this place. In the name of Jesus, Father God I pray that if this is of the devil that you bind this attack and not let it take place. But if you will allow this calamity to take place in Dallas I pray Father God that you will have mercy upon the people. Have mercy for thy names sake, for the sake of your people the church. Father God I plead the blood of Jesus over every school house, over every church building, over every policeman, fireman and emergency medical worker. I plead the blood of Jesus over all the businesses and the houses in Dallas. Father I plead the blood of Jesus over the land, the trees and the waterways that they remain pure to drink for the people. Father I plead the blood of Jesus over the hospitals, nursing homes and government buildings. I pray that the watchman will sound the alarm and that the people will have ears to hear what the Spirit is saying to the world today. Father we know that you have told us that these things will occur before your return. The day of the Lord is upon us and the world must surely repent. I thank you for pleading with us because you love us and do not want to see the people perish."

Betty layed down to sleep but it was hard for her that night. She had spoken with the Lord and He had also put a burden upon her. She didn't quite know how she would tell John and when would the time be right. He had so much on his mind as well. But it had to be done. Jesus had given them a task to complete and they were going to complete it. Somehow she managed to fall asleep. The next day they would be packing up the tent and moving on to Dallas. That morning Betty felt somewhat refreshed. She had not realized how tiring the ministry was. She just never let herself think much about being tired she just kept going like the energizer bunny. There was much work to be done before the Lord's return. She would not stop for one minute. She knew that Jesus must have gotten tired at times as well but he kept in front of Him at all times the Father's business.

Just as Betty woke up the phone rang and she sat up to take the phone call. Samuel had called to say that Bro. John had taken ill and they were on their way to the hospital. She was startled and said that she was on her way back. She got the name of the hospital and said that she would get directions and meet them there. Her mind was racing back and forth. John had never been sick much the whole time they had been married. He was probably just tired and needed to rest. She hoped that it was just a head cold or something. That probably wasn't it if Samuel had to take him to the hospital. She had better start praying now before leaving the room.

"Father I plead the blood over this situation. I know what you have told us to do. If you have given us an assignment then we will be able to make it. Send your healing grace into his body today. I rebuke the devil today and this sickness that he has brought our way. I know that he is just trying to keep us from obeying your commandments Father. We shall be about the business of the Father and no weapon that is formed against us shall prosper. In Jesus Mighty name. Amen."

Betty quickly got dressed and made her way to the hospital. When she arrived Samuel told her that John was waiting for the doctor to come and check on him. He had started vomiting blood terribly and felt like he was going to pass out. He didn't want to go to the hospital but Samuel insisted that he get checked out before going back on the road. He hoped it wasn't serious but it was best to check it out thoroughly. Betty went into the room to be with him and was quite amazed when she saw that his face didn't have much color at all.

"John how are you doing?"

"I just feel really weak. We had another great service last night. I felt fine when I layed down but when I got up this morning it just hit me. I felt dizzy, and just terribly sick to my stomach. Samuel came over and found me almost passed out. I don't know what would have happened if he had not come over for breakfast. I might have been out cold in the room. Divine intervention I hope."

"Yes. The Lord knew that you needed help. I cannot ever remember you being ill like this ever."

"Your right. I am getting old you know. Don't worry the Lord is here and so are the doctors. He should be here any minute. Let me just lie here for a while. They'll run some tests and we will be on our way. Perhaps you might want to call Bro. Thompson and tell him that I'm ill but that Samuel can run the meeting if I don't have the strength to do it myself. Okay?"

"Okay John. It can wait until I know what the doctor has to say."

The door opened and the doctor walked in with a big smile.

"Hi Mr. Brubaker, I'm Dr. Stallings seems like you have a bit of a problem with your stomach. It sounds like a bleeding ulcer. Do you have a history?"

"No doctor. And I feel dizzy as well. I've never felt like this before. I almost passed out at the hotel. And no I don't have a history until now."

"Well these things have a way of laying idol until one day they surface.

"Yes. I guess that's how it works. I don't feel very good. I need to use the restroom."

Betty helped John get into the bathroom. He was vomiting blood again. She and he were very alarmed now at this point. The doctor wanted to order some tests and hold John over night for observation.

"I think we had better run some extensive tests on you Mr. Brubaker. It could be several things wrong with you all of which I don't like. If you have any plans you might as well cancel them. John had a worried look on his face.

"See Betty. Every time God has given us a specific task that devil comes in like a flood and tries to keep us from doing it. I know it was God now that told us to go overseas. Some ugly demons aren't happy about it. Now their making me sick but we are going to be about the Father's business. You go out there and tell Samuel to get the team ready to go to Dallas. Nothing the devil does is going to keep us from getting the gospel to the people. Jesus didn't take any sick days and neither are we. Paul didn't stop preaching just because he got thrown in jail and we aren't going to stop either. You tell him that we'll meet him there as soon as the doctor says that I can travel and tell him to start the meeting on schedule as planned. We should never keep the Father waiting, he didn't say I can't go to the cross today because I have something else to do. We cannot let Him down ever. Go on."

John was serious as a heart attack. He wasn't able to travel but the team could. He didn't want them to think that there was any excuse why they should be all standing around worrying about him. They should go on and get the meeting started the Lord was waiting.

Betty had not gotten a chance to tell John all that the Holy Spirit had told her. She had a warning to give to the people and here she was stuck with a sick husband. But if she had told him he would have told her to go on and tell the people what God had said. She didn't know what to do but she had a message from God. God knew that John was going to get sick why did he tell her to give this message. He knew she would not want to leave him there. Hopefully all would be well by the time the meeting was going to be over. She could rush in and give the message. She would have to pray and seek the Lord quickly before the team left. They took John upstairs and put him in a room. They would start his tests right away. He didn't want Betty to worry so he told her to just take a seat and when the tests were over she could come and sit with him and pray that all would be well. He knew how she would just worry over him. He didn't want her to see any kind of fear or worry on his face. But he was definitely worried about what was happening to him.

Betty told Samuel that John wanted them to pack up the tent and all the gear and get ready to leave for Dallas. She told Samuel that she was having quite a dilemma because God had given her a special message for Dallas. She didn't know what to do because she didn't want to leave John. She didn't know what to do. She knew what she had heard. But she also knew that at times the prophecy was not to be fulfilled right away so they most likely had time. So she decided to tell Samuel to tell the team to take a day off and leave tomorrow. This would give them time. Perhaps they could do the tests and she and John could join them after all. Samuel agreed and they would hold a vigil all night praying for John to get out of the hospital in the morning. If not they would leave in the afternoon.

Samuel left to tell the rest of the group what was happening. He knew that they would all be worried.

Betty went to the hospital chapel so she could pray and get her bearings. It seemed as if everything was happening all at one time. But John was right when they first stepped out into ministry all of their friends turned against them and told them they were crazy going into the tent ministry. Terrible things were being said about them and they had done nothing wrong but answer the call of God for their lives. It was quite discouraging and perhaps that is what the devil wanted to happen to them but it just made them want to show everyone that God was on their side. Since the old days they saw many saved, healed and baptized in the Spirit. Being about the business of the Father was no easy task. They had suffered a lot at the hands of the beloved who did not believe in what they were doing.

Samuel had the task of going back to tell the team that their leader was going to stay in the hospital for observation. John Jr. had stayed behind with the rest to make sure that all was well with the equipment. They could not leave it alone of course lest vandals walk away with everything. He really didn't think that it was anything serious otherwise he would have come along.

"You think that I should go and be with mom? I'm sure she is very worried about how this is going to turn out."

"No, your father was very serious about us getting things packed up and ready to go. He does not want to let the Father down. He wants the revival to go on whether he can make it out of here on time or not. But Sis. Betty said that we should wait a day to see if maybe he can get out in the morning. She has asked that we pray for him that all will go well, something about she has a special word from God for Dallas."

"Oh boy. The last time mom had a special word for someone it wasn't good. We had a revival in Kansas City and God had told her that there would be a terrible earthquake there. The people of course didn't receive the word from the Lord but mom knew that she had heard from the Lord. Well of course it came true and instead of the people being grateful they smeared mom and dad all over the place and asked that they never return to Kansas City. It was as though they believed that they brought the earthquake to the place. We both know that prophecy is of God. Mom was just the vehicle used to give the word of the Lord to the people. I never could understand the mentality of that whole thing."

"Well you know John most people today don't believe in the prophecy of the bible. They do however unfortunately believe in the personal prophecies that are being given all over the place. If you notice the difference between the prophecies given by the real prophets God is using today the message is so not like what the false prophets are giving to the people. Many people want to hear the nice personal prophecies that say all is well with the world and that they are going to receive rich rewards here on earth. While some of them are true there are still some not so nice prophecies that God is giving to his servants that we must deal with as well. I myself have received many words from the Lord that I have been afraid to speak because I'm afraid that the beloved will stone me to death if you know what I mean."

"I sure do. I'm wondering now what God told mom. Well we had better start breaking down the tent and the equipment. Dad will be very angry if he knew we were standing around talking. He is very serious about what he does and we will want to be ready to go in the afternoon if that is what mom wants. I'll call Bro. Thompson and ask him to have the church pray for mom and dad. He'll be concerned when he doesn't see us there. But I will tell him that we will start the revival on time."

"Thanks John."

"No thank you Samuel for taking dad to the hospital. As soon as we get things wrapped up we should all get together and have supper and then pray that dad will get out tomorrow. He said that he had a special word himself for Dallas. When he says that hold on."

The two young men went to gather up the rest of the team to tell them that Bro. John is in the hospital but that they would be leaving if he cannot get out of the hospital the next morning. They would all get together that evening for diner and prayer that all would go well.

The doctor ordered John's test right away. He felt that it was nothing but an ulcer but just to make sure he ordered some more testing. Betty took the time to pray for John that God would give her the strength to make it through yet another test from the devil. They had been through so much but God was faithful to his servants. When Betty walked into the chapel there were several people on bended knees praying for their loved ones. She didn't particularly feel like ministering to anyone that day, in fact she felt that she needed the priest to come and pray with her but she knew that was not the way she should feel. People all over the world are in need of a word from God in these last days. More and more people are getting sick from one disease or another. It is sometime through these hard times when we reach out to help someone else that we get the healing we so desperately need ourselves. The days before the Lord's return is getting shorter and shorter and the things He spoke about in Matthew 24 were coming with greater intensity. The world was in a panic from one thing or another. The prophets of God were speaking what the Spirit was saying to His church and it wasn't good. The chosen people of God were called to minister a message of love and hope to the world. Unfortunately, God's people could get caught up in forgetting the hope which is Christ Jesus and start panicking like everyone else. Betty sat down quietly and tried to blend into the room without disturbing the other's prayers. To the corner of her eye she saw a nun and a priest talking quietly. When they saw her they just smiled and nodded so she would know they were available if she needed something.

She thought to herself it must be difficult yet rewarding to be about the business of the Father in a hospital environment. So many sick people and so little time to help them all. She thought that maybe she could pray that God would send them the finances and the help to build a small clinic where they were being reassigned by God. Many people in foreign nations do not have the medical facilities that are commonplace in America. Good medical treatment is a necessity for any society but they cannot afford it. Many doctors and nurses are joining medical mission teams sent throughout the world. She would have to talk with John about this when he gets better. It just felt good to sit for a while and pray for John. Betty was always doing something for the ministry and it just felt good to sit and pray. Betty was true to her calling though so she couldn't help but think about what the others were praying for, perhaps she could just utter a prayer for them as well. The bible said that if two or three are touching and agreeing on anything that God would do it. She wanted to join in prayer with them that what they were asking God would do. She just knew in her heart that her John would be okay. He had not been sick much a day in his life. He had the hope which is Christ Jesus as healer for him but what about these people? Were they true believers or had they just come before God in a time of need. It was the responsibility of every believer to come to the throne of grace for those who really had no right to come before the throne of God because they were not of His own. Only the children of God had the right to come to their Father in prayer and ask for help.

After quite a few hours had passed Betty went back to John's room to see if the testing was over. He was back in his room but he was sleeping. Betty took a small bottle of oil out of her bag that she carried around just in case. She took some out, put it on her finger and layed hands on her husband asking God to heal him while he was sleeping. She must have sat there for a few minutes and found herself dozing off. In her dream she saw Jesus riding on a white horse. He said that He was going about throughout the earth checking on His bride to see if she was remaining faithful to the commission. He said that His reward will be great for those who stay faithful to the end. He said that the mark of the beast was coming quickly and to warn the people not to take the mark of the beast for it will mean certain death to all who take it. They must remain clean and walk in the Spirit. This is the only way that they will escape the judgment that will come upon the world. He rode off into the clouds the same way that He came.

Betty woke up forgetting that she was sitting at John's bedside. This was a dream unlike any that she had ever had before. The Lord was coming to talk to her more and more these days. This told her that the time for the Lord's return was getting closer and closer and He was preparing His church, His bride to be with Him in glory.

Chapter 26

SAMUEL AND THE REST OF the group had finished taking down the tent and putting all of the sound equipment into the bus. They started praying for Betty and John that all would go well and they could all leave together. No one wanted to sleep but it was going to be a long day on the road so they all retired early after they heard from Betty. The tests had gone well and John would be able to leave the next afternoon providing that he promised that he would not work too hard and take the prescribed medicine. The Lord had answered their prayers and everyone was praising God. Samuel was thinking about what he would minister since John and Betty were so tired. Maybe John Jr. would minister as well. He wasn't much like his dad. He liked being in the background of the ministry. That was okay he guessed. Maybe that was his calling. No need to do something you are not anointed to do. The ministry had lots of work to do in other areas. Every person was important though. In the Book of Romans Paul talked about all of the different offices that worked in the church and that all of them worked together for the good of the church. The hand had its purposes while the foot had a purpose all of its own. The body is lead by the head Jesus. It is an amazing analogy of how the church works. But it seems that the church of today has lost its head and has taken on another head.

What happened to the church of today? It seemed like if you study church history that whenever the church was being persecuted and truly relied on the Father for strength and support they were a thriving church. This is why in the Book of Revelation the Laodicean church which is the church age of the latter days was accused by Jesus of being neither hot nor cold. The problem as Jesus saw it is this, that the beloved are rich not having any need of anything. But in the eyes of the Father he says that they didn't know that they were wretched, miserable, poor, blind and naked. This is not a very good picture for the latter day church before Messiah's return. The Lord orders the church to repent that they may sit with Him on His throne. Samuel's mom told him before she died that before he was born the Lord came to her in a vision to tell her that Jesus had come to her and began weeping with great anguish. He told her that the church had become sluggish and had fallen away from their original purpose. He said that the world did not know Him anymore because the church had begun to preach a watered down gospel, a gospel that He did not teach his disciples. The church had lost its power because they didn't demonstrate the power of God through the gifts God gave them for the church. Some of the churches still believed that they walked in the power that the apostles were given and that the miraculous works of God were still being orchestrated in the church today. And then many didn't believe in the miraculous gifts of God at all it was a dead issue. It was no wonder that the world was turning to all other manner of spiritual mediums because the church had nothing to offer. Samuel wanted to call the church to repentance. He would talk with John about it as soon as he could. Jesus and many of the saints had died for this church and there was a need for a true revival in the people of God or else many would die because the true gospel was not being preached as it ought to be preached.

The morning came sure enough and Betty and John made it back to the hotel for the whole team to leave for Dallas together. They all didn't know what to do when they saw the car pull up. It was a joyous day to see the sun shining and the man of God on his feet again. He looked a bit tired but that was to be expected. John Jr. drove with his mom and dad so that Big John would not have to drive all the way to Dallas, he was not up to it. Because of his condition they decided that they would stop so that he could rest a while and then continue on to Dallas. They still had a few days in between so there was no rush. They had expected before all of this happened to get there early so that the team could rest but this would work as well. The weather forecast called for a big storm to be heading in their direction so they didn't want to get caught up in it. They hoped that it would pass quickly so it wouldn't inhibit the people from coming out to the revival. But it seemed that when the man of God stepped onto the holy ground the Lord took care of the rest.

The team put up for the night at a local motel on the way to Dallas so that Bro. John could get some rest. The forecast was not good there was a tornado moving right outside of Dallas. Betty was apprehensive of how things were going to work out but they would pray and God would tell them what to do. They had not had this problem before. There were times when there was a light storm but that in and of itself would not stop the revival. The tent they had now was a new one and it was very strong. So far it held up very well and the people stayed dry. A tornado was another story. Nothing could withstand those kinds of winds and rain. The team had to think quickly what they were going to do. First they should get in touch with their host and see what he had in mind.

"Hey my friend how are you doing?"

"Well we are doin but this tornado is heading our way and we are all getting everything ready. They say that we might have to evacuate the place. That's a lot of people to evacuate but they want to play it safe."

"What should we do? Do you think we should wait it out where we are until this thing blows over and then see where we are?"

"I think that would be the wise thing to do. Why take chances. The good Lord said not to test Him. Give me the name and number of the hotel and then when this thing blows over we'll get in touch and we'll see where we are at that time."

"That sounds like a plan. I can catch up on some rest and if it is God's will we will have a revival. If not we'll have to change the date for another time. I've been ill for the first time in quite a while. Maybe this is all happening for a reason. The doctor did say that I need to lay low. I guess I'll be doing what the doctor ordered huh?"

"Well now you take it easy ole boy. You old timers don't know quite how to sit down when you need to. Remember that God created the heavens and the earth all by himself and he'll be alright if you need to take a rest now."

"You crazy ole boy. You can't sit down either. Remember when you preached that revival with a broken leg. We had to carry you to the hospital kickin and a screamin. So don't tell me about it."

"Those were the good ole days. Back when preachers were really preachin something. Now adays they get up there with three points and a prayer and that's it. We used to go for hours and hours. We couldn't get those people off the grounds. Revival went on for days and days. People used to camp out for real. Nowadays they have a bunch of people in a building three days and they call it camp meeting. I don't know what has happened to the church Johnny. It just ain't like it used to be. We need to get back to the ole time religion. Give me that ole time religion any day. This new fangled stuff ain't getting nobody saved."

"You said a mouth full Karl. The Lord is not pleased with what has happened to His bride and something is going to be done about it one way or the other. I don't want to be in the way when the judgment is ruled out against the church. What can we do brother about this? We gotta get to the people and let them know what is really going down. The pastors and the leadership must be held accountable for what is happening. We are responsible for the sheep. If we don't get this thing back on track a whole lot of preachers are going to be held accountable to God for not taking care of His flock."

"I don't quite know what to do. I as an individual just keep on preaching the way I know that it should be done. Do you know that they got churches out there right now that have homosexuals in the pulpit? This is an abomination before God and they are going to pay a big price for this. Who would have ever thought that in our day there would be states lobbying for same sex union? And then instead of the church setting the example they are following right along with the world's standards. Their standards are not our standards Johnny. The Lord thy God He sets the standards for his church not the world. We are to be in the world but not of the world. Is that not what the bible says?"

"Yes sir it sure does. I can't believe it either. And then there are church folk who don't want to speak out against sin anymore. It's like there afraid or something. The Lord said fear me and not the devil. He can take your life but after that can do nothing. God can take your soul for all eternity. We had better wake up to the fact that the church is in deep trouble and its getting worse. The church of old were not liked by the world at all. Why was this? Because they were a peculiar people. They were different from the world. The women dressed holy back in those days. Now adays you don't know the Christian women from the worldly women."

"Talk about it. I can't understand what has happened to us."

"We have gotten comfortable Karl. That's the problem. Much, too comfortable. The Lord has been telling me a lot of things of recent. I have more dreams than I ever have. I believe it's because God is warning the people of great things that are coming. The reason for this is because He is trying to get our attention."

"Oh Johnny I have been so busy I have not been keeping up with you. I have been having the same things happening to me. God is talking full strength now. It's the Book of Joel man. It's kind of scary. God told me not many years ago that there is going to be a massive earthquake right here in Dallas. Man I'm ready to get out of here, but where do you go? He's touching every state in the U.S. You might as well get prepared and plead the blood over your house and keep on praying until this thing is over."

"You ain't kiddin. There are going to be many earthquakes, tornadoes and everything to wake the people up. You see as long as the people have their money and power they think they don't need God. But when He shakes the very foundation of their strength they have nothing else but God to look to. Now he can talk to them and tell them to stop sinning before Him. The world does not realize that a holy and righteous God created this earth and He is not going to stand for anything else but holiness and righteousness from His creation. It's just that simple."

"That's right brother. Every knee is going to bow and every tongue is going to confess that Jesus is Lord to the glory of the Holy Father. They can come easy or they can go the hard way. If they would just trust Him and know Him. They would see that He is the glorious Father that loves all of His creation. He loves us too much to let us continue going in the direction that we are going. Every day there is something terrible happening in the world. CNN doesn't have any problems with news to report."

"You aint' kiddin. There sure isn't any shortage of bad news in the media today. In fact it seems like in recent years it has gotten progressively worse I would say. There isn't one town in the world that doesn't have a drug problem. More and more we are hearing about little children being snatched from their home or neighborhood. Old women are being raped in their homes. Churches are being burned down by teenagers who have no respect for God. The day of the Lord is coming that He is going to put a stop to all of this. The world is out of control. And this is not just a problem in the United States but all over the world."

"It's a sad state of affairs Karl. What's happening with the weather? You think that we'll ever get out of here?"

"I don't know right now Johnny we might have to go to the designated shelter. I'm an old man. I can't mess with these things like I used to. Mother and I will call you in the morning, okay?"

"Okay Karl. You guys get to a safe place. We'll talk with you hopefully in the morning."

Dallas had not seen a storm like this in many years. People had to leave their homes and go to shelters to be safe. Of course many decided to ride out the storm at home and many evacuated all together. The highway was a nightmare but by the time the storm hit many had gotten out of town. There was much damage but it had come in with a furry and after a few hours it was all over. There was so much damage that many would not be able to return to their homes for quite sometimes. There actually was nothing left to many of them. The governor of the state declared it to be a state of emergency. The national guard was called out to maintain order. In situations like this there would be looters and all kinds of mayhem in the aftermath of the storm. Bro. John didn't know quite what to do he would have to talk with Betty about what they should do next. There would be certainly much more of this in the years to come.

John and Betty came together with the team and came up with the idea to put some money together and to buy as much non-perishable items as they could afford for those who had lost the use of their homes. Many were without electricity so they had to have can items they would not have to refrigerate. They would leave for Dallas as soon as they could and set up the tent as a make-shift area where people could come and get food, prayer, bibles and what other items they could purchase. This would be more fitting than a revival service. As time went on if all worked out then they could turn it into a revival service. It would be like the old days the people could come and camp out and they would praise the Lord that no one died in the storm and that the light of day would bring along with it renewed hope for the future. John and Betty had not told the team that they would be going overseas but John thought maybe this is what they could start off doing in Africa. Many of the areas in Africa had food shortages and if they planned ahead they could come up with some money from some of the churches they were affiliated with to send food and other supplies to minister to the people along with giving out bibles and ministering the word. They could come for prayer and receive the Lord and get prayed over for healing in their bodies. There was not one place on the earth where people did not need prayer for sickness.

The team headed out the next day for Dallas. They were indeed grateful that they were headed for this area at that particular time. The church would have to put on a new face and act like the church of old who took care of its people and others in need when the need arose. Paul often took up offerings to take to one congregation or another. The love of Jesus is not just in the preaching of the gospel but in the taking care of the every day needs of people who were in need. Jesus had great compassion for those who were sick, hungry, naked and in prison.

Chapter 27

He told his disciples that if you do this for the least of the brethren you have done it for me. The face of the true church of God has to come outside of the walls of the church and minister to the needs of the people in the world. There is a hurting world out there and the church is called to give the world the hope which is in Jesus. The whole team was excited. They had never taken on a project like this before. There was so much to consider. They purchased food items, water, baby diapers, clothing items for men, women and children and plenty of bibles. There is nothing like the word of God to quench the thirst like no other water could. When Jesus came upon the woman at the well he asked her for a drink of water. Here Jesus stops to talk to a woman that had had many husbands and the one that she presently lived with was not her husband. It's not until Jesus walked into her life that she received a word that would change her entire life. And not only that she was so changed that she went into the town to tell other people about this great man that she had met. Jesus had asked her for a drink of water but then he told her that if she knew who He was that she would be asking Him for a drink of living water. She was puzzled because He had just asked her for some water and then said that He in turn had a better water. Where was this water that Jesus spoke about? He was the living water. In Him was all that she needed to change her life for the better. He told her that with this water she would never thirst again. If only the church could get the people of the world to see that you cannot find a thirst quencher more better than Jesus. Some look to alcohol and other substances to quench the thirst they have in life and that will not do it. Some look to other people to fill the void in their life but only God can fill any void that they have in life. In these last days critical times are happening every day. Only God has the answers to life's problems.

Bro. John and Sis. Betty and the team felt really good about the transition. It felt as if this is what they should have been doing all along. It took the disaster of a storm to let them see that there was something more they could do for the people of the world. That tent became a tabernacle where the people could come and have a little talk with Jesus. They could tell Him all about their sorrows and they would know that He was right there working through His servants to tackle whatever the problem was. If they didn't have the answer right there they would walk with them to get the problem solved. Many of the people had lost the home that they had lived in for a long time and all of their possessions. They had nothing left that made them feel secure. To get that bible with the word of living water made a big difference for them. They had a place where they could cry on someone's shoulder and know that the good Samaritan had arrived that cared about their loss. Families were scattered and loved ones didn't know where each other was. This is a cause for much stress but just a kind word will get them through the next minute.

At one point the people were lined up in cars for miles and miles Bro. John was afraid that they would run out of supplies before the next day. He got on the phone and started to call pastors from all over the country that he knew to ask for donations for the help ministry that they had started. They could wire him the money or send it directly to his account so he could get access right away. The need was greater than he could ever imagine. At one point they cut the line off and told the people to please come back the next day when they could replenish the supply of needs. He also took a list of things that they needed just to get them by until the Federal Government could get trailors for them to live in. Many other

231

ministries were doing the same thing. It was amazing how so many people came to the aid of those that were in need in such a short period of time. They were there on the scene about 24 hours after the storm had ended. It was truly a miracle.

Many people ask the question where is God in the midst of trouble. The answer to that question is that God is right in the midst of the trouble the whole time. Most times we want the trouble to never come and we pray and pray for God to not let the hurricane or tornado take place. But allowing people to go through troubled times is also a part of God's plan whether we like it or not. Good weather and bad weather are all a part of life. You cannot escape it no matter how much you try. Even a regular rainy day can have its downfall but you learn how to make it through. Some days are worse than others but you learn how to get through. Many who live in the coastal areas know all about the weather being difficult but they love the place they live and they work to survive through the difficult times.

Unfortunately the difficult times will be more frequent in the last days. It is God's way of waking the world up. Why does the world need a wake up call? When Jesus came the first time He came to die for the sins of mankind and to provide a way of redemption for the world. This world of course needed redemption because it has been so polluted with sin. The God of all creation will not and cannot stand for sin to continue in the world. The Bible says that the wages of sin is death. This is definitely true when we see how many people are killed for one reason or another. The Kingdom of God shall be a place where there will be no sin, no killing. It will be a place of love and peace for all mankind. This was the way the world was to be before sin entered into it. Everyone on earth wants peace for their families. The problem is there is no system of government that knows exactly how to accomplish this great feet accept God. God made heaven and earth not man. When God made man He made man that he should take care of the earth but He didn't say that He should be left out of the process. This is what has happened to the world that they have forgotten the role of God in life much to the detriment of every society on every continent. God must take control of the world again and get it back on track.

It was disheartening for Sis. Betty to see the women and children with nothing but the clothes on their backs. Mother's with newborn babies with no milk or diapers to care for them was hard. But the old people who had nothing to show for all the years they had raised children and some grand children was the worse. There were sick people who had no medicine and with all the help that was available it was just not enough to take care of all the needs of the people. This was a whole new level of homelessness. But in the midst of it all people were coming together to pray for one another. The young people were holding on to one another as they sang hymns to the Lord as they comforted one another. This is the joy of the Lord that no matter what the situation is they will trust in Him for help. The blessed Father is always there to help his children in times of trouble. The wonderful Father says do not worry about what you will eat or what you are to drink for your Father who is in heaven knows that you have need of these things.

As in Paul's day he took up offerings when needed for those who were in need in Jerusalem and he delivered that money to them. The beloved church of today is called to that same task. Bro. John received offerings from all over the United States and was able to go quite a few days just feeding the people and helping with whatever he could. At night for those who kind of stayed close to the tent he would just go around like a pastor and just listen to the stories of the people who lived in the area and some who just came out to help.

Wanda Close heard about the terrible devastation and decided to take some time off of work to come and help. She felt like it was the neighborly thing to do. She was not a Christian but she just felt it in her heart that she wanted to be of service. She remembered that when she was a little girl her family lost everything in a fire and they got help from the Red Cross but if not for that she didn't know how they would have made it through.

Wayne heard about the storm and came down on his break from school to help. He and some of his buddies knew how to fix houses and so that's what they were there doing. There was an older woman who lived alone in a very small house, not very fancy and the roof came completely off. She didn't have any money or insurance and she had no family that she could stay with. They did the best they could to clean the house for her the best they could and get a make shift roof on for her until they could finish the real work. She was so grateful. They were presently going to a Christian university and just wanted to show the love of Jesus to someone that was in need.

There were many stories just like these all over the place. People loving and caring for one another. In the last days this is what the church must do. You can only do so much through prayer. James said don't pray about it if you can do it yourself. Don't say to the mother who has three children, no husband and no job that the Lord will provide. Yes the Lord will provide but he might just be asking you to be the provider. There is a great blessing to those who take the time to take care of someone in need. God put us here with all the abilities that we need to survive. We look to Him so much when we can take care of a lot of things all by ourselves. We get mad at Him sometimes when it feels like He is not responding to our prayers. But the fact of the matter is God is not responding because He doesn't want us be dependent upon Him. He wants us to be independent creatures able to do things on our own. Some people have to pray about every matter as though they don't have any common sense of their own. This is not the kind of children that God wants us to be. He wants us to take the reign and ride the horse with ease ourselves. There is nothing wrong with a little perseverance or hard work. A little hard work never killed anyone. It's laziness that will kill a society much quicker.

Chapter 28

It was hard for the team to make the decision to leave Dallas the need was still to great. Bro. John got on the phone and started coordinating with other pastors and ministries to come and take the horse by the reign. God had called them to go overseas and he didn't want to keep God waiting another minute. His health had been restored and it was time for the team to get ready for the new mission. The pastors and churches rallied to the call and it was time for them to leave. Actually this experience had opened up their eyes of understanding how to move into the new ministry. Betty told John about what she had been thinking about them liquidating all of their assets to take the funds they had to Africa with them and start the Hand of Help clinic, school and church. He thought that was a great idea and they started the preparations for the trip. They also called all of the pastors and other ministries they had been acquainted with over the years and asked them if they would like to pledge donations for the ministry. God had answered their prayers and they had taken up much more than they could have ever imagined. Now it was time to get in touch with some of the pastors and ministries affiliated with the ministry in Africa to get things started. They had enough workers to begin with but they would need as many local pastors and ministers as had time to help them get started. God was always faithful to complete the visions that he had in mind.

Bro. John spoke with the whole team about the new ministry and they all wanted to stay on board. Many of them did the same who had the means and also donated what they could for the ministries success. It was now time for them to leave America and go into all the world as Jesus admonished in His word to the church. The team was about to fulfill what Jesus had said to His disciples "go ye therefore into all the nations baptizing them in the name of the Father, and the Son and the Holy Spirit." This is a direct commandment from God to go into all of the nations of the world. The church from its birth has been instrumental in spreading the gospel into the world but of recent because throughout time many missionaries have been martyred for the sake of the Christ many have slacked off from going into the nations. The world has become so evil and many nations who are not predominantly Christian will not allow the Christians to come in and evangelize the people. Many have had to use other means like benevolence ministries to get into these countries. They bring in teams of doctors and nurses and they do medical missions. Many of these same nations are plagued with many diseases and injuries that we can help them with so this is a means to come into the country and then share the gospel with the people. Some nations will let the Christians in to feed the starving people of their nation and then they can share the gospel of Jesus Christ with the people. When the Jewish Christians go into some areas to minister to the Jewish people they use the Feasts of the Lord as a means to come in and tell the people that the Messiah has truly come and that they need not wait any longer for His arrival. So there are many ways by which the nations are being opened up to the gospel. But the fact of the matter is that there are so many Muslim nations that still have a large population of people who have not heard the gospel and it is the heart of God that all people get a witness of the gospel before the end should come.

All means must be used such as television, the internet, satellite television whatever new technology is coming out to get this gospel to the world. Many in Korea, China, Iraq, and Iran are able to receive the gospel from the internet because after all of these years many nations still wants to put a chokehold on the gospel reaching its people. But God has ways and people to get around what these governments are doing to keep the Christians out. It is amazing that the church has still thrived in these countries despite all odds against keeping the gospel out of the country.

It was a long flight to the Sudan from America but the whole team was so excited. When they arrived one of the missionaries was their waiting for them at the airport. The Sudan had been in an uproar for a long time now. Bro. John had not had sufficient enough time to investigate the place that God had sent him too. Perhaps it was best because he would later find that the Sudan was not a place where Christians were liked. The government was in a disarray and the people were fleeing for their very lives. churches and villages were being burned to the ground. Many hundreds of thousands were dead and literally millions were displaced and in refugee camps. The devil was certainly busy in the Sudan. Bro. John could not understand for the life of him why God had sent them their. He was in over his head in the Sudan. He certainly did not have enough money to feed all of those people.

"Welcome to the Sudan Bro. John."

"Thank you so much Bro. Kivebulaya. I thank you for helping the team with this mission. We are sure that God has called us to the Sudan. Why we do not know but here we are?"

"Well Bro. John many of these people here are Christians but there are still so many that have not come to the Lord. The need is great everywhere especially in Africa. It is such a large continent. Perhaps he will send you to other parts of Africa like Bro. Besel. He is very prominent all over Africa. It is a hard place though don't get me wrong. People are not easy to adjust to outsiders especially for the gospel. It's like the devil is fighting hard to maintain his territory in Africa. There must be something special about you that God has sent you here."

"Well I don't know about that. But I do have a burden for the lost souls of the world. There's certainly a need here in the Sudan. With all of the problems here they need a lot of prayer. Only God can change this horrible situation around. Whatever He wants us to do we will do it. It's going to take a lot of time but we have lots of that. God has something special he wants to be done here in the Sudan. How's about we work hard for God and make Him happy."

"Sounds like a good thing to do. Why don't we get you all situated and then we can take some tours of the place and see where you might want to set up."

"That sounds wonderful."

The situation was one that Bro. John could not fathom. He had been on the gospel field for a long time but he had never experienced anything like this before. There were people everywhere living in conditions that was worse than anything the United States ever had. There were women, men and children as far as the eyes could see. Why did God send them there? He certainly did not have the means in and of himself to combat this situation. It reminded him of what Moses must have felt like leading the children of Israel out of Egypt. It is said that there were literally 3 million people. They all had to cross the Red Sea, go through the wilderness and then into the promised land. Moses had no money, no food and no Walmart to sustain that amount of people. God had provided provisions for them and He would have to do it now. But this was different many of the women had been raped and treated so badly by the armed military that ravaged the land. They were in such dire need of mental, spiritual and physical help. Most of the team were men and they only had two other women besides Sis. Betty. They could spend a life time trying to heal the brokenness of these women. The children were also traumatized as they saw their fathers get killed and maimed to the point where many of them had lost hands, arms and legs from the war. This was the worst case of genocide that Bro. John had ever heard about in these recent years. How could one person do something so horrendous to another person? These were poor people they didn't have anything. What could they possibly get from hurting them? Well Bro. John knew one thing that this war was not about land, farms, churches or money. There was something greater going on here and he had to turn to the Lord to tell him how to combat this kind of evil.

Chapter 29

THERE HAD TO BE SOMETHING going on in this nation that the devil was waring so hard against these people. It was not just about money which you can see that on the surface but the climate in the whole world showed that the devil was waring like never before to kill these people. Many of the African nations were that way and it was not about black people against white people. Many make that mistake. The war is about Lucifer and the Most High God. From the beginnings of time Lucifer wanted to take over the throne of God. Of course he could not achieve this. He was kicked out of heaven by God to the earth. The bible says that he took one third of the angels with him. These are the dark forces that are waring against God to destroy everything that God made. We might think that it would have been so easy if God had just destroyed Lucifer and the other angels that came against the heavenly kingdom but God chose not to do this at that particular time. To understand why He did not is to get into the heart and mind of God. Only He alone knows why He makes the choices that He does. But one can only say that He and He alone is sovereign over all that He has made. But in any case these are the factions that man is fighting against here on the earth. The devil only has a short period of time because although God allowed them to still exist on the earth He does have a set time that they will be bound and thrown into hell. But in the mean time it is the life purpose of Lucifer to destroy the earth. If the people of all nations band together and served God with all of their heart, soul, mind and strength the plans of Lucifer could be cancelled out and the Kingdom of God would be in force one hundred percent. But what Lucifer does is that he keeps people at odds with one another all the time. The world has never seen such hatred amongst people of varying nations. The Muslim radicals of the world hate the free world all together. It is their life goal to make every nation of the world Muslim by any means necessary. They don't realize that Lucifer is using them. The men, women and children are being taught to hate all people who do not follow the ways of their nation. Of course not all Muslim people think the same way but this is a problem in the world today. This is a very big problem for the United States and Europe. The word from the prophets is that there will be a war between the United States and Iran before the end of the Obama administration. Many who do not listen to the Christian prophets can see this from the way things are escalating in the war in Iraq. This war was supposed to have happened because Saddam Hussein was said to have had weapons of mass destruction and had his hands in the World Trade Center bombing. Whether this was true or not does not deal with the war of Lucifer on the world against God. This is the real problem that mankind has to deal with and they don't even know it is a real problem.

The people of Israel seem to have every Muslim nation in the world trying to control them and put them out of Israel again. The Bible is very clear that this land was given to the descendants of Abraham and that it is a covenant forever. The problem with them is that Abraham had two sons Isaac and Ishmael. The children of Isaac were given the land and the children of Ishmael are fighting against their brothers for the land that was not promised to them. This problem will only be resolved when the Messiah returns at the battle of Armageddon. Then Jesus will set up His Kingdom and all of these problems will be resolved. The reason for all of this is that Lucifer hates the nation of Israel because the Messiah, Jesus came through that lineage of Abraham. His desire is to wipe the Nation of Israel off of the planet which he cannot accomplish so he will do everything he can to make their lives miserable. He used Adolf Hitler to accomplish this goal. Many say why did God allow this to happen? Well according to history if we would take the time to look at it God has always informed many nations of people what would come against them. The people were warned about Hitler and what he was about to do but many would not heed the warnings. Many Jews did get out before the bombs were dropped and the people put into camps but many did not listen to the warnings. God cannot be put responsible when he warned them what was to happen. First we must understand that God has from the beginning of creation made mankind free moral agents. He did not just create the world and then just sit back and watch while we destroyed it but He is there to help us. The world was created for man and man was created to take care of the earth. The problem is that man has done a terrible job taking care of the world and now wants to point the finger at God because of the mess that has been created. That's usually how it goes make a mess and then blame someone else for the repercussions. Everyone wants to be in charge but nobody knows what they're doing. Lucifer wants to be in charge but he has a mean and evil heart. His heart is so evil that he cannot possibly run the world like the God who is loving who created it. God has the best interest of His creation at heart while Lucifer is nothing but evil and has nothing good at heart. Mankind has both evil and good at heart and so it's the luck of the drawer what they will do.

The Sudan and Lebanon have a problem with displaced people. These camps are a terrible solution to the problem. The United Nations and the church are having a time taking care of the people in these camps. It is not good to put that many people in such a confined area without sufficient water, food and jobs to take care of them all. This is causing problems of mass proportions between the people in the camps as well. Time will only tell what will be the outcome of the whole thing. But one thing we know for sure is that Jesus will soon come to set up His Kingdom here on earth. All the nations of the world will have to bow to Jesus one way or the other and Satan will be bound from operating in the earth.

Chapter 30

WHEN GOD CALLED ABRAHAM TO be the Father of many nations he told him that his descendants would be bound into slavery in Egypt for 400 years. After 400 years in bondage God called a man named Moses to be a light to his people and to lead them out of slavery. God had heard the cries of the people that were being enslaved by Pharaoh in Egypt. Today there have been many people who have been enslaved in one nation or another. The Africans came as slaves to America. God heard the cries of the people and through many men and women who answered that call black men and women are free in America today. The cries of the Palestinian people and the Sudanese people have been heard at the very throne of God and he is calling on his people and the people of the world to have mercy on such ones and let them be free from the bondage of slavery.

Bro. John could not for the life of him understand what God wanted him to do for these people. He didn't have sufficient anything to handle the masses of people. Whenever God gives you a task that is too big you need to stick close to Him and he will unfold what needs to be done little by little. He took the time one afternoon to just pray and seek God. He needed to know why God had sent Him to Africa after all of these years. He had been preaching under that tent for many years and he was comfortable doing it. Maybe that was part of it. He had become comfortable and maybe God wanted to take him from comfort to discomfort to get the pure oil out of him. The oil that was used to give the light from the lamps in the tabernacle came from olives. It was from the crushing of the olives that produced that oil that gave the light. It was time for him to do something different for God and he felt like a fish out of water. During his time with God, the Lord told him about the many missionaries that gave of their lives totally for the service of the Lord. There was a great missionary named Dumitru Duduman who lived all of his life in Romania. He grew up in a Christian home but upon graduation from high school he entered the military. He grew up in a poor area all of his life and entering the military would give him a good job and maybe one day he would have a family and be happy. He served in the Navy and the ships would come in with missionaries bringing bibles in for the people of Romania and Russia. It was his job and the job of his crew to confiscate the bibles and get rid of them. But one day he heard a voice say "Dumitru I have put you here so that you can help your brothers." At first he thought that he was hearing things and he got scared so he ran out of the room. But when he got to the other room he heard the voice even louder. This caused Dumitru great anguish. The voice told him to let the missionary go with the bibles despite the fact that he could lose his job. So this went on for some time and he would listen to the voice and let the missionaries go. In time a mandate came down that all Christians should not be allowed to serve in the military. Dumitru lost his job as a military officer. He was so angry and saddened by this that he went home very angry with his family. He went home and told his mother that he had lost his job because he was a Christian. He wanted to talk with his father who had been at the church at the time. He went to the church very angry expecting to tell his father all that was in his heart. When he entered the sanctuary his father and the rest of the congregation looked up to see him entering the sanctuary. Surprised he just sat down in the back while they finished the sermon. As his father preached he began to cry and so he asked his father "why am I crying." His father replied "we have been praying that you would return home." Despite Dumitru's anger he did not realize that God was working in his life all along and that He had a purpose for his life from the very beginning. From that day forward Dumitru rededicated his life to the Lord and began serving Him as he had wanted for so long.

Dumitru knew that he had to get back on the docks so that he could help the missionaries get the bibles into the country. It was pertinent that the word of God get into the hands of the people. This is the way that the captives get set free. The Romanian people were a praying people and God heard their cries for the word to get into their country and into neighboring Russia. This was no easy task now that Dumitru was no longer in a position to help them. He thought that he would go back down to the docks and ask for any job that he could get. He humbled himself and went back to his old boss to ask for any job that he would give him. He gave him a job as a cook for the officers that he had once been a part of. This was very hard for Dumitru but he was able to continue helping to get the bibles into the county and that was all that mattered.

As the years went on Dumitru and many of the other Christians that were helping him were countless numbers of times thrown into prison. There families were targeted all the time and they were being watched every day by the police. But this did not stop Dumitru. He saw the power of God working in his life when many times the police would break into their homes looking for the bibles and would not see them although they were sitting in plane sight. The Lord had put blinders on the eyes of the oppressors so that the Kingdom of God would prevail.

Dumitru would spend a lot of time in jail and be beaten much like the Apostle Paul but he still stood strong. One time the police came to his home and took him to jail and beat him so mercilessly that he almost died. The Angel Gabriel would come to him and minister to him so that he could go on. This is the kind of Christian that God wants to make of all of his people. One's that are strong and will fight the fine fight of the faith no matter what the cost. Dumitru would later be called after many years of this to America to speak to the churches of America that the Day of the Lord Is Come. He was told of God to tell the people of God that judgment was coming to America and they needed to repent. Dumitru did all that God asked of him until the day that he went home to be with the Lord.

Bro. John had never heard a testimony quite like Dumitru. He realized that all that he had done for the Lord was as filthy rags and that he thought he had really served God with everything he had but that there were voices crying in the wilderness and God had to call him so that he could hear them. There are people in the world who are hungering for God and the Christians in America many of them do not hear them. They do not know of the countless numbers of missionaries whose blood cries as well from the ground in many countries around the world who gave of their lives wholeheartedly for the sake of the Gospel of Jesus Christ.

Bro. John knew now what he was called to do. He knew that he had to pray with all of his might for these people and do everything he could to keep the Gospel alive in that country despite all that was working against it. He too would shed his blood for Christ if it came to that. This was the ultimate sacrifice that a man should give his life for another.

Samuel knew all to well that his father had given his life for another during the World Trade Center bombing. He felt in his heart that he was exactly where God wanted him to be. To see the looks of desperation on the people's faces in the camp in Sudan. He just wanted to lift them all out of the despair that they were in. He was not God but he was a worker of the Kingdom and he destined that he would give his life for these people.

Day in and day out Samuel, Bro. John and the rest of the team worked long hours ministering to the sick, feeding the hungry and spreading the Gospel of Hope to the downtrodden. These people were broken and crying out for help. They knew that it would be a long task and that it would not change over night. But there hearts were hopeful that the day would come when the United Nations and other nations would rise up and take a stand against the type of atrocious conditions these people were living under.

Each day Bro. John had to think of new ways to get more supplies into the country and around the militia who many times would steal some of the supplies that they had coming. Bro. John

spent a lot of time in prayer because he needed the protection of
the angels to assist them in just getting the supplies into the camp
without them being stolen. The people were crying daily about what
they needed. The mothers especially were in distress over how to take
care of their children. It was a never ending situation.

Chapter 31

BRO. JOHN HAD NOT SEEN so many people in such a destitute situation. He felt so small in comparison to the level of madness looming all around him. Men, women and children had makeshift dwellings made out of whatever they could find. Some of the ministries had donated tents and the people lived in the tents. It was almost like a military camp. Bro. John had served in Vietnam and that was what it reminded him of. There were no bathrooms so you could smell the stench of human feces in the air. The people didn't have sufficient water so it was hard to stand too close to anyone because they had not washed in weeks many of them. The water had to be used sparingly for drinking and cooking purposes. Bro. John thought how did Moses make it with all of those people. The answer was he could only make it with the help of the Lord. God had provided manna from heaven and water from a rock. If He could do it then, He could do it now. Ministry after ministry was sending food and medical supplies. It seemed like it was not enough but they were happy for what came in. God knew all about their needs, He said so in his word and He was going to provide. God was providing, the ministries were helping, the prayer warriors were praying but the powers that be had to make some governmental changes so that the war could stop and great change could be made over night. The people were willing to work. They were not just looking for a hand out. But as long as the war ensued they could not go back to a normal life.

Bro. John talked with family after family who had a reasonable home and farm and were getting along when the militia came in and slaughtered just about everyone in the village except those who escaped. Houses, churches and business were burned down and men, women and children killed. One little girl had to crawl under the dead bodies and play dead in order to survive. She made it to the camp barely alive when Bro. John and his crew arrived. The stories were so horrendous it was amazing that many of the people were alive. Many of the men had legs cut off and arms cut off. For what purpose would one human being do this to another? They wanted to maime them so that they could not fight. These men watched in horror while their wives and young daughters were raped mercilessly. The scars will never heal without the help of the Lord for what has been done to these families. But the Lord has said that vengeance is mine and He will repay for what has been done to these people.

Every morning before Sis Betty and the other missionary women started their days busying doing one thing or another they would gather as many of the women who could come to an area that was designated as the healing room. They would come there and pray and wail before God for the people of their nation. Prayer is the way to change things. God moves the hearts of man to work according to His purposes. This was the way they started off each day. It was amazing that in the midst of such a terrible situation that the women could come together and kneel before the Lord and receive grace sufficient for the day's activities. The younger women would cleave unto the older women for support. The older women had known much sorrow but had somehow learned how to be strong in the midst of the stress of staying alive moment to moment. These were the real warriors of the faith. These women would never know what it was like to have a job where they had health benefits, 401K plans, vacation days and an honest wage for a days work. They didn't have the luxury of having their nails done and their hair fixed at the hair parlor. They didn't have fancy homes with microwave ovens, televisions and nice cars. They suffered in a way that no one should.

But yet when they came before the throne of God they reverenced God in a way that Sis. Betty had not ever seen. They cried out not just with tears of anguish but with tears of love because they knew that their Lord had suffered in a way that they had not. They knew that His blood was shed for their sins and that He was coming back for them. They knew that it was man that had forsaken them and not He. They knew that He had gone to prepare a place for them and if they did not make it in this life that when they closed their eyes they would walk on streets of gold with Him. They were tears of sorrow but yet tears of joy that no man could understand but them.

The rest of the day was filled with all kinds of activities. Sis Betty had started a counseling session held a few days a week for the women who had lost husbands. The grief in the camp was like a thick blanket that had to be taken off of these women in order for them to survive. One thing that had to happen was that they had something to do every day like a job that kept them busy and working for others instead of just thinking about themselves. She told them the story about Mother Theresa and how one little woman made the difference in the lives of many of the people of India. She had to think about Mother Theresa herself. God had led her to this story to give her courage. Mother Theresa was a nun but when she joined the many other missionaries in India she saw the harsh conditions many of the people lived in. Moved by the Holy Spirit she took some classes in nursing and stopped teaching to care for the sick people of Calcutta. She didn't have any money, much education or even the help of her peers but the love that she had in her heart was so strong that she couldn't help but reach out to them. Despite all odds she was able to get help little by little from shop owners and other people to get food, and other supplies to help the people. Mother Theresa is known as one of the most important women in our time. It was the work of the Holy Spirit in that one woman that made the difference for many hundreds of thousands of people in India. She told them that they too could rise up like women like Harriet Tubman and Sojourner Truth who were slave women who helped hundreds of other slaves go free. It was due to the help of God that these women remained strong and accomplished what they did. They must refuse to be victims and become victorious in Christ Jesus from whence comes their help.

The numbers in the camp increased daily but then many succumbed to sickness and died also. There was not one day since they arrived at the camp that someone did not pass away. The harsh conditions were just too much for some of the older ones and the young children to withstand. They needed a hospital the size of the Mayo clinic to keep up with the sickness and disease that was spreading rampant in the camp. But day after day the missionaries continued to work diligently to help the people any way they could. What they needed were schools for the children, several hospitals to take care of the sick, churches so the people could worship and jobs for the men to take care of their families. This all took lots of money and ingenuity. How could this be accomplished when the militia would probably just come and tear everything down again?

Samuel fought back the tears as he felt like most of the others that they were in over their heads. They could not leave but the famine and the pestilences that were literally killing the people was too hard to bear. Samuel remembered when he was just a small boy dying from cancer and how Jesus came and healed him. He started to cry out to God and ask Him would he give him healing power to help some of the people. He knew that it would be a great testimony to the people to see the hand of God at work in the midst of their situation. Samuel and the others too needed to see a move from God to lift their spirits. They so wanted to go on but after weeks of staring death in the face it has a way of robbing you of any sense of accomplishment. The children were bored and scared. The women were sorrowful and worried. The men felt destitute and powerless. For weeks there had been no rain and Bro. John and some of the men of the camp were desperately trying to farm so that they could have another means of feeding the people. One evening as they prayed and fasted for rain to come it finally came and the whole camp was in an uproar. Water had finally fallen from heaven and they knew that God had answered their prayers. Some times it's just the little things. People were running around in the rain like little children.

The crops began to grow and there was joy for a little while that things might just be getting better.

Samuel wanted more. He was getting angrier by the moment. His countenance had changed and he began to withdraw. Little John was starting to worry about him and he too started to pray for something more than the rain. They really needed it but the overall atmosphere in the camp was just not good. Samuel and Little John had the task of teaching school on a daily basis for the young men and the young women. This was very difficult without paper, pens and books. They had only their bibles which was good but they so wanted more for the children. Samuel wrote to many of the ministries that would give out free books but for the amount of students they had they could only get a few books in to teach them with. It was however the most rewarding thing that Samuel had ever done with his life. He wanted that someday these young people could rise up and come through this like the children who were born in the wilderness. They were the ones that ended up going into the promised land. This was the Joshua and Caleb generation and he was honored to be a part of the process. If they could make it through this they could make it through anything. These would be the warriors God would send out throughout the earth to teach others how to come through adversity. One day as Samuel was teaching a lesson on forgiveness a young girl stood up to address the class. Little Sarah said that she could not forgive the men that killed her parents and raped her and her mother. She said that she could never pray for them and that Jesus could not possibly love the people who would do such a thing. Samuel stood dumbfounded, he realized that so many of them had gone through something so terrible that it would take a long time for them to be able to forgive the pain went so deep. So he told little Sarah that God understood her pain and that she didn't have to worry about it at the moment. Then another little boy stood up and said "but the bible has said that we must forgive or else we cannot ask God to forgive us for the sins that we have committed." He said "Sarah do you remember that man that you shot and killed after he killed your father. You did the same thing to him that he did to your family. Which one of you is worse him or you?" She looked at him and she said "he is the one who started the whole thing. I would not have killed him if he had not killed first." But he said it doesn't matter. You have also to come before God and ask for forgiveness because you have also killed a man."

Samuel just allowed the conversation to go on because he knew that Sarah would get the understanding of what her brother was saying. She then said "Samuel I must ask God to forgive me for killing this man. He was wrong but I was wrong also. Do you think that God will forgive me?"

Without thinking Samuel ran over to Sarah and he embraced her tightly. They both began to cry uncontrollably and Samuel and the rest of the class said a prayer for the family members who had died and also for the militia men who died also. This brought a lot of healing to the class that day. Samuel felt that the Holy Spirit had been working in the class that day and it somehow lifted his spirit that he was doing a most precious work with these young people.

Before the class was over that day there was a sound that sounded like gunfire. All of the children started running for cover. Samuel tried to maintain order but that just was not going to happen. Oh he was so angry the children were starting to break through the fear and now this. He could see armed men in tanks and trucks riding and shooting. They were not shooting the people but just shooting into the air. Samuel just crouched down and started to pray that God would send his mighty angels into the camp to take care of these men. He felt that they had no right to live the way they were treating these people. They were like wolves coming in to kill and steal the sheep. That's just what the Lord said of Lucifer. He comes to rob, steal and destroy. Samuel had to get his thoughts together. He really wanted to pray that God would kill everyone of those men but he had to remember what he was just teaching the children about forgiveness. He prayed that God would forgive him for his evil thoughts against these men and he started to pray for their deliverance. Perhaps one day some of these men will hear the gospel and mend their ways. They will be a testimony of the grace of God for anyone to repent before the end comes. His sin was no different from their sin it was just manifest in a different form. He might not have killed or raped someone but if the record were told he had sin in his life as well.

Samuel hoped that the children would return after things had calmed down but it was not likely this happened before and it was a few days before they felt safe to come and have school again. It was like two steps forward and one giant step backwards at times. But it was the two steps forward that made all the difference in the world. He knew that he was doing a good thing and he saw the results in the children's overall attitude about life. The word of God gave them hope that soon the Lord would be coming back to set up His Kingdom and they would no longer be hungry and have no place to live. They knew that God loved them and that it was the evil men of the world and the devil that brought this upon them. They knew that the end was near for all the people in the world who were suffering like them.

Chapter 32

ONE MORNING AS BRO. JOHN was walking through the camp in the wee hours of the morning he started to cry out to God that he could get some help. He needed animals to help with the plowing and more supplies for the clinic, the school and the church. One of the missionaries said to him that he might have a breakthrough coming and that they should just pray.

Bro. John wasn't sure what the breakthrough was but knew that they needed one soon. The supplies were dwindling and he had all but exhausted all of his pastor friends. They were helping all that they could. The help was a drop in the bucket compared to the need. That afternoon came a plane which held a young man and his wife that had started a ministry called Samaritans Purse. They had both made quite a substantial amount of money in the business world. From what he heard they had more money than Donald Trump and were very eager to help them with the project in the Sudan. They had heard a lot on the news about what was going on and wanted to help. The bible says "give and it shall be given back to you good measure, pressed down, shaken together and running over shall men give into your bossom." Bro. John and the team had given all that they had in the world to this project for God and He was not slack concerning his promises. This was the answer to much needed prayer. The Blossoms were not quite 45 years old but they had done quite well for themselves. They had both grew up in a Christian home but soon lost their way to the life of money, fame and fortune. But one day Joseph and Evelyn realized that they had made so much money there was nothing left for them to accomplish. The businesses were going well, the children were blessed and then God started to speak to Joseph. He told him that He had called him to a much greater purpose and that it was time that he started to obey the word of the Lord or else He would lose everything. Joseph knew that God had called him into the ministry when he was a young boy. He used to have dreams of far off countries and he could see himself flying in planes bringing food to the people and he saw buildings and schools and churches and God told him that he would build these places up for him. When he was young of course this was hard for him to fathom because he was just a young man not even out of school yet. But he had great aspirations to attend university and be an accomplished entrepreneur. He met Evelyn while in college. It was love at first sight. She was attending a little church while at school and invited him to attend with her. She promised herself that she would not date anyone that was not attending church. She liked Joseph he was tall, handsome and had great promise. But he was not attending church and he was hanging out with the wrong crowd according to her. She felt that if he would at least attend church with her she would see where it would go. Joseph really liked Evelyn and hoped that one day she would be his bride so he stuck with church. To his surprise he really liked the pastor there and he would soon give his life to the Lord. He and Evelyn both finished business school and went into management out of college. Joseph went into the hotel business and realized that there was a lot of money to be made in the business. He started from low level management and after two years he was managing a full service hotel. He wanted of course to own his own hotel but he didn't have the collateral. He was blessed of the Lord to purchase the hotel from the present owner. He had made a lot of money off of that hotel and was ready to let it go. He had many others beside that one. So Joseph was able to purchase his first hotel and the rest was history. Now at 45 years of age he now owned almost 150 hotels across the world. Business was never better.

He had made his pie in the sky and now it was time for him to do what God had given him the blessing to accomplish. He was worth over a billion dollars at the present time and the sky was the limit.

Bro. John was introduced to them by Bro. Johnson. He had been a missionary in Africa for several years before Bro. John and his group got there. He was the sweetest person that Bro. John had met in a long time and dedicated to the cause of Christ Jesus. He had actually gone to church at one time with Joseph and Evelyn. His daughter and son worked for them when they were home on summer break from school. He knew a lot about them and never ever asked them for anything. But the Lord told him to call Joseph and Evelyn that they would be glad to help and it was no time before they boarded their private jet to come and see what God was doing in the Sudan.

"My God this place is huge and look at all the people. They look so destitute. It makes me feel bad to have so much. I cannot imagine what its like to not have food for my wife and children."

"Joseph this is Bro. John. He and his wife and his team have come here to help us."

"It's a pleasure to meet you Bro. John. You and Bro. Johnson are the true body of Christ. My wife and I are here to find out what you need. God has been speaking to my heart that He has blessed me that I might be a blessing to others. He has given me more than Evelyn and I could possibly spend in a lifetime. It's time that we put this money to use for these people and other people around the world. And I have other friends too that can join in this great battle against homelessness and poverty."

"Many thanks to you Joseph and you Evelyn. I have got to get my wife and the rest of the team. These people have been working so hard and they are getting tired because we just don't have the funds to take care of the many needs these people have. We need a full scale hospital to meet the needs of the sick. We would love to start building some real homes for the people. We just about need everything Joseph. Whatever you can do we would be grateful. Please let us show you around. When you see the deplorable conditions these people are living in your heart will ache. I can't sleep most nights knowing that I was living in the United States with a roof over my head, food on the table and these people are literally starving to death. Little children are dying for no reason at all. We have got to open our hearts to these people. This is the commandment of God to take care of the widows and orphans of the world."

"My brother you are right about that. My wife and I have been in this ministry for about 5 years now and have seen the most horrendous cases of malnutrition and poverty that we could have ever imagined. And this is not just outside of the United States but inside the United States as well. The tornadoes and hurricanes are doing great damage to many areas of the United States and according to the Bible this is only the beginnings of sorrows. God has showed me many things that I am afraid to even speak about. It saddens me that many of the churches are still having business as usual church and are not listening to what the Spirit of the Lord is saying to the church. If we would listen to the Lord many lives could be saved. People are taking these last days as a time of folly. But the wrath of God is nothing to play with trust me."

"Bro. Joseph you are a God send. I too have heard many things from the Lord and you are right the Day of the Lord is Come. But this is a time to wake up the people of the world that the Kingdom of God is at hand. The whole world is about to go through a major shift and they need to be informed so that they can get as ready as they possibly can. It's a time for prayer and a time to get our lives right with God."

"Your right Bro. John. I'm so glad that God sent me a wife filled with the Holy Spirit. If it were not for her I would not be where I am today. All I was worried about was making money and having a good time. We have made lots of money and we have had a good life but it is nothing without the Lord. Many during these last days are going to look to their money and fame and find out that it has no worth when up against God. Our real treasure is in Him."

"Please come let's take a walk around the camp and let us introduce you to the rest of the team."

"That sounds fine. Please tell me what you have in mind. You know the needs of these people more than we do. Although I might say that this is not uncommon to us. We have seen many camps such as this around the world and the needs are basically the same. We can tell you what we have accomplished and if that sounds good to you then we can get to work right away."

Bro. John and Bro. Joseph came together with the other members of the team to plan a strategy and have a time of prayer. Each team member prayed and expressed their concerns for the particular area that they were ministering in. Samuel wanted more for the school, Bro. John wanted more for the men to have work and to produce a larger food supply so that they would not have to always look for outside help. Bro. Johnson wanted better housing and places for the people to worship. The women were concerned about the psychological trauma that the women and children had suffered and wondered what more could be done in the healing process for them. It was a large undertaking but this is what God called them there to handle.

Bro. Joseph told them what they had been doing in other parts of the world in situations just like this that had been working for the short term to deal with the displacement of such a large number of people. It was a set up just like the military would do when they went in to a country for their soldiers. Everything was in a tent. The purpose of this was because if and when things got better the people would want to return home. There was no need in taking good money and constructing buildings so they would use the tent system so that they could just tear them down for useage again elsewhere. These were the best tents in the world. They could construct tents for sleeping, eating, bathing and just about anything that they needed. This idea didn't start with the military but it started with God in the wilderness. The Nation of Israel wondered in the wilderness for forty years. They lived and worshiped in tents. If it worked for God it would work now. They didn't need laborers because they had all the laborers they needed right there. The people would do the work of setting the tents up, cooking the food for the others and policing the area against the militia. They would however need some outsiders to train nurses for the hospital and other areas of the hospital. They would also need to train some of the men to guard the perimeter this was essential for the safety of the women and children. They would hire some ex military personnel to come in and do the training and work along with the men as well. Otherwise the people would do the jobs themselves.

Bro. Joseph and his wife came in for a few days and would return home to get the process rolling. They would send as much food as they could to get things started and get the necessary work orders for the tents and other necessary equipment right away. They had done this many times before so they knew exactly what the missionaries needed. When it was time for them to depart Bro. John and Bro. Johnson felt like now they were going to be able to better take care of the needs of the people. They were praising and thanking God for providing for the needs they had been praying for.

They wished Bro. Joseph and Sis. Evelyn a safe flight home. They would be hearing from them in just a few weeks. It would take time to get the supplies boarded on planes and to the sight as well as the tents. They would send some people to oversee erecting the tents and putting everything in place. There was customs and other arrangements that had to be made to get things rolling. It was amazing how difficult these things could be so Bro. Joseph told them to pray that all would go well.

Chapter 33

THOSE THINGS THAT SEEMED EASY most often times were not easy at all. Bro. Joseph had to call several senators and congressman to get the necessary paperwork he needed in order to get the food and other supplies into the country. He had gone through this several times before so he knew the red tape that was involved. The leader of the country of course needed to know what would be brought in and how much and there were fees that had to be paid of course. Bro. Joseph didn't care about negotiating prices he just wanted to get the supplies to the people so they could live just a little bit better. It would take a lot of time to get the tents up and get everything running. Meanwhile the people were starving and desperate. Bro. Joseph spent many hours in prayer during this time. It was a matter of God opening doors so that things could run smoothly. He realized that all things were done in God.

It seemed like months before Bro. John and Bro. Johnson heard from Bro. Joseph again. It seemed like the opposition was just great in connection to bringing the supplies into the country. Bro. Joseph had never had so much opposition. It seemed as though the devil was just going to fight them tooth and nail on this one. He had paid the necessary fees and had talked with all the right people and it just seemed as if it was going to take forever before he got the necessary paperwork to start the ball rolling. He had already made all the contacts and the materials were ready to be shipped but he could not do anything without clearance from customs officers and government officials. He just said to keep on praying.

Finally after about 8 weeks of waiting and praying Bro. Joseph finally got the necessary paperwork for the project. This was a major project that required not only paperwork to bring in supplies but also paperwork for digging wells for the water source, permission for electrical wiring, permission to bring in bibles and other religious material and the food must be inspected. It was amazing how difficult it was to help the people they didn't care much about.

The planes were all loaded and ready to get underway. It took of course several hours to make the trip and Bro. John and his wife would be coming out later to make sure that everything was going okay. When the planes touched down of course there was major trouble and the pilots and the workers were being detained and they didn't know why. They had all the paperwork they were supposed to have and it was a fiasco. Bro. Grisco had been working for Bro. Joseph for many years and had done this many times before. He had had trouble at times but always knew how to get around it. But this time it seemed like they would never get the problems resolved so that they could unload and get the supplies to the camps. The officials would not talk to them in English and that made things even more difficult. They were surrounded by tanks and gunmen and they didn't know whether they would get out alive.

The commander came over to one of the pilots and struck him on the face. He hit him so hard that he fell to the grown. His face was burning from the open wound that was now gushing with blood. He had knocked out some of his teeth and broken his nose. Shawn didn't know what quite hit him and he certainly did not know what to do next. The commander bent down and started shouting at him but Shawn didn't know the language so he could not respond. He motioned for one of the other soldiers to come and interpret for him.

"What are you doing here?"

Shawn looked up still stunned by the blow to tell him that they had received clearance to bring in food and medicine for the people.

"What clearance? We have not received the word for this clearance. Let me see the paperwork."

Shawn motioned to Mark one of the missionaries on board to get the paperwork and to give it to the commander. He looked at the paperwork for quite a while.

"I don't know about this paperwork we will have to detain you until we have this all sorted out."

Shawn was worried that they just wanted to steal the plane and its content and kill them all. No one would ever know what happened to them. He quickly thought about what he said to his wife the last time he saw her. He longed to be with his children again. He knew that one day one of these missions would land him in a place like this but he continued for the sake of Christ. These people were desperate and he knew that his life was being placed in jeopardy for their sake. But this was what the love of Christ was all about giving of one's life for the sake of another.

They were all ordered off of the plane and marched to a camp where they would be detained. Shawn had no way of getting in touch with the brothers in the camp or Bro. Joseph to tell them what was happening. They were supposed to get in touch with him as soon as they made contact with the missionaries in the camp. He would be worried and hopefully would try to track them down.

The place where they were being detained was like a dungeon. It was just a large room with no windows and just a door. They didn't know whether they would feed them, give them water or what they would do next. It seemed like hours before someone came in to talk with them again. In fact it wasn't until the next day that someone came in to say anything. One of the soldiers came in to bring them some bread, meat and water. They were so happy, they had not eaten for hours. This was a gesture of peace to a certain degree. The soldier assured them that they would not be harmed. This has happened before and they were just following orders. Shawn felt a bit better but wanted to retrieve the plane and its contents and get on with the mission. He decided that since this young man was being peaceful that he would ask him that he could get in contact with his people at home so that they would know that they were okay. He didn't know how that would go but he would try anyway.

"Sir I don't mean any harm but is there a way that we can phone home to tell our boss that we are okay and that we are having a problem with the paperwork?"

"I'm sorry but this could cost me my life. These people are nothing to play around with. I am a Christian just like you and God has placed me with these people so that I can help in situations just like this one. Please just sit tight and God will work this thing all out. Just pray and that is the best thing that you can do right now."

This was the best news that Shawn and the rest of the people could have heard. A man of God that God had working in the field to help in situations just like this one. He wondered how many lives this one man had saved working behind the scenes. He gave them some very good advice and they would do just that. If they prayed God would answer. He knew that this was going to happen. But he certainly wanted the mission to be accomplished so all would be well. They had a wall to get around and they would pray that this wall would come down. When the young soldier left Shawn thought about Paul and Silas and how when they were in jail they prayed and praised God and God caused an earthquake to take place and the chains were broken off and they were able to minister to the prison guard and be set free. How often we find ourselves in trouble and thinking in the flesh instead of thinking in the spirit. God would bring them out of this thing if they would have faith in Him to do what He has promised.

Shawn talked with the rest of the team and told them that they don't know how long they will be in this situation so they had better think wisely and pray so that God would bring them out and they would have an even greater testimony than they had ever had before. Each morning when they woke up someone would start off the prayer and they would sing and praise God. They would each take turns preaching a sermon that came from the very depths of their souls and it would build up the group tremendously. They would do the same thing after each time that wonderful soldier came to bring them meat, bread and water. It was like God was feeding them like He did for Elijah by the brook. They only hope that it would not dry up and that it would stay constant. They didn't want to grow weak. No one came but that one soldier to tell them anything. He didn't say much but left the food and gave them encouragement.

Each day was difficult. They were only allowed a few minutes out of the room to make use of the bathroom and to stretch for a few minutes. Darryl the eldest of the group had served in Vietnam and was a great source of help to the others. He told them stories about how difficult it was serving in Vietnam and how the Christian soldiers fought to keep their standards of living in Christ Jesus in tact. There was a lot of drinking, smoking and drug abuse in Vietnam. They used it to get them by the fear of death steering them in the face every day. These were just young boys that were sent into the greatest battle that American soldiers had ever seen. The only thing that they had was their word and God. It was amazing how difficult it was not having the written word right at your finger tips. The group would every day recite whatever word they had in themselves. It was truly a great test to see whether they had done their homework. Many Christians don't take the time to read the word daily. If a situation arose where they needed that word they would not have any word deep down to rely upon. It taught them that when they got out of this situation that they would spend more time reading the word and praying to the Lord because when the chips get down that is what will keep the saints of God.

One day when the group had a chance to get outside they noticed that there was a plane that was flying overhead. Darryl had noticed it before but didn't pay much attention to it and thought that maybe Bro. Joseph had a search party out looking for them so they had to devise a way that they could maybe leave some clue that this was where they were. His military training gave him a sensitivity to things that the others didn't think about. He noticed little things that they were oblivious too. There wasn't much time when they weren't alone and they didn't have any kind of materials to build a signal for the plane. They would have to think.

The most important thing was to pray and not give up. The soldier continued to bring the food every day. They were able to get outside but not to get in touch with anyone. They wondered what Bro. Joseph was thinking and doing by now.

Bro. Joseph knew that something was wrong when Shawn and the crew did not get in touch with them. They started calling government officials, hospitals and anyone that might have seen the plane or got a distress signal from them. There was nothing. It was as if they had dropped off the face of the planet. He knew this was not so. The plane was in good condition, and the pilot had been flying for years. There was no way that they had just vanished. He finally got in touch with a Senator friend of his who knew people in very high places. They were bad people but sometimes they had to use these methods to get the job done. This friend told him that the plane had been intercepted by some militant rebels and that they wanted money to release it. Bro. Joseph was furious that his people were being detained but he knew that anger was not going to solve the problem. He wanted to go with this person to make the payment to ensure that the people would be freed.

All of the arrangements were made and the Senator, his contacts and Bro. Joseph boarded a plane to get his crew and the missionaries released from imprisonment. It took several hours to reach their destination and then more red tape that went on for quite a few days but Bro. Joseph was praying the whole way. He wondered whether they were being tortured, were they eating, how were they doing? He fought back the tears day and night for weeks now. His brother Shawn was the lead pilot and he would not forgive himself if something had happened to him or any of the other missionaries. He knew that one day this might happen but God had been good to them up until this point. He knew that God would never fail them now.

Finally they were taken to the plane and he was able to see that everything was in tact. The militant commander took the payment and said that the next day they would be shown where the group was being held.

The days went into a week and the week went into another week. They wanted to get worried but decided that this was not the thing to do. If they started to lose faith all would be lost for the group to maintain the strength they needed to go on. Finally one day came that another soldier came to tell them they had gotten everything taken care of and that the next day they would be released to go on to the camp. The whole group just started jumping up and down they were so happy that this was finally coming to and end. God had been faithful to them and they kept strong because of the simple words of one soldier to keep the faith and to pray.

The next morning they were surprised when the door opened and Bro. Joseph and the Senator was standing there waiting to greet them. Shawn ran to his brother and hugged him like they had never hugged before. He hugged him, kissed him and told him how much he loved him and that he would never take life for granted ever again. He knew that God was with them but he didn't know whether this was going to be the last mission that they would go on.

The whole group was just glad that part of the ordeal was over and they could now get the supplies to the people who needed it.

Chapter 34

THE NEXT MORNING CAME AND the team was up and ready to go. Bro. Joseph had the plane taken to a safe location and took the whole team to a nice hotel where they could wash and have a good meal and a good nights sleep. It had been a harrowing ordeal sleeping on the concrete floor for the past few weeks. Shawn told Joseph about the soldier who came to bring them food every day and encouragement in the Lord. He couldn't believe that one of those guys could possibly be a Christian but he was sure glad that God had someone watching out for them.

The night before they would leave God gave Bro. Joseph a vision of seven angels. He asked God what did it mean? God told him that there would again be an attack against the team but that they should not fear because the holy angels of God would be there to protect them. He was sure glad that God had warned him because he had just about had it with the militia. They were nothing but greedy thugs that took advantage of people by the use of fear and guns. This was not the way that God taught his people to be but these people presented a problem for the missionaries around the world. But God had a few tricks up his sleeves too that they didn't know about. The angels were out there working tirelessly with the saints of God to help them accomplish the will of the Father to set the captives free in the world as well.

The whole group boarded the plane ready to get to the camp and see where they would start setting up the tents. Bro. Joseph had not told them about the dream that he had it would only worry them. He would tell them when the time was right. All he knew was that God told them not to fear and he would not fear. It was amazing how close they actually were to their destination. It took just a matter of hours before Shawn could see the camp in sight. He began to get excited. This was the moment they all were waiting for. The missionaries and the people were always so happy to see the plane land and see the supplies coming off of the plane. There was much work to be done so it kept them busy until things got up and running.

Bro. John, Bro. Robertson and all of the rest of the group stood back while the plane landed. They had gotten word from Bro. Joseph that the group was in trouble so they had started praying around the clock that all would go well. God had answered their prayers and there were shouts of joy around the camp that day. They decided that since God had delivered them from sure death that it was appropriate to have a night of festivities to thank the Lord for what He had done for His people. Bro. Joseph had state of the art equipment and he had a refrigerator unit on the plane. They brought out some of the food and had a big cookout for the camp that evening complete with all the fixins. The people danced and praised God until the wee hours of the morning. Even those who were not Christians were glad that the Christians were there that day. They were sure that in time many of them would come to the Lord.

The problem between Christians and Muslims has a very long history. And the problem between Jews and Muslims is one that will never be totally solved until the Messiah, Jesus Christ returns. They will always be enemies but Christians must remember that Jesus does not hate the Muslims but want them to come to a working knowledge of Christ Jesus that they too might be saved. This was the reason why the militants detained the plane. They don't want the Christians coming in because they know that the people will convert. They just do not realize that if they were right the people would not convert. Jesus comes to set them free from poverty, sickness and slavery. Who would not want this? Jesus followers have the freedom to serve Him or not. He does not have to use terroristic methods to keep them in line. He does not have to use fear to keep them in bondage. Jesus is a God of love and it is His hearts desire that people will serve Him because they love Him as Father and because He takes care of His own children in love. He wants that His children will live in peace and joy forever with Him in His Kingdom.

The following morning Bro. Joseph and the Senator had to return to the states. He wanted Shawn to always have a plane ready to go just in case anything really troubling happened he could get all of the missionaries out safely. Bro. Joseph had many projects he was working on and so he bid them farewell. He and Shawn hugged for the last time and his private jet came to get him and the Senator. It was harder leaving him this time after what happened but he knew that he had to leave him in the hands of the Lord. He still had not said anything to them about what the Lord told them. He just admonished them to stay vigilant in prayer and to let him know every day if things changed just the slightest bit. He knew that some trouble was coming but he didn't know when or what was to occur.

The first project was to get all of the tents set up. The medical facilities, cooking facilities, the school and the church would be first. They would deal with more tents for the people to live in and washing and bathroom facilities as well. They didn't have to bring many people because there were so many people there already that could help put everything together. These tents were not difficult to put up. After this was accomplished there would be two or more planes coming to bring more equipment such as cots for sleeping and other supplies necessary to make things a bit more comfortable for the people. The climate in the camp changed overnight. The people could see that they were being cared for and that things would slowly get better as time went on. This is all that people in the camps want on the short term. They want to have a purpose for their lives. They used to have a real life getting up every day and working their farms and caring for their families. Now they just sit around wondering when things will get better and seeing nothing being done about it. It seemed to them like no one was listening to them or cared about their situation. Many of the Muslims were angry that their own people were the cause of them losing their homes. They were distrusting of the Christians because they had been taught to hate them for so long. It was very confusing for them. The love of Jesus Christ would break through that eventually. Hopefully when the fighting stopped they could go back to set up their villages again and they would aid them in that venture as well. Bro. Joseph was working on that very thing in another area where things were starting to get better for the people. They were being transported to areas group by group. Samaritan's Purse started building small villages and bringing in animals to start working the land and the people could get their lives back again.

Within weeks it was time to send for the other planes to bring in more supplies. This was a big project but it was coming along quite nicely. The children were starting to feel more comfortable. Samuel was happy that soon he would have books, paper, pencils and other supplies to aid in teaching the children. He might even ask for some toys that they could be children again. He remembered as a boy that he and his mom would play ball together. She tried to be the best dad that she could considering that he never had a dad around the house. Perhaps this was why he understood these children who many had already lost their fathers at such a young age. They were so vulnerable and sad a lot of the time. The games and school would give them something to keep their minds on. The Muslim children stood firm in their faith but even they were starting to question life and Samuel was right there to answer them.

The other planes had arrived and there was joy filling the camp like never before. Marcus the leader of the mission had been working also with Bro. Joseph for quite a number of years. He had been a pilot for American Airlines but received the call of God to go into missions. He didn't know what he could do for God but when he met Bro. Joseph it all came together. It amazed him that God could use him in this capacity. But not only could he fly that plane but he learned how to set up the tents, and he was willing to jump in and do whatever someone needed him to do. He learned that ministry wasn't as difficult as some people thought. He also learned that God would take care of his needs. He was like many who believed that he would be poor doing ministry for God and that he would not be able to feed his family. This was far from the truth. God had met every need that he had since leaving American Airlines. Bro. Joseph was very fair to all of the ministers. They were not pilots or electricians or cooks but they were all ministers of the Most High God. He knew that God was able to supply all of their needs according to His riches in glory. They had not missed one payment of one bill yet to date.

Marcus absolutely loved being a minister of the Lord. He was able to do something that he absolutely loved doing and that was rebuilding broken lives and teaching them the love of Jesus Christ. Before God got his attention he used to go to church with his family every now and then when he was at home which wasn't very often. He missed out on so much of his children's lives because he was always working. He loved flying and he loved the money and he felt that he was providing well for his family so this should make them happy. But one day his little girl said to him very frankly that the day of the Lord is come and that people who didn't go to church will have to stand in judgment before God. He couldn't believe what he was hearing. What kind of things were they teaching at that church? He didn't want his little girl talking like that. She was supposed to be singing the Jesus loves me song and that was about it. But for some reason it really bothered him that his little girl probably knew more about God than he did. So he tried his best to get to church more often and it was a shock to him what God started to say to him.

Marcus started by reading his Bible faithfully every day. Before the beginning of each day he took the time out to pray for his family, his co-workers and his church. He was amazed at how different he felt about people. As he started to pray his eyes of understanding began to open up and he could see things about people that he could not see before. He started to love people at a different level than he had ever before. He and his wife started tithing like the pastor was teaching and he was actually seeing that God was blessing them more than ever. The children were healthy, their marriage was stronger than ever and their relationship with God was better than they could have ever imagined it could be. Blessings are not just about money but about relationships and growth. Paul says that we are new creatures in Christ Jesus and they could see it working in their lives. They were truly new people in Christ Jesus. This all happened because his seven year old challenged him one day. She was of course his favorite.

So one day Marcus heard the call of God to go into the ministry but he had no idea what he could do for God. God gave him a vision just like Bro. Joseph of flying to different lands and ministering the love of Christ to them. He though that he would have to go into debt for buying a plane of his own so he prayed to God about it. One day another pilot told him about the ministry and that he should call Bro. Joseph to see if he needed any more help. The rest was history. Marcus had been working with Samaritan's Purse and planned on staying with them forever.

It was much the same with the other members of the group. Many of them felt that they could not possibly be used of the Lord but Jesus had other plans for them. He can use truck drivers, prayer warriors, nurses, doctors, housewives, writers and cooks. Whatever a person can do can be used for the glory of God.

He was however troubled about this trip. He had been receiving a reoccurring dream about being surrounded by tanks. There were people running, children crying and someone that he did not know had been wounded terribly. He remembered putting this person on the plane and flying to the nearest place where there was a hospital. All he could remember was that the Lord said do not be afraid that all would be well. It just kept coming back periodically and all that he would do was pray and not worry. He had his church praying for him all the time.

He had a new dream that was bothering him as well. He would wake up in a cold sweat. The camp again was surrounded by tanks. But this time he could see off in the distance seven angels with swords of fire coming and surrounding the camp. When the soldiers saw the angels coming they all fled. He liked this dream but it was scarey all the same. These angels were tall as trees. They had hoods over there heads and they were not laughing. You don't play with angels with swords of fire in their hands. He was surely glad that they were there to protect them. God was showing him that he was there with them to protect them.

Marcus had a special calling on his life and God was revealing himself more and more as the times got greater in the world. Marcus knew deep down that the work they were doing for the Lord was of utmost importance. These people needed to hear the gospel of Jesus Christ before the times of the gentiles ended or they just would not make it.

Tent City in the Sudan was in the making and God's soldiers were on the move. There is much work to be done in the world and God is using his saints to do it.

Chapter 35

Bro. John and Bro. Roberts could not believe the change in the camp over the last year. God was on the move and they were so excited about what he was doing. Unfortunately, there was no end in site to the fighting going on in the country. It seemed like the world was at war and it just was never going to end. They had built a barrier around the Tent City now and had guards posted in different places to watch over the camp morning, noon and night. They wanted the men, women and children to feel secure in the City, that no one would ever hurt them again.

The City was booming. The people were happy and all seemed well for quite a few months. The camp had running water and electricity. The people were being fed well and they now had the hope of a better life that they had not had before. The men were working, the women were taking care of their families and the children were in school.

One evening Samuel had a dream about the camp. It had seemed as if God had stopped talking to him like he had in times gone past. But this particular dream was so disturbing that he knew that it was God. He knew that God was warning him that something was about to happen and that they needed to fast and pray that all would go well. It almost seemed as if he was awake but he wasn't and he was walking through the camp at night just walking and praying over the people as he often times would do. He and Bro. John and his son were walking and praying over the people and all of a sudden off to the distance there were seven angels with swords drawn. They could not believe what they were seeing. They all fell prostrate to the ground out of reverence for God's servants. Off into the distance they could hear guns firing and bombs going off, they were terrified. As the sound got louder the angels stopped looking at them and with great speed surrounded the camp so that the militia could not get through. Samuel, Bro. John and little John started running to wake up the men so that they could get ready to fight if necessary. But then one of the angels motioned for them to stand down. Just when the army got upon the camp they saw the mighty angels standing ready to fight and they fled. The angels stood there for what seemed like a few hours before they left the camp. They all fell to the ground praising God and thanking Him for the victory over the enemy. He now knew how important it was that they continued to keep the watch and pray over the people because the enemy was out to destroy the work that God was doing there. Samuel never told anyone about the dream but kept it to himself. He didn't want the rest of the team to be afraid. There was so much that they had to deal with already.

The next evening Samuel had a dream that was even more horrifying. Bro. John had a death in the family and he little John and his wife had gone back home to attend the funeral. He could see that they had gone home on the plane but were detained by the authorities when they were to come back into the country like Shawn and the others. They held them in prison for quite some time. Samuel could not discern how long the time was, he could just see them in the prison. The Lord showed him that they would go through great torture and that Bro. John because of his age would not make it. They were going to lose him. This caused Samuel great sorrow for he had learned to love Bro. John as if he were his father.

Each day after receiving this word from God Samuel was very depressed and everyone saw his sorrow but he would not tell anyone what it was all about. His grandmother was ailing so he told them that his grand mother was sick and that he was worried about her. How would he possibly tell them that the Lord had told him that

Bro. John and his family would be imprisoned and that Bro. John would later die and leave them?

Samuel thought about how difficult it must have been for the disciples when he had to constantly remind them that He was going to the cross. The disciples could not understand why their master had to die. But if Jesus had not died then He would not have accomplished the will of the Father for His life. Perhaps it was the will of the Father that this take place and that He had a purpose that Samuel could not understand so he sought the Lord to see what could this possibly accomplish for the Kingdom of God to take this great man of God whom he had come to love so much.

One thing Samuel realized that day was that every person would die at some time or other. He just never looked at life that way that one day he too would die and go home to be with the Lord. Death is a hard thing no matter whether a person is sick and dies from illness, or whether they lived a long or short life. Death is still something that in the heart of every person is hard to accept. God never meant for man to die. Man was created to live forever. When Christ died he conquered not only sin but he conquered death. When a child of God dies they go on to be with the Lord in heaven and when the Body of Christ returns to rule and reign with Christ for 1000 years they shall never die again. But until that time all men and women will die at their appointed time and that time is in God's hands not man.

Samuel started coming to turns with the message that God had given to him but he still felt sorrow that he would not see his friend until it was his turn to go to heaven himself. Then he would see his father, whom he had not met and his mom whom he missed so terribly. He thought about the many saints who had given their life like Bro. John to serve the Lord. There could be no better way to live your life than for the Lord and no better way to die than to die in the Lord. Many people in the world from the beginning of time until the present days think about what will happen to me when I die? The question is a question that many have asked but few had the truth about the matter. The true answer to this question can only be found in God. The important thing is to be living each day for God.

Samuel had to get himself together because God had already told him that there were dangerous times ahead and that one of their elders would be taken from them. He had to grow up and continue to do the work that God had sent them there to do. He would not falter nor would he give up. The Day of the Lord had come and He needed the saints to stay strong. He had already showed him that He was with them by sending his mighty angels to rescue them so there was no need to fear. He also showed him that some of the team would be in great danger and that this was a time to pray and not be fearful.

Many had been receiving visions of the end times and how difficult those times would be for the Body of Christ. Samuel could never have dreamt that he too would be having these kinds of dreams. But his mom told him that his grand-father and his father received words from the Lord all the time. He guessed that the anointing flowed to him. God was showing the Body of Christ that just before the rapture that there would be a great time of testing for the church. The only bad thing about it was that many did not believe it. One young man received a vision before he got saved where God showed him that the church of America would be persecuted and that the government was a part of the conspiracy against Christians. One man after he got saved said that he was ashamed that he had been a part of putting the conspiracy together. They were already setting up camps where the Christians would be detained and killed. Not in America? Well this is the word of the Lord.

Three weeks after Samuel received the word from the Lord about the militia coming up against them in the camp it happened. But true to the dream the angels of the Lord were standing around the camp waiting for the army to arrive. When they saw the angels standing with their swords drawn they could not have gotten out of there quick enough. They were falling all over each other trying to get out of the way. Bro. John, Samuel and little John fell to their knees and praised God for the victory. God was true to His promise and the whole camp and the team talked about that night for a long time. They knew that their God was with them just like He said that He would be.

Now Samuel was afraid that the other dream would be coming true as well. This one sure did and he cried out to God to extend the man of God's days like He did for Hezekiah the King. He didn't know whether the Lord would do it or not but he asked anyway. The day came when Bro. John got word that his mentor had died and that he was asked to return home and attend his home going. Bro. Presley was Bro. John's spiritual father. He died at the ripe old age of 102. Bro. John was broken up about it and didn't talk to anyone for quite a few hours after he heard the news. Nothing could comfort him. Bro. Presley was like a father to him and they had been through a lot together. He loved him more than life. They boarded the plane to return as soon as they could. Samuel was sick because at the worst time of his life the devil was going to attack him again. He prayed and prayed while he was gone that God would give them the strength they need to persevere. He wanted to tell someone but he knew that he could not.

Chapter 36

AFTER ONE WEEK OF BEING away Bro. John contacted the team to tell them that they were on their way back to the Sudan to continue the work that God would have them do. He said that he had doubted for many days whether he would return or not because the grief that he had in his spirit and soul was so overwhelming he didn't want to live. They all understood and would have understood if they had not returned. Samuel wanted to tell him not to return because he was going to be imprisoned and die but he had no right to interfere with what God had sent Bro. John there to do. His reward was to be great in the Kingdom of Heaven. He could see him now walking with Jesus and his beloved Bro. Presley whom he loved like a father. He felt a bit better now for some reason because he knew that there would be so many waiting for Bro. John whom he had led into the Kingdom and many who loved him who had led him into the Kingdom of God as well.

When Bro. John, his wife and little John stepped off of the plane they expected that they would take a day and then one of the team members would be there to pick them up. He didn't feel good when the customs officer started asking them all sorts of questions about why they were there and how long they expected to be in the country. Bro. John didn't mean to but he got a bit indignant with the customs officer which was not the thing to do. All of a sudden they had dogs sniffing around their bags and they told them that they would be detained while they checked on their status and passport information.

Bro. John could not believe that this was happening. He should have known the devil was going to pull a stunt like this. They were away from the team and there was no one to help them. But he would pray and the Lord would deliver them like he always had. He looked at his wife who had fear on her face to reassure her. His son was there and they would come through this together.

The customs officer came back after quite a few hours to say that they would be detained by the police, that there visas had expired and that they would be getting in touch with the consolate to get things fixed for them. Not to worry that all would be well in just a few hours. Well after a few hours no one from the United States consolate showed up and all they could do was wait. A military officer came into the office after almost 24 hours and said that they could not located anyone from the consolate and that they were being moved to the jail until someone could be contacted.

This made Bro. John very angry and he demanded a phone call home to let someone know what was happening. Of course he never received a phone call. His wife was starting to get nervous that no one would ever find them again. He tried to comfort her but she wasn't easy to comfort. They had heard some terrible stories about terrible things that happened in many countries to so many missionaries who never returned home and never were found again. He knew that Samuel would not stop until they had been found. He would surely get in contact with Bro. Joseph before long and he would come to find them like the crew before. It would all work out but they would have to keep their heads and put their trust in God.

The first day in jail it seemed like a terrible nightmare. They had not eaten in two days and the place had no real bathroom facilities only a whole in the ground. It was a rude awaking to them all to live this way. They had never had to lose their dignity in such a way even when they got to the camp they could go behind a tree. Bro. John started thinking about how difficult it was for Jesus and the disciples. He never thought about it but had they hotels and places to stay all the time while they were out preaching from city to city. The Lord did say that the Son of Man did not have a place to lay His head. All of a sudden he realized something about his life. He had been coddled all of his life. He always had a roof over his head, food on the table, his family was healthy. He had never really suffered a day in his life for the Lord. Yet the Lord suffered terribly for him. How dare he even think about questioning God about this matter? Of course no one wants to suffer but in the last days, critical times were to come for the whole world including Christians. How many would suffer like James admonished. He said that whenever trouble comes your way, let it be an opportunity for you. For when your faith is tested, your endurance has a chance to grow. So let it grow, for when your endurance is fully developed, you will be strong in character and ready for anything. Bro. John knew that this was the time to see what type of Christian he really was. Would he curse God and die and lose out on all that God had purposed and built in him? Would he finish the race with the same steadfastness that Jesus did? Would he run away and abandon God like so many did when He went to the cross? There were so many people in the Holy Scriptures that received from Jesus. He gave sight to the blind, fed the 5,000 and raised the dead. But where were these same people when he died on the cross? Would he be one that would be there with Him or would he say I do not know you Jesus?

He was sure that he would not be one of those. He loved the Lord with all of his soul, mind and strength and he would die for him if it came to that. He felt though like he was dying inside and his family felt the same way. He told them though that this is the only way that they would be like Christ is that they must die to self. God came from His mighty throne in heaven and came to earth to suffer as a servant for all creation.

By the third day they started to get hungry but prayed that God would put them on a divine fast of the Holy Spirit just in case it took much time before they would get at least some bread and water. This was certainly the time for a fast. They needed help from the Lord and murmuring was not the way. This was the time that they needed to use their faith in God that they would be delivered.

By the fourth day a young man came in and brought them some bread and water and told them that all would be well. That they must have faith that God would deliver them and that he would.

"Hey are you the young man that is a Christian? Some of our people were detained a while back and they said a young Christian soldier brought them bread and water."

"Why yes. I am that same man."

"What are you doing working for these people?"

"God had sent me here for such a time as this to help his people. This is why I am here. Keep the faith. Tougher times are coming to the Body of Christ. God has sent you and many others before you to do this same work. Fear not for His Kingdom is soon to come and there will be no more martyrs for the Kingdom. Finish the race with all diligence and you will receive the prize."

With that he was gone. Bro. John and his family was so glad that God had sent this angel to them. Sometimes we might not like the situations that we find ourselves in but God has all things in His hand and putting our trust in Him is the key. There is nothing that we should fear because God has not given us the spirit of fear but of power, love and a sound mind. They rejoiced that day that God had sent someone to watch over them.

Day four and day five were not much different. No one from the consolate came to speak with them, they didn't received a phone call neither were they able to go outside. It would just have been nice to see the sunshine. Each day was difficult but the family sang hymns, praised God, prayed and ministered to each other what was in their hearts.

One evening while Bro. John layed down to ponder over his life he remembered a dream that God had given to him. He was in a room and there was no furniture in that room. A man walked into the room with a chair and he sat down in the chair. The man began to ask him all manners of questions about what it was like to be a Christian and that if he could have a good meal and a bed would he renounce his faith in Christ. He told the man that he most definitely would not renounce his faith in Christ. At the time he would not understand who that man was and what was going on but now he understood what God was trying to tell him.

Within seven days a man walked into the room and asked Bro. John to follow him. Bro. John kissed his wife and went with the man. He had already told his son that if he did not live that he should continue on in the ministry and take care of his mother. They were going to make it no matter what happened. It was the first time that Sis. Betty let her emotions go. She didn't want her husband to see her break down. He had been ministering so hard that they would not give up hope. She had listened to all that he had said but at this point she could not hold back any longer. She thought that she would never see him again. They had been through so much together, the cancer, the birth of their son, entering the ministry together. Could it all really end like this? She thought of the other missionary wives whose husbands were taken in the middle of the night and never returned back to the villages where they lived and worshiped together for years. Only to return back to the states without them ever knowing what happened to them. Little John wasn't much help either at the moment. He thought he was seeing his father for the last time too and he began to cry like a baby.

It was night when they came to get Bro. John so he could not see anything but trees and a few huts like the one they were being kept in. There were a few men with guns telling him what to do and he just followed. He was afraid but he was not going to let them know it. They put him in a jeep, blind folded him and they drove for what seemed like just a few minutes and he was told to get out. Why were they moving him? Would he see his wife again, his son? What was happening? His heart was beating so hard he thought he was going to pass out. He started to sing in his mind to calm himself down. He didn't want to have a heart attack right there. He wasn't going to give them any satisfaction. In any case he started to calm down.

He felt a hand take his arm, they had put the blindfold on and he couldn't see to walk. He just walked carefully as he was being directed. When he got inside the hut his blindfold was taken off and he was instructed to sit down in the chair. It was just like in the dream. But God had not shown him everything. I'm sure he knew that he would not have taken the assignment if he knew all the details. He was so glad that he had the opportunity to serve these people but what was ahead he was not ready for.

"Your wife and son are waiting for you. You can get out of here in just a few minutes if you will renounce Christ. We will give you, food, water and a free plane ride home if you will leave here never to return."

Bro. John just looked at the man. All of his flesh wanted to say put us on the plane and we will never return but he could not renounce God that way. He knew that it would mean his very life if he renounced God. He would rather die now than have to deal with God on judgment day.

He looked the man in the face and said "I cannot renounce Jesus. He is my Lord, my God and in Him will I put my trust." He remembered Jesus on the cross and Stephen when he was being martyred and in his heart he said "forgive them for they know not what they do."

One soldier came over to him and put a gun to his head.

"You can go the easy way or you can go the hard way. We will leave you and let you think about it for a while."

The blindfold was put back on Bro. Johns' face. When the men left the room a light shown so brightly that Bro. John knew that a brighter light had been turned on than was on before. He did not know what was happening but all of a sudden an angel started to speak to him. He took the blindfold from over his head and he could see him as clear as day. The angel told him that this would be the last but greatest test that he would have to endure for God. He told him that God had sent him to this place to further the work of the Gospel and that God was pleased with his diligence and that his reward would be great. He told him to stand fast no matter how hard things got. He told him to remember what his master, Jesus Christ endured. That he would have the same strength that He did because the Holy Spirit lived within him. The angel told him to plead the blood of Jesus for his protection.

In a moment in a twinkling of an eye the angel was gone and Bro. John sat with the blindfold over his eyes praying that God would rise up in him like never before and give him the strength to remain faithful to the gospel. Bro. John did not know how much time had passed before a man came back into the room. He took the blindfold off of his head and told him that he should give himself up for the sake of his family or else they were going to kill him. Bro. John was scared to death but he said "I cannot do this."

"I've tried to help you. You have only one life to live. You must think about your family."

"Young man I am thinking about my family. All of these years I have served my God and I have told my wife and my son that we will always be faithful to our God. If I change now and turn my back on my God then I will not only hurt my God but all of the people who trusted the very word of God that I have lived all of these years. I would rather die than turn my back on Jesus Christ. You should know Him. He is the great I Am. He is the one true God. He is the one who gave His life for me."

"Well I am only trying to help you. I must go. I wanted to give you time to change your mind. They will be here in a moment."

The time slipped by and Bro. John actually fell asleep in the chair. Eventually a few soldiers came into the room and began interrogating him again and again. They would not stop trying to get him to turn against his God. They stood him up, took off his shirt and began to beat him mercilessly. This took place for several hours. By the time they had finished Bro. John had passed out and wished that he were dead. But he remembered John when he was on the aisle of Patmos. He had been imprisoned and before that he had been thrown into scalding grease to try to take his life but God had other plans for his son. Bro. John knew that he would make it through this somehow to testify to the world that his God is great. He remembered that Abraham was imprisoned and when he would not renounce the God of all creation he was thrown into the fiery furnace. They were astonished when they saw the man Abraham walking in the midst of the fire. God had spared his life. But he also knew that if God wanted to let him go that he would be walking on streets of gold with the Lord Jesus Christ whom he had been serving all of his life.

God had allowed him to see exactly what it felt like when he was whipped as he drug that cross to Golgotha. It was indeed a privilege to suffer for Christ as He had suffered for him that he might have life and have it more abundantly. Bro. John was now giving his life and shedding his blood that those people might have the light of Jesus shining brightly for them and their children and those to come.

Just when he felt that he wasn't going to make it the light shown again brightly in the room and that same glorious angel came to tell him that he was about to be delivered and sent back to his family. He told him that help was on the way and not to give up.

Chapter 37

SAMUEL WAS BESIDE HIMSELF AFTER Bro. John and his family did not arrive back on time. He investigated to find out that they had boarded the plane but that when they arrived they had not gotten in touch with anyone. He knew that something was wrong and immediately he got in touch with Bro. Joseph. The rest of the team was praying and Bro. Joseph immediately boarded the plane to see what had happened. He got in touch with the consolate and they had not heard anything. Immediately they started making phone calls to see where they might be held. This had happened so many times before. The Muslim factions did not like the Christians in the country so it was an on going battle. Bro. Joseph would have to work very hard because time was not on their side. They had been missing for quite sometime now and could be dead but they were hoping for the best. The Senator and his not so scrupulous contacts was all that he had beside the Lord. It had worked before and he hoped that it would work this time.

They found out that they had been being held and that it was not going to be easy to get them out. Bro. Joseph had brought some money with him and hoped that he could purchase their release. It worked most of the time but who knew. In any case they had made some contacts and found out where they were holding Sis. Betty and little John. By the time they got there they were beside themselves because Bro. John had been gone for quite a few days and they had no idea where he was being held at that point. But they were glad that they were being released. Now it was time to find Bro. John. The soldiers were afraid at this point to tell them where Bro. John was being held. He had been beat almost unto death and this wasn't good. He wasn't far away and time was running out. Bro. John was losing blood and he was very weak.

While Bro. John was laying in a pool of blood, he could see the streets of gold. He saw many of his friends and he saw the Lord Jesus Christ high and lifted up, his train filling the temple. Oh how beautiful it was. He longed to be with Christ but was worried at the same time about his wife, son and the rest of the team. It was out of his hands, he knew that and was ready for whatever was to take place. The angel appeared to him again to tell him that he would be going home soon but that he would see his family again for a short time. He was going in and out of consciousness not knowing when anyone would find him. But the angel said that he would see his family again. This gave him hope. He hurt like never before and felt that he wasn't going to make it.

There was one soldier that told Bro. Joseph where Bro. John was being held and said that they must hurry because he was in terrible danger. It didn't take them much time but when they arrived Bro. John didn't even look like himself. He was laying with no shirt on in a pool of blood. His back had been torn to pieces by the whip that they had used on him. It was so bad that they did not want Sis. Betty to see him that way. Little John could not believe that had happened to his father. There was no reason why they had to do this to him. He never did any harm to any one. Hatred started to form in the young mans heart against those who had beat his father this way.

They had to airlift Bro. John to the nearest hospital before he died. He did not even know that he had been rescued. He was in and out of consciousness for several days before he lapsed into a coma. While he was in a coma the Lord came to him and told him to not be angry for what has happened to him. He told him that He gave his life and that many would have to give their lives to win the war for the souls of men. The time would come when it would all be over and that many lives would be saved because many were willing to give of their lives for the sake of others.

"Remember my son that in the end we win. Satan will no longer have any power to do harm in this world. We will live in everlasting peace forever."

"Father I just pray that I have brought glory to your name. I just want to know that I have made a difference in this world. There are so many who do not realize that this thing is not going to end for Christians like they think."

"I know my son. They must learn for themselves. The Day of the Lord is come. I will not tarry with man much longer. So as it was in the days of Noah so it is in the world today. I must put an end to all of this suffering. But don't you worry about this. You have done well my son. I am proud of you."

"Thank you Lord."

Bro. John felt at peace for the first time in a long time that he was okay with the Lord and that it would be okay to leave. His family would miss him but his work was finished.

The doctors watched him around the clock. Betty never left his side, neither did little John. He never ever thought about his father dying. They had a good life and he just thought that they had many more years to go. There was so much that he had never told his father and now he might not ever get the chance to tell him. Isn't that how it always ends. One day a loved one walks out the door never to return and you never get that chance to say "I love you". Samuel didn't want to leave the children but he took the time to come with them to the hospital. They were so understanding and prayed with him before he left that Bro. John would one day return to them. Samuel knew the extent of his injuries and had already received word from the Lord that his mentor and spiritual father would go home to be with the Lord. He had some time to prepare unlike the others.

After several weeks in the coma Bro. John opened his eyes to see his lovely bride of 50 years holding his hands and praying for his recovery. Betty had not realized that her husband had opened his eyes until she had stopped praying long enough to look at him.

When she realized that his eyes were opened she woke up the whole hospital so that the doctors could come and check on him.

"John can you hear me?"

He just looked up at her with tears streaming down his face.

"Betty I've seen the Lord. Heaven is so beautiful. There is nothing to be afraid of Betty. It is not painful and what a pleasure to see the Lord that we have served all of these years."

"Don't talk so much John. You are weak. We are going to pull through this and we are going to focus on the family from here. God will understand."

"No Betty, God will not understand. I'm sorry darling but I will not be with you much longer. The angel told me that I will have a time with my family again but that my work is done here. I'm going on to be with the Lord."

Betty became hysterical and started crying. Little John tried to console her but she was not to be consoled. She and big John were inseparable. She could not see her life without him. Bro. John fell back asleep for a while. The doctors told the family not to excite him and to let him sleep.

It was not easy but Samuel convinced Sis. Betty and little John to go to a hotel and get a good nights rest and a good meal. They had spent every day with Bro. John since he entered the hospital. He told them that he would stand watch and he would call if he woke up again.

While they were gone Bro. John woke up and spoke with Samuel for a while.

"Samuel you take care of my family. You are much stronger than they are. Betty will probably fall apart and little John too. You must continue the work that God has sent us to do with these people. When God releases you to do something else then and only then should you leave. Be faithful to Him and he will be faithful to you."

"I will do what you have asked Bro. John. I thank you for all that you have meant to me over these past few years. You are the father that I never knew. I am proud to be called your friend."

"And you are more than a friend you are a son. Oh Samuel, Samuel God told me many things as I layed there on that floor close to death. You must go and tell the people, warn the people that there is much danger coming for the Body of Christ and that they must get prepared or they will suffer greatly. But there is a glorious time coming when the Lord is going to poor out his grace upon the whole world and they shall know Jesus in a way that they could not have imagined. The whole world will see what is in store in the coming Kingdom of God. God is going to give the whole world one last chance to repent before the end of this world comes. Oh Samuel it's going to be a glorious time for some and an awakening for others."

"I understand Bro. John. Rest, don't get yourself too excited. Do you want me to call Sis. Betty back to see you one last time?"

"Samuel it won't help. No matter how many times I see her she is not going to be able to let me go. I will just go now. My angel is standing by to escort me back to the great city. Samuel I love you and I will be waiting for you on streets of gold."

At that moment Bro. John crossed over into heaven to be with the Lord. Samuel just bowed his head and let the tears stream like rivers of waters. He left the room and went to the nurse station to tell them that Bro. John had passed away.

The next step was to tell Little John and his mom. The phone call came just after midnight.

"Sister Betty, this is Samuel."

"Samuel is everything okay?"

"Well Bro. John has gone home to be with the Lord."

Sis. Betty just sat down in the chair and she began to weep.

"Sis. Betty, are you there?"

"Yes Samuel I am here. Did he go peacefully?"

"Yes he did. He was ready for it. He said that he had seen the Lord and that he was not afraid. He told me to take care of you and that we should continue the work that God started. He wants us to warn the world of what is about to take place and that God is preparing to do a greater work such as mankind has never seen before. I miss him already."

"So do I Samuel. Well I guess we had better make his funeral arrangements. He didn't tell me what he wanted so I'll call Bro. Joseph and have him flown back home to be buried alongside his mother and father."

"Okay. Why don't you try and get some rest. There is nothing that you can do for him right now. He is walking on streets of gold. He is worried about you but I know that you have more strength than you think."

"Oh I don't know Samuel. I'll take it one day at a time."

Precious in the sight of the Lord is the death of his saints. It was a hard time for Sis. Betty, her family and the whole camp. The world was a better place because of a great man of God who lived what he preached to the world. He gave all that he had to the work that God had set before him. He didn't ask for much but only hoped that in his life and work that people would see the God that he served and loved. Life would no longer bring tears and sorrow because he was now crossing over to a new life that is promised to those who serve Jesus Christ.

This was the message of the man who taught the word of the Lord. The message of the cross is a message of hope to the world that Bro. John saw going down a terrible road. He saw a world full of poverty, sickness and wars in one place after another. The good news of the Gospel of Jesus Christ is that this world will be one day transformed into the Kingdom of God. This Kingdom of God will be like it was in the beginning, a beautiful garden made by the hands of an Almighty God.